YOU
ARE NOT
ALONE

Greer Hendricks spent over two decades as an editor. Prior to her tenure in book publishing, she worked at *Allure* magazine and earned her Masters in Journalism from Columbia University. Her writing has been published in the *New York Times* and *Publishers Weekly*. Greer lives in Manhattan with her husband, two children and very needy dog, Rocky. *You Are Not Alone* is her third novel.

Sarah Pekkanen is the internationally and *USA Today* bestselling author of several novels including *Skipping a Beat*. A former investigative journalist and feature writer, her work has been published in the *Washington Post*, *USA Today* and many others. She is the mother of three sons and lives just outside Washington, D.C.

The two women began working together in 2010 when Greer became Sarah's editor. They formed an instant connection, which grew into a close friendship, and they now write *New York Times* bestselling psychological thrillers together.

By Greer Hendricks and Sarah Pekkanen

The Wife Between Us
An Anonymous Girl
You Are Not Alone

YOU
ARE NOT
ALONE

GREER HENDRICKS

AND

SARAH PEKKANEN

MACMILLAN

First published in the United States 2020 by St. Martin's Press, New York

First published in the UK 2020 by Macmillan
an imprint of Pan Macmillan
The Smithson, 6 Briset Street, London EC1M 5NR
Associated companies throughout the world
www.panmacmillan.com

ISBN 978-1-5290-1078-7

Authors' Note: The data in this novel has been culled from a variety of sources and
is true to the best of the authors' knowledge.

1 3 5 7 9 8 6 4 2

A CIP catalogue record for this book is available from the British Library.

Printed and bound by CPI Group (UK) Ltd, Croydon, CR0 4YY

MIX
Paper from
responsible sources
FSC® C116313

Visit **www.panmacmillan.com** to read more about all our books
and to buy them. You will also find features, author interviews and
news of any author events, and you can sign up for e-newsletters
so that you're always first to hear about our new releases.

From Greer:
For Robert, who always encourages me to break down walls

From Sarah:
For Ben, Tammi, and Billy

PART
ONE

CHAPTER ONE

SHAY

Numbers never lie. Statistics, charts, percentages—they don't contain hidden agendas or shades of gray. They're pure and true. It isn't until people start meddling with them, spinning and shaping them, that they become dishonest.
—Data Book, page 1

TWO WINEGLASSES ARE ON the coffee table, evidence of a romantic night. I clear them away, rinsing the ruby-colored stains pooling at the bottom of the goblets. The coffee is brewing, filling the galley kitchen with the aroma of the dark roast beans Sean introduced me to when I moved into his Murray Hill apartment eighteen months ago.

I turn my head at the sound of a key in the lock, and a moment later he comes in, stepping out of his flip-flops. He's humming, like he does when he's happy. He's been humming a lot lately.

"Hi there," I say as he sets down a shopping bag from Whole Foods with a bouquet of purple tulips peeking out of the top. "You're up early."

His thick, gingery hair is sticking up a bit in the back, and I suppress the urge to reach out and run my fingers through it.

"Thought I'd pick up breakfast." He unpacks eggs and croissants and strawberries.

As I reach for the carafe of coffee, Sean's bedroom door opens.

He quickly gathers the tulips as his girlfriend, Jody, walks into the kitchen.

"Good morning," she says, stretching. She's wearing a pair of Sean's boxers, which are almost covered by one of his big hoodies. Her curly hair is up in a high ponytail, and her toenails are painted bright pink.

Sean gives her the tulips—and a kiss. I quickly turn away, busying myself opening the fridge and pouring almond milk into my travel mug.

"Enjoy breakfast," I say. "I'm heading out to get some work done."

"On a Sunday?" Jody crinkles her pert little nose.

"I want to revise my résumé. I have an interview tomorrow."

I grab my tote bag containing my laptop off the bench by the front door. Beneath the bench, Jody's sandals are nestled next to the flip-flops Sean just removed. I use my toe to nudge apart their shoes.

Then I descend a flight of stairs and step outside into an already-muggy August morning.

Not until I'm at the corner do I realize I left my travel mug on the kitchen counter. I decide to treat myself to an iced latte instead of going back to the apartment. These days, I spend as little time there as possible.

Because numbers never lie. And two plus one equals . . . too many.

I pull open the heavy glass door to Starbucks, noticing it's packed. Not surprising: Seventy-eight percent of American adults drink coffee every day, with slightly more women than men consuming it regularly. And New York is the fourth-most coffee-crazed city in the country.

I can't help myself; I often see the world through stats. It's not just because as a market researcher I analyze data to help companies make decisions about the products they sell. I've been this way since I was a kid. I started keeping data books at age eleven, the way other kids kept diaries.

Wow, you gained twelve pounds since your last visit, my pediatrician told me when I went in for a strep throat test the summer before middle school.

Shay, you're the tallest—can you stand in the back row? my fifth-grade teacher instructed me on class photo day.

Neither said it with a negative tone, but those comments, along with others I often heard, made me aware that numbers affect the way people see you.

I used to chart my height, my weight, and the number of goals I scored in each soccer game. I collected other data, too, like the categories of coins in my piggy bank, the number of library books I read every month, *American Idol* voting rankings, and how many gold, silver, and bronze medals the United States won in the Olympics. These days, I've come to mostly accept my body—I've turned my focus to my health and strength—and now, instead of what the scale shows, I record my 10K race times and the pounds I can deadlift.

I glance around the coffee shop. A woman leans over her laptop, typing purposefully. A couple sits side by side, her leg draped over his, *The New York Times* splayed across their laps. A father and a young boy sporting matching Yankees caps wait at the counter for their order.

Lately it seems like the stats are against me: I'm thirty-one years old, and I'm not dating anyone. When my boss called me into his office last month, I thought I was getting promoted. Instead, he told me I was being downsized. It's like I'm caught in a slow spiral.

I'm fighting as hard as I can to turn things around.

First, a job. Then maybe I'll join a dating site. There's a void in my life Sean used to fill. Before he met Jody, we ordered in Chinese food at least once a week and binge-watched Netflix. He's forever misplacing his keys; I instantly know from the way he calls "Shay?" when he needs help finding them. He waters the plant we named Fred, and I bring up the mail.

Sean's the first guy I really liked since I ended things with my college boyfriend. I began to fall for Sean months ago. I thought he felt the same.

When the barista sets my latte on the counter, I scoop it up and push my way through the door.

Even at a few minutes after nine A.M., the heat is thick and oppressive; it engulfs me as I head to the subway station on Thirty-third Street. When I feel my hair sticking to the back of my neck, I stop to dig an elastic band out of my bag so I can tie it up.

That simple act costs me twenty-two seconds.

As I descend the stained stairs into the tunnel, I see the train I just missed speeding away from the station. A few people who must've disembarked from it climb the steps opposite me. I reach the platform and feel the last of the train's breeze in its wake. A fluorescent light above me flickers, and trash overflows from a garbage bin. Only one other person is waiting, about ten yards from me.

Why didn't he catch the train that just left?

When someone conjures unease in you, there are usually good reasons behind it. A man with a goatee and backpack lingering on a deserted subway platform on a Sunday morning isn't enough to make my pulse quicken.

But the way he's looking at me is.

I watch him out of the corner of my eye, alert for any sudden movements, while my brain spins: The stairs are directly behind me. If he wants to harm me, I might be quick enough to run up them. But I could get stuck at the turnstile.

I can't identify any other escape route.

The man takes a slow, deliberate step toward me.

I whip my head around, hoping someone else is coming.

That's when I see we aren't alone after all. A woman in a green dress with white polka dots stands farther down on the platform, in the opposite direction of the man. She's partially camouflaged by the shadow of a large support beam.

I move closer to her, still keeping the guy in my peripheral vision. But all he does is continue walking toward the stairs, eventually disappearing up them. I chide myself for overreacting; he probably mistakenly entered the downtown platform instead of the uptown one, which I've done before. Odds are, he was looking at the exit the whole time, not at me.

I exhale slowly, then glance up at the green-hued LED display. The next train is due in a couple minutes. A few more people drift onto the platform.

I can hear the distant rumbling of the wheels of the inbound train—it's a familiar soundtrack to my daily life. I feel safe.

The woman glances my way and I notice she's about my height—five feet ten—and age, but her hair is shorter and lighter than mine.

Her face is pleasant; she's the kind of person I'd ask for directions if I were lost.

I break eye contact with her and look down. Something is glinting against the dull concrete of the platform. It's a piece of jewelry. At first I think it's a bracelet, but when I bend over and scoop it up, I realize it's a gold necklace with a dangling charm that looks like a blazing sun.

I wonder if the woman dropped it. I'm about to ask her when the roar of the incoming train grows louder.

She steps close to the edge of the platform.

My mind screams a warning, *Too close!*

In that instant, I realize she isn't there to ride the subway.

I stretch out my hand toward her and yell something—"No!" or "Don't!"—but it's too late.

We lock eyes. The train appears in the mouth of the tunnel. Then she leaps.

For a split second she seems frozen, suspended in the air, her arms thrown overhead like a dancer.

The train shoots past, its wheels grinding frantically against the tracks, the high-pitched shriek louder than I've ever heard it.

My stomach heaves and I bend over and throw up. My body begins to shake uncontrollably, reacting to the horror as my mind frantically tries to process it.

Someone is yelling over and over, "Call 911!"

The train stops. I force myself to look. There is no sign of the woman at all.

One second she existed, and the next, she'd been erased. I stagger over to a bench by the wall and collapse.

During everything that follows—while I give my statement to a police detective with an impassive face, am escorted past the crime-scene tape up to the street, and walk the seven blocks home—I can't stop seeing the woman's eyes right before she jumped. It wasn't despair or fear or determination I saw in them.

They were empty.

CHAPTER TWO

CASSANDRA & JANE

AMANDA EVINGER WAS TWENTY-NINE. Single. Childless. She lived alone in a studio apartment in Murray Hill, not far from Grand Central Station. She worked as an emergency room nurse at City Hospital, an occupation so consuming and fast-paced it prevented her from forming close ties to her colleagues.

She seemed like the perfect candidate, until she threw herself under the wheels of a subway train.

Two nights after Amanda's death, Cassandra and Jane Moore sit together on a couch in Cassandra's Tribeca apartment, sharing a laptop computer.

The clean lines of the living room furniture are upholstered in dove gray and cream, and accented with a few bright pillows. Floor-to-ceiling windows invite plenty of light and afford sweeping views of the Hudson River.

The apartment is sleek and elegant, befitting its two occupants.

At thirty-two, Cassandra is two years older than Jane. It's easily apparent the women—with their long, glossy black hair, gold-flecked brown eyes, and creamy skin—are sisters. But Cassandra is composed of sleek muscles, while Jane is softer and curvier, with a high, sweet voice.

Jane frowns as Cassandra scrolls through potential pictures. The only ones they possess of Amanda are recent—within the past few months: Amanda sitting cross-legged on a picnic blanket in Prospect Park; Amanda lifting a margarita in a toast at Jane's birthday party; Amanda crossing the finish line of a charity walk for breast cancer research.

In most of the photos, she's surrounded by the same six smiling young women—the group the Moore sisters have methodically been assembling. The women have different occupations and hail from vastly diverse backgrounds, but they have more important, hidden qualities in common.

"We need one of Amanda alone," Jane says.

"Hang on." Cassandra pulls up a picture of Amanda holding a calico cat, sitting in a pool of sunlight spilling in through a nearby window.

Jane leans forward and nods. "Good. Crop it a bit and no one will be able to tell where it was taken."

The sisters fall silent as they stare at the photo. Just a few weeks ago, Amanda was sprawled in the gray chair adjacent to this very couch, which was the spot she usually chose when she came over. She kicked off her shoes and stretched her long legs over the chair's arm as she talked about the elderly hit-and-run victim she'd helped save with four hours of frantic treatment. *His daughter brought in dozens of homemade cookies today and left us the sweetest card!* Amanda had said, her words tumbling out with her usual exuberance. *It's times like this when I love my job.*

It seems impossible not only that Amanda is gone, but that she chose to end her life in such a spectacularly violent way.

"I never saw this coming," Cassandra finally says.

"I guess we didn't know Amanda as well as we thought," Jane replies.

For the sisters, Amanda's suicide triggered frantic efforts to answer questions: Where had she gone in the days before she died? Who had she talked to? Had she left any evidence behind—like a note of explanation?

They searched her apartment immediately, using their spare key to gain entrance. They retrieved Amanda's laptop and asked one of the women in their close-knit group, an operational security consultant, to unlock it. She ran a dictionary attack, cycling through thousands of possible passwords until she cracked Amanda's. Then the sisters examined

Amanda's communications. Unfortunately, Amanda's phone was destroyed by the subway, so it couldn't be scrutinized.

Within two hours her building was put under surveillance. The first visitor to it, Amanda's mother, who took the train in from Delaware, was invited to tea by one of Amanda's grieving friends. No helpful information was gleaned, even though Amanda's mother changed the venue to a bar and stretched the conversation over two hours, during which time she consumed four glasses of Chardonnay.

The memorial service, which will take place on Thursday evening at a private club in Midtown, is a precautionary measure. It was Cassandra's idea to hold the simple, nonreligious ceremony. Anyone connected to Amanda will likely show up.

The sisters, who now have access to Amanda's contacts, will invite everyone Amanda corresponded with during the past six months.

Cassandra and Jane also plan to post printed invitations on the main door to Amanda's apartment building, in the nurses' break room at City Hospital, and in the locker room of the gym Amanda frequented.

At the memorial service, a guest book will be used to gather names of the mourners.

"We'll get through this, right?" Jane asks Cassandra. Both sisters are exhausted; faint purple shadows have formed beneath their eyes, and Cassandra has lost a few pounds, making her cheekbones even more pronounced.

"We always do," Cassandra replies.

"I'll get us a glass of wine." As Jane stands up, she gives Cassandra's shoulder a squeeze.

Cassandra nods her thanks as she fits the photograph of Amanda into the template of the memorial-service notice on her screen. She proofs it a final time, even though she knows every word by heart.

Will it be enough? she wonders as she hits the print key.

If Amanda revealed something she shouldn't have to someone—*anyone*—in the days before her death, will that individual feel compelled to come to her service?

The phrasing below Amanda's smiling photograph was debated by the sisters before this simple message was agreed upon as bait: *Please Join Us. All Are Welcome.*

CHAPTER THREE

SHAY

NYC Subway System Stats: More than 5 million daily riders. Open around the clock. 472 stations—the most of any subway system. Seventh busiest in the world. More than 665 miles of track. 43 suicides or attempted suicides last year.
—Data Book, page 4

I LET MYSELF INTO the apartment and look around. It seems impossible that I've been gone only two hours. The violet tulips are in a cobalt vase. The frying pan soaks in the sink. Sean's and Jody's shoes are missing from beneath the bench.

I walk straight into the bathroom and strip off my red T-shirt and khaki shorts. As I stand under a stream of hot water in the shower, all I can think of is her. Her pleasant face and pretty polka-dot dress. And those empty eyes.

I wonder how long it will take for someone to miss her. When her husband arrives home to a dark apartment? When she doesn't show up for work?

But maybe she wasn't married. Perhaps she didn't have colleagues she was close to. It might take a while for her absence to register.

Just as it might take time for anyone to notice mine.

As I lie in bed that night, I can't stop replaying the scene, starting with the moment I edged toward the woman to get away from the guy with the goatee. I keep berating myself for not doing something differently. I should have reached out to grab her or yelled *"Don't!"* sooner.

When I spotted the woman with the pleasant face, I only thought about how she could save me. But I should have been the one to save her.

My room feels like it's closing in on me in the darkness.

I reach over and flip on the nightstand lamp, blinking against the sudden sharpness. I have to sleep—my big interview at Global Metrics is at nine A.M., and if I don't get this job, I'll have to keep temping. I'm lucky to have a part-time gig in the research department of a white-shoe law firm, but the pay isn't great, plus the health benefits I carried over from my old job expire in a few months.

But I can't rest. I reach for my phone and try to listen to a TED Talk to distract myself, but my thoughts keep creeping back to her. *Who was she?* I wonder.

I type "NYC 33rd Street Subway Suicide" into a search engine. The tiny news brief that appears doesn't answer any of my questions. I only learn she was the twenty-seventh person in New York to jump in front of a subway train this year.

So much suffering, hidden like a current beneath the loud bustle of my city. I wonder what compels someone to cross this final, desperate line.

Was it a sudden tragedy that led her to the edge? Or maybe she also felt like she was caught in a slow spiral?

I put down my phone. *Enough,* I tell myself. I need to stop looking for comparisons between the two of us. She isn't my future.

I wait until seven A.M., then I brew extra-strong coffee, put on my favorite gray suit, and dig out the little Sephora makeup palette my mom got me for Christmas.

As I close the apartment door behind me, I realize I never updated my résumé. I tell myself it didn't need much tweaking, and that I can compensate with a strong interview.

While I'm walking, I'm rehearsing how I'll explain being let go from my last job—five of us were downsized, which I hope will put me in a better light—when I glimpse the familiar green subway pole marking the tile stairs that descend underground.

I rear back, feeling as if I were electrocuted.

"Hey, watch it," someone says, brushing past me.

It's like my feet are stuck in cement. I see other commuters disappearing into that dark hole, just as I did yesterday—as I've done thousands of times before. But now, splotches form before my eyes, and a rushing sound fills my head. I can't even bring myself to walk over the steel grates between me and the entrance.

The longer I stand there, trying to will myself to move forward, the more my panic swells. When I hear the muffled sound of a subway train pulling into the station, it's hard to breathe. My armpits dampen and my glasses slip down on my nose.

I pull out my phone: 8:25 A.M.

I walk on shaking legs to the corner and hail a cab, but it's rush hour and the streets are clogged. I arrive at Global Metrics ten minutes late, rattled and jittery. I take deep breaths and wipe my palms on my suit pants while the receptionist leads me to the office of Stan Decker, the head of human resources.

People generally form an impression about others within the first seven seconds, so when I meet him, I make sure to stand up straight, offer a firm handshake, and maintain eye contact—signals that convey confidence.

He looks to be in his early forties, with a receding hairline and a thick gold wedding band, and a lot of framed photos are on his desk. They're all facing him, but I imagine they're of his wife and kids.

"So, Shay, why do you think you'd be a good fit here?" he begins once we're seated.

It's a softball question, and one I anticipated. "I love research. I've always been intrigued by how unconscious factors affect people's habits and decisions. I majored in statistics, with a minor in data analytics. I can help your company by doing what I do best: gathering and deciphering the information you need to craft messages that will resonate with your target consumers."

He nods and steeples his hands. "Tell me about a few of your most successful projects." This is another of the top ten most common interview questions.

"At my last company, one of our clients was an organic-yogurt company that wanted to expand its market share by wooing millennials."

My phone buzzes inside my bag. I flinch. I can't believe I violated one of the most important rules of a job interview: Turn off your cell phone.

Stan Decker's eyes flit to my tote.

"I'm so sorry. I must have forgotten to turn it off after I phoned to let you know I'd be a few minutes late."

I want to kick myself as soon as the words leave my mouth: *Why remind him of that?*

I fumble in my tote for my phone. Before I can turn it off, a notification pops up on the screen. I have a voice mail from an unfamiliar number with a 212 area code.

I wonder if it's the police detective who took my statement yesterday. She'd said she might need to follow up today.

"About the yogurt company?" Stan prompts.

"Yes . . ." I feel my cheeks grow hot; they must be blazing red against my fair skin.

I try to regroup, but it's impossible to focus. I'm acutely aware of the message waiting on my phone.

It seems like that call uncorked the noises and sights of yesterday—the grinding screech of the train wheels, the flutter of the light green polka-dot dress as the woman jumped. I can't stop reliving it all.

I fumble through, managing to finish the interview, but I know even before I leave the building that I won't get an offer.

As soon as I'm on the sidewalk in front of Global Metrics, I pull out my cell phone.

I was right: It's Detective Williams. She wants to go over my statement on the phone again. Once we're done, I ask for the dead woman's name; somehow it feels important for me to know it.

"Her next of kin has been notified, so I can do that. It's Amanda Evinger."

I close my eyes and repeat it to myself silently. It's such a pretty name. I know I won't ever forget it.

I walk the forty blocks home, forcing myself to craft a plan for the rest of the day: I'll update my résumé and send it to a new batch of headhunters. Then I'll go for a run for a hit of mood-boosting endorphins. And I should pick up a little baby gift to give my friend Melanie, who invited me over later this week for a drink.

I do one other thing on my way home: I plan my route to avoid stepping over any subway grates.

CHAPTER FOUR

CASSANDRA & JANE

A FEW DAYS AFTER Amanda jumped in front of the train, Jane receives an urgent call: Someone other than Amanda's mother has shown up at her apartment building.

Jane rushes into Cassandra's adjoining office, clutching her phone. It's a busy morning at Moore Public Relations, their boutique firm on Sullivan Street. Up until now, their workday appears to have been business as usual—they've met with an up-and-coming purse designer, fine-tuned the details on a gallery opening for an artist they represent, and assembled a list of influencers to spread the word about a new Asian-fusion restaurant.

But all the while, they've been on high alert, their cell phones always within reach.

Stacey, who at twenty-nine is the youngest member of their group, is on the other end of the line. Stacey dropped out of school after the eleventh grade but later earned a GED and has taught herself so much about technology that she is now in demand as a cybersecurity consultant. With a small, wiry build that belies her physical prowess, and a rough, occasionally profane way of speaking that distracts from her razor-sharp mind, Stacey is often underestimated.

The sisters agree she was one of their most valuable selections.

Stacey was the one who hacked into Amanda's laptop. She's also savvy enough that she was able to install a security camera on a streetlight just outside Amanda's building and remotely access the live video feed. From a coffee shop a block away, Stacey has simultaneously been working and surveilling.

While Stacey rattles off information—"She didn't stay long, didn't speak to anyone"—Jane rushes through the open door of Cassandra's office.

Cassandra's long, elegant fingers, poised above her computer keyboard, freeze as she catches the expression on Jane's face. Cassandra leans forward in her chair, her hair spilling over her narrow shoulders.

Jane shuts the door and puts Stacey on speakerphone.

"I'm with Cassandra," Jane says. "Take us through it from the beginning."

The Moore sisters learn that at 11:05 A.M., a woman—thirtyish, tortoiseshell glasses and brown hair, tall and athletic looking—climbed the steps of Amanda's apartment building. While the visitor stood looking at the old brownstone, which had been cut up into small apartments, her actions were captured by Stacey's camera. Stacey didn't recognize her, which set off alarm bells.

The visitor didn't press any of the buzzers. After approximately ninety seconds, she lay a single yellow zinnia on the corner of the top step, just a few feet from the laminated memorial-service notice created by the sisters.

Then she turned and left. Stacey—who was already packing up her things in an effort to run toward the apartment and follow the woman—was too far away to catch her.

"Please send the video immediately," Cassandra directs. "If she comes back—"

"I got it," Stacey interrupts. "She's not going to give me the slip again."

The video is scrutinized the moment it comes in.

Cassandra pauses on the clearest frame of the young woman. It fills her computer screen, just as Amanda's image recently did.

"Their coloring is different, but she's tall, like Amanda was, too," Cassandra says. "Could she be a relative we never heard about?"

Jane shrugs. "Amanda had secrets. Maybe this woman is one of them."

Taking in the mysterious visitor's widely spaced blue eyes and the faint cleft in her chin, Cassandra leans closer. She reaches out, tracing a fingertip along the curve of the woman's cheek.

Cassandra's voice is whisper soft, but her gaze is intent and unblinking. "Who are you?"

CHAPTER FIVE

SHAY

552 suicides were reported in New York City last year; approximately
one-third were female. 48 percent of the women were single. Among women,
white females had the highest suicide rate. And within the five boroughs,
suicide was highest among Manhattan residents.
—Data Book, page 6

A FEW NIGHTS AFTER my botched interview, I'm in the kitchen of Mel's Brooklyn apartment, twisting off the cap of the bottle of Perrier I brought.

Her colicky baby daughter, Lila, is strapped to her chest, and Mel gently bounces up and down to soothe her while I fill a glass for each of us and take cheese and crackers out of my shopping bag.

Her place is cluttered but cheery, with a pink-and-yellow Boppy pillow on the couch and burping cloths stacked on the kitchen counter. An electric swing is wedged next to the small round dining table. The Beatles' "Yellow Submarine" plays in the background, on the record player Mel's husband bought last year.

I hate bringing the horror of Amanda's suicide here, but Mel knows something is wrong. I've never been good at hiding my emotions.

"Shay, I can't even imagine how awful that must have been," she says, shuddering, as I finish the story. She hugs Lila closer.

I don't reveal that I took a bus, then a twenty-five-dollar Uber, to get here instead of the subway. The panic descended again tonight, just like it did when I tried to ride the subway to my interview on Monday and my temp job yesterday. As I approached that forest-green pole, my heart exploded and my legs refused to move forward.

Logically, I know I'm not going to witness another subway suicide—the stats prove how rare they are. But the one I did see keeps replaying in my mind.

"I went to her apartment this morning," I say. "Amanda's."

Lila spits out her pacifier and Mel pops it back in, jiggling faster. "You did what? Why?"

Mel looks tired, and I'm sure I do, too. Last night a bad dream jarred me awake. The onrushing rumbling of wheels was the backdrop of my nightmare. I looked up Amanda's name on the white pages website when I couldn't fall back asleep, which is how I found her address.

"I wanted to know more about her. To kill yourself that way is so violent . . . so *extreme*. I guess I'm just trying to make some sense of it."

Mel nods, but I can tell from her expression she thinks my behavior is odd. "Did you learn anything?"

I toy with the Fitbit around my wrist. My steps have nearly doubled in the past few days now that my usual mode of transportation has been eliminated.

"There's a memorial service tomorrow night," I say instead of answering Mel directly. "I'm thinking about going."

Mel frowns. "Is that a good idea?"

I can see why it seems weird to her, here in the cozy apartment with three-bean chili warming in a pot on the stove and a postcard for a Yoga with Baby class affixed to her refrigerator.

Amanda wouldn't have haunted Mel; they have nothing in common.

I fight the compulsion to touch my Fitbit again. The devices used to be ubiquitous; now not many people seem to still wear them. But in the photo of Amanda by the front door of her apartment she had one strapped to her wrist, too.

When I noticed it, my stomach dropped. Yet another link between us.

I don't tell that part to Mel, either. Mel used to know me better than anyone; we were roommates our freshman year at Boston University, and we shared an apartment when we first came to New York. But our worlds don't intersect anymore, and not just because of geography.

"Let's talk about something else," I say. "How do you feel about going back to work? Did you find day care yet?"

"Yeah, there's a great one a block away from my office. I can visit Lila every day during my lunch hour."

"That's perfect!" I say. "Just promise me you'll eat more than strained carrots."

She laughs and we chat awhile longer, then Lila's fussing grows louder. I can tell it's hard for Mel to focus when her baby is upset.

"I should let you go." I put down my empty glass.

Mel picks up the little stuffed elephant I brought Lila and waggles it at me. "You know you can call me anytime."

"And vice versa." I give Mel a kiss on the cheek, then I lean over to kiss Lila's sweet-smelling head.

I walk toward Manhattan until it begins to grow dark, then I call an Uber. The driver has on the air-conditioning, for which I'm grateful.

My mom left me a message while I was with Mel, so I dial her number.

She answers immediately. "Hi, sweetie. I wish you were here! We're having Mexican night. Barry and I made guacamole and skinny margaritas!"

"Fun!" I try to match her enthusiastic tone.

I can picture her in cutoff jeans and a tank top, her wavy chestnut hair pulled back with a bandanna, lounging on the brick patio Barry built a few years ago. My mom is petite, with an olive complexion. I inherited my father's broad-shouldered, rangy frame. Growing up, I sometimes wondered if people who saw us together realized we were mother and daughter, not just because we looked so different, but because she was much younger than the other moms at my school.

She had me when she was only nineteen. She was a receptionist in Trenton and my father was a twenty-one-year-old economics major at Princeton. They broke up before I was born. He comes from a wealthy family, and he paid child support. But I've only seen him a handful of times in my life because he went to business school at Stanford and has remained in California ever since.

My mom's life is so different: She worked for a construction company and married Barry, who was a foreman, when I was eleven.

"What have you been up to?" my mom asks now. "I haven't talked to you all week."

"She's probably too busy napping at that cushy temp job," Barry calls from the background before I can answer.

Barry's the main reason I don't go home to see my mom as often as I should.

I pretend to laugh at his comment. A minute later, when Barry calls my mom to come eat quesadillas, I'm glad for the excuse to hang up.

I remove my glasses and rub the bridge of my nose, then put them back on and lean against the seat, taking in the Manhattan skyline as we cross the Brooklyn Bridge. It's a sight I never grow weary of, but at twilight, with the majestic buildings rising into the purple-and-orange-tinged sky, it seems especially beautiful.

Every year, people are drawn to this bridge to enjoy the beautiful views or a relaxing stroll.

Or jump to their deaths.

The thought zings through me like an electric shock.

I jerk my gaze away from the steel beams and shimmering darkness of the East River below.

I keep my eyes fixed down, staring at the Uber's rubber floor mat, until the bridge is well behind us.

CHAPTER SIX

CASSANDRA & JANE

AN HOUR BEFORE AMANDA'S memorial service begins, five women assemble in a private room at the Rosewood Club to mourn the emergency room nurse with the effervescent personality who tracked her steps on a Fitbit to offset the sweets she loved.

They sit on sofas and chairs in a semicircle, softly talking. One weeps, her shoulders shaking, as another comforts her by stroking her back.

They're the same women who appeared with Amanda in Cassandra's photographs.

Only one is missing; she isn't attending the memorial service because she has a more important assignment tonight.

Cassandra and Jane survey the room. Everything is in place: The corner bar is stocked with plenty of alcohol—which will loosen tongues. The buffet holds a cheese board and tea sandwiches. Perched on an easel is the enlarged photograph of Amanda holding the calico cat. Beside it, the guest book is splayed open on a small table.

Cassandra closes the door, then strides to the center of the room and stands silently for a moment. Her ebony silk dress hugs her tall, lithe body. The only splash of color is her red lipstick.

Somehow the strain and pressure of the past days haven't dimmed her sharp, unconventional beauty. If anything, her features seem even more finely chiseled, and her amber eyes are mesmerizing.

"I know Amanda's death was as devastating to each of you as it was to Jane and me," Cassandra begins. She briefly bows her head. "Amanda was one of us."

The women murmur in agreement. Cassandra lifts her head and looks at each of them in turn:

Stacey, so small and scrappy and smart, who possesses at least a dozen Marvel T-shirts, a temper quick to flare, and a reservoir of loyalty that appears bottomless.

Daphne, who at thirty-two owns a chic boutique in the West Village and has the sort of innate sophistication that makes it easy to imagine her charming clothing designers and selecting styles that will entice her clients. Daphne always appears camera ready; her buttery-blond locks are professionally blown out twice a week, and her makeup is flawless.

And finally Beth from Boston, a thirty-four-year-old public defense attorney who often seems to be overwhelmed and a little flustered—her purse filled with crumpled receipts, half-eaten granola bars, hair bands, and loose change—but who possesses a sharp, uncanny intuition about people.

Cassandra admires these women greatly. They are smart and loyal. They have something else in common, too: All have overcome obstacles that range from job loss to assault to cancer.

"I just can't believe it," says Beth. Despite the strains of her occupation, Beth is quick to laugh. But today, tears glisten on her cheeks. "The last time I went to her place she baked the most amazing butterscotch cheesecake"—Beth pronounces it butta-scotch—"because, y'know, Amanda and sweets. And we made plans to see the new Julia Roberts movie. I'm still in shock. I keep thinking I shoulda done something differently—tried harder to get her to talk."

"Look, I know things spiraled out of control," Jane says. "It's no secret that Amanda was upset by our . . . experience."

"We all wish she'd come to us instead of shutting us out." Cassandra clears her throat. It's time to reclaim the women's focus. "We don't want to alarm you. But we have to consider the possibility that Amanda may have talked to someone about our group."

What the sisters haven't told the others is that Amanda's necklace—the one Cassandra designed and created—didn't disappear beneath the train wheels when Amanda died.

A GPS tracking device was inserted inside the sun-shaped charm the sisters had given to all of the women. It was a precaution, intended to protect them during the sometimes-dangerous work they performed—but perhaps it was also the result of a faint premonition. Other than the sisters, none of the women know that their necklaces aren't simply a piece of jewelry.

When the sisters checked the location of Amanda's tracker on their phones a few days after her suicide, they expected to see nothing: Surely the necklace had been destroyed.

But a gray marker on Jane's phone screen revealed the tracker was transmitting from just a few blocks away from the Thirty-third Street subway station, in a small apartment building in Murray Hill.

Cassandra's face had blanched when Jane told her the news. She'd grabbed Jane's arm.

"*Who?*" Cassandra had whispered. "Who would Amanda have given it to?"

Two dozen people lived in that building. Any of them could have the necklace.

Now Jane distributes copies of a photograph of the young woman with tortoiseshell glasses who laid a single flower on Amanda's doorstep.

Stacey glances at it. Her head snaps up. "Hey, that's from the video I took the other day," she blurts, then crosses her arms and stops talking. The streak of color in her blond hair is purple now—she changes it every few months—and her mouth is a thin, hard line.

Stacey isn't typically one of the more vocal members of the group, and given her background and the recent events in her personal history, it's unsurprising that she feels uneasy in this posh setting.

"Has anyone else seen this woman before?" Jane asks. One by one, the others shake their heads as they study the picture.

"Was this taken in front of Amanda's apartment?" asks Beth. "I recognize the entrance."

Cassandra awards her an approving nod. "Yes, this woman went to Amanda's building yesterday and left a yellow zinnia by the front door."

Jane's gaze shifts to the bouquets on the buffet and mantel, composed of dozens and dozens of yellow zinnias. This was Cassandra's touch. If the flowers are significant in some way, and the visitor appears, they may provoke a reaction.

Daphne—the member of the Rosewood Club who reserved the room for the occasion—lifts her hand, her Hermès cuff bracelet slipping down from her wrist. Until fairly recently, Daphne favored Hermès scarves, too, but she can no longer tolerate having anything around her throat, other than the most delicate of necklaces.

"Is this the woman you think Amanda talked to?" Daphne asks, her voice tight with anxiety.

"We don't know if Amanda talked to anyone yet," Cassandra replies. "But we need to find out exactly what links this woman to Amanda."

Stacey speaks up again. "Seems weird she's sniffing around right after Amanda died." Her foot begins a rat-a-tat-tat against the hardwood floor.

"Agreed," Beth chimes in.

Jane nods. "We can anticipate some of the people who will come today—Amanda's mother and her aunt, of course. Maybe a few coworkers. Perhaps this mysterious woman. Or Amanda may have reached out to someone else entirely." Jane pauses. "That's where you all come in."

"Mingle among the crowd," Cassandra instructs. "Strike up conversations with questions like 'How did you know Amanda?' 'Had you seen her recently?' 'Did she seem any different?' If something seems off to you—not just a response, but anything you overhear—come find me or Jane right away."

Cassandra's eyes sweep the room, again landing on each of the women in turn. Jane watches the effect Cassandra has on them—it's as if her gaze infuses them with a clear, bright energy. A few sit up straighter or begin nodding.

"And what if someone asks one of *us* how we knew Amanda?" asks Daphne.

"Good question," says Jane.

"Let's see. She used to go to Al-Anon, because of her mother," Cassandra says. "That would be a natural spot for us to have met her . . . but, no. Let's not go that route. She liked the sunrise yoga class on Tuesday mornings at her gym on Forty-second Street, so . . ."

Cassandra shakes her head. "No, that won't work either. Someone from her gym may show up tonight. Let's take the role of book club members. Everyone comfortable with that?"

"Sure," says Daphne.

Jane continues, "We haven't known each other long, but we've become close friends. Sticking to the truth will make it simpler. The last book we read is *Pride and Prejudice.*"

Stacey clears her throat. "Uh, I'm not really sure I'm the book-group type."

"Don't worry if you haven't read it," Cassandra replies. "A lot of people go to book clubs just for the wine and conversation."

For the first time since they've assembled, a laugh ripples through the room.

Then Beth speaks up. "Should we add other details? Like those lemon bars Amanda used to make . . . should I say she brought them to book club?"

"Sure, that would be a nice touch," Cassandra says. "We're here today as mourners, too. Our feelings of loss and pain are real. Remembering the qualities that made Amanda special will help us honor them."

Cassandra glances at her watch. "We have a little more time. Why don't we have a private remembrance now?"

She sinks onto an empty chair, crossing her legs, and Jane claims the seat next to her.

Cassandra's husky voice takes on a soothing tone. Her hands remain easily clasped in front of her. Her measured affect is a testament to her self-control.

"A loss like the one we've endured can cause fissures," Cassandra begins. "Right here, right now, let's make a vow that we won't let that happen. With Amanda gone, it's more important than ever we stay aligned. . . ."

Cassandra reaches out to take the hands of Jane and Beth, who are closest to her. They in turn reach for Daphne and Stacey, forming a circle as they listen to Cassandra's words:

"Let's remember why we came together in the first place. Let's embrace the safety in our sisterhood."

CHAPTER SEVEN

AMANDA

Ten days ago

AMANDA LAY IN BED, her knees curled tightly against her chest, her eyes squeezed shut.

Fresh memories pulsed through her mind: The smiling man clinking his glass against hers. The bitter taste of whiskey prickling her tongue. The two of them, hand in hand, stumbling slightly as they left the bar together, heading toward Central Park. A breeze cutting through the summer's night air, raising goose bumps on her bare arms.

A loud buzzing sound interrupted the vision. She lifted her head. Someone in her lobby was insistently pressing the button for her apartment.

She tensed, barely breathing.

She pressed her hands over her ears, but the unyielding buzzer reverberated through her mind.

They won't ever stop, she thought.

Then the noise abruptly ceased.

She looked around the shadowy apartment. Her shades were drawn, her windows locked, her door chained. All of her lights were off. She hadn't left her apartment in days; it was possible that her place might appear empty to anyone watching.

There could still be time to save herself.

Her brain felt muddy due to lack of sleep and food, but she tried to formulate a plan: the call she needed to make, the supplies she'd take, the safest route to get there.

She had almost convinced herself it could work when a soft, chilling noise thrummed through the air.

Knuckles rhythmically tapped against her door. Then the scrape of a key turning in the lock.

A voice called out, barely above a whisper, "We know you're in there, Amanda."

CHAPTER EIGHT

SHAY

About 50 percent of people who try to kill themselves do so impulsively.
One study of survivors of near-lethal attempts found that more than roughly
a quarter considered their actions for less than five minutes.
—Data Book, page 7

I WEAR A SIMPLE black dress to my temp job on Thursday, even though I haven't decided if I'm going to the memorial service.

At least that's what I tell myself.

My supervisor leaves early to meet a client for dinner, but I stay a little longer, until I've finished proofing some new materials for the firm's website. It's not something he asked me to do, but I figure an extra set of eyes never hurts. I circle a typo on one of the sheets and walk into his corner office.

I leave the sheet on his desk and sneak a Reese's mini-peanut-butter-cup from the glass jar he keeps on top of his desk for visitors. Then I take the elevator down to the lobby and step outside.

A late-afternoon thunderstorm has washed the sidewalks clean and broken the oppressive heat.

I should head to the grocery store—I'm out of everything—then go home and do my laundry.

But I'm already walking in the direction of the memorial service.

The address is easy to remember. It's a palindrome—the numbers are the same forward and in reverse.

Fifteen minutes later, I enter the Rosewood Club. Behind the plain exterior, the grandeur of the inside comes as a surprise. Thick, patterned carpets hug the floors, and an impressive spiral staircase winds to the second floor. Paintings with gold frames hang on the walls, each with a plaque beneath it.

I quickly read one—JOHN SINGER SARGENT, 1888—as a young man in a gray suit approaches me. "Are you here for the memorial service?" he asks in a tone that's both authoritative and welcoming.

"Yes," I say, wondering how he knows. Maybe it's the only event here tonight.

"Second floor," he says, gesturing to the staircase. "The room will be on your left."

I'm only going to stay a few minutes, I tell myself as I tread soundlessly up the carpeted stairs. I can't pinpoint exactly what I'm after. I guess I'm hoping to learn something that will assuage my guilt and close this chapter for me.

When I reach the landing, I turn to the left. The door to the room closest to me is open, and I can see people mingling inside. It looks like there are fewer than twenty. I'd imagined rows of chairs, with a speaker eulogizing Amanda. I'd thought I could slip in and take a seat in the back unobtrusively.

Coming to this intimate gathering was a mistake; I don't belong, no matter what that flyer on Amanda's apartment door said.

Before I can take a step back, a woman approaches me. Even in a city populated by models and actresses, she stands out. It isn't simply that she's beautiful. She radiates something indefinable, an aura that feels magnetic. She's around my age and we're both wearing black dresses. But she seems like she inhabits a different world.

"Welcome," she says in a slightly throaty voice, reaching out to take my hand. Instead of shaking it, she folds it between both of hers. Despite the air-conditioning, her skin is warm. "Thank you for coming."

It's too late now. I have to muddle through this. "Thanks for having me." I realize it sounds inane. It's not as if she personally invited me here. She keeps my hand in hers.

"I'm Cassandra Moore." Her almond-shaped eyes are golden brown, and her cheekbones are high and sharp. Her shoulders are pulled back, and her posture is so flawless I can almost imagine a book balancing perfectly on the top of her head.

I realize I'm staring, so I quickly say, "Shay Miller."

"Shay Miller." Cassandra somehow makes my name sound exotic. "And how did you know Amanda?"

I can't tell her the truth—she'll probably think it's strange, just like Mel did. So I clear my throat and glance around the room frantically.

I notice two things: The first is that other than two men, everyone here is a woman—and almost all of them are around my age.

The second is the poster-size picture of Amanda holding a calico cat.

"We had the same veterinarian," I blurt. "We both had cats."

Cassandra releases my hand. "How sweet."

I immediately wish I hadn't lied. Why didn't I just say we lived in the same neighborhood?

Before I can turn around her question and find out how she knew Amanda, she says, "Why don't you have a drink and something to eat. There's plenty." She gestures toward the corner, where I see a bar and a buffet table. "And please make sure to sign the guest book."

I smile and thank her.

"Shay?" she says as I turn away.

I look back at her, and I'm struck anew by her vibrant presence.

"It really is so kind of you to come tonight. We were expecting a larger crowd, but people are so busy these days. . . . We're all so disconnected, living our separate lives. But you took the time to be here."

Her words do more than wash away the embarrassment and shame I felt only moments ago.

They make me feel like I belong.

My posture straightens as I head to the bar and ask for a mineral water, then I wander through the room. There isn't a program, or any other photograph of Amanda. It's such an odd memorial.

I do a double take when I notice the big bouquet of yellow zinnias next to Amanda's photograph. *This one,* I remember thinking as my hand reached past the lilies and roses to select it to lay on her doorstep.

My heartbeat quickens. Why did I pick that particular flower over all the other options displayed in buckets at the corner deli I passed on the way to Amanda's apartment? Maybe she shopped at that deli, too. Could it actually have been her favorite flower?

I tear away my gaze and sign the guest book, as Cassandra asked. I write my full name—Shay Miller—but leave the spot for my address blank. The information is probably being collected for Amanda's family, maybe so they can send thank-you notes to her friends for attending the memorial, or simply to keep in touch with them.

I put down the pen, then walk over to Amanda's picture. I stare at it for a long time.

My impression of her in the subway is confirmed: She looks kind.

I wish I could have helped you, I think. *I wish I had noticed sooner. I'm so sorry.*

I feel a tear slide down my cheek. Then I notice something: In the photo, Amanda is wearing a gold charm on a fine chain. The charm is shaped like a sun.

Goose bumps rise on my skin as the realization slams into me: It's the necklace I found on the subway platform.

Where is it now? I wonder. The hours following Amanda's suicide are a blur. Maybe I put it in my shoulder bag. I reach into my tote and try to discreetly feel around, but my fingertips don't catch on any small, sharp edges.

I probably dropped the necklace in the shock of the moment, but just in case, I'll check my bag again later, I decide.

By now, two other women have come up to look at Amanda's photograph.

"I'm going to miss the way she always teased me about my accent," one says.

"I can still hear her asking if 'ya pahked ya cah in Hahvad Yahd,'" the other adds.

Then a third woman comes over and wraps her arms around the other two. Other than that they all appear to be around thirty, they have almost nothing in common physically. The woman with the Boston accent looks a little like an unmade bed—her shirt is rumpled, her red hair is untamed, and she's holding a wad of crumpled paper napkins. The woman who imitated her accent is small and tough looking, with a purple streak in her dirty-blond hair. The third is the kind of woman I think of as a glossy girl—from the tips of her fingernails to the delicate straps of her blush-colored sandals, she's perfectly put together.

The affection between the trio is tangible. And Amanda—again, appearing so different from all of them—was obviously part of their group.

Maybe they were all sorority sisters in college, I think.

I wonder if Amanda, who clearly had such loyal friends, reached out to them for help. They obviously cared deeply for her. But I guess whatever she was grappling with was too strong for her to overcome, even with their support.

I watch as the three women lean their heads close together again, talking, then the one with the purple streak in her hair turns to look at me, her close-set eyes narrowing. The two others do as well.

I quickly move away in case they intend to approach me to talk about Amanda. Even though Cassandra welcomed me, I'm still an impostor.

As I begin to walk toward the door, yet another woman appears in my path. "Are you okay?" She gives me a sympathetic smile and a dimple appears in her right cheek. "I'm Jane. You met my sister Cassandra earlier."

I would've guessed they're related: They share not only the same ebony hair and luminous skin, but the same magnetic quality. Jane is more petite than her sister, with softer features and a gentle voice.

"Thanks." I take the tissue she offers. I reach beneath my glasses to dab at my eyes. "I guess . . . I just wish I could have helped Amanda."

Jane takes a step closer to me and I inhale the sweet smell of her floral perfume. "I know," she says, her voice confiding. "A lot of us are grappling with complicated feelings today. I certainly am."

Perhaps everybody second-guesses themselves in the aftermath of a suicide, I think.

I'd give anything to take back my lie about how I met Amanda, but since I can't, I'm honest with Jane now. "I didn't really know her well, but I can't stop thinking about her. I suppose I came here to learn more about her."

"I see." Jane cocks her head to the side, like something has just occurred to her. "You know, a bunch of us are going out for a drink after the service. You should come."

"O-oh," I stutter, so surprised by the invitation I can barely talk. "I, uh, have plans."

She looks disappointed. "That's too bad. I know we just met, but I have a feeling we might have a lot to talk about."

Before I can reply, Cassandra breaks away from her conversation with a tearful older woman holding a glass of wine who looks like she could be Amanda's mother. Cassandra gives the woman a hug, then strides toward us, her gaze fixed on me.

She touches my arm, keeping her hand there. "My sister and I know what it's like to struggle with loss. Please reach out if you ever want to talk. Connecting with each other is one of the most essential things we can do. I only wish Amanda . . ."

I find myself nodding. "I would really like that." Cassandra awards me a full, genuine smile.

"Here." She's holding out a business card with her free hand. The embossed black letters stand out sharply against the crisp white rectangle: CASSANDRA MOORE. Instead of any business contact information, there's just a phone number and email address.

"I hope we'll see you again, Shay." Cassandra removes her hand, but I can still feel the heat of its imprint on my bare forearm. Suddenly I don't want to leave.

It's no longer about the connection I feel toward Amanda. It's the connection I *want* to feel with her friends.

CHAPTER NINE

CASSANDRA & JANE

CASSANDRA AND JANE LEARN two things about Shay during their brief encounter with her.

She is a bad liar; her cheeks flushed and she avoided eye contact when she fabricated the story about the veterinarian.

And Shay has a strange and alarming attachment to Amanda.

Immediately following the memorial service, Shay walks to a bistro and sits at the bar. She is watched by Valerie, the sixth and final member of the group—and the only one who didn't attend the service.

Valerie, who was an actress in Los Angeles before moving to New York, is employed by Cassandra and Jane at their PR firm. She assists them with many professional assignments, as well as personal ones.

There is little danger of Shay noticing that she is under observation. Valerie is a chameleon; tonight she wears a simple navy dress with her hair tied in a low ponytail. She stands near a high bar table populated by a group of tourists and effortlessly blends in with them.

Initially, Shay's story about having plans appears to be true. But as the minutes pass and no one joins her, it becomes obvious this is yet another lie. Shay sips a beer and eats a burger and occasionally looks down at her phone.

After about an hour, she exits the restaurant. The credit card slip she signed was quickly retrieved by the bartender before her name could be verified.

Shay walks thirty-eight blocks to her apartment with a loping, athletic stride, not even pausing at several subway stops that would quicken her journey.

It's another curious detail about her. Perhaps the subway carries a dark reminder of Amanda.

She disappears into a five-story white-brick residential building.

The same building that, according to the sisters' tracking device, holds Amanda's necklace.

Valerie continues to watch the entrance, but Shay remains inside, keeping with her any secrets she might be holding about Amanda.

Valerie is raising her cell phone to take a picture of a man as he enters Shay's building—he might be a neighbor who could provide useful information—when an incoming call from Cassandra registers on the screen.

"I'm with Daphne," Cassandra begins.

Valerie's hand reflexively clenches the phone at Cassandra's tone.

"A police detective left a message for her while we were at the memorial service," Cassandra continues. "She asked if Daphne could give her a call to answer a few questions."

Valerie sucks in a breath. "About Amanda?"

"No. About a man named James whom Daphne went on a blind date with ten months ago."

CHAPTER TEN

DAPHNE

Ten months ago

DAPHNE STOOD IN THE FOYER of the small Italian restaurant, adjusting the vintage scarf around her neck. No matter how many first dates she went on, her stomach always fluttered at this moment.

She'd pulled a winter-white wool dress and high-heeled boots from the showroom of her West Village boutique and had gotten a blowout at lunchtime. *I think you two will hit it off,* Kit, the customer who'd set them up on a blind date, had said. *James was in the same fraternity as my husband in college, and they recently reconnected. He's a really fun guy.*

The door opened and a tall, broad-shouldered man walked in. "You must be Daphne." He broke into a wide smile and leaned down to kiss her cheek. "I'm James."

He was as attractive as Kit had indicated. Plus James had been so complimentary and warm in the texts they'd exchanged that she felt the night held promise. He'd told her he liked her name and suggested they eat at a restaurant that would be convenient for her.

"The gnocchi here is insane," James said as the hostess led them to an intimate table by the fireplace.

Another point in his favor: A lot of guys would have suggested meeting for a drink. James seemed to want to get to know her.

"Should we get a bottle of wine?" he asked, and when she agreed, he ordered Pinot Grigio.

She preferred red wine, but she let it go.

As a busboy filled their water glasses, James launched into a funny story about his buddy's wedding to Kit, recounting how the band's lead singer didn't show up. "So we all took turns grabbing the mic and performing."

"What did you sing?"

He started laughing so hard it was contagious. His laugh was wonderful—warm and inviting.

"Tell me!"

"'My Heart Will Go On.'" He could barely choke out the words.

"By Celine Dion? You did not!"

"'Near, far, wherever you are . . . '" he sang in a falsetto.

"Please tell me there's video!" She finally composed herself, taking a sip of the wine, which tasted good after all. James was solicitous, offering her a bite of his gnocchi and coaxing her to tell stories about her customers.

It was, she thought, the best first date she'd been on in a long time.

As he lifted the wine bottle to refill her glass, she said, "Oh, just a splash for me." She had an early morning tomorrow; she was opening the boutique.

"C'mon." He filled it up. "It's the weekend." As he put down the bottle, she noticed his fingers were thick and strong looking.

Nothing set off alarm bells for Daphne during dinner. That was one of the worst parts; later she would go over the night obsessively in her head, asking herself if she'd missed a clue. A whiff of danger that had swept past her.

When the bill came, James reached for it so quickly she didn't have a chance to offer to split it, which made him seem chivalrous.

As they stepped outside, James said, "Can I walk you home?"

For a brief moment, she wondered how he knew she lived nearby. Then she remembered he'd chosen a restaurant in a location she'd said would be convenient. Naturally, he'd deduced it was near her apartment.

He talked easily as they walked, stopping to pet a Standard Poodle as the smiling owner looked on. Then he slipped Daphne's hand into his. His grip felt firm and welcome.

By the time they reached her apartment building, Daphne was hoping he'd kiss her good-night.

"This was really nice," she said as they reached the entrance of her apartment. She looked up at him, feeling a little shy. She was picky; she hadn't kissed a man in months. "Thank you for dinner."

He leaned in and kissed her, slowly and softly. She brought her hands to his shoulders. He pulled her in more closely. The kiss lingered, his tongue teasing apart her lips.

It felt so good to be touched. To be wanted.

When they broke apart, she smiled. "Thanks again," she said, and turned to walk into her lobby.

"Hey," James said, and she turned back around. "Do you mind if I use your bathroom real quick?"

She blinked. It felt like a strange request.

"Sorry, it was that last glass of wine." He laughed.

How could she say no to this nice man who'd just taken her out to dinner; this guy who liked dogs and held open doors for her? "Sure."

She felt a moment of awkwardness when they passed the doorman, Raymond, who greeted her with no indication that he was surprised to see her bring home an unfamiliar man even though he'd never before seen her return at night with one.

Raymond had probably been watching as she and James kissed; they were clearly visible through the glass-walled lobby entrance.

"Good night," she said to Raymond as they passed.

"Night," James added, which had seemed odd to Daphne—after all, he'd be leaving in a minute—but maybe he'd just spoken the word automatically.

James put his palm on the small of her back as they walked to the elevator. So low it grazed her butt.

Daphne flushed, wondering if Raymond was watching this, too. She reached back and removed his hand.

They stood side by side as they rode the elevator to the tenth floor. The easy conversation between them stuttered. James was staring straight ahead, no longer smiling.

Had he been expecting more?

They'd flirted all night, but that didn't mean she wanted to sleep with him so soon.

She decided to leave the door to her apartment open and stand by it. She could gesture to show James the way to the bathroom; there was one in her hallway. Then she would motion him out; he'd get the message clearly.

That's exactly what Daphne started to do. She heard the toilet flush, then the sink faucet running—she flashed back to his strong-looking hands—then James reappeared.

She was halfway out the door. There was no way he could misread her signals.

James approached. She shuffled a bit to let him pass. Still with one foot in her apartment, and one in the hallway. But he paused right in front of her.

Now he was straddling the threshold, too.

James leaned down to kiss her again. She made the split-second decision to allow this; it seemed like the easiest way to get rid of him.

It felt almost as if she were kissing a different man; his lips were no longer tender, and he pressed his body against hers. She could smell the garlic from his gnocchi on his breath.

Her customer Kit had mentioned her husband recently reconnected with James. How well did they know him?

Daphne didn't even know *Kit* all that well, she realized.

Daphne pulled away. "Thanks again."

But he didn't move.

The hallway was well lit, but her apartment was not. James's face was half in the shadows, half in the light.

"Does it have to be over?"

Her heart began to pound, but she forced herself to smile. "I've got an early morning."

Daphne saw something enter his eyes that made her instincts finally scream the warning they'd been whispering ever since James had asked to come upstairs.

"I'm just really tired." Anxiety filled her voice. "But I'll call you."

"Sure you will." He still didn't move.

Adrenaline flooded her body. No one else was within view. The doorman was ten flights away. She prayed for the sound of the elevator ding, announcing that a neighbor was coming. But the hallway was still.

He kept staring at her, his face expressionless.

"So . . ." Her voice faltered. "It's getting late. . . ."

The instant he stopped blocking the door, she'd slam it and quickly engage the dead bolt. She'd also phone Raymond to make sure James had really left the building.

After what seemed like an eternity, he finally lifted his foot and stepped into the hallway. But he didn't turn his back to her. Instead, he edged sideways. Still, at least he was no longer in the threshold.

Daphne leaped back into her apartment and began to slam the door.

But his arm shot out and pushed it violently in the other direction while her palms were still on it. She tumbled backward, unsteady on her heels.

It was James who slid home the dead bolt.

In the days that followed, Daphne picked up the phone a half dozen times to call the police. But she always hung up before dialing.

She kept experiencing the sensation of James's hands closing around her throat while she lay there, unmoving. His ugly words reverberated in her mind: *I know you like it rough.*

The only evidence she had was the faint bruise on her neck. She imagined a prosecutor asking, *Did you tell him to stop?*

It would be her word against his. Even her doorman likely saw them kissing, and definitely saw her leading him into the elevator. She knew the legal system had failed other women. She couldn't trust that justice would prevail.

Late one night, she reached for her phone and sent James a text: *I hope you rot in hell.* Then she blocked him. It felt like such an inconsequential reaction, but she didn't know what else to do.

She told no one at first. Daphne was an only child, and she wasn't close to her parents, who'd had her later in life. They hadn't been trying for a child and didn't seem particularly pleased to be raising one, even a quiet, self-sufficient little girl.

She tried to lose herself in long, exhausting runs along the West Side Highway, and she began dropping weight. Food held little appeal. She couldn't meet the eyes of Raymond whenever she passed through her lobby.

Then one day, a few weeks after the attack, a chime sounded in her boutique. Daphne had taken to locking up when she was alone and leaving a sign directing shoppers to press the doorbell.

It was a slow Tuesday afternoon on a slushy winter day, but somehow, none of the dirty gray snow or salt on the sidewalks marred the high leather boots of the two women who strolled in. Daphne had never seen them before, but she immediately guessed they were sisters.

"We've walked by your shop a million times and we've always wanted to stop in," Cassandra gushed.

"I can already tell this place is going to be my new favorite addiction!" Jane said, running her fingertips over a stack of cashmere sweaters.

They'd stayed for nearly an hour, chatting easily as they tried on clothes and sipped from the flutes of champagne that Daphne brought out for good customers. They were much friendlier than most of the shoppers who passed through Daphne's door; the sisters seemed truly interested in getting to know her.

By the time she was packing their purchases into glossy shopping bags, Daphne felt a little lighter, as if the presence of these warm, vibrant, strong women had somehow provided a barrier against the emotions battering her.

"We'll be back soon, Daphne!" Jane promised as the sisters left.

And they were, a few days later.

A week or so after that, they'd invited Daphne to Jane's apartment for drinks. It felt natural and spontaneous, like an extension of the drinks and conversation they'd shared in the boutique.

Daphne hadn't intended to reveal James's assault to the sisters. She barely knew them after all. But something about them—she couldn't quite put her finger on what—invited her confidence. They seemed to know exactly what to say to draw her out. As Daphne sat on Jane's couch, stroking Jane's pretty little calico cat, Hepburn, Daphne felt less alone.

Cassandra's eyes had darkened. "James is a criminal. He raped you, Daphne."

Jane had wrapped an arm around Daphne: "What can we do to help?"

"I don't know," Daphne had whispered. "I just want him to pay for this."

Later the sisters told Daphne that was the moment they knew she was one of them.

They were a group of five: First Cassandra, Jane, and Valerie, then Beth—whom Valerie had gotten to know because they were neighbors in an apartment building—had joined the circle. And shortly thereafter, Beth had brought in Stacey.

Their vote was unanimous: Daphne would become the sixth member.

CHAPTER ELEVEN

SHAY

Strategies to alleviate panic attacks:
1. *Breathe in through your nose to the count of five, hold it for the count of five, and breathe out through your mouth to the count of five.*
2. *Count backward from 100 by 3's.*
3. *Tune into four things you can see, three things you can touch, two things you can smell, and one thing you can taste.*

★Attempts to enter subway without a panic attack: 12 (none successful)

—Data Book, page 11

I THOUGHT AMANDA'S MEMORIAL service would provide a sense of closure, and things would get better.

But they're worse.

Nearly two weeks have passed since I saw her jump, and I still can't get close to a subway. Home is no respite; Sean rarely spends time at Jody's place because she lives in a tiny two-bedroom with two other girls. So they're always around, cooking dinner or cuddling on the couch in front of the TV.

I walk and take buses when possible, but sometimes taxis are the only option—like the other day when my bus broke down and I was running late to my temp job. The fares are whittling away at my bank account.

Geography is shaping my choices: I feel like my life is tunneling inward. Instead of visiting the Brooklyn Botanic Garden over the weekend, which always brings me peace, I went to a smaller park a few blocks away. My favorite CrossFit class is in SoHo, but I've begun frequenting a little gym that's only a few blocks away.

Sometimes, when I reach into my tote bag, I think I feel the scrape of a tiny, sharp edge against my fingertips and I'm convinced I've found Amanda's necklace. But it's just the ridge on my Chap Stick tube, or the bend in the stem of my sunglasses, or the uneven seam at the bottom of my bag. I've turned my tote inside out more than once, but it's never there. I wonder if it's still glinting somewhere down in the Thirty-third Street subway station.

I dread falling asleep, knowing nightmares await. The worst one yet left me drenched in sweat: I was running down the subway platform, desperately trying to stop Amanda from jumping and knowing I wouldn't get there in time. Just as I reached for her arm, clawing at empty air as she pulled away, she turned to look at me.

But instead of *her* face, I was staring into my own.

That's what made me finally pick up the phone and schedule an appointment with a psychologist. I'd like to say I selected her based on her academic credentials or a referral, but the truth is, I chose my therapist because she is covered by my insurance—and the walk is only eight minutes.

My first session with Paula revolved around goal setting. I was a little nervous when I sat down in her small, utilitarian office on East Twenty-fourth Street, but I reminded myself how common it is to seek therapy: 42 percent of Americans have been in counseling. One in five millennials currently see a therapist—although I never have before.

Paula suggested I set a small objective to work on, and she agreed the one I selected seemed doable.

"It'll be a good first step," Paula had said, and I'd smiled, confident I was finally on the right track.

But now, at the start of our second session, as I sit aimlessly moving a tiny rake through a little Zen sand garden while Paula looks over her notes from our last session, I feel as if the hope she offered me has floated away.

Paula finally looks up and smiles. "Okay, then. Did you achieve your goal of touching the green subway railing?"

I put down the rake and cross my arms over my chest, rubbing my hands up and down my bare arms.

I'm aware of Paula's gaze on me, but I can't meet hers as I shake my head. "I only got to the edge of the grate." I feel my throat thicken with the words.

She writes something in her notebook, then takes off her reading glasses. "Have you been trying the other techniques we discussed?"

I lift up my left hand to show her the blue rubber band around my wrist. Paula had told me to snap it hard when the panic began to descend. *It'll distract your mind,* she promised. It was one of many remedies she'd suggested, from a gratitude journal to tackling my phobia by breaking it down to a series of steps.

None of it is working. The only thing that has helped me at all is the Ambien I bought off a sketchy Canadian pharmaceutical website. I took it for the first time last night. It delivered oblivion and left me so groggy I slept through my alarm, but at least that's better than a nightmare.

We talk awhile longer about how to scale down my goal.

"Maybe you can look at pictures of subways on your computer at home. It could help desensitize you. And then perhaps attempt to walk over a subway grate."

Even though I nod, I already know I'm not going to be able to do it. Just the thought of it causes a hitch in my heartbeat.

What's happening to me? I want to cry out.

I try to swallow down the wobble I know my voice will contain before asking, "I guess I was wondering how long you think it's going to take me to feel better. . . . I have another job interview next week, but if I'm hired, I'd have to take three buses to get there."

Paula closes her notebook, and I see her sneak a glance at the clock on her desk.

"Shay, you came in here because of one specific incident, but I believe there's something deeper going on."

My gut clenches because I know she's right. I've tried to put what I witnessed into perspective by analyzing the data, by framing Amanda's

tragedy in facts: More than two dozen other people leaped in front of
New York City subway trains this year alone. A hundred pedestrians
were fatally hit by vehicles in my city last year, along with dozens of
bikers. Jumping from a tall building is the fourth-most common way to
commit suicide in New York, and homicides occur here daily.

There are witnesses to almost all of these horrific deaths; I read some
of their quotes in the newspapers. While it seems certain that other ob-
servers are also affected—how could they not be?—I wonder if it's a
natural consequence for onlookers to be as traumatized as I seem to be.

Maybe it isn't what I witnessed that's causing all of this, I think as I
sink lower into the chair across from Paula. Perhaps the tragedy of
that muggy Sunday morning and the bad luck that preceded it simply
flipped some kind of a switch in me that was waiting to be activated.

"I'd love to give you a specific timeline for healing, but I can't,"
Paula says.

"But—like weeks? Months?" I ask desperately.

"Oh, Shay." She seems truly sorry. "There's no quick fix in therapy."

Just like that, the wispy tendrils of hope float even further away.

I walk home in the sundress and flats I wore to my temp job, hoping
Sean and Jody are out so I can have the sofa to myself. All I have the
energy to do is make microwave popcorn for dinner and watch mind-
less television.

When I enter the apartment, one of my wishes is granted: The apartment is empty.

I head into my bedroom to strip off my sundress. I pull a pair of
shorts off the top of my basket of clean laundry, hesitating when I realize they're the same ones I wore the day Amanda died.

But this is a challenge I can surmount. I pull them on.

The pockets are bunched up from being swished around in the
washing machine, so as I wander into the kitchen to grab a seltzer, I
absently stick my fingers into them to flatten them out.

My feet stutter to a stop.

I checked my tote bag several times, shaking it upside down and running my hand along the seams. But I never once thought to look in the pockets of what I'd been wearing that day.

As I slowly draw out my right hand, I know what I'm going to see even before my fingers clear the top of my shorts.

It was here all along, inches from me. Waiting to be discovered.

If I'd gotten rid of these shorts to avoid the reminder, I would never have found it.

The necklace is heavier than I remembered. Maybe that's because I feel like it's bearing the weight of all the emotions I've experienced since the moment I first picked it up.

I must have shoved it in my pocket sometime after Amanda stepped toward the edge of the platform and I heard the whoosh of the oncoming train.

It was the last thing I did before everything changed.

My lungs feel as if a vise is squeezing them.

I stare at the gold necklace with the sun-shaped charm dangling between my fingers.

The one I'm now certain belonged to Amanda.

CHAPTER TWELVE

CASSANDRA & JANE

THE SISTERS ARE STEALTHILY ransacking Shay's life—scouring the internet for every wisp of her electronic footprints, dissecting her routines, canvassing her contacts, and delving into her background.

From her LinkedIn account they learn Shay has held three jobs since she graduated from Boston University, but now temps for a Wall Street law firm. By tracing the tentacles of her Facebook profile, they discover that her best friend, Mel, has a new baby and lives in Brooklyn.

They learn even more by following Shay, like the fact that she enjoys the falafel from the Greek restaurant a few blocks down from her apartment, and that she works out almost every day. "Her roommate, Sean, is in a serious relationship," Stacey reports after following Sean to a bar, where he met his girlfriend for happy hour. "He's trying to start his own college-prep tutoring company."

Their scrutiny extends to encompass her family: Her mother, Jackie, isn't shy about posting bikini shots on Instagram, and her stepfather tinkers with his Ford Mustang in his spare time.

What the sisters still don't know: how the mysterious woman who clearly goes out of her way to avoid even getting near a subway station is linked to Amanda.

"She can't be a relative or she would have acknowledged Amanda's mother at the funeral. She can't be a close friend because she wasn't even listed in Amanda's contacts," says Cassandra.

The two women's lives have no other natural intersections. They didn't grow up in the same town or attend the same college.

"They lived near each other," Cassandra says to Jane as the Town Car they've hired for the evening pulls up in front of a Chelsea art gallery. "Six blocks apart."

The sisters are careful to sanitize their conversation in case the driver is eavesdropping: no names or identifying details.

"That doesn't mean they ever met. New York can be a city of strangers." Jane keeps her tone light, as if they are gossiping about acquaintances. "Do you know the names of everyone in your building? Or in our yoga class?"

Cassandra nods to acknowledge the point as the driver opens the back door.

Right now, Shay is a bigger concern than even the police detective who reached out to Daphne to ask about Daphne's date with James.

Daphne had been badly thrown by the call, but the sisters had coached her well, and Daphne had handled herself beautifully during the brief police interview.

Daphne had told the detective, a woman named Marcia Santiago, that she'd gone out on a single date with James that previous fall. She'd found him handsome and charming. They'd ended the romantic evening in her apartment.

Then had come the tricky question: *Why did you send that hostile text to a man you say you liked?*

Daphne had given her practiced answer: *He never called like he promised. I was upset.*

Detective Santiago had stared at her for a long, unsettling moment. Then she'd closed her notebook, saying, *I may have some follow-up questions.*

That was two weeks ago. There has been no further contact.

There's no reason to worry that the police are continuing to investigate any connection between Daphne and James.

Cassandra and Jane thank their driver, then step out of the sedan and walk toward the entrance of the gallery.

The balmy early-September air caresses Cassandra's shoulders, which her slinky red halter top leaves bare. She wears butter-soft leather leggings and high-heeled sandals. Jane's fitted dress accentuates her hour-glass shape, and her delicate gold and platinum bangles clink as she pulls open the door.

The gallery is hosting an opening for the promising young mixed-media artist the sisters represent, Willow Tanaka. She was profiled in this week's *New York* magazine.

Heads turn as the sisters step in—shoulders back, high-wattage smiles in place. They are completely at ease in this cultured, sophisticated environment: They know which clothes to wear, the correct way to eat the oysters offered by a passing waiter, and how to gracefully extricate themselves from unproductive conversations.

Seeing Cassandra and Jane in this moment, no one would ever guess the details that compose their backstory: Their father died when Jane was still an infant. Their mother scrambled to make ends meet. The girls wore hand-me-downs and often ate peanut butter sandwiches for dinner alone while watching television.

But the sisters possess something money can't buy. Something grittier than perseverance and more powerful than determination. It carried Cassandra and Jane through college, as they cobbled together scholarships and loans and part-time jobs, and led them to an enviable life in one of the world's most dazzling cities.

As Cassandra accepts a glass of champagne from a waiter, she looks at the collage hanging on the wall, priced at seventeen thousand dollars.

The canvas, one of fifteen on display, depicts the water's edge. Rough, foamy waves crash into gray boulders under a bleak sky. It's delicate yet assured and stark—at least at first glance.

When they glimpsed Willow's work in the small, turpentine-scented apartment that doubled as her studio, they were mesmerized. Layered into her paint strokes are curious objects: a feather, a typewriter key, and a dried mushroom.

Right now, Willow is just a few feet away, talking to a prospective buyer. She's as compelling as her creations: Willow's blunt bob is dyed white-blond, which contrasts with the thick red liner winging her eyes and her midnight-black dress.

"This one is my favorite," Cassandra tells her sister, pointing to a piece featuring the Kiso Mountains.

The collage holds the eyes of a puffer fish, a *Nerium oleander* flower, and the silver mercury from a thermometer, all woven so seamlessly into the brushstrokes that it takes several moments for the eye to distinguish them.

As with all of Willow's work, the seemingly disparate elements share a common denominator: They are linked to death. Even the key is from the typewriter of a serial killer.

Without the relevant information, though, the ingredients appear innocuous.

Maybe there's a lesson here, Cassandra thinks. They've been assembling facts about Shay. But they're missing the invisible ingredient that will link all the disparate parts together.

Shay also appears innocuous. But is she?

Cassandra's thoughts are interrupted as Willow rushes over to give them both a hug.

"Cheers," Jane says, lifting her champagne glass and handing one to Willow. "Tonight is a triumph."

"The *Times* review is going to be a rave," Cassandra says.

The sisters want to savor the moment, but the alert tone for Valerie's texts—one that's distinct from the sounds assigned to everyone else in their contacts—is erupting on both of their phones.

Valerie is keeping an eye on Shay tonight—or more accurately, the tracker in the necklace that Shay somehow got from Amanda.

Cassandra and Jane don't look at each other, but a cord of energy pulses between them. Cassandra murmurs an excuse to Willow while Jane turns and pulls her phone out of her purse as a second text sounds.

Shay just left her apartment with the necklace.

Then: *She's heading uptown. I'm 20 minutes away from her. Getting a cab.*

As Cassandra stares over Jane's shoulder at the phone, a new text lands: *She's past the Starbucks now, going toward the subway.*

It's the exact route Amanda took on the last day of her life.

The sisters weave toward the door—waving at an acquaintance, sliding their champagne glasses onto an empty table, dodging a man who steps in front of them with a smile, never stopping but never giving the impression they're rushing out of the gallery.

Why now, so many days after Amanda's death, is Shay moving the necklace? And, far more important, where is Shay taking it?

They're almost at the exit when a hand lands on Jane's arm.

"Darlings! You're not leaving so soon? The evening's just getting started!"

It's Oliver, the owner of the gallery and the one other person here besides Willow that Cassandra and Jane can't rebuff. When the sisters first started out, they splurged on an abstract painting for the entryway of their new offices. Oliver sold it to them—and became enamored of them, announcing, "I'm going to be your fairy godfather!"

Oliver, a slim Brit, throws lavish but intimate dinner parties, pulling in a mix of some of the most relevant people in the city. In addition to Willow, he has connected the sisters with two other good clients.

"Come with me," he commands, gesturing toward the thick of the crowd. "There's someone you must meet!"

Again, the identical sound erupts on their phones. It's barely discernible amid the noise of a dozen conversations in the gallery. But it's all the sisters can hear.

Jane sucks in a breath. Cassandra's grip tightens around the handle of her purse.

Another chime. The sisters can feel tension rising not just in themselves, but in each other.

"I'm so sorry, but we have to rush off," Jane tells Oliver.

"I'm afraid I'm coming down with something." Cassandra puts a hand to her stomach. All the color has drained from her face, supporting her fib.

"Poor girl, go get some rest." Oliver blows them kisses.

This time, they manage to depart without any interruptions.

They pull out their phones and read the new texts from Valerie:

At 49th Street. Just saw Shay crossing street.

Where are you two??

Then: *Out of cab. I'm right behind her now.*

Jane phones their driver and instructs him to pick them up as quickly as possible.

Cassandra types to Valerie: *We're in Chelsea, coming as fast as we can.*

"Come on!" Jane says, pacing the sidewalk and craning her head to see if the driver is approaching. But traffic is clogged—it's still the tail end of rush hour—and the Town Car isn't in view.

Has Shay been playing them, with her shy manner and quiet life? She could destroy everything the sisters have built.

The final text lands.

Jane grips her sister's arm as Cassandra whispers, "No."

Shay just walked into a police station.

CHAPTER THIRTEEN

SHAY

Loneliness is spreading to more and more people, almost like a virus. These days, roughly 40 percent of Americans report feeling isolated on a regular basis—double the approximately 20 percent in the 1980s. One survey found Gen Zers (those born 2001–now) to be the most lonely, followed by millennials (those born 1980–2000—my generation).
—Data Book, page 15

I'VE NEVER BEEN INSIDE a police station before, but television prepared me for the Seventeenth Precinct: Two rough-looking benches line the hallway walls, the floor is composed of scuffed linoleum squares, and a uniformed officer eyes me from behind a glass partition.

He continues to regard me steadily as I approach, but waits for me to speak first. "I'm Shay Miller. I spoke to Detective Williams earlier today and she asked me to drop this off."

I reach into my purse for the letter-size white envelope that contains Amanda's necklace. I wrote *Detective Williams* on the outside so it won't get lost a second time.

I'm about to slide it through the opening at the bottom of the glass when the officer says, "Hold on," and reaches for the phone. He turns slightly, and I can't hear any of the conversation.

He hangs up and swivels to face me again. "Detective Williams will be out soon."

"Oh." From my conversation with her earlier, I assumed I'd just be dropping it off so she could return it to Amanda's family. But maybe she wants to collect it in person.

I look behind me, at the long, scarred wooden benches. They're bolted to the floor.

I stand there for another second, then walk over and sit on the edge of the closest bench, still holding the envelope. I can feel the metal chain and the intricate charm through the thin paper.

Before I called Detective Williams, I stared at the necklace for a long time. It still looked to me like a blazing sun, with rays firing out in all directions. The gold is strong but delicate. It seems expensive, and I thought Amanda's family might want it back as a memento.

I'd noticed one other thing: The chain was broken.

Maybe that's why it had fallen off Amanda's neck in the subway. But other possibilities had occurred to me on the walk to the police station: Someone could have ripped it off her neck. Or she could have yanked it away herself.

"Shay?" I look up and see Detective Williams striding through the security door. She's got unlined dark skin and a close-cropped Afro. She's wearing a crisp blue pantsuit—similar to the gray one she had on when I first met her—and the same impassive expression she wore when she questioned me on the subway platform after Amanda's suicide.

"Come with me, please," she says in her soft voice.

My brow furrows. What else can she need from me?

I follow her down a hallway lined with a few small, spare rooms—probably places where suspects are questioned—and into an open area filled with desks and chairs. It smells like french fries, and I spot a Mc-Donald's bag on the desk of an officer who's simultaneously eating dinner and filling out paperwork.

"Have a seat." She gestures to a chair. Her words could make it an invitation, but her tone straddles the edge of an order.

She walks around to the other side of the desk and sits down. She pulls her chair in closer, her movements slow and deliberate.

When she reaches for a notebook and pen in her top drawer, then fixes me with her inscrutable dark brown eyes, my mouth turns dry.

I can't shake the sense that I'm in trouble.

The detective can't suspect *I* had something to do with Amanda's death. Can she?

She turns to the first blank page of the notebook. "Tell me again how you came to realize the necklace belonged to Amanda Evinger."

"I saw this picture at her memorial ser—" The realization hits me: Detective Williams must be wondering why I went to a memorial for a woman I never met.

I haven't done anything illegal, I think frantically. *I was just in the wrong place at the wrong time.*

But I'm holding a broken necklace that was on Amanda, and I was beside her when she leaped to her death. When I reached out to try to grab her, could someone have thought I was pushing her?

My breathing is so ragged I worry it'll seem like evidence of my guilt. Detective Williams is waiting. Not saying a word.

"I know it sounds strange," I blurt. "I just felt this—this connection to her because I was there right before she . . ." I can barely choke out the words. "That's all it was. I went to pay my respects."

The detective writes something down in her notebook. I'm desperate to see it, but I can't read her tiny, squiggly letters—especially upside down. It seems to take her forever.

She lifts her head again. I can't tell if she believes a word I've said. "How did you know about the memorial service?"

Inwardly I cringe. I'm digging myself into a deeper hole. My upper lip and brow are sweaty. My heart is pounding so hard I feel as if Detective Williams must be able to see it pulsing through my shirt—as if it's another piece of evidence in the case she might be compiling. I doubt innocent people panic like this.

"Do I need a lawyer?" My voice is shaking.

She frowns. "Why would you think that?"

I push my glasses up higher on my nose and swallow hard. "Look, I just—I found her address after you gave me her name. I was wondering about her, and she lived near me. So I took a flower and left it on her doorstep. That's where I saw the notice about the memorial service."

I wonder if the detective already knows about the yellow zinnia I left, and the way I lied at the service about how I knew Amanda.

Detective Williams looks at me for a long, steady moment. "Anything else you want to tell me? Are you still hanging around her apartment?"

I shake my head. "No, just that one time." I'm near tears. "That's the whole story, I swear."

She closes her notebook and stretches out her hand. For a moment I think she's reaching for mine, but she just wants the envelope. I give it to her, noticing it's now crumpled and damp from my sweaty palms.

"That's all I need for now." She stands up.

I do the same, my legs weak with relief.

As we retrace our steps down the hallway, Detective Williams asks me one final question: "You still seem really shaken up by all this. Is there someone you can talk to?"

No, there isn't anyone, I think an hour later, as I sit across from an empty chair at a table for two at my favorite Greek restaurant a few blocks from my apartment.

After I'd left the police station, I'd stopped at a deli to pick up a six-pack of Blue Moon—Sean's favorite beer, and one I like, too. I thought I'd remembered him saying something about Jody being away, and I'd hoped to catch him alone.

My fingertips had skipped past Cassandra Moore's card as I'd reached for my Visa tucked in the slot behind it.

"Oh, I forgot an orange," I'd said to the cashier, running back to scoop one up. We always drank Blue Moon with a slice of the fruit down the neck of the bottle for extra flavor, ever since a bartender served it to us that way.

I was curious about the origin of that garnish, so I looked it up a while back: The cofounder of the company came up with the idea after he observed some bartenders serving beer with lemon wedges. Although Americans don't drink as much beer as they used to, in recent years consumption of Blue Moon has nearly doubled. By changing up the fruit, the cofounder added a distinctive association to Blue Moon.

As I accepted my bag from the cashier, I'd imagined Sean and me sitting on the couch and talking, the way we used to. Sean is as kind as he is analytical. He wouldn't judge me. He'd try to help.

But when I unlocked the door to our apartment, I heard laughter. Jody's silver sandals were under the bench—along with two pairs of shoes I didn't recognize.

"Want some sangria?" Sean said after he'd introduced me to the other couple in our living room. "Jody made it. We're just having a quick drink before we head out to dinner."

"There's plenty," Jody had added. But her tone didn't quite match her welcoming words. I'd glanced at the pretty glass pitcher and the pink cocktail napkins with WHY LIMIT HAPPY TO AN HOUR? written in gold lettering.

"Thanks," I'd said brightly. "Wish I could, but I've got plans, too."

Then I'd shoved the six-pack, bag and all, into the refrigerator and got out as fast as possible.

Three weeks ago, I dined at the same Greek restaurant where I'm now sitting.

Then, the room felt warm and welcoming. It's a family-owned place and Steve, the patriarch, had brought me a complimentary second glass of wine, as he sometimes does for regular customers. He'd asked me about the Malcolm Gladwell book I was reading on my phone, and I'd explained Gladwell's ten-thousand-hour rule: An individual needs to work at something for ten thousand hours before developing an expertise in it. Steve had joked that since the recipes he used were handed down from his grandmother, they met the "century rule." As I dug into my hot, savory falafel, I'd told him I agreed.

I'd lingered, the conversations from nearby tables wrapping themselves cozily around me.

Tonight I'm eating the same dish, sipping the same inexpensive white wine, and sitting only a few tables away.

Another stat from my Data Book: The percentage of adults who routinely eat on their own is estimated at 46 to 60 percent. Some studies show that eating alone is more strongly associated with unhappiness than any other factor, except mental illness.

This has never bothered me before.

As I pick at the falafel and a side of sautéed spinach I usually devour,

I wonder if Sean and Jody and the other couple have left yet. All I want to do is take an Ambien and slip under my covers.

I'm about to ask the waitress to box up my food and bring me the check when a woman swoops past me, calling out, "Sorry! Sorry!"

I turn to look as she joins a table of four other women, making her way around to hug each in turn. They're all around forty or so, and they seem to have the easy familiarity of old friends.

"Don't worry, I already ordered you a vodka tonic, extra lime," one says.

"You've always been my favorite," the woman shoots back.

They continue the merry banter, their heads close together, their voices overlapping, warm laughter ringing out.

The waiter delivers my check, and this time when I reach for my Visa, I pull out Cassandra's card, too.

Snippets from the memorial flash through my mind—the three women studying Amanda's photo, their arms wrapped around each other; *Pahked ya cah in Hahvad Yahd*; Jane's dimple flashing as she smiled at me; the warmth of Cassandra's hand on my bare forearm as she told me to call her anytime.

Cassandra's words echo through my mind: *Connecting with each other is one of the most essential things we can do.*

I took for granted what I used to have: the college boyfriend who wanted to marry me; Mel flopping onto my bed while we talked; even the coworkers from my last job, who gathered on Thursday nights for happy hour.

One by one, they've all slipped away.

I run my fingertips over the embossed letters of Cassandra's name.

Jane had invited me to join them for a drink that night.

I'd give anything to go back and change my answer to yes.

CHAPTER FOURTEEN

SHAY

In a study of people who witnessed a suicide, 60 percent said they thought about the event without meaning to. 30 percent had physical reactions when they were reminded of the event, including sweating, nausea, and difficulty breathing. Almost 100 percent said the experience had a significant impact on their lives.
—Data Book, page 17

I MAKE MY USUAL banana-and-almond-butter smoothie for breakfast and leave my apartment by eight A.M., my routine on the days that I temp. My tote bag holds my lunch—a turkey sandwich, apple, and pretzels. I've stopped seeing Paula because even with insurance she's expensive, but I'm trying to do some of the things she suggested. Last week I even made it halfway down the stairs of the subway—the one near my temp job.

I've also got the phone number of a new headhunter Jody said her brother had used.

I'd thanked her when she'd offered the lead, but I suspect Jody's motives aren't completely altruistic. I'm sure she'd like me out of the apartment more so she and Sean could have it all to themselves.

Plus, there's this: A few days ago Jody was drying dishes in our kitchen—she's a professional organizer, and our place is a lot neater since she started coming around—and she grabbed a little towel out of a drawer. It had a TOUGH MUDDER 10K logo on it.

"Which one of you maniacs ran this?" she asked, waving it in the air.

A small, internal twinge made me pause.

But Sean blurted out, "We did it together. Last August, right, Shay? Man, were we sore."

"Yet I somehow managed to heroically stumble to the beer tent," I joked.

Jody gave one of her tinkling little laughs. But her face pinched. She'd continued cleaning the kitchen, throwing away the unused chopsticks from a take-out meal and the almond milk that Sean and I both drank—Jody preferred half-and-half—even though I'd just used it and knew a good splash was left.

I'd found an excuse to leave, which I've gotten pretty good at doing. But as I closed my bedroom door, erasing the view of Jody sponging down the now-bare countertops, I couldn't help feeling like another piece of clutter Jody wanted to get rid of.

Jody gave me the headhunter's contact information shortly after that.

I plan to call him on my lunch break.

As I set off toward my bus stop, I notice the shift in the city: It's early September, and Manhattan, which empties out in August, is bustling again. Commuters with to-go cups of coffee wear earbuds as they stride down sidewalks, and little kids with new-looking backpacks hold the hands of their parents or nannies as they head to school.

The air is thick and warm, and the sky is gray, swollen with another late-summer storm. I feel a drop hit the top of my head and decide to duck back inside and grab my umbrella.

Then I see her.

Her golden brown hair hangs loose around her shoulders, and her green polka-dot dress sways gently as she walks.

Amanda.

I'm unable to breathe, to think, to move. Then, as if a cord is connecting us, I begin to walk, following in her footsteps.

It isn't really her, I tell myself, battling the icy fear engulfing my body. But I've seen that dress so many times in my nightmares. The shade of grapey-green; the simple shift that nips in at the waist. It looks identical.

Two women in New York might own the same dress. But what are the odds that they have the same hair color, the same hairstyle, and the same physical build? The data doesn't compute.

My chest constricts, but I push on. I can't let her out of my sight. That polka-dot dress is like a beacon, weaving through the crowd of dark suits and raincoats, leading me around a corner.

Toward the Thirty-third Street subway station.

Could this be a dream? I wonder frantically. *One of those nightmares that feel so true to life even after you wake up?*

I snap the rubber band on my wrist, hard. The pain registers. A few light raindrops hit me, and I smell the aroma of the crêpes from a food cart on the corner. It's all real.

So she must be, too.

The world pitches and whirls around me, but I press forward, almost staggering, my eyes fixed on her like she's the only person in this entire city.

She keeps advancing, never turning her head. Not rushing but never pausing; her steps as steady as a metronome. I'm a quarter of a block behind her, and although I could catch up to her if I ran, I'm terrified at the thought of seeing her face.

The rain comes down harder, drops coating my glasses and blurring my vision. I push my hand over my eyes, wiping away the dampness.

She is close to the entrance of the subway station now.

I can see the forest-green pole ahead, and stairs descending into that dark hole. I quicken my pace and slip on the wet pavement, my ankle wrenching beneath me. I scrape my palm as I catch my fall and leap up again. Umbrellas pop open all around me and I lose sight of her.

Where did she go? I twist my head left and right, frantically searching. Then I see her.

She's taking the first step down the subway stairs.

"Stop!" I try to cry, but my voice is stuck in my throat. It comes out as a hoarse whisper.

I grab on to the subway pole, so dizzy my vision swims again. I want to run after her, to pull her away. But my body betrays me by shutting down. I'm encased in cement again. Completely immobilized.

Tears stream down my cheeks, mixing with the rain. My clothes are plastered to my skin. People keep pushing past me, in a rush to get cover in the subway station.

By now she has almost completely disappeared. I crane my neck to get a last look at her before the hole swallows her.

She's gone.

I begin to hyperventilate, my breaths loud and raspy. I huddle into myself, my hands over my ears, unable to do anything but wait for the screech of the subway car.

Then the rain abruptly disappears.

Someone is standing next to me, holding a large umbrella over us.

I turn my head and blink and my vision clears. The woman next to me comes into view.

Cassandra Moore.

"I . . . I . . ." I stutter.

Beside Cassandra is her sister Jane, looking at me with the same worried expression.

"Shay," Cassandra says in her low, husky voice. "Are you okay?"

It feels like a miracle: The only two people I'm acquainted with who also knew Amanda are standing right beside me.

Cassandra puts her hand on my elbow, steadying me. Her eyes—brown and gold flecked, like a tiger's—are filled with concern and kindness.

"Amanda," I gasp. "I—I just saw her. She went into the subway."

I point but both sisters keep their gazes fixed on me.

"Who?" Cassandra asks.

"Amanda? It couldn't have been . . . " Jane says.

"Please," I beg. "Can—can someone go check?"

"Shay—" Jane begins, but my sobs cut her off.

"We have to help her," I whisper.

Cassandra stares at me with her unblinking eyes. Then she does something extraordinary. "Wait here." She hands me her umbrella. "I'll go look."

I watch her descend in quick steps, her bare legs flashing beneath her poppy-colored, belted raincoat.

In the distance I hear the approaching rumble of the train.

Hurry, I think, even as I acknowledge the impossibility of what I've just seen.

"Could it have been someone who just looked like Amanda?" Jane asks.

I shake my head. My teeth are chattering. "She was the same—I swear I saw her—I'm sure of it. . . . But how could it be her?"

I stand under Cassandra's umbrella, my stomach clenching as the train's brakes scream. But then, a moment later, I hear the train pull away from the station, the thunder of its wheels growing fainter and fainter.

Nothing happened. It was an ordinary stop for the subway train.

I'm almost beginning to wonder if *any* of it happened, if my mind betrayed me. But Jane is still standing beside me, and my skirt and top are soaking wet, and I'm clutching the smooth wooden handle of Cassandra's oversize umbrella.

Cassandra reappears, climbing the stairs—first just the top of her glossy black hair, then her strong, symmetrical features, then her slender frame.

"Everything's okay, Shay." She puts a hand on my arm, just like she did at the memorial service. Her touch is the only source of warmth on my body. "I didn't see anyone who looks like Amanda down there."

"Are you sure?" I ask desperately. But my heartbeat is slowing. The sisters are helping the world to stop spinning.

I see Cassandra give Jane a quick look before shaking her head. "I don't think so, but maybe I missed her. She might've caught the subway before I got down there?"

That's impossible; only one train came in between the time the woman descended the stairs and now.

I start to try to explain again what I saw. But just before I get to the part about the polka-dot dress, I cut myself off. It might make sense that I spotted a woman who resembled Amanda. But one in the exact same outfit? I'd seem crazy—especially given how I must look in my drenched outfit with my bedraggled hair sticking to my face. So I just nod.

"You're probably right." I swallow hard. "I'm really sorry. . . . I don't know what happened. . . ."

Cassandra links her arm through mine. "Our morning meeting was canceled. Are you in a rush?"

"We were just going to grab tea," Jane adds. "There's a little café around the corner. Why don't you join us?"

I look at them, stunned. After all this, they want to be with me?

It's more than an act of kindness. It feels like a gift.

What are the odds that I'd run into the Moore sisters at this exact juncture; that they and Amanda would somehow intersect in my life again? It seems impossible. Yet here they are.

I'm going to be late for work, but I find myself nodding. I'll call my temp job and claim an emergency, and I'll make up my hours tonight.

I'm not going to turn down an invitation from these women again.

CHAPTER FIFTEEN

CASSANDRA & JANE

SHAY—TREMBLING, SHATTERED, and unsteady—grips Cassandra's arm as the sisters lead her through the misty, rain-dampened air toward a café.

The hostess tries to seat them by the window.

"Actually, could we have that booth?" Cassandra points. "It looks cozier and our friend is soaking wet."

It's also more private; a few other customers are in the upscale diner.

The hostess matches Cassandra's smile with one of her own. "Of course."

After Shay is seated, Cassandra takes off her raincoat and drapes it over Shay's shoulders. "You've got to be freezing in this air-conditioning. Do you want anything to eat?"

Shay shakes her head as Cassandra slides onto the opposite bench, so both sisters are facing Shay.

In another few moments, with the dry jacket wrapped around her and her hands cupping a steaming mug of chamomile tea, Shay's shivering ceases.

But she still appears fragile and dazed—exactly how the sisters wanted her. When people feel vulnerable, they're more likely to spill their secrets.

"You must really miss Amanda," Jane begins gently. "I know we do. We talk about her all the time."

Shay looks down at her mug of tea. Despite her obvious chill, her cheeks flush. "Um, the truth is . . ."

Tension floods Cassandra's body. Jane perches on the edge of the bench, her fingernails clutching its wooden rim. But the sisters' faces remain placid. Shay has to feel safe and unhurried.

"I don't know why her death is affecting me so much." Shay starts to say something else, then she lifts her mug and takes a sip.

Cassandra exhales, so slowly and softly she doesn't make a sound. Jane doesn't move a fingertip. Shay is on the brink of something pivotal; they don't want to sway her in the wrong direction.

Shay keeps her eyes on her cup. The sisters wait, not daring to even sneak a look at each other.

"Amanda and I weren't friends," Shay whispers. "I actually didn't know her at all."

Neither sister reacts outwardly—a tremendous effort, given that both feel as if the wind has been knocked out of them. If this is true, how would Shay have known where Amanda lived? Why would she have felt compelled to put a flower on Amanda's doorstep? And why would she appear so haunted by Amanda's death?

Clearly Shay feels guilty; she's almost cringing. Is this because she's telling another lie?

The stakes feel higher than ever. The sisters may only have this chance to obtain answers. One false move and Shay could shut down, or flee.

"Oh?" Cassandra's word is so gentle it could almost be a breath. "But you said you shared a vet?"

Shay's tortured eyes rise to meet Cassandra's. Then Jane's.

Shay nods. "Yeah, um, I saw her there once or twice, but that's not exactly why I came to the memorial. . . . The thing is, I was actually standing next to Amanda on the subway platform when she—when she died. I can't get her out of my head. . . . I think about her all the time. I can't stop wondering what would cause her to do something like that. . . ."

Shay leans back, slumping, looking as if she expects to be reprimanded.

Some of the tension drains out of Cassandra's body. Jane releases her grip on the bench.

Shay was simply in the wrong place at the wrong time. The sisters' minds begin to fire, assembling the pieces.

"Oh, Amanda suffered from depression off and on her whole life," Jane says gently.

Shay nods.

"So how did you find out about the memorial service?" Cassandra reaches over and freshens up Shay's mug of tea from the pot. Cassandra's hand is trembling slightly from accumulated tension, so she quickly tucks it in her lap.

Shay doesn't appear to have noticed; she's still blinking back tears. "I went by her apartment to leave a flower, just as a tribute, and I saw the notice. . . ."

"But how did you know where she lived?" Jane interrupts.

Cassandra gently pats her sister's hand: *Slow down.*

"There's this detective who questioned me at the subway after . . . well, after everything. Anyway, the last time I spoke with her she told me Amanda's name and I figured out her address from there. . . ."

At the mention of the detective, Jane sucks in a quick breath. Shay's word choice indicates she has had multiple conversations with the police, plus there was her recent visit to the Seventeenth Precinct.

Before, there was one pressing question: How did Shay know Amanda?

Now, there is an even more urgent one: What did Shay tell the police?

They already knew Shay had left the necklace at the Seventeenth Precinct, since the gray dot on Valerie's phone remained at that location even after Shay exited the building. But her subsequent movements that evening were so ordinary they were curious: If Shay had dropped a bombshell at the police station—if she'd described the events that had led to Amanda's suicide—then surely she would have been more skittish. She wouldn't have leisurely strolled home, alone. She wouldn't have cut through a quiet, shadowy walkway between buildings without once checking behind her.

Shay misreads their silence. "Are you angry? I'm so sorry I misled you. I just didn't know what to say when I showed up at the service."

Jane shakes her head. "We're not mad. And no way would we ever judge you for that."

"It was really nice of you to come pay your respects," Cassandra adds.

Shay's expression turns wistful. "I remember thinking Amanda looked like someone I'd want to be friends with."

More pieces fall into place: On the days Shay temps, she walks to a bench at lunchtime and pulls a foil-wrapped sandwich out of her bag, eating by herself. When she rides the bus to work or walks to the gym, she doesn't chat on a headset—instead, she usually appears lost in thought. She stays in her apartment most nights.

Shay is desperately lonely.

Cassandra files away that key observation to discuss with Jane later, though she suspects Jane has already come to the same conclusion; the sisters' thoughts are often in sync.

"Amanda was a really good person," Cassandra says. "Did you two ever talk at the vet's?"

Shay shakes her head rapidly. "No, not really—and my cat died last year, so . . ."

"Ah," Cassandra says. "Well, you would have liked Amanda, and she you."

Jane takes a sip of tea before steering the conversation in a new direction. "No wonder you panicked when you saw that woman walking into the subway station a little while ago."

"I haven't been able to ride the subway since that day. It's hard to even get near the stairs. . . . And that woman looked so much like Amanda." Shay's face creases. "But . . . I guess I imagined it all."

Cassandra's gaze meets Jane's. The sisters had noticed Shay's eyes well up as she'd stared at Amanda's photograph at the memorial service, and later they'd seen her repeatedly cross the street seemingly to avoid subway grates. She'd also been observed leaving an office that was later identified as belonging to a therapist.

The illusion the sisters had created was as effective as they'd hoped. By now, Valerie is on her way back to her apartment to take off her wig and the heels that added several inches to her five-foot-six frame, remove the expertly applied makeup that made her nose appear narrower and her eyes wider, and change out of the polka-dot dress she'd pur-

chased from an online retailer. In a few moments, Valerie will have transformed from an Amanda look-alike into a different thirty-something
woman—pretty, but forgettably so—who blends into a crowd. Her
performance is over. The dress will be stored in the back of Valerie's
closet, in case it's needed again.

If Shay had answered all of the sisters' unspoken questions, they
would have given her the parting gift of peace. Cassandra would have
pretended she, too, had thought she'd seen Amanda the other day and
had felt a little unhinged afterward. Jane would have said, *I suppose it
must be common for people to imagine things like that after a death.*

But they don't. Instead, Jane presses her hand against Cassandra's
under the booth. Cassandra understands the signal: This engineered
meeting with Shay has not tied up the final loose ends surrounding
Amanda's death, as the sisters hoped. They can't simply finish their tea
and walk away, never looking back.

Shay still claims she first encountered Amanda at the veterinarian's,
which the Moore sisters know is a lie.

She says she barely knew Amanda. Yet somehow she had Amanda's
necklace.

What else is Shay lying about?

Cassandra gazes at Shay's cell phone, which is facedown on the
table. She wonders what information it holds.

Stacey would be able to hack it quickly; she's an expert at installing
spyware on cell phones, as she has already proven to the group.

It was no coincidence that Cassandra and Jane wandered into Daphne's boutique shortly after she sent a one-line text—*I hope you rot in
hell*—to a man named James Anders.

The sisters had been watching James for a long time. Tracking him.
Creating a log of his schedule and habits—such as his routine of going
to a bar called Twist most Thursday nights. Eventually, thanks to the
spyware Stacey had installed on his phone one night when he'd left it
unattended, they'd had the capability to read his texts.

While they'd been contemplating different ways to punish James,
that searing text from a number with a 917 area code had landed simultaneously on his cell phone and on their computers.

Valerie had intuitively felt it was from a woman James had harmed; the sisters already knew of at least one other instance in which he'd tried to commit rape.

Stacey had tracked the number of the text's sender and found it listed with a boutique called Daphne's, owned by a single woman in her thirties. Shortly thereafter, Cassandra and Jane had visited the shop and struck up a friendship with its owner.

It didn't take long for Daphne to let down her guard. When she did, the sisters' suspicions about what James had done to Daphne were confirmed. They then folded Daphne into their group.

Now Cassandra tears her eyes away from Shay's cell phone. It's too bad Stacey isn't with them; it's a missed opportunity to dig into Shay's secrets, Cassandra thinks. They'll have to create other opportunities.

CHAPTER SIXTEEN

STACEY

Fourteen months ago

THE BUTTER HIT THE frying pan with a sizzle.

Stacey lay three slices of American cheese on whole wheat bread, glancing at the cell phone vibrating on the chipped linoleum counter next to her. The text read, *Need dog food now.*

She placed the sandwich in the frying pan and licked her fingers before she picked up the phone to reply, *In fifteen.*

The junkie jonesing for his crack fix would have to wait. She hadn't eaten all day.

Through the thin apartment wall came the sound of her neighbor's young daughter singing along to *Pitch Perfect* in her high voice as she rhythmically clanked something: "'When I'm gone, when I'm gone . . . You're gonna miss me when I'm gone. . . .'"

"Stop banging those spoons," the girl's mother snapped.

Stacey flipped her sandwich. The underside was golden brown and cheese had started to ooze out. Her stomach rumbled. She pulled a plastic cup out of the cabinet with the Philadelphia Eagles logo emblazoned on the front. Her boyfriend, Adam, remained fiercely loyal to their hometown team, even though they'd been living in the Bronx for years. She filled it to the brim with Pepsi.

Tomorrow was Saturday, visiting day at the prison. It meant a two-hour bus ride each way, with the same weary-faced wives and kids and girlfriends she saw every month. She got an hour with Adam, their hands entwined across a tabletop, under the watchful eyes of guards.

"'I got my ticket for the long way 'round . . .'" the little girl sang.

"I told you to shut your trap," the mother ordered, but without a lot of heat in her voice—at least compared to other times Stacey had heard her. Stacey had seen bruises on the girl, who looked to be about eight, from time to time. Once a cast was even on the girl's arm. Stacey had tried to ask her about it, but the child skittered away like a timid mouse.

"You only told me to stop banging. You didn't tell me I couldn't sing," the little girl said.

Stacey pressed the spatula down on the sandwich.

The junkie texted her again on Adam's phone: *How long? My dog's hungry.*

She'd taken over Adam's clients while he was gone, not expanding his business but making enough to pay the rent until she could find a real job, one that paid at least minimum wage. She'd filled out dozens of applications. But a woman like her—a high school dropout, an outcast from her solidly middle-class family, not much to look at—didn't get a lot of opportunities.

She took a long sip of Pepsi and glanced over at the wall. It was quiet next door. Even the music had stopped.

She was sliding her sandwich onto a plate when she heard the scream.

Stacey closed her eyes and gritted her teeth.

"I'll stop! Don't!" the little girl shrieked.

Stacey's grip on the handle of the frying pan tightened as the little girl cried out again.

Then the high, piercing scream ceased.

Its absence felt even more alarming.

Stacey's skin prickled. She didn't hesitate. She picked up the frying pan and ran out the door, bursting into the neighboring apartment. She had a clear view into the kitchen. The wild-eyed mother was holding her daughter's head down in a sink full of dirty water and dishes.

"Get off her!" Stacey bellowed, swinging the pan like a baseball bat. It connected with the mother's head and she collapsed to the kitchen floor.

The little girl's head popped up and she drew in raggedy breaths, then began to cough, water streaming down her face and onto her Princess Elsa nightgown.

Stacey lifted the pan to swing it again, but the little girl begged her to stop. So she lowered it.

When she looked around again, the little girl had run away through the open apartment door, disappearing as she'd probably done numerous times as a survival mechanism during her short, violence-filled life.

Stacey returned to her own apartment, leaving the mother slumped on the floor. She wasn't even finished with her sandwich when two uniformed officers burst through her door.

She tried to explain about the little girl, but the mother claimed Stacey had robbed and assaulted her. It didn't help Stacey's case that she had a baggie of crack on the counter next to her, ready to deliver to Adam's client.

The next day she was leaning against the hard bench that served as her bed, staring into space, when the guard rapped on the bars of her cell and told her she had a visitor.

She'd blinked at him in surprise. Nobody knew she was there. She hadn't even used her single phone call. Adam was unreachable. Her father and two uptight, social-climbing sisters hadn't spoken to her in years, ever since she'd brought Adam, who was high, to her nephew's first birthday party, where he'd dug a big serving spoon into the cake and scooped out the first bite for himself. And her mother—who maintained secret contact with her despite her father's wishes—was in the early stages of Alzheimer's.

Stacey let the guard cuff her and lead her to the small room where inmates received visitors.

A woman with short, frizzy red hair was waiting by the small table.

"Hi, Stacey, I'm your public defender," she'd said, her Boston accent sharpening her words. "My name is Beth Sullivan."

Despite Stacey's excellent legal counsel, the evidence against her was overwhelming. Still, Beth got Stacey's sentence reduced to four months in jail since no signs of drugs were in Stacey's system—she never used—and the prosecutor couldn't prove she was actually selling crack.

"It's bullshit," Beth had said when the judge handed down his verdict. "You saved the kid's life."

Beth had shaken her head as she'd told Stacey that she'd become a lawyer because she wanted to give a voice to people who didn't have one. But instead, she'd watched too many guilty individuals go free and innocent ones end up behind bars. Instead of giving, she'd had something taken from her: her trust in the judicial system.

"I think you should meet Stacey," Beth told the Moore sisters at one of their regular gatherings. Ever since Valerie had introduced Beth to Cassandra and Jane, they'd become a tight-knit group of four.

When Beth had brought Cassandra and Jane to meet Stacey in the medium-security prison, they were immediately taken by the small blond woman whose eyes constantly flitted around while they chatted. It was as if Stacey always needed to see what might be coming at her, as if she was accustomed to being viewed as prey.

"She deserves another chance," Cassandra had said to Jane as they watched the guards round up all the prisoners at the end of visiting hour. "Beth was right."

When Stacey was released from jail, she expected her prospects as a broke, convicted felon—one whose scumbag boyfriend had moved on to some prison groupie he'd met online—to be even more dismal.

Instead, a small studio apartment in Alphabet City awaited her. Soft, fresh sheets—heavenly compared to the scratchy ones in prison—were on the sofa bed. The refrigerator held fruit and yogurt and bread. Cassandra and Jane, who had several more times come with Beth to visit Stacey in prison, had learned of her prowess with computers, and they hired her to help them in the office.

Once she'd proven herself to the sisters, they gave her stellar references. Stacey found work as a consultant quickly and insisted on paying back every penny the sisters had spent on her behalf. Even so, Stacey considered herself forever indebted to them.

She'd lost one family, but she'd found another.

CHAPTER SEVENTEEN

SHAY

On average, women report having eight close friends. Studies have found that, when under stress, women tend to seek out these female friendships. Instead of simply experiencing the adrenal-based "fight or flight" response, women also secrete the "bonding hormone," oxytocin. This phenomenon has been termed "tend and befriend."
—Data Book, page 18

I LEARNED SO MANY THINGS about Cassandra and Jane Moore at the café this morning: everything from the flavor of tea they drink—jasmine for Cassandra, and rose hip for Jane—to how Jane's eyebrows tilt up slightly when she listens, to how gracefully Cassandra gestures with her slim fingers.

As they hugged me goodbye, Cassandra told me to keep the raincoat for now since she had her umbrella. "Just text me and we'll figure it out," she'd said, right before the sisters hurried to the curb and hailed a cab. Naturally, one pulled over within seconds.

While I sat on the bus to work, I wondered if I should have just come clean and admitted I didn't have a cat. At least I'd undone part of my lie by explaining I'd been by Amanda's side when she'd jumped, and that was why her death had so affected me. But I was such a wreck when they found me clutching the subway pole; how could I admit

I'd completely fabricated the story about sharing a veterinarian with Amanda? I'd sound pathological.

Especially to these women; not only are they glamorous and magnetic, they're highly successful. When I googled them, I learned they founded their own boutique PR firm while still in their mid-twenties, and that they represent a couple of names even I recognize. Cassandra is thirty-two and Jane is thirty, so my age puts me right between them, which makes their accomplishments even more impressive.

I also discovered that the yoga class Cassandra frequents requires more raw strength than it does a Zen mind-set.

"Downward Dog into a plank," the instructor at Yoga Flow commands, walking over to adjust my form. I'm wearing the leggings and tank top I packed for the spin class I had planned to take that evening. After I found the receipt for a package of ten classes from this yoga studio in the pocket of Cassandra's raincoat along with a tin of cinnamon Altoids, I altered my plans.

When I called the studio to reserve a mat at the eight P.M. Ashtanga class, I told myself it would be grounding and relaxing—exactly what I needed after the intense distress of the morning. But that's not the real reason I'm here.

Cassandra and Jane are powerful, confident, alluring—everything I'm not.

I guess I just wanted to take a tiny step in their shoes.

I run my tongue over my teeth, still tasting the faintest trace of cinnamon. The tin of Altoids was almost completely full, so I knew Cassandra wouldn't notice if one was missing.

"Let's prepare for Savasana," the instructor says.

I glance at the woman next to me to get a cue for the pose, then lie on my back with my palms faceup.

"Today's word is *gratitude*. Allow your mind to be filled with something or someone you are grateful for," the instructor continues. He rings a chime four times, the crisp, delicate notes reverberating through the air.

Cassandra and Jane, I think instantly. If they hadn't magically appeared this morning outside the subway, I don't know what would have happened. I felt as if I were shattering, and they put me back together.

I know women as in demand and special as Cassandra and Jane don't need me as a friend. But I can't help thinking about how that word sounded coming from Cassandra's lips when she told the hostess we wanted a booth.

Even their names have the sound of mantras.

I close my eyes and feel my body melt into the mat.

When the instructor rings the bell again, I slowly get up and gather my things from the locker, including Cassandra's raincoat. It kept me warm today, but I know that, like Cassandra and Jane's company, it isn't mine to keep.

I reach for my phone and slowly type in a message: *I wanted to thank you and Jane again for today. I can drop your jacket off tomorrow if that works.*

I stare at my phone for at least a minute, but there's no reply.

It's nearly nine-thirty when I return to my apartment. I climb the flight up to 2C and fumble through my bag for my keys. Before I can unlock the door, Sean opens it.

I take a step back, surprised. "Oh, are you heading out?"

"Actually, no, I've been waiting for you." He clears his throat. "Do you have a moment to talk?"

"Sure."

His eyes flitter away from mine. His speech is more formal than usual. He doesn't seem to know what to do with his hands; he finally clasps them in front of him.

All of this signals he's going to deliver bad news.

"Want a beer? I was about to open one."

I don't, but I grab two of the Blue Moons I brought home the other night while Sean slices up the orange I toss to him.

"So, what's up?"

He walks over to sit down on the couch and I feel my heart plummet.

But when he finally tells me what it is, I force myself to smile. I even hug him. "No problem. I get it. And I'm happy for you."

Sean suggests we hang out on the couch and watch a movie like we used to.

"Sure," I say. "I didn't have dinner, so you pick something out and I'll go buy some snacks."

As soon as I reach the corner, I collapse against the side of a building, my face in my hands.

Jody's lease is up next month. They want to live together. *I'm sorry. I know you've been going through a lot with the job stuff and everything,* Sean had said. *She and I can look for a different apartment. . . .*

But I told him I'd move out. *You've been here forever. It's really your place.*

Take as long as you need, he'd replied.

No job. No relationship. No home.

I stand there for a long moment, unsure of what to do, gulping in breaths.

Then I hear a chime—a crisp, faint sound that reverberates through the air, reminiscent of the bell from yoga class.

I reach into my tote and pull out my phone. On the screen is a brand-new text: *Sure you can drop off the jacket, or you can join me and Jane for drinks this Thursday and I'll get it then? xo, C*

I read it twice. Then I straighten up and push away from the building.

I make myself wait another thirty seconds, then type, *I'd love to join you!*

My breaths are steadier now; my despair is receding.

As I walk to the deli to grab a few bags of microwave popcorn, I wonder why they're interested in spending more time with me. But then I remind myself that Amanda didn't seem to be as glamorous as Cassandra and Jane, yet they were close friends.

So maybe there *is* room for me in Cassandra and Jane's world.

CHAPTER EIGHTEEN

SHAY

We tend to like people whom we perceive as similar to us. And the less information we have about a person, the more important these perceived similarities are in influencing our approval.
—Data Book, page 19

I'VE SPENT ALL MORNING and some of the afternoon searching for studio apartments online, and I've even gone to look at a couple. The first had mousetraps in the run-down lobby and a puddle of water under the refrigerator. The second—described as "quaint"—was so small I wouldn't have room for any furniture other than my double bed and dresser.

I'd be completely demoralized and anxious if I weren't meeting Cassandra and Jane for drinks tonight.

After I finish checking out the apartments, I stop by Zara, a store that sells designer knockoffs. Both times I met the sisters, they were chic without being trendy. Although the kind of clothes they wear are far outside my budget—the raincoat Cassandra lent me had a Stella McCartney label and my Google search revealed it sells for twelve hundred dollars—I can at least up my game.

I ask the salesgirl for help, and she puts together an outfit from head to toe, including shoes and a bracelet. She shows me a cute pair of matching earrings, but I tell her I don't have pierced ears. I wince at the total, but hand over my credit card anyway.

Next I pop by Sephora and ask a saleswoman for some tips. She ends up overdoing it—my eye shadow is too bright, and my lined lips look strange to me—but I buy a tube of lip gloss and grab a few tissues to tone down the makeup before I leave.

I swing by home to change into my new clothes and drop off my bags, then I splurge on an Uber to take me to our meeting spot. It's warm out, and I don't want to show up sweaty and undo all my efforts. I pull up the restaurant's menu on my phone so I can pick what I want to drink.

A jalapeño margarita sounds delicious, but I'm only going to order it if I'm the first one the waiter asks. Otherwise, I'll follow the sisters' lead, because people tend to feel more comfortable with those who make similar choices. My slim black pants and gauzy sleeveless top, my coppery eyeliner, even the manicure I gave myself—I can't pretend it isn't designed to make these women like me.

Tons of studies have found that attractive, well-groomed individuals are assumed to possess positive qualities that aren't even related to their appearance—they're perceived as being more intelligent, more interesting, and more trustworthy. This is sometimes called the halo effect.

Maybe that's why I've prepared more for tonight than I ever have for any date, school reunion, job interview, or even Mel's wedding, where I was maid of honor. I hope it's enough.

The Uber pulls over to the curb and I step out. Cassandra gave me an address and the name of the bar—Bella's—but I don't see any sign indicating where it is.

Then I notice a black door with simple silver numbers on it: 242. That matches the address I have.

I pull open the door and walk to the hostess stand. It's still light outside, but in here, it's dim and homey. Instead of the usual booths, it's like being in someone's living room—clusters of couches and chairs are grouped together. The furniture is eclectic, but even I can tell it all works together.

"Do you have a reservation?" the hostess asks.

A grin spreads across my face. "Actually, I'm meeting some friends."

Then I hear my name being called from across the room: "Shay! Over here!"

Cassandra and Jane are standing at a low, round table toward the back, waving and smiling. I hurry toward them. Their arms open wide to hug me before I even reach them.

"It's so good to see you!" Jane says.

"You look *great*!" Cassandra adds.

I feel my skin betray me by flushing again, but this time, it's with pleasure. I once read that a sincere compliment is so powerful because it activates the reward centers in the brain, creating the same reaction that receiving money does. It truly does feel like a gift.

I'm especially glad I made such an effort, because Cassandra is in a chic dress with a skinny alligator-patterned belt, and Jane wears a fitted cream leather jacket with dark-rinse jeans and heels. A few guys are sitting at a nearby table, and I see one swiveling his head to check them out. The sisters don't even appear to notice; this sort of thing must happen to them all the time.

They've claimed the chairs opposite each other, which means I'm in the middle.

"Oh, before I forget." I hand Cassandra a sturdy bag from Lululemon. I'd gotten it when I picked up a pair of running tights on sale last year and I'd saved it because it was so much nicer than the usual plastic or cheap paper bags stores give out.

Now Cassandra's poppy-colored raincoat is carefully folded inside. Her yoga card and Altoids are in the left pocket, where I'd found them.

"Thank you!" Cassandra exclaims, almost like I've given her a present rather than simply returned the item she lent me.

"Your arms are so toned!" Jane adds. "That explains the Lululemon bag. Do you have Michelle Obama's trainer?"

"Thanks." I laugh, feeling a little embarrassed. "This place is really cool." It's crowded, but the tables are far enough apart that it feels private.

"Wait until you try the cocktails," Jane replies. "We love the Moscow Mules."

I don't even know what the ingredients are, but when the waiter comes by, I order one.

Cassandra leans closer to me. "So, how are you feeling?"

Better than I have in a long time, I think. All my worries about my job, my living situation, even my new phobia, have suddenly receded. I was so distracted getting ready for tonight that it pushed those nagging issues out of the forefront of my mind.

But I just say, "I'm good. Thanks again for the other day—I hadn't slept well and I was going through a rough patch."

"We've all been there." Jane touches my forearm. "A few months ago, this investment banker I thought I was going to marry broke up with me. I couldn't even get out of bed, but this one"—she jabs a thumb at Cassandra—"kept bringing me lattes and dragging me to work. If it hadn't been for her, I'd still be hiding under the covers."

It's hard to imagine anyone breaking up with Jane, I think, watching her full lips curve into a smile, revealing perfect white teeth. But Cassandra nods and says, "Hey, that's what sisters are for. Well, that and stealing your favorite clothes."

We all laugh, and my little breakdown the other day doesn't feel as humiliating.

"Three Moscow Mules," the waiter says, setting down copper mugs garnished with limes and fresh sprigs of mint.

Cassandra lifts her mug. "Cheers."

I clink mine against theirs, then take a sip. It's icy and refreshing, with a nice kick of ginger.

The number one rule for getting people to like you is to ask them about themselves. So I lob a question to them.

"Do you guys work around here?" I already know that they do. By now I've checked out their website and even googled a few of their clients: a handbag designer, a gallery owner, and a young actor who has a part in an upcoming independent film.

They chat for a while about their company, then ask about me. I describe my work as a data analyst and explain I'm temping at a law firm. But I make it sound like I have a lot of leads and it's only a matter of time before I end up somewhere new and exciting.

Cassandra and Jane lean toward me, listening intently. Jane keeps smiling, her dimple flashing, while Cassandra nods encouragingly.

Something strange starts to happen: As I talk about my potential opportunities, I begin to believe they will materialize. I feel more expansive; more self-assured. It's like their confidence and success are infectious.

The waiter appears with three more copper cups. "Another round of Moscow Mules, compliments of the gentlemen over there."

I glance at the table of men, and one of them raises his glass to us.

"Cheers, guys," Cassandra calls, then she turns back to me. It's like she's thanking someone for opening a door; she's gracious but completely nonchalant. This, too, must happen to them all the time.

I start in on my new drink. I feel warm and glowing inside, but I can't tell if it's from the alcohol or if I'm just high from their company.

Cassandra has left a perfect crimson crescent near the lip of her mug. One of the differences between her and Jane is that Cassandra seems to favor a more dramatic look, while Jane is softer. Her lipstick leaves a faint pink mark, like mine.

Even Cassandra's jewelry is striking: a chunky cocktail ring with an onyx stone on her right hand, and dangling gold earrings. But the necklace she's fiddling with is—

I do a double take.

It's a simple gold chain with a sunburst charm.

I'm too stunned to speak.

First Amanda disappeared, then I thought I saw her reappear going into the subway. Then I gave her necklace to the police, and now it's back.

Cassandra notices me gaping and pulls away her hand, giving me a better look.

"Your necklace—it's—"

Cassandra gazes down at it, as if she hadn't even thought about what she was wearing.

"Amanda had the same one," I finally manage to say. It's the only explanation.

Jane's eyes widen. "Actually, she didn't. I had a matching one and I lent it to Amanda. Our mother gave them to us as Christmas gifts when we were teenagers."

Cassandra smiles, looking as if she's reaching for a memory. "Mom told us we were her sunshine. I guess we cherish them because of that, even though we're not close to her now."

At my look of surprise, she shrugs. "There was a rift in our family years ago."

Jane says wistfully, "I guess mine was lost along with Amanda."

I want to sink into my chair. I gave away Jane's special necklace. I have to tell her, to explain there was no way I could have known.

I swallow hard. "I think—I mean, I know where the necklace could be."

"You do?" Jane gasps. "How?"

"Right before Amanda—before I saw her—I found it on the floor of the subway station. I forgot I even had it until a few days ago."

Jane leans forward and grabs my hand. "You have it? I would give anything to get it back."

Cassandra is smiling at me, like I've just solved all their problems. "Fate must have brought us together."

I clear my throat. "The thing is, since I thought it was Amanda's, I brought it to the police."

I expect the sisters to be upset—maybe even angry. But they look strangely relieved. Jane exhales slowly and recrosses her legs. Cassandra takes a long sip of her drink before finally speaking again.

"That makes sense."

"I can try to get the necklace back for you," I blurt.

"You can?" Jane gasps.

"I'll go back to the police station and explain to Detective Williams that I got it wrong, that the necklace doesn't belong to Amanda. Besides, that's the truth."

I flash to Detective Williams leading me down that long, silent hallway. But I push back against the quick jab of fear in my gut: Being afraid has already interfered too much with my life; it doesn't have any place at this table.

"That would be incredible," Cassandra says.

"I would be so grateful," Jane adds.

I'm riding something—endorphins, or maybe it's the second cocktail—that makes me feel like I can accomplish almost anything tonight.

I'm desperate to know more about the sisters and about Amanda—to discover the intimate details you can't find online. So I ask how they met her. I got the impression they'd known her since childhood, maybe because Cassandra and Jane hosted Amanda's memorial and I saw Cassandra hugging the woman who must have been Amanda's mother.

But when I ask if they were family friends, Cassandra and Jane look surprised.

Jane shakes her head. "No, she was from Delaware. We met here in the city."

Cassandra chimes in, "It's funny, we hadn't even known Amanda all that long, but we just clicked."

I nod eagerly, leaning forward.

"She had a rough time growing up," Jane confides. "No one ever really cared for her, which makes it so admirable that she became a nurse to help other people. Her father died when she was five, and her mom started drinking heavily. She never remarried. Would you believe poor Amanda used to come home from grade school and find her passed out on the couch? She started making her own dinners when she was just a little girl."

"Maybe we connected so deeply because Jane and I don't really have parents, either," Cassandra says. "It's hard to understand if you're close to your family and you've got grandparents and cousins you adore. . . . But those of us who feel a bit more alone in the world tend to recognize each other."

Her words hammer into me. She's speaking to my deepest longing.

"In a way, Amanda became another sister to us," Cassandra finishes.

With those few words, Cassandra has just articulated everything I've been yearning for—not just lately, but for my entire life: A place to belong. A home that has nothing to do with a physical structure and everything to do with a feeling of love and acceptance.

"I do know," I whisper. "I'm an only child. . . . I'm not all that close to either of my parents."

I've never said those words before. I guess I've never wanted to admit them, even to myself.

Jane and Cassandra look at each other, then they both turn to me with what feels like heightened interest. "I didn't realize we had so much in common," Jane says.

Her words hover between us, like a gossamer thread. I'm here with these two incredible women who seem to be turning into friends. It seems that the data is true: Sharing personal information and emotions leads to increased feelings of closeness.

We talk for another hour, and I'm surprised by how interested the sisters are in everything about my life—from my weakness for chocolate to how Jody clearly feels discomfort with my presence in Sean's life.

All the while, I hold tight the knowledge that I now have a reason to see them again.

I tried to make my appearance mirror theirs tonight.

But it's much more powerful to know that the deeper, hidden parts of us match.

CHAPTER NINETEEN

CASSANDRA & JANE

Twenty years ago

"This is your room, Cassandra," their stepfather said, opening a door to reveal what looked like a page out of *Teen* magazine: The center-piece was a white canopy bed with a frilly pink duvet and decorative pillows. There was also a glossy white dresser and matching desk. Seashell-colored paint—so fresh the scent still filled the air—covered the walls.

"And, Jane, yours is here." He crossed the hall and opened another closed door to reveal an identical bedroom.

The sisters looked at each other before moving in separate directions, their socks gliding soundlessly over the thick carpeting. They'd never not shared a room.

But they knew what was expected of them even before they felt their mother's sharp nudges: "Thank you!" they chorused.

"It's so beautiful," Jane added.

Their stepfather nodded—he was a man of few words—and turned to descend the stairs, which creaked heavily under his weight.

The fancy bedrooms were just the beginning of the changes that lay ahead: Their mother had already told them that new clothes, a transfer to their town's private school, and piano lessons would soon follow.

"Why don't you girls freshen up. Dinner is at six," their mother instructed as she hurried to catch up with her new husband. "I'm making Dover sole and asparagus."

Even their mother was different now—she used fancier words, and she'd stopped smoking. She'd begun going for manicures in town rather than painting her own nails. She gestured a lot more, too, with her left hand—the one with the big diamond on it.

Cassandra looked at Jane and shrugged. It was as if their mom had been replaced by Carol Brady. But their stepfather was no Mike Brady; his slightly bulging eyes and full lips reminded them of a frog.

"What's Dover sole?" Jane whispered, and they both burst into giggles.

There was one other big change: They now had a stepbrother, a handsome, golden-haired, athletic teenager who came to spend every other weekend with them. Even his nickname—Trey, because he was the third male to inherit the same name after his grandfather and father—was cool.

The first time they saw him, the sisters were sitting on the edge of the pool in the backyard, dangling their feet into the cool chlorinated water. He raced through the yard and cannonballed into the deep end. When he broke the surface, the girls were laughing and shaking droplets from their hair.

"Hey," he said, effortlessly treading water. "Want to see who can hold their breath underwater the longest?"

During those two weekends a month, Trey breathed life into the house that felt like a museum when their stepfather was around. Trey hoisted them up and carried them around on his shoulders and whispered secrets about his father—such as that he kept a bottle of Viagra in his nightstand. In the basement game room with the big wooden bar and giant TV, Trey taught them to play pool, leaning over them and adjusting the angle of their cues. "Don't rush your stroke," he'd say.

Trey snuck shots of Jack Daniel's or tequila from the bar and handed them his glass, laughing as the sisters took the tiniest sips possible and crinkled up their noses.

He complimented their mother and always opened doors for her—winning her over instantly. He called his father "sir" without any trace of sarcasm. When Trey spotted the cleaning lady struggling to carry the heavy vacuum up the stairs, he leaped to his feet to help her. Adults adored him.

"Trey is a true gentleman," their mother was fond of saying. "I couldn't have asked for a better stepson."

Then, a few months after the sisters moved in, Cassandra and Jane discovered a small sparrow lying stunned on the patio, having crashed into the glass doors.

"The poor little bird!" Jane cried.

Cassandra took charge. "It's looking at us. We have to help it."

They ran inside and found a sturdy shoebox—their mom had acquired quite a few by now—then began filling it with paper towels from the roll in the kitchen.

"We can feed it worms," Cassandra said as their stepbrother sauntered into the kitchen in his lacrosse uniform from his Saturday-afternoon game.

"Feed what worms?" Trey grabbed the container of milk out of the refrigerator and drank it straight out of the carton.

"We found a bird," Cassandra told him. "It's hurt so we made it a nest."

"His name is Tweety," Jane added.

Trey put the milk down on the counter and followed them outside.

The bird was in the exact same position, its shiny dark eyes staring up at them. The girls squatted next to it.

"Should we just pick it up?" Jane asked.

But neither girl made a move to do so.

"You guys are so lame." Trey laughed. "Want some help?"

"Could you put Tweety in the box?" Cassandra asked.

He'd stepped closer to the bird. He bent down and looked at it. "Hi, little guy."

Then his foot—still in his lacrosse cleats—lifted high into the air and came down.

A sickening crunch filled the air.

Jane and Cassandra stared, uncomprehending, as their stepbrother said, "It was gonna die anyway."

Trey turned and walked away, leaving them kneeling on the stone patio, as their shock turned to tears.

They sobbed while they wrapped the little bird's body in another layer of paper towels, and while they wrote TWEETY in Magic Marker on the box they'd intended as an infirmary bed but that was now a coffin. They decorated it with drawings of flowers and rainbows and picked the prettiest spot in the garden, under a yellow rosebush.

After they finished smoothing the dirt over the grave, Cassandra and Jane held hands.

"We're sorry," Cassandra said. "We should have protected you."

They avoided their stepbrother as much as possible after that. But he was still drawn to them. He'd snap the strap of Cassandra's training bra and, when he passed Jane in the hallway, call out, "Plain Jane coming through!" Even though he had a bathroom of his own, he often went into the one Cassandra and Jane shared when they were getting ready for bed.

"Just looking for the Tylenol," he'd say as he pushed open the door without knocking. It always seemed to happen when one of them was in the shower; he must have listened for the running water. The sisters would try to cover themselves as he leered at them through the rippled glass.

But they didn't have to avoid Trey for long. Seventeen months after their mother had put on a long white lacy dress—as if she were a first-time bride—and wept prettily while saying her vows, their stepfather kicked them out of the house and filed for a divorce.

The changes and chaos in their life bound them even more closely together, especially as their mother turned bitter and even more remote. Cassandra and Jane, entangled by secrets and similarities, never let anyone else into the protective bubble they erected around their sisterhood. They were always together. Supporting each other. Defending each other. Loving each other.

Protecting each other.

CHAPTER TWENTY

SHAY

*There are 1.3 million stepfathers in the United States. More than 1,300
new blended families form each day, and more than 50 percent of children
under 13 live at least part-time with one biological parent and
one stepparent.*
—Data Book, page 21

Twenty years ago

ON MY ELEVENTH BIRTHDAY, which fell on a Saturday, my mom took
me shopping at the local mall. She told the saleswoman at Lord & Taylor
that I needed a special outfit for a special occasion. I wasn't the kind of
girl who dreamed about pink ruffles or tulle—I preferred soccer and
math puzzles. But when I tried on the royal-blue knee-length dress
with the sash around the waist, I felt special.

I wore it right out of the store, to the nail salon, where my mom
and I sat in big leather recliners and got mani-pedis. A little later, as
we pulled up to the ranch-style home where we now lived with Barry,
I saw my stepfather standing on an aluminum ladder, wearing faded
jeans and a Bruce Springsteen T-shirt, hammering in a loose roof shin-
gle. I felt Barry's stare as I walked toward the front door.

"Welcome back, Fancy-Pants," he called down to me, and I gave him an awkward wave, keeping my head low.

I was still wearing the velvet dress that felt so soft against my skin when my mom called me to dinner—my favorite, spaghetti and meatballs—so I carefully spread a napkin over my lap to protect it.

My mom usually served Barry first, but tonight she filled my plate before his.

"Hey, hon, can I have a little more gravy for my pasta?" Barry was from the Bronx and always said *gravy* instead of tomato sauce. After I first heard him use that term, I wrote it down along with other regional sayings in my Data Book, such as *bubbler*—which a girl in my class who was from Rhode Island called the water fountain—and *pop* instead of soda, and *freeway,* which people on the West Coast and especially in California call highways.

"Of course," my mom said, spooning more tomato sauce atop his spaghetti.

Barry went through two Coors at dinner—and I'd seen him throw out an empty can on his way to the table. Two beers a night wasn't unusual. But three or more meant trouble: He was angry . . . with the boss who didn't pay him well enough, the jerk in the BMW who'd cut him off on his commute home, or the politicians who kept taxing his hard-earned money.

When my mom went to the kitchen to get dessert, Barry followed her and brought back a fresh can: The tab made a popping sound as he opened it.

"'Happy Birthday to you,'" my mom began to sing. She held a platter with a dozen chocolate-frosted cupcakes: another of my favorites. I closed my eyes, wished for a puppy to cuddle, and blew out the candles.

"Let's see if your wish came true!" she said brightly. "Come on, the present your dad sent is in the backyard." She set the platter down on the table, and I was so excited that I didn't mind waiting for the delicious-looking cupcakes.

She held my hand as we walked, still moving with the grace of the dancer she used to be. I already had two inches on her by then—and I was rapidly gaining on Barry. The only features I'd inherited from her were a cleft in my chin and a narrow, slightly upturned nose. By contrast, she and Barry—who was short and muscular, with thick dark hair and Mediterranean coloring—were a perfect physical match.

A shiny red ten-speed bike with a big bow on the seat leaned against the garage.

"Surprise!" my mom shouted.

I felt my eyes prickle—a dog would be my best friend and would always keep me company—but I recovered fast, biting my lower lip hard so my mom wouldn't know.

"Can I ride it now?"

My mom looked at my dress. "How about we have dessert, then you change and go? It'll still be light out."

Barry hadn't moved from the table when we returned. He was holding his can of Coors with his left hand. He'd lost the tip of that pinkie to a circular saw on one of his construction projects years ago, and the nail was missing. "Like your gift?"

Something in his tone held a warning. I nodded and slid into my seat, carefully arranging my napkin so I didn't have to meet his eyes. I suspected the monthly child support my father paid to my mom was a pretty good-size amount, judging by what I'd overheard Barry say about it.

"I got a bike when I was a kid. But I paid for it myself. Earned the money on my paper route."

"Barry," my mother said softly. "Let's have dessert."

She put the first cupcake on his plate, then she served me and herself.

The icing was thick and gooey, with crunchy rainbow sprinkles on top. I licked some of it off, savoring the sweetness, because it was my favorite part.

At the exact instant I opened my mouth to take a big, greedy bite, Barry spoke up again. "If you're gonna wear a dress like that, you need to lay off the cupcakes."

I froze. Then I carefully put my cupcake back on my plate.

"Barry! That wasn't nice!" My mom turned to me. "Sweetie, it's your birthday. Eat as many as you want."

Barry spread out his arms, as if he didn't mean any harm. "Hey, I'm just trying to help. Guys don't like girls who are bigger than them."

I couldn't stop the tears then. Even though I didn't make a sound, my mom saw them rolling down my cheeks. She jumped up, her face flushed. I'd never heard her yell at my stepfather, but she let loose. "What's gotten into you? Don't talk to her that way!"

I slipped out of my chair. "It's okay," I said quietly. Barry didn't even look at me; his apology was only to my mom. "I'm sorry, babe. I don't know what came over me. I just had a really rough week."

I ran into the backyard and climbed aboard my bike. As I passed the dining room window, I saw Barry pulling my mom into his lap, nuzzling his face into her neck. She wasn't smiling, but she was letting him do it.

I rode around aimlessly until it began to grow dark, then I pedaled home. I put my bike in the garage and quietly entered the house. Barry was watching TV in the living room, but my mom was waiting for me upstairs. She gave me a big hug and whispered, "Barry's really sorry. And I left a cupcake on your desk with a glass of milk."

I ate it, but it wasn't nearly as good as that first sweet taste.

I've been so lost in the birthday memory that my feet are leading me, almost unconsciously, toward the Seventeenth Precinct.

As I pass a glass storefront, I notice my reflection. My shoulders are hunched, and my arms are crossed. I know what I'm doing; I'm trying to make myself smaller. That's the legacy Barry left me with, even though after that birthday, he was careful to save his barbs for moments when it was just the two of us.

I stop and turn to look at myself face on. I uncross my arms, letting them hang freely at my sides. I straighten up and square my shoulders.

I reclaim the woman I was only a few minutes ago, when I sat with Cassandra and Jane.

Barry's words are extinguished by the ones Jane uttered: *Your arms are so toned! Do you have Michelle Obama's trainer?*

I reach the precinct and step inside, past the parallel wooden benches. This time the officer manning the entrance is a woman. She lifts her eyes to look at me but doesn't speak, and I'm reminded again of what an intimidating place this is.

But I press on: "Hi, I'm here to see Detective Williams."

"She isn't in."

I'm instantly deflated, but I recover and ask if I can leave her a note.

The officer nods and I find a pen and an old receipt in my tote bag. *Please call me,* I scribble. *The necklace actually didn't belong to Amanda.*

I write down my cell phone number, just in case Williams no longer has it.

I've already got a plan in place in case the necklace is now in the hands of Amanda's mother. I can research her. I can find out her phone number and address and explain what happened.

I won't tell the Moore sisters about the lengths I went to to get it back. I'll just deliver the good news.

CHAPTER TWENTY-ONE

CASSANDRA & JANE

THE SISTERS ONLY LIE when absolutely necessary.

Making Shay feel better about herself was essential, which was why Cassandra invented the story about Jane's heartbreak—*Jane* had ended the relationship with the handsome banker who grew too demanding of her time.

The only other fabrication they concocted concerned the true owner of the missing necklace. Jane's was resting in her jewelry box.

Shay had seemed so eager to get it back for them. The sisters expected to hear from her quickly—especially since Valerie followed Shay when she departed Bella's and observed her going to the Seventeenth Precinct police station, presumably to retrieve the necklace.

But the rest of that evening passed without a single word from Shay. By now, hours have stretched into days, and still Shay is silent. As soon as Shay left the necklace at the police station, the sisters stopped monitoring its location. They can't risk leaving an electronic trail in case the police have discovered the tracker.

When Cassandra and Jane's assistant interrupts them by knocking on their door during a strategy session to announce they have an urgent call, for a moment both sisters think, *Shay.*

Instead, Daphne is on the line, hyperventilating so furiously she can barely get the words out: "Kit—the customer who set me up with

James—she—she just called. The police stopped by—they asked her about—"

"Wait!" Cassandra interrupts. The line might not be secure; this is something Stacey warned them all about.

Daphne seems to get it. "Sorry." Her voice is still ragged but her words are more circumspect. "Kit's on her way here—to my boutique."

Cassandra and Jane are scheduled to have lunch with a new columnist for the *Post*. But they can't let Daphne handle this alone. Cassandra phones the restaurant to change the reservation from three to two people, while Jane runs outside to hail a cab.

By the time Kit comes rushing into the boutique, pushing her oversize dark sunglasses onto the top of her head, Jane is in the back, browsing the rack of fall blazers. No other customers are in the small boutique.

Kit flings her arms around Daphne. "Can you believe it?" she cries, her voice carrying easily in the small space. "I opened my door this morning to go to Pilates and there's this man standing there with his fist raised!"

Daphne nods and crosses her arms over her chest. Clearly this understated reaction isn't what Kit is seeking.

"He was just about to knock, but still, it gave me such a fright. Anyway, he pulls out his badge. It's bigger than it looks on TV when it's in your face, I'll tell you that. He asked a bunch of questions—how did we know James, yada yada—and then he wanted to know about *your* date with James. Isn't that weird?"

"Careful," Jane breathes, too softly for either woman to hear.

"Why would the detective ask about that? I only went out with him once."

"I know!" Kit exclaims. "And that was forever ago! You said he was cute, but not really your type. And James never brought you up either. I explained all that to the cop—"

A loud crash from the back of the store makes both women spin around.

"So sorry!" Jane calls. "I can't believe I'm such a klutz!"

Daphne hurries to help Jane, who is kneeling beside the fallen torso of a display mannequin adorned with crisscrossing scarves and belts.

"Don't worry about it," Daphne says.

Jane notices Daphne's hands are shaking as she begins to pick up the accessories. Kit comes to hover beside them, practically vibrating with impatience.

"I'm trying to find some new pieces to wear to work," Jane says to Daphne. "Could you help me?"

"Of course." Daphne rises and sets the half mannequin back on the table. "Do you prefer dresses or slacks?"

"Both. I pretty much need a whole new wardrobe."

Kit, disappointment written over her features, looks back and forth between Jane and Daphne. "I better get going. I'll call you later!"

Daphne and Jane watch until Kit is out the door, then Daphne collapses onto a tufted chair by the display table. "I can't believe the police are still asking about me." Her face is drawn and pale.

The detective had surely homed in on the huge discrepancy in Daphne's story: Daphne had told the police that James never contacted her after what she described as an intimate night that ended in her apartment. She'd explained that was the impetus for her angry text telling James to rot in hell. But Kit had revealed a different version of the evening. She'd said Daphne had told her that the date was pleasant, but that she hadn't felt a spark with James.

This tiny, nagging thread could unravel everything.

"You're handling everything beautifully," Jane assures Daphne, putting a hand on her shoulder. "I promise you don't have anything to worry about."

This lie was also necessary; they can't have Daphne start to spiral the way Amanda did.

CHAPTER TWENTY-TWO

SHAY

Most people lie in a conversation when they are trying to appear likable and competent. One famous study found that 60 percent of people lied at least once during a ten-minute conversation. If you're going to tell a premeditated lie, here's how to do it:

- *Make it believable.*
- *Practice saying it.*
- *Keep the lie short.*
- *Be confident.*

—Data Book, page 24

JODY ISN'T SUPPOSED to move in until the end of the month, but her presence is all around me when I walk in the door: New floral throw pillows adorn our brown cracked-leather couch, and a Monet water-lily poster hangs above the bench where we put our shoes. A silver-framed picture of her and Sean sits on the end table; only yesterday, all the table held was coasters.

It's all a reminder—as if I needed one—that my time here is limited. I spent two hours today searching sites such as Apartments.com and Trulia. I finally found a place that looked promising—but when I called the real estate agent, she told me a new tenant had signed the contract an hour after the listing went up.

I hear Jody's voice as I take off my shoes. She and Sean are in his bedroom with the door shut, but the walls are thin.

"It's called the one-minute rule." Jody's voice sounds a little higher and shriller than usual. "If it takes less than sixty seconds, then you should do it immediately. That's why there are dishes in the sink and clothes flung over your chair."

I can picture Sean running his hands through his gingery hair. He's not a messy guy, but he sometimes lets the recycling pile up or he leaves nonperishables in grocery bags on the counter for a few hours.

His voice is deeper and softer, but I think I can detect annoyance: ". . . work . . . want to relax . . ."

If it only takes a minute, why don't you just do it, Jody? I think.

"Well, I can't relax when things are so messy!" She's definitely snippy now.

A tingle of excitement runs through me. This is the first time I've heard them fight. If they break up, then I won't have to move.

There's the rumble of Sean's voice again. Then Jody laughs. And just like that, the moment's gone.

He's so good with quick quips.

It's one of my favorite things about him.

I change out of the pants and top I wore to work and put on running shoes and tights and an old T-shirt. I love to jog along the East River when the weather's on the cusp of fall.

I grab my headphones and tie a light jacket around my wait. Before I head out, I do one more thing. I phone Detective Williams.

She hasn't responded to the note I left. I called a couple times yesterday, but she was out in the field and I was embarrassed to leave my name again. She's probably dealing with murders and burglaries. Returning my message is on the bottom of her to-do list.

This time, she answers.

I've got my little speech all planned. It comes more rushed than I want because just hearing her voice makes me nervous. "Hi, it's Shay Miller. I'm just calling because the necklace I gave you wasn't actually Amanda's. Another friend lent it to her. So could I just swing by and pick it up?"

She doesn't reply and I can only imagine what Detective Williams thinks of me. She told me to let all this go and suggested I could use professional help.

The silence is so heavy I begin babbling. "I—I know this all sounds strange, but I ran into a couple of friends of hers, and we got to talking, and they told me the necklace didn't belong to Amanda. . . . I really need to get it back to them. . . . I promised I would—"

"Wait a second." Her voice is so commanding I flinch. "You're talking to Amanda's friends?"

"I just bumped into them on the street. . . . We recognized each other from the memorial service."

Detective Williams sounds annoyed. "Look, Shay, stop talking to Amanda's friends. I already mailed the necklace back to Amanda's mother. You need to let all this go."

Her tone has a finality to it.

I've run into a dead end. I think about Jane's delighted expression when I told her I'd get back the necklace. I remember Cassandra saying, *Fate must have brought us together.*

"I'm sorry," I say to Detective Williams just before she hangs up.

I'm not apologizing for bothering her.

I'm apologizing because I'm not going to let this go.

"Hi, I'm Melissa Downing," I say to the woman behind the ER desk at City Hospital. "I was hoping to speak to Amanda, that nice ER nurse."

The woman's eyes widen. "Oh." She hesitates and I can almost see her thoughts scrambling. "May I ask what this is in reference to?"

I stretch my lips into a smile. *Keep the lie believable.* "I was brought here a few weeks ago. She was the nurse on duty. She took care of me, and she was just so wonderful. I wanted to come back and thank her."

In my hand is a bouquet of flowers. Yellow zinnias again.

I avoid covering my mouth, chest, or stomach—all clues that someone isn't telling the truth.

"I see. Can you give me a moment?"

"Sure." I step back and take one of the plastic bucket seats, making sure my movements are nonchalant.

It's more than a moment. I stay in that chair for at least fifteen minutes while the woman at the front desk first murmurs into the phone, then goes back to working on her computer, her eyes avoiding mine.

The TV in one corner is silently tuned to CNN, with captions scrolling below. A few others are waiting, but nobody appears to be in terrible distress. Still, I can hear someone's faint moans from not too far away, then a man shouting.

It must take an extraordinarily compassionate person to work in this sort of environment—not to mention a highly competent one. I looked into stats on nurses before I came here and found a study that showed 98 percent of hospital nurses describe their work as mentally and physically demanding.

I wonder if Amanda was one of them. Witnessing near-constant suffering and death must be overwhelming. Another article I read showed nurses are 23 percent more likely to commit suicide than women in general—perhaps because many nurses have easy access to lethal doses of medicines.

Amanda must have had such access: fentanyl, OxyContin, Valium, Percocet, and Vicodin. Yet she chose to leap in front of a subway train.

I jotted all this down in my Data Book. Even if her suicide makes a little more sense to me now, her method does not.

"Melissa?"

I don't react until my name is called a second time. I look up and see a nurse in pink scrubs standing there. Her hair is in a ponytail, she wears no makeup, and she looks completely exhausted. I have even more respect for her profession now—nurses are as underpaid as teachers.

"Oh! Sorry, I was just lost in thought." I get to my feet. I look at her quizzically, hoping she gets the impression I was expecting Amanda.

"I'm Gina. I was Amanda's supervisor. Why don't we talk over here." She leads me to a relatively quiet corner. "You were a patient of Amanda's?"

"Yes," I lie. "Ruptured appendix."

I'd prepared this story because I knew it was highly unlikely a hospital employee would share any personal information about Amanda if they knew my true connection to her.

She nods and I'm grateful no one ran my name through the system to verify that I'd actually been admitted here.

"I'm sorry to have to tell you this, but Amanda died a few weeks ago." For a moment I'm taken aback by her matter-of-fact delivery. Then I realize she probably has to give news like this all day long.

"Oh my gosh! What happened?"

"It was sudden and unexpected." Gina pushes a loose strand of hair behind her ear. She glances at a man walking through the door, his leg bandaged, leaning on the arm of a younger woman, then turns back to me. "But I'm sure she would have appreciated your visit. She truly cared for her patients."

I shake my head as if in disbelief. I look down at the flowers in my hand. "I was going to give her these. She saved my life."

The mournful wail of an ambulance trails off as the vehicle pulls up on the other side of the wide glass doors. I know I don't have much time left; Gina has probably already given me more than she can afford.

I lift my head and blink. "I'd like to write to her mom, Mrs. Evinger. I feel like I should send her a sympathy card and tell her what a wonderful nurse Amanda was."

Gina starts to respond, then a staticky announcement comes over the intercom. "Why don't you leave a card at the front desk and we'll forward it." She takes a step away from me.

I'd assumed Amanda and her mom had the same last name, since the Moore sisters indicated her mother never remarried after the death of Amanda's dad. Gina didn't correct me when I called her Mrs. Evinger, so I feel confident that piece of information is correct. But I still need more data.

"Could I just get her mother's first name? So I can personalize the note."

The announcement comes on again and I can barely hear Gina's distracted response over it: "Um, it's Ellen. . . . Wait, no, it's Eleanor. Just leave the note at the desk and I'll forward it on."

Eleanor Evinger.

I already know she's from Delaware. There can't be too many of them. All I need to do is find the right one.

CHAPTER TWENTY-THREE

VALERIE

INSTEAD OF TIDYING UP in anticipation of her visitor's arrival, Valerie begins to create chaos.

In the master bedroom of her apartment in the East Village, she gently tosses the contents of her dresser drawers and mixes her summer and winter clothes together in her closet. She removes the light-green polka-dot dress from a back hanger, hiding it in a Bloomingdale's shopping bag under her bed. She scatters a few pairs of shoes on the floor and throws a couple of light jackets over the back of a chair.

Securing this appointment with the professional organizer wasn't difficult. During the introductory phone call to arrange the meeting, Valerie had claimed to be free anytime in the late afternoons or evenings. Which was true—Cassandra and Jane had told her this was far more of a priority than any work waiting at their PR firm.

Jody had suggested four P.M. the next day. "My clients make the most progress with a three-hour window, since any more than that is fatiguing."

"I'm excited," Valerie had replied, smiling over the edge of her cell phone at Jane and Cassandra, who were leaning in close. "I know you're going to be so helpful."

There has been no word from Shay despite her vow to retrieve the necklace. And the police seem to be circling nearer to Daphne. The sisters need to go on the offensive. Perhaps Sean's girlfriend, Jody, can provide some insight into his mysterious roommate.

Now, less than twenty-four hours later, Valerie takes a final walk through her apartment, tucking away personal photos as well as pieces of mail with her identifying information on it. She also plans to pay in cash.

Valerie dresses in an outfit that suits her character of being a newly divorced, somewhat idle, well-off woman: ballerina flats, slightly distressed jeans, and a two-hundred-dollar T-shirt. As an added precaution, she wears her hair in a messy bun so its length and style can't be identified, and she puts on fake eyeglasses.

Valerie heads to the lobby ten minutes before the appointed time. When Jody arrives, Valerie greets her with a warm smile and begins chatting about the weather as she ushers Jody past the doorman.

Most visitors give doormen the name of the person they're going to see, but this can't happen today. Valerie isn't using her real name.

Valerie presses the button for the sixth floor and turns to Jody with a smile. Jody is exactly as she imagined—petite, bubbly, with an air of professionalism that feels slightly affected. Shay described her well to Cassandra and Jane, down to the high ponytail that bounces when Jody walks.

"Oh, Deena, your place is beautiful!" Jody exclaims after Valerie unlocks the door and welcomes her in. "I love the color scheme. And those granite counters! Your kitchen is a dream."

"Thanks."

Jody walks over and touches a white vase on the kitchen counter that holds bright peonies. The vase is in the shape of an upside-down hand, with a hollow wrist to hold the flower stems.

"What a fun vase! Do you mind if I ask where you got it? I'm always looking for things to recommend to my clients."

"Oh, it was a gift."

"Looove it." Jody draws out the word, and Valerie responds with a light laugh.

After they chat for a few more moments, Valerie leads Jody to her closet. "As you can see, I need help."

"Oh, this isn't bad at all. You should see some of the closets I've worked with! Now, the first thing we're going to do is pull out everything you own and put it on the bed."

"Even bras and panties?"

"Everything!"

"Nobody else has seen my panties since I got divorced last October." The divorce part is true; the timing is not. Valerie and her husband split up more than a decade ago.

"Oh, I'm sorry."

"Thanks, but don't be." Valerie injects a confiding tone into her voice as she begins pulling out dresser drawers, heaping T-shirts and socks onto her bed. "I'm happy to be rid of him."

"Ugh. Well, good riddance. Let's get rid of some other unwanted stuff now!"

They laugh in unison. The first seed has already been planted.

The two women begin sorting the clothes into three piles as Jody directs: Keep, Donate/Toss, and Repair/Alter. They talk the whole time, with Valerie weaving in tidbits about her life—some real, some fiction—and asking Jody questions, too.

Jody is candid and chatty, telling Valerie how she became an organizer—"It isn't that easy, you have to get certified and everything"—and she confides that she is about to move in with her boyfriend.

Once a few green Hefty bags have been filled and all that remains are the Keep items, Valerie suggests a glass of wine. Jody demurs without a lot of conviction in her voice.

"Oh, come on, it's after five. You're not going to let me drink alone!"

"Maybe just one."

Valerie brings in two glasses and an uncorked bottle of good Sancerre. She fills the glasses generously, then hands one to Jody. "Cheers! To new beginnings."

Jody takes a sip. "Ready to move on to accessories?"

"Let's do it."

They continue chatting as they sort through Valerie's shoes, then handbags.

Jody is admiring a metallic clutch when Valerie looks at the bed and frowns. She picks up a beige sweater from the stack. "This should actually be a toss. My ex bought it for me, and I don't want the reminder of him. I was wearing it when I caught him cheating on me."

"Oh yeah?" Jody takes another sip of wine. It's clear she is eager to hear a juicy story.

"Can you believe that jerk slept with our neighbor? She wasn't even that pretty. They claimed to be just friends." Valerie uses her fingers to put air quotes around the word *friends* and shakes her head.

This is a lie, but Valerie is so convincing: Her jawline tightens and her eyes grow momentarily flinty.

"That's awful!" Jody puts her wineglass on the dresser and begins folding a T-shirt. "You really had no idea?"

"I mean, in retrospect, there were a few signs. They both loved golf, which I hate, so they played together now and then. . . . What do you think? Can men and women truly be friends?"

"Well . . ." Jody flattens her palms, aggressively smoothing out another T-shirt against the bed. "My boyfriend is actually living with another woman, and they're just friends. At least, he's just her friend. But I think she's secretly in love with him."

Valerie nods. "Women always know. So what's she like? The roommate."

Jody slides the T-shirts into a dresser drawer and shrugs. She reaches for her wineglass again and takes a healthy sip. "She's nice. I mean, she doesn't really have much of a social life, though. . . ." Jody hesitates.

Valerie smiles encouragingly. "Come on, out with it."

"The truth is, she's a little weird."

"Ooh, like how?"

Jody's voice drops, even though they're alone. "She's got this strange book she carries around. When I first saw it, I thought it was a journal. But once she left it out . . ."

"I bet you couldn't resist peeking. I know I wouldn't be able to." Valerie tops off Jody's wine.

"I thought maybe she'd written something about Sean. Or me. But it isn't like that at all."

Valerie's body tenses.

"She just has these crazy statistics written down."

"Statistics?" Valerie frowns. "Like what?"

"I'm not sure if that's what you call them, but it's stuff about phobias and how many people commit suicide. There's a whole page about nurses, too. Like what percentage of nurses commit suicide, and what kind of drugs they have access to when they do it. I mean, who researches stuff like that?"

Valerie is too stunned to speak. Luckily Jody mistakes this for shock at the revelation.

"She's obsessed with death, I think. It's just really creepy, and I wish she'd move out."

"Yeah, I can see why." Valerie turns around under the guise of filling her glass again to buy time to compose herself.

She's desperate to rush Jody out so she can call Cassandra and Jane, but she can't. Jody could be an important resource in the future. Valerie has to behave normally for the next thirty minutes, until Jody's allotted time is up.

They spend it chatting, sipping wine, and putting the clothes away. But all the while, Valerie's mind is consumed by questions.

Why is Shay continuing to obsess over Amanda's suicide? And how much does Shay actually know about what happened to Amanda Evinger?

CHAPTER TWENTY-FOUR

SHAY

Nearly 500 million pieces of mail are delivered each day and 146 billion pieces are delivered every year. Mail theft is a felony punishable by up to five years in prison, and up to a $250,000 fine. Some estimates are that one in three people have had packages stolen from their homes. To combat this, some police departments use "bait" packages with a hidden GPS locator, left on the porches of volunteers. As soon as the package is moved, officers get an alert and can track it.
—Data Book, page 25

I FIND SEVERAL WOMEN with the name Eleanor Evinger, but only one who is the right age.

With a little more research, I discover an online site that verifies she is related to Amanda.

She lives in Wilmington, Delaware, about two hours from Manhattan.

On my next day off, I rent a Zipcar, which I've only done a few times before.

Traffic isn't too bad, since I leave the city after rush hour. I keep the speedometer at a steady sixty miles per hour as I head south on I-95. I listen to a TED Talk by a man named Daniel Kish to distract myself not only from the problems that feel like a dull, constant ache in my mind—my lack of a job, not to mention an apartment—but also from what I'm about to do: pay a surprise visit to a grieving mother.

My plan is to be honest with Amanda's mom. I've told too many lies lately, and they only make things worse by twisting around me, ensnaring me. I'll just explain that I found the necklace, I thought it was Amanda's, and it's not actually hers. When I practice saying it like that, it sounds so simple.

It also sounds coldhearted. But I don't know what else to do.

I turn down Pine Street two hours later. The quiet neighborhood has nearly identical single-story brick homes filling both sides of the street. I find the right house—it has a little wooden front porch—and pull up to the curb across the street.

I pick up the bouquet of zinnias that I've been keeping fresh with a damp paper towel wrapped around the stems—by now I associate the flower so strongly with Amanda—and step out of the car. I reach for my blazer, since it seems more respectful than just wearing the plain shirt I have on, and smooth back my hair.

The first thing I notice is the bedraggled look of the lawn, as if it hasn't been weeded or mowed in weeks. A peeling wooden two-seater swing is in the side yard.

It's so similar to the house my mom and Barry live in—the one we moved to when I was ten—except that Barry scrupulously maintains the yard. I see a few fuzzy white dandelions growing by the front walk, and I picture Amanda as a little girl, picking one and blowing away the fluff. Just the way I used to.

The tinge of guilt I felt earlier expands. I force myself to keep moving.

I open the screen door to the porch, wincing as it loudly creaks. I intend to take the few steps to the front door and knock.

But I can't help looking around first. It's crowded with a rocking chair and a few other pieces of furniture, including a side table cluttered with stacks of mail, magazines, and newspapers. A recycling bin next to it is close to overflowing.

In the corner, asleep on a wicker settee, is the woman I've come to visit. Amanda's mother. I recognize her from the memorial service, where she sat in a chair near Amanda's picture, accepting a hug from Cassandra.

Her mouth is slightly open, and she's lying on her side with her hands curled up beneath her chin. On the table before her is a mostly empty bottle of Chardonnay, an overturned wineglass, and a half-eaten tuna sandwich. I hear the drone of a fly buzzing around the sandwich.

It feels voyeuristic seeing her like this; there's an intimacy in watching someone sleep. She looks so vulnerable, and much older than the fifty-something I imagine she must be.

I wish I'd called to let her know I was coming. But I'd figured the element of surprise wouldn't give her time to come up with a lot of questions. Or worse, tell me I should stay away.

I step toward her, then stop. To be shaken awake by a stranger on your front porch would alarm anyone.

Maybe I should go back to my car and wait. But this doesn't look like a catnap. I could be here for hours.

I consider a few options—clearing my throat loudly, going back outside and knocking on the porch door—but then I look at the stacks of mail again. They appear to have been piling up for some time.

I already mailed the necklace back to Amanda's mother, Detective Williams had said.

I edge a little closer, my breathing turning shallow.

The first item on top is a Sears catalog in a plastic wrapper. I see the corners of envelopes beneath it, but it's impossible to tell what they hold.

The detective could have sent it in the plain letter-size envelope I gave her, or maybe she put the necklace into a thick padded mailer.

I glance at Amanda's mom. She hasn't moved, and her breaths are slow and even. I gently set down the flowers on the coffee table, next to the wine.

Then I take another step closer to the table, which is just inches from her head.

My hand hovers above the catalog. If I pick it up, there's going to be no plausible explanation for my actions.

I ease my fingers beneath it and slowly lift it. There's nowhere to set it down, so I hold it in my left hand while I reach for the next piece. It's a water bill.

Detective Williams's envelope could be anywhere; there's no organization to the stacks. I hope it's near the top, with the more recent mail. But it might not even be here at all.

The fly buzzes past an inch away from my nose and I flinch, batting at it with my hand.

Amanda's mother makes a soft noise. I hold my breath. All she has to do is open her eyes to see me looming above her. But she remains asleep.

I pick up the water bill and shift it into my left hand, on top of the catalog. Then I lift up the next few pieces of mail quickly. With each one, I'm aware I'm getting in deeper and deeper.

It's like I've tumbled into the something called the snowball effect, which I researched a while ago. Basically it means that people who commit small acts of dishonesty find it easier to tell more lies. As your fabrications pile up, your anxiety and shame start to disappear.

The first time I met Cassandra, I lied to her. Then, when I had tea with her and Jane, I continued the lie about sharing a veterinarian with Amanda. After that, I concocted a story when I went to the hospital and saw Gina. Now this.

It'll be the last time, I vow. It ends here.

When I try to pull away a magazine, the stack topples. A dozen letters and bills slide to the floor, making a shuffling noise.

I cringe as Amanda's mother shifts over, onto her other side. One of her arms rises and for a moment I'm terrified she's going to grab me. But it just flops above her head, so close her fingertips almost graze my leg.

After an agonizing moment, I scan the items that fell to the floor. Two are in pretty pastel envelopes, the kind that come with Hallmark cards. They must be sympathy notes.

Hot shame engulfs me. But I can't stop, not when I'm so close. The necklace has to be in here. And Detective Williams is so busy she probably didn't even call to explain she was sending it. If so, Amanda's mother won't ever know it's missing.

I lift up another six or seven envelopes. Then I see a long white one with a preprinted return address in the upper left-hand corner: NYPD 17TH PRECINCT, NEW YORK, NY 10022.

I stretch out my hand and slowly lift it. It's so light, but I can feel something hard inside through the thin paper.

If it was important to her, she would have opened it, I tell myself.

Slowly, I ease the stack of mail in my left hand back onto the table. It's impossible to do so soundlessly and I wince. But Amanda's mother doesn't move.

I slip the envelope into my tote bag.

Opening up someone else's mail, let alone stealing it, is a federal crime.

But I'm not really stealing, I tell myself. The necklace never belonged to Amanda at all.

I look down at the pieces of mail scattered on the floor. I can't risk making any more noise by picking them up, so I just leave them. Maybe she'll think a breeze blew them off the table.

I take small, quiet steps toward the door. When I reach it, I look back at Amanda's mother in her shapeless housedress. Sadness overtakes me. This poor woman lost her husband, and now her daughter. And she seems to have lost herself, too.

She is utterly alone.

I wish I could spend a few hours here, cleaning her porch and bringing her a cold glass of water. It wouldn't make up for what I've done, but it would be a way of apologizing.

I ease open the door, bracing myself as it creaks.

Then I step outside, into air that feels fresher than it did in the cluttered screen porch with the old sandwich.

I walk briskly toward the Zipcar, feeling with every step that I might hear Amanda's mother call out. My hands are shaking when I pull the key out of my tote bag.

As I open the car door, I realize I left the flowers on the table. I'm about to risk going back to get them when I hear someone call out, "Hello!"

I spin around, my heart exploding. A woman in jeans and a flannel shirt, with short white hair, is kneeling in the garden edging the sidewalk. She's obviously the neighbor who lives directly across the street.

She stands up and approaches me and I take an instinctive step back.

"Are you a friend of Amanda's? We were so sorry to hear the terrible news." She clearly wants to talk; maybe she even watched Amanda grow up in this neighborhood. But I can't get into a conversation with her.

"I'm sorry, I'm in such a rush." I slide into the car. "Nice to meet you." I wave through the open window as I drive away.

In the rearview mirror, I see her staring after me.

I slowly let out my breath as I turn the corner too quickly, my wheels squealing. I drive another few blocks, then pull over and reach for my phone.

I got the necklace back from the police, I text to Cassandra and Jane. *Happy to bring it to you anytime!*

I put away my phone and step on the gas pedal, more lightly this time.

My vow to stop lying lasted less than ten minutes.

CHAPTER TWENTY-FIVE

AMANDA

Two months ago

"MOM, I'VE GOT TO GO," Amanda said over the wail of an incoming ambulance's siren. "My break's over."

It wasn't, but she wanted to get off the phone. The slur in her mother's words caused Amanda's stomach to clench reflexively. And she had far more pressing things on her mind today than her mother's complaint about a neighbor's son who'd blocked her driveway again.

Amanda tucked her cell phone into the pocket of her scrubs.

It's now or never, she told herself, feeling a hitch in her heartbeat.

She walked back toward the hospital, triggering the ER's automatic glass doors.

The uniformed security guard behind the desk nodded. "Heat's on today."

She flinched before realizing he was referring to the temperature outside.

"So hot the chickens are laying hard-boiled eggs," she replied, swiping her key card to gain entrance into the ER.

She hoped the guard didn't notice that her hand was shaking.

It had all seemed so simple when she'd been at Jane's apartment, sitting next to Cassandra and feeling the eyes of the other women on her. *I can do it,* she'd offered. *No problem.*

Oh, Amanda, you're the best, Cassandra had responded, leaning over to give her a quick hug. She'd felt Cassandra's silky hair sweep across her cheek as she inhaled the notes of rosemary and mint from Cassandra's shampoo. Amanda knew the precise brand; she'd once peeked into Cassandra's shower and medicine cabinet, wondering which beauty products Cassandra used.

Amanda had five minutes left in her break.

I do this every day, Amanda reminded herself as she walked toward the medication room that contained the hospital's arsenal of narcotics.

In other departments, nurses typically dispensed medication on the even hours—ten A.M., noon, two P.M., and so on. That meant the half hour before those time slots were the busiest, as nurses hurried to collect the various drugs their patients required.

Things were different in the ER; predictability didn't exist here.

Right now, the room was empty. But another nurse could rush in at any second.

Quickly, Amanda told herself.

Her body felt icy as she pressed her fingertip on the keypad, then punched in her ID number. She retrieved the bottle of liquid morphine sulfate she needed for the burn victim who'd been brought in earlier today; he was due another dose soon. Up until this moment, she'd done nothing wrong.

Now came the tricky part; the moment she crossed the line.

Her fingers closed around a second bottle of morphine. She slipped it alongside the first in the pocket of her scrubs.

She closed the cabinet and exited the room, walking briskly toward her locker at the end of the hallway, her Crocs squeaking on the glossy linoleum floor.

Her chest felt tight; eyes were everywhere in the hospital, from security guards to other employees to cameras. But no one had any reason to be watching her, a nurse who'd diligently worked there for several years.

She pushed through the door to the break room. Her luck held: No one was there.

She opened her locker and retrieved an empty travel-size container of mouthwash from her insulated lunch bag. Carefully she transferred sixty milligrams, trying to still her shaking hands. She then replaced the Listerine bottle alongside the scalpel she'd wrapped in a medical towel earlier today.

A wave of exhilaration rose inside her, pushing down her anxiety, as she envisioned texting Cassandra and Jane as soon as she left the hospital: *I got it!*

Each of the seven women in their group had special skills, but only Amanda could perform this particular task. Liquid morphine extinguished pain, and it also typically caused extreme drowsiness. This stolen dose would be used for those precise qualities.

Her hand, with the mostly full bottle of morphine, moved toward the pocket of her scrubs.

"Hey, girl, hungry again?"

She fumbled the bottle, almost dropping it. She closed her fingers around it tightly and swept her hand behind her back as she spun around.

"Gina! You surprised me."

Was her supervisor looking at her strangely?

Amanda tried to smile. "Just grabbing a snack."

Gina walked to her own locker. "Me, too." She pulled out a granola bar. She unwrapped it and sat down heavily on the bench in the center of the rows of lockers. "Did you see the guy who almost cut off his thumb slicing a bagel?" Gina shook her head as she bit into her granola bar.

"Another one? We usually get those on Sundays." Amanda turned back around and eased her hand into her pocket, hoping her body had blocked Gina's view. "See you back out there." Amanda stepped toward the door.

Gina was definitely looking at her strangely now. "What happened to your snack?"

Amanda felt her cheeks heat up. She shrugged. Tried to come up with a quick joke, but her mind was blank. "I'm not really that hungry," she finally responded.

She hurried out of the room before Gina could say anything more.

CHAPTER TWENTY-SIX

CASSANDRA & JANE

TONIGHT WAS SUPPOSED TO be a triumph for the Moore sisters. It's the Manhattan premiere of a film featuring one of their clients, an actor named Dean Bremmer, who is being compared to a young Denzel Washington.

However, instead of sipping champagne in their offices while getting their makeup done, the sisters spent the hour before the premiere strategizing.

Daphne called twice today, her anxious voice soaring into a higher octave, convinced a police officer in a cruiser was staking out her boutique. But when Valerie broke away from reconfirming RSVPs to the premiere to hurry to the West Village, the officer had already driven away. It was probably nothing, the sisters agree. The officer could have been doing any number of things, including simply taking a break.

Still, neither Cassandra nor Jane can eat dinner. "I'll skip Dean's premiere and stay by my phone," Jane says.

Cassandra agrees that one of them has to be reachable at all times; too many land mines surround them.

After Cassandra leaves—her hair slicked into a high ponytail, since she canceled her appointment for a blowout, and the black stilettos she'd planned to change into forgotten beside her office sofa—Jane sits at her glass-and-chrome desk, trying to catch up on the paperwork that has piled up.

But it's impossible to focus. Every time her phone vibrates with a text or email, she flinches.

Then a sharp sound cuts through the silence: The office phone is ringing, even though it's after business hours. Jane checks caller ID: *City Hospital.*

Amanda's former workplace.

Jane slips on her headset and immediately accepts the call.

It's Gina, who was Amanda's supervisor in the ER. As soon as Gina explains that Amanda's mother gave her the PR firm's number, Jane's shoulders unclench.

"We finally cleaned out Amanda's locker earlier this week," Gina says. "It took her mom a few days to call me back. And she wanted me to ask if you and your sister could take Amanda's things. It isn't much— some clothes, an umbrella, and a few toiletries."

"Of course." Jane can imagine how the conversation played out: Amanda's mother has been all too willing to abdicate responsibility to the sisters for everything from clearing out Amanda's apartment to organizing and paying for the memorial service.

The sisters are more than willing to take responsibility for anything relating to Amanda.

"I can swing by tonight," Jane offers.

"Oh, I'm just about to leave. Would sometime tomorrow be okay?"

"Sure."

Gina was one of the few people outside of the group that Amanda sometimes texted—forwarding a cartoon joke about nurses, or coordinating details about a baby gift for a colleague. Gina couldn't attend the memorial service because it conflicted with her shift.

This is an opportunity.

"I still can't believe she's gone," Jane says.

"Yeah, me, too."

"I guess I feel like I should have picked up on something, but I didn't notice anything different about her. Did you?"

Gina hesitates and Jane can hear the hospital's noises through the phone: the static preceding a loudspeaker announcement, a distant siren, voices rising and falling. "She did seem a little . . . well, *off* isn't quite the right word, but it's the best I can come up with. I guess I started noticing it a couple weeks before she died."

"Mmm . . ." Jane grabs a yellow notepad and a pen. She can't transcribe the conversation on her computer because Gina might hear the clicking of the keys.

"And then, right before she died, she was acting really strangely. She made a few mistakes, which was unlike her. And on our last shift together, she raced out midway through. I never saw her after that."

Jane's body is rigid. "I wonder what was going on."

"I really have no idea. It was all so out of character." Gina exhales.

Jane does, too.

"It's such a terrible loss. She was a wonderful nurse. It's easy to get burned out, to put up a buffer between you and your patients so you don't get your heart broken if they don't make it. But Amanda didn't do that."

"I know. She really cared, especially about the underdogs of the world." Jane puts down her pen and stands up. Her water glass is empty, so she heads to the small Deer Park cooler by the reception desk to fill it up.

"Just the other day, this woman showed up with flowers to thank Amanda for saving her life."

"That's sweet." Jane presses the water tap. She'll wrap up work soon—she's too distracted to get much done—and uncork a bottle of wine at home, then check in with Daphne.

"Yeah, she seemed really affected by Amanda's death."

Jane freezes. Then she shuts off the tap, though her glass is only half full. She quickly returns to her desk, struggling to keep her voice casual: "Is that so?"

"Anyway, I should get going—"

"Sorry," Jane interrupts, her pen poised over her page again. "The woman with the flowers—was she tall, with brown hair and tortoise-shell glasses?"

Jane can feel Gina's surprise swelling through the phone lines. "How'd you know?"

Jane grips the pen. *Shay,* she writes, underlining the name so heavily that her pen rips through the page. "It's a long story and I'll explain

everything, but could you just quickly let me know what else she did?"
Jane's stomach tightens as she waits for the reply.

"Nothing really." Gina sounds puzzled now. "She asked for Amanda's
mom's address so she could send a sympathy card."

Jane closes her eyes. "Did you share it with her?"

"No, I told her I couldn't give it out, but I'd be happy to forward
the letter on."

Jane is already grabbing her bag and coat. "I don't want to alarm you,
but this woman has been doing some really strange things," Jane blurts.
"She showed up at Amanda's memorial and lied about how she knew
her. I don't believe she was ever a patient. I don't know what she could
be writing to Amanda's mother, but it's definitely not a sympathy card."

"Oh, wow, are you kidding me? I had no idea. She was so convincing."

"Her name is Shay Miller. If she shows up again, please call me
right away, okay?"

"S-H-A-Y? She gave me a different name, started with an M, I
think. Hang on, I'm going to get to a computer and check something."

There's silence for a few moments. Then Gina says, "No one named
Shay Miller was *ever* a patient here. I searched our records."

"I'm going to reach out to Amanda's mom now. She can't open that
card."

"Wait." Gina hesitates. "Come to think of it, she never did drop it
off."

"There's a reporter from *E! Entertainment* heading this way," Cassandra
says to Dean Bremmer, the twenty-two-year-old actor by her side.
"He's going to ask two questions. The first is what it was like to work
with Matthew McConaughey. And then he'll ask what drew you to
your character. You've got this; you've answered these questions a
dozen times before."

Dean nods. "Is this ever going to get easier?"

"Definitely." Cassandra smiles at him.

The bright lights of the *E!* camera have just illuminated Dean when
Cassandra feels a hand grip her elbow.

Jane leans in close. An onlooker might imagine she's whispering to her sister something about how much she enjoyed the movie.

"I just spoke with one of Amanda's coworkers, Gina, then I called Amanda's mom," Jane murmurs.

Cassandra smiles, as if delighted to hear it.

"What was it like to work with Matthew?" the reporter asks Dean.

"Oh, a total nightmare!" Dean cracks, flashing a winning smile.

Cassandra nods at Dean as Jane whispers again.

"A few days ago, Shay went to the hospital and pretended to be one of Amanda's former patients. She was trying to get Amanda's mother's address."

Cassandra stiffens almost imperceptibly.

The *E!* reporter asks the second question Cassandra has approved in advance: "What drew you to play this complicated and sometimes infuriating character?"

"It was all about understanding his truth," Dean replies earnestly.

Jane continues, "Gina didn't provide the address and I phoned Amanda's mother on my way here. She hasn't heard a word from Shay. But she said today, when she woke up from a nap, she found a bouquet of flowers on the front porch."

"I don't understand," Cassandra murmurs. "Someone left Amanda's mother flowers, but didn't try to talk to her?"

Jane speaks four words into her sister's ear:

"She brought yellow zinnias."

CHAPTER TWENTY-SEVEN

SHAY

*One of the best ways to get someone to like you is to ask them to do a
favor for you. In one study conducted in both the U.S. and Japan, people
who thought they were working on a joint project ended up reporting liking
someone more when that person asked for their help with the task. This is
called the Benjamin Franklin effect. The phenomenon is named for the way
the founding father used this tactic to appeal to a political rival, by asking the
man to lend him a book from his library.*
—Data Book, page 32

WHEN THE INTERCOM BUZZES, I press the button to let in the Moore
sisters.

I'm holding Jane's sun charm necklace, thinking about how I
couldn't tell them the truth: that I'd gone to the trouble and expense of
renting a car and driving four and a half hours to retrieve the necklace.
It would make me seem desperate. Plus, how could I admit I'd basically
stolen it back?

Now I look around my apartment, realizing how small and unso-
phisticated it appears. I consider hurrying downstairs to meet them,
but that seems rude.

Sean and Jody are sprawled on the sofa, her feet in his lap, watching
a Tina Fey movie. They don't even look up at the sound of the buzzer.

They probably think I've ordered in Chinese food. I haven't had a visitor in months, since Mel came over for dinner before her baby was born.

I clear my throat. "Hey, um, someone's coming by to—"

There's a single, sharp rap on the door.

I open it and see the sisters looking as if they just stepped off the runway. Cassandra wears a black-and-white-patterned sheath, and Jane is in a belted suede minidress with over-the-knee boots. Their hair is shiny and smooth, despite the fact that it's a windy day. The vision of the two of them standing in my narrow doorway with the peeling paint feels almost like a mirage.

"Come on in." I smile.

Their heels click against the wood floor, and the faint scent of their floral perfumes mingle in the air.

Jody sits up instantly, yanking out her scrunchie to release her ponytail, her attention no longer on the movie. Sean clicks it off and looks back and forth between the sisters.

"Cassandra and Jane, this is my roommate, Sean, and his girlfriend, Jody."

"Nice to meet you," Jane says.

"How do you all know each other?" Jody's puzzlement is obvious.

I have no idea how to answer.

But Cassandra gives one of her high-wattage smiles: "Oh, we met a few weeks ago and became instant friends."

Jody looks at me as if she's never before seen me—or maybe it's just that she hasn't seen me in this particular light: as someone whose company is sought after by these cool, mysterious women.

"Here." I hand Jane the necklace.

"You're the *best*." She hugs me tightly.

Cassandra reaches for the chain and fastens it around her sister's neck. The pendant rests in the hollow space between Jane's collarbones.

"Perfect," Cassandra says.

"Do you want anything to drink?" Sean says. He and Jody are both standing up by now.

I see Cassandra and Jane take it all in: the matching wineglasses in front of Sean and Jody, the blanket that had been covering them, and the absolute lack of anywhere else to go in the apartment.

"That's so sweet of you," Jane says. "But we're going to pass."

My heart sinks. When they leave, they'll take the light they brought with them into my apartment. I'll probably spend the evening alone in my bedroom, searching Apartments.com again. But that's not the worst part. Now that they have the necklace back, I don't have an excuse for trying to get together with them again.

A lump forms in my throat, but I swallow it down.

I'm about to thank them for coming when Cassandra wraps her arm around me. "Hope you don't mind if we steal Shay."

An hour later, I stand in the middle of a small but stylish apartment, feeling as if my luck is finally beginning to turn around.

The fourteen-story doorman building on East Twelfth Street has everything a single woman in New York City needs, and more, including a little gym in the basement.

The efficiently designed kitchen is stocked with an espresso maker and a Vitamix, along with the usual dishes, pots, and pans.

In the living room, an L-shaped sofa faces the flat-screen TV and built-in bookshelves, which are filled with novels and memoirs. Against the windowsill is an iron plant stand displaying several delicate-looking orchids, and a small aquarium with a few brightly colored fish.

"The master bedroom is over there, but here's the guest room you would use," Jane says, opening a door.

When the Moore sisters told Sean and Jody they were stealing me, I expected to go out for drinks again. Instead, they said they had a surprise for me: a house-sitting job, if I wanted it.

Now I step inside the bedroom, knowing I don't even need to look at it to say yes. I'd be happy sleeping on the sofa in the living room.

The double bed is made up with a crisp white comforter and fluffy pillows. It looks so cozy I wonder if I'll even need my Ambien. A window with a built-in seat overlooks the rain-dappled street below. In the corner, a small desk hugs the wall. A candle is on the nightstand, with a red tulip in a bud vase.

It looks like the kind of place I'd splurge for on the Airbnb site.

"There's an empty closet." Cassandra gestures. "And a little guest bathroom with a shower."

"It's perfect," I tell Cassandra and Jane.

"I'm sorry she isn't going to pay you for this, but you'd be doing us a favor, truly," Cassandra says.

"Oh my gosh, are you kidding? I'm thrilled!"

We walk back into the kitchen again, and I imagine making my coffee without having to put on a robe—or worrying that I'm going to hear intimate noises coming from Sean and Jody in his bedroom.

"It was meant to be," Jane says, leaning against the granite counter.

Everything in here is so bright and spotless. Even though it's temporary, it feels like a fresh start. I can hardly wait to go home and pack a bag.

"All you need to do is feed the fish and water the orchids every other day. The flowers are a little temperamental, so just put an ice cube on the soil," Cassandra says.

"I'm happy to do anything else your friend needs. Steam clean her carpets? Renovate her kitchen?"

They laugh, and I add, "I hope your friend's sister gets better soon."

"I have a feeling she will," Cassandra replies as we step into the hallway and she locks up. "And she'll be thrilled to know her home will be watched over."

When we exit the building, I hug the sisters goodbye. I stand there for a moment, feeling the whisper of the sky's last few raindrops against my skin, as if it is washing me anew, too.

CHAPTER TWENTY-EIGHT

BETH

Twenty-two months ago

THE SOFT PATTER OF the shower running in the next room was as sooth-ing as a light rainfall. Beth lay in bed, warm covers wrapped around her, listening to its gentle rhythm.

She could stay snuggled here for another two hours, drowsing away the morning; her first court case wasn't on the docket until eleven A.M. It was a tempting thought. Ever since her chemotherapy had begun more than a month earlier, exhaustion had overpowered her usual exu-berant energy.

But she also hadn't been intimate with her husband, Brett, since she'd started treatments. It had been even longer than that since they'd show-ered together, which used to be one of their preludes to lovemaking.

So she eased out of bed and pulled her long-sleeved flannel night-gown over her head, catching a glimpse of herself in the full-length mirror on the back of her closet door. She could see the sharp edges of her rib cage and hip bones; her once-curvy body had become almost unrecognizable to her.

She stepped toward the bathroom, wondering why she felt a little nervous. She and Brett had been together for five years, married for three; they'd begun talking about starting a family, although those con-versations had been put on hold once her doctor phoned with the results of Beth's mammogram. This wasn't the first crisis they'd weathered. Brett supported her when her parents refused to attend their wedding, since Beth had defied their wishes by having a justice of the peace instead of their family priest perform the nondenominational ceremony. When publisher after publisher rejected Brett's poetry collection, it was Beth's turn to stand by her husband. She not only encouraged him to keep writing, but agreed to move from Boston to Brooklyn so he could immerse himself in literary circles. He cooked dinner, since his part-time job as an instructor at a writing center left him with more free time, and she covered most of the bills.

They were, she often thought, a beautiful team.

She slowly pushed open the bathroom door. Steam filled the room, and she could smell the fresh, sweet scent of shampoo. Brett's glasses rested on the edge of the sink, and his pale, lanky silhouette was visible behind the frosted-glass shower door. His head and neck curved down, like a question mark.

He wasn't moving; he just stood there, letting the water beat down on his head.

Maybe he was concentrating on the perfect metaphor for his latest poem, she thought.

She felt a surge of tenderness for this sensitive, creative man who so loved words and could happily get lost in his own mind on the fifty-mile bike rides he took on his days off. He watched only the History Channel and old black-and-white movies; he did the crossword puzzle in ink. He was so different from her—she hated exercise and loved romantic comedies as an escape from the darkness of her job as a public defender—but that was what also made them work.

She took a deep breath and pulled open the shower door.

Brett was staring at the drain.

Or more accurately, at the clump of bright red hair clogging it.

Beth instinctively touched a hand to her head. Her hair was thinning and patchy, but she still had some.

"Oh, hey," Brett finally said. His eyes met hers, then skittered away. "I'm about to get out so it's all yours."

She knew it pained him to see her struggle. He touched her so gingerly these days, as if he worried she might break. He packed homemade puréed vegetable soup in a thermos for her lunch—it was one of the few things she could keep down—and he'd even taken to sleeping on the couch so she could get better rest.

But she didn't want him to see her as an invalid or a patient today. She wanted him to see her as a woman.

She didn't know how to say it; he was the one who was gifted with words, not she. So she simply stepped aside to let him move out of the shower.

When she finger-combed conditioner through her curls, a tangle broke loose into her hands. She inhaled a shuddering breath. *It'll grow back,* she told herself. *It's only temporary.*

She turned off the water and wrapped herself in a thick robe—she was always cold now—then used a wad of tissues to gather all the hair from the drain and bury it in the trash can.

The next day she met with a few clients—a woman caught soliciting an undercover cop in a prostitution sting, a nineteen-year-old charged with second-degree battery—and while she sipped her soup at lunchtime, she made an appointment to get a wig. Maybe she'd surprise Brett by showing up as a blonde, she thought.

But he surprised her first.

Two days later, she arrived home from work and called out, "Brett?"

There was no answer. None of the Wagner he adored playing over the stereo, no smell of sweet potatoes roasting or bread baking.

In the bedroom, his usually cluttered desk was clean. The antique gold clock that was always atop it was missing.

A note was propped up on the dresser they shared.

Dear Beth,
I'm so sorry. I can't do this. I can't be what you need. You deserve better. I'll always love you.
Brett

She read the words a half dozen times, but they still didn't make sense.

She hadn't shed a tear when her parents had railed against her for being so different—for marrying outside the Catholic faith, for being a liberal, for always speaking her mind. She hadn't broken down when the oncologist confirmed she had Stage 2 breast cancer.

But as she stared at the words on the ragged-edged paper she recognized as having been torn out of the leatherbound notebook she'd bought Brett to draft his poems, her body collapsed and she sobbed.

A few weeks later, as Beth was struggling to carry two bags of groceries through her lobby—by now she could only stomach ginger ale, bread, and vanilla pudding—the heavy bottles of soda caused one of her paper bags to split.

A bottle rolled across the tile floor. It came to an abrupt stop under the sneaker of a woman roughly her own age, clad in black exercise clothes.

"Can I give you a hand?" the woman offered as she bent down to collect Beth's groceries.

"I'd really appreciate it," Beth said, looking at the ruined bag. It would take her two trips to get everything up the stairs by herself, and she was bone weary. "I'm just up in 3F."

"No problem, neighbor," the woman said, straightening up.

She looked directly at Beth, and Beth suddenly had the sense that the woman saw straight through her, past the clothes that hung loosely on Beth's body and the scarf that covered her now-bald head, and into her very core, glimpsing it all: her cancer, her betrayal, her loneliness.

"Nice to meet you. I'm Valerie. I just moved here from L.A. a few months ago."

CHAPTER TWENTY-NINE

SHAY

About one-third of all injuries occur at home, and one of the most dangerous areas is the kitchen. Two of the most common kitchen injuries include burns and knife cuts. If a wound keeps bleeding after you've applied direct pressure for five to ten minutes, you may need stitches.
—Data Book, page 34

THE BLADE SLICES INTO my skin so quickly that I begin to bleed before the pain registers.

I grab a paper towel and wrap it around my fingertip, wincing.

The cut isn't too bad. I was just using a little paring knife to chop up a red pepper for my salad. But I need some Neosporin and a Band-Aid.

I walk through my bedroom into the guest bathroom, but the cabinet over the sink is empty. My toiletries bag is stuffed—I packed Advil, tampons, shampoo, and everything else I thought I might need, but I overlooked first-aid supplies.

A red splotch is already seeping through the paper towel, even though I doubled it up. If I keep pressure on the cut, the bleeding will stop. So I could make do without a Band-Aid.

But I was using the knife against a cutting board I found propped by the sink. And I once read a horrifying statistic that I've never been able to get out of my mind: Cutting boards can contain 200 percent more fecal bacteria than a toilet seat.

I guess I could run out to the drugstore to pick up some antibacterial cream. But I've just stirred ziti into a pot of boiling water. And I don't even know where the nearest Duane Reade is.

There's one other option.

I walk back into the living room and look at the closed door to the master bedroom. There must be an en suite bathroom, because Cassandra described the one I'm using as the guest bathroom.

The Moore sisters didn't explicitly tell me *not* to go in there. Surely just grabbing a tube of ointment and a bandage won't do any harm, I think.

Still, I'm oddly reluctant.

As I make my way across the living room, I'm aware of the utter silence. The walls here are composed of thick plaster, and the floors are lushly carpeted. It's so different from the place I share with Sean, where noises from neighboring apartments and the street below infuse the air so regularly I barely notice them.

I reach for the door handle to the master bedroom, wondering what the room beyond will look like. Then it strikes me that Cassandra and Jane never gave me the apartment owner's name. I guess I don't need the information, but it feels strange to be drinking out of coffee mugs and sleeping on sheets that belong to a stranger without even that simple formality.

I hesitate with my hand resting on the cool metal knob. *I'll be in and out in two minutes, tops,* I tell myself. *And I'll leave everything exactly the way I found it. No one ever needs to know.*

A loud rattling sound comes from the kitchen. I flinch and whip around.

It's my cell phone on the kitchen counter, vibrating against the granite. I hurry over and see *Jane Moore* flashing on the screen.

I'm smiling even before I answer.

"Shay!" Her sweet voice bubbles over the line. "I'm so happy I caught you! What are you up to?"

"Just making dinner." I wrap the paper towel more tightly around my finger. "How about you?"

"Everything's great. But Cassandra and I have been thinking about you, and how you don't ride the subway anymore. It just hit us that there isn't a bus stop that's really convenient to the apartment."

I can't believe Cassandra and Jane spent time considering my situation.

But they're right: My route to my temp job this morning was completely meandering. There's a subway stop just a block from this apartment, which would make the commute so much easier.

"Oh, it's not a big deal," I say, giving a little laugh.

I cradle my phone between my ear and shoulder to free my hands. I remove the paper towel and turn on the sink tap, letting cold water run over my finger.

"We have an idea." Jane's voice is soft and inviting; I feel like she's sharing a confidence with me. "I hope this doesn't feel like we're overstepping. But we've got this friend. You'd love her, she's really great. Anyway, she helped us with something personal that we were really struggling with a long time ago, and a few of our other friends have turned to her when they've had difficulties. I bet she could help you with this."

I already tried counseling—I flash to Paula's rubber band—and it didn't help. I'm not sure that meeting with their friend would be any more effective.

But when I open my mouth, I find myself saying, "That would be amazing."

Cassandra and Jane have already made a huge difference in my life in such a short time, I think, looking around the serene, lovely apartment. *Maybe they can find a way to fix my fear of the subway for me, too.*

"Are you free tomorrow morning? I bet she could make that work."

The Moore women don't waste time. I mentioned a tough living situation, and they found me a temporary apartment. Now they're tackling my phobia.

And tomorrow isn't one of my temp days; I'm completely free.

I'd planned to spend the day searching for rental apartments because being here—spreading out on the sofa, singing in the shower—makes me realize how chipped away I feel with Jody and Sean around all the time. But being with one of Cassandra and Jane's friends seems almost as good as being with them.

"Sure, I could make that work. I'd love to meet her. What's her name?"

"Hmm? Oh, it's Anne. Anyway, how's the apartment? Are you finding everything you need?"

By now my finger has stopped bleeding. It doesn't even hurt.

Some antibacterial soap is by the sink. I can just wash my hands with that and keep a clean paper towel around it tonight. I'll pick up a box of Band-Aids tomorrow.

"The apartment's perfect. I don't need a thing. I was just making some pasta and I'm going to flop on the couch and watch a movie in a few minutes."

"I'm going to do the same." Jane laughs.

We chat awhile longer, then Jane promises to give her friend Anne my phone number so we can make plans to meet tomorrow.

A little later, after I rinse my pasta bowl and put it in the dishwasher, I walk past the master bedroom on the way to my room to grab my phone charger, since my battery is low.

I abruptly stop a foot away from the closed door.

A tiny splotch of my blood is on the glossy wooden floor by the bottom of the door frame.

I rush back to the kitchen, dampen a paper towel to clean the blood up, then I drop to my knees by the door and start scrubbing. It comes right off.

I lean back on my heels. If I'd gone in that bedroom, I could've dripped blood onto the floor—or worse, an expensive carpet—and I might not even have noticed.

But surely the owner of this apartment would have.

I search the area around the door again, double-checking the handle. But everything is clean.

Then I head into the kitchen to toss out the paper towel, thinking, *Thank goodness Jane called at the precise moment she did.*

CHAPTER THIRTY

CASSANDRA & JANE

STACEY WAITS UNTIL VALERIE texts to say the apartment is empty before she strides into the lobby of Valerie's building, a toolbox in one hand and a baseball cap tipped low on her forehead.

"I'm the contractor for Valerie Ricci," she tells the doorman, who has been instructed to anticipate her arrival. He hands over the spare key, and Stacey is heading up in the service elevator within moments.

She'll have roughly an hour to work, while Valerie, who is posing as a woman named Anne today, distracts her houseguest.

Stacey's instructions are clear: Install an extra camera behind the couch where Valerie's guest likes to sit typing on her laptop, and a key logger program on her laptop, which will automatically send everything she types to the sisters. Get the Bloomingdale's bag from beneath the bed in the master bedroom. Find the houseguest's leather notebook and photograph every page, making sure the words are clearly visible.

Stacey didn't question why Valerie would invite someone into her home and then invade the person's privacy. Nor did she ask why Valerie was using the alias Anne.

Her formidable streak of loyalty runs wider for the sisters than for anyone else, except maybe Beth, who was Stacey's court-appointed defense attorney when Stacey was charged with aggravated assault and drug possession.

By the time Valerie and Shay conclude their outing to the Thirty-third Street subway station ninety minutes later, Stacey is already on a different subway, heading to Moore Public Relations.

The moment she arrives, Jane ushers her into Cassandra's office.

"No interruptions, please, unless it's an emergency," Cassandra instructs her assistant, who can't resist sneaking glances at Stacey, clearly curious about this small, swaggering woman with an emerald-green streak in her hair and a metal toolbox.

As soon as the door is closed, Stacey pulls a laptop out of her toolbox and opens it to reveal the first page of Shay's Data Book. Without being asked, she steps aside to give the sisters privacy to review the contents.

They scan the entries rapidly:

Roughly 40 percent of Americans report feeling isolated . . .

In a study of people who witnessed a suicide . . .

If you're going to tell a premeditated lie, here's how to do it . . .

Nurses have access to fentanyl, OxyContin, Valium, Percocet, Vicodin . . .

Some police departments use "bait" packages with a hidden GPS locator . . .

Cassandra's eyes widen as they rise to meet Jane's.

Ever since the sisters first scrutinized the photograph of Shay on Amanda's doorstep holding a yellow zinnia, Shay has seemed cloaked in different personas, morphing from threatening to innocuous and back again. She is an optical illusion, like the famous black-and-white picture that flips between two different illustrations—the old crone and the beautiful young woman—depending on how the artist's lines are interpreted.

This new evidence does nothing to solidify the contrasting images.

Shay's masquerade as a former patient at City Hospital was not recorded in her notebook.

Nor was her bizarre trip to Amanda's mother's house to drop off a bouquet of flowers. Why that long journey for a simple errand that could have been handled by a florist? Shay is obsessed with Amanda and suicides; perhaps she went to Delaware to dig more deeply into Amanda's background.

Shay is highly inquisitive and overly analytical. Her curiosity and determination to make sense out of seemingly disparate facts are dangerous.

The sisters have a lot to discuss, but they don't want to talk in front of even Stacey.

"Can you send us the full file for our records?" Jane asks.

Stacey nods and steps forward. She clicks a few keys. "Done. And here's your Bloomie's bag."

Cassandra reaches for the bag and tucks it under her desk. "You're amazing, Stacey. Thank you."

Stacey, uncomfortable with praise, shrugs. "Oh, I put the additional camera in an air-conditioning vent. If anyone uses a laptop on the couch, you should be able to see their screen."

As Stacey heads toward the door—she has a busy day ahead of her, with three clients stacked back-to-back—Jane calls out, "Let us know how the appointment goes for your mom next week."

The sisters secured Stacey's mother a consultation with a top Alzheimer's specialist in her hometown of Philadelphia. At just fifty-six, Stacey's mother no longer recognizes her daughter.

"Thank you." Stacey's voice is uncharacteristically soft. "I hope he can help her."

Stacey hides her pain well. Few people know she always carries it with her.

Stacey leaves the door open behind her, so Jane hurries to close it.

They need to scrutinize every word in Shay's notebook. But they've barely begun when they receive a phone call from Oliver, the gallery owner.

"Lovelies! Strangest thing. A police officer just came into my gallery. At first I thought she could be a stripper, but it isn't my birthday. Plus you two would know she wasn't my type."

Oliver's laughter dies away when the sisters don't join in. Jane reaches over and grabs Cassandra's hand, squeezing it tightly. Cassandra stares straight ahead, her expression resolute.

"Anyway," Oliver continues, sounding subdued, "she had some questions about that exquisite friend of yours, Daphne, you sent in a couple months ago. She wanted to know what time she came in and how long she stayed. Luckily I had a copy of the receipt from the little watercolor she bought, and I even had the selfie of us on my phone that she suggested I text to you. Darlings, is she in some sort of trouble?"

For once, the sisters have no answer.

CHAPTER THIRTY-ONE

SHAY

The term déjà vu *means "already seen," and as much as 70 percent of the population reports having experienced it. The rates seem to be highest among people aged 15 to 25, and déjà vu experiences decrease with age. When it comes to what* déjà vu *really is and what causes it, there are more than 40 theories—ranging from reincarnation to glitches in our memory processes.*
—Data Book, page 36

I'M A DIFFERENT PERSON here in this apartment.

At night, I stretch out in the blissful quiet of the guest room, with its soft blue walls and blackout shades.

I brought along my bottle of Ambien just in case, but it remains untouched on my nightstand. I don't need the drug to fall asleep.

And—I can hardly believe it—I'm riding the subway again.

This morning, I made my favorite banana-and-almond-butter smoothie, using the Vitamix on the kitchen counter, the one that rests near a weird vase in the shape of an upside-down hand. Then I met Cassandra and Jane's friend, Anne, on the corner. I thought Anne might be one of the women I'd seen at the memorial service, but I didn't recognize her. She didn't have any distinguishing features: Her hair was medium brown, and neither long nor short. It was midway between wavy and straight. Her eyes were brown, the most common color, and she wore simple black pants and a black top—like half the women in New York.

She strode toward me with a big smile, and I instantly liked her.

"So good to meet you!" she'd said. I detected a slight Southern accent as we chatted for a bit. Anne had an exuberant personality; she gestured expansively and spoke quickly. She was married with two kids in elementary school, she told me, and she'd left her job at a law firm after her second one was born. That explained why she had free time in the middle of a workday to help me.

"How long have you known Cassandra and Jane?" I asked.

"Those two?" She threw back her head and laughed. "Feels like I've known them forever!"

We began walking toward the green pole marking the Thirty-third Street station and continued down the concrete stairs. "Let's do this!" she said, and took my hand.

I didn't even have time to hesitate; I was pulled along in her undertow.

"You're doing awesome!" She kept up a steady stream of chatter as we pushed through the turnstiles and walked onto the platform. Panic kept rising in me like a set of waves, but she helped me battle it. "Breathe," she'd say, or she'd distract me with questions like "What's the strangest food you've ever eaten?"

Right as the train roared into the station, she cracked a joke: "This station is shaking more than my vibrator!"

I actually *laughed*. The tension coiled within me broke; it felt like a physical snapping. The next thing I knew, we were stepping onto the train together, just as I'd done thousands of times before.

The way I now knew I would do thousands of times again.

"Hope to see you again soon!" Anne said, giving me a hug as she left me on the corner. I waved as I watched her go, then stood there almost in disbelief.

Cassandra and Jane had irrevocably changed my life in a week.

I had to keep up the momentum. I wanted to tell them about my day when I thanked them for introducing me to Anne. I wanted to seem busy and interesting, like them.

As Anne disappeared from view down the street, I hurried into my temporary Twelfth Street apartment, grabbed my gym bag, and rode the subway to my favorite CrossFit class in SoHo.

"Where've you been, Shay?" the instructor said when she spotted me in the front row.

"Just a little under the weather," I fibbed. I offset it with a truth: "But I'm better now."

All the time I've spent planning my routes and sitting on slow-moving buses is mine again; I'm going to reclaim my life.

I decide to use some of it tonight to check out various dating websites. I imagine turning it into a funny story for Jane and Cassandra, and hearing them laugh again.

When I get home, I take a warm shower, then change into clean sweats. I pop a frozen veggie pizza with cauliflower crust into the oven, grab a beer, and settle onto the couch. I begin collecting data, trying to analyze which dating sites are best for women in their thirties who want a lasting relationship. I jot everything down in my notebook. I don't create a profile—I need better photos than the ones on my phone—but at least I've made a start.

I get off the couch, feeling the welcome burn in my thighs from the intense CrossFit class, then I walk over to the mirror hanging by the entryway and take a good look at myself. I pull off my glasses and squint.

I could give contact lenses a try again. Mel urged me to, telling me I shouldn't hide my pretty eyes. But after I got an infection once that left my eyes red and sore, I went back to glasses.

I tilt my head to one side. Then something in the corner of the reflection catches my eye. I lean closer and confirm it: The apartment isn't exactly as I left it this morning.

I've been back here for hours, but it's only now—with the living room and bedrooms behind me at a certain angle—that I notice the master bedroom door seems to be the slightest bit ajar.

I put on my glasses and walk over to it.

It's barely cracked open, but it's definitely not tightly shut, as it was last night. I'm certain of this. I stood here, my hand on the knob, for several seconds.

Could I have inadvertently twisted it just enough to release the catch? I wonder.

But I know I didn't.

Someone must have been in the apartment. They could even be here now.

I back up, fast.

"Hello," I call out, my voice wavering.

No answer.

I force myself to consider the facts: I've been here for several hours, and nothing has happened. I've even taken a shower. I haven't heard a sound. And nothing's out of place in the apartment. Maybe the super needed to check on the radiator or something. I wouldn't have been notified, but rather the apartment's owner.

Just to be safe, I grab my phone and text Cassandra and Jane: *Hi guys, hope you're doing well. Everything's great here, just wanted to let you know I found the master bedroom door cracked open. You may want to double-check with the super in case he came by when I was out.*

Almost immediately, three dots appear, indicating one of them is typing back.

Oh, we should have told you! It was the super, he needed to check on a leak. But it was all fine, Cassandra types.

I breathe a sigh of relief and walk back over to pull the master bedroom door shut. Then I return to the mirror in the hallway.

I remove my glasses again and pull my hair up with my free hand, wondering if I should get it cut. I've worn it long and straight, all the way down to my bra strap, since high school. I imagine it layered around my shoulders.

The oddest sensation—something akin to déjà vu—creeps over me as I stand there, twisting my head from side to side. My glasses are off, and my hair is flatter from the shower. I remind myself of someone, but I can't pinpoint who.

My mind scans through the possibilities: Maybe a woman I went to college with? A former colleague? An actress I glimpsed on TV?

Finally I give up trying to figure it out. I let down my hair, fluff it up, and put on my glasses. Just like that, I look like me again.

CHAPTER THIRTY-TWO

CASSANDRA

She looks like Amanda.

Cassandra stares at her computer monitor, her skin prickling.

Shay is staring almost directly into the camera installed at the top of the hallway mirror.

Cassandra leans in closer, barely breathing. Weeks ago, when she flipped between the photograph of Shay carrying a yellow zinnia and the image of Amanda holding a calico cat, she noticed a passing resemblance—the height, the general shapes of their faces.

Now, with Shay's hair up and her glasses off, Shay could *almost* be Amanda's sister.

Cassandra snaps a screenshot to capture Shay in this moment.

When Cassandra clicked on the icon on her computer to access the cameras in Valerie's apartment right after Shay texted about the door that Stacey must have left cracked open, Cassandra expected to capture Shay typing on her computer or writing in her notebook.

Instead, Shay's face looms so close it almost appears as if she is peering back into Cassandra's computer.

In her mind, Cassandra further alters the image, lightening Shay's hair and cropping it to a layered bob that hits her collarbone. Instead of baggy sweats, she envisions Shay in a dress—the kind of feminine, flowy style Amanda used to favor.

Cassandra studies Shay, her pulse quickening, as Shay tilts her head from side to side. Amanda's eyes weren't as widely spaced as Shay's, and she didn't have a cleft in her chin. But with the right clothes, the right hair, the right *coaching* . . .

Cassandra reaches for her phone and dials Stacey, who picks up immediately.

"Do me a quick favor?" Cassandra's words are terse and clipped. "Can you access Shay's calendar off her computer?"

"Hang on." It's silent except for a rapid clicking. "Got it. What do you need?"

"Send me a screenshot for the month of August."

Almost before Cassandra finishes the sentence, Stacey replies, "Done."

Cassandra pulls up the calendar, her eyes sweeping across it as she searches for a specific date.

She holds her breath when she finds it.

She's almost scared to look.

One of the threats facing the group is Detective Santiago's interest in Daphne's connection to James.

The other is Shay, and her unrelenting probing into Amanda's life.

There may be a way to join together these menaces and extinguish them both simultaneously.

Cassandra reads the entry for a specific date: *Temp, dentist, 6-mile run.*

Cassandra exhales slowly. Her skin tingles.

Everything is snapping into place so beautifully it's almost as if the chain of events were preordained—as if an unseen hand had guided Shay onto the Thirty-third Street subway platform to stand next to Amanda on that fateful Sunday morning.

Initially, the sisters believed Shay was the worst possible person to become entangled in the aftermath of Amanda's suicide. Now the opposite seems true.

She is perfect.

All this time, they have been struggling to figure out who Shay was.

Now the sisters will turn all their focus onto who she could be.

PART
TWO

CHAPTER THIRTY-THREE

SHAY

The average woman spends about $313 per month on her appearance—and about a quarter of a million dollars over her lifetime—according to a study funded by Groupon. Women are most likely to splurge on facials, followed by haircuts, then manicures and pedicures. Another study, this one conducted by Clairol, found that about three-quarters of women dye their hair. And 88 percent of women say their hair has an effect on their confidence.
—Data Book, page 41

"YOU LOOK . . . PERFECT," JANE SAYS, sounding a little awed.

The stylist, Philip, unfastens my black cape and whisks it off to the side. Then he runs his hands through my hair while I gape at myself in the mirror.

"Isn't she gorgeous?" Philip asks as he looks to Cassandra and Jane, clearly seeking their approval.

What a difference it made to chop off four inches, add layers, and lighten my hair by two shades. "I totally see you in this color," Jane had said as we'd walked to the salon, showing me a tear sheet from a glossy magazine that she'd pulled out of her purse. I'd given it to Philip, and he'd matched the shade perfectly, added a few blonder streaks around my face that make me appear like a more polished, pretty version of myself.

"Your eyes really pop now!" Cassandra exclaims, leaning in close to me to get a better look.

Philip shaped my eyebrows, too, at Cassandra's suggestion. "Defined brows will help frame your face," she'd explained. All these beauty tricks made a huge difference.

As with most of the other good things happening to me lately, I have Cassandra and Jane to thank.

It started so simply: When Cassandra called me a few nights ago with the good news that I could have the apartment for another week, we'd chatted for a while. I'd just received an email from the head of human resources at the Avenues Agency asking me to come back for a second interview, and Cassandra couldn't have been more encouraging.

"What else have you been up to?" she'd asked.

So I told her about my investigation into online dating, making it sound like a lark. "I just hope I don't wind up in someone's freezer."

Cassandra laughed. "Oh, I've always been curious about those dating sites. Which one are you joining?"

"I'm thinking about Cupid. Apparently a lot of people sign up for more than one at a time, so I might do a couple. Now I just need to take some better photos of myself. My corporate headshot can't compete with all the bikini pics I keep seeing on the sites."

"Oh, shut up, you look great." Cassandra had laughed. Then she'd paused. "But if you really want a makeover, you've got to let us help! Jane and I live for this stuff. We do it for a lot of our clients."

I hadn't even mentioned a makeover—I was just thinking about putting on some eyeliner and a cute outfit and maybe getting a trim.

But the enthusiasm in Cassandra's voice ignited something in me, a sense of excitement at the possibilities.

Who better to guide me through this than the gorgeous Moore sisters? I'd thought as Cassandra told me she'd try to get an appointment with a stylist she knew for Saturday.

"Even if he's booked up, he'll find a way to squeeze you in. And don't worry about the price—we send him so much business that he always gives us a huge discount."

Now, as I look at myself in the mirror—with Cassandra and Jane standing behind my shoulders, staring at me with approving smiles—I think about how I've felt like someone else ever since I began house-sitting in the apartment.

Maybe it's only natural that I start looking like someone else, too.

I leave Philip a big tip, since he refuses to charge me anything. Then we head out the door and Jane links her arm through mine.

Next up is an appointment with the optometrist. After a quick eye exam and a vision test, he gives me a pair of sample contacts on the spot and tells me my order will be in next week. I'm surprised by how easy it is to put them in.

When I walk into the reception area, where Jane and Cassandra are trying on sunglasses, I feel a little naked. Maybe I didn't only use my glasses to improve my vision; maybe they provided a shield for me to hide behind.

Cassandra lowers oversize Ray•Bans and gapes at me, while Jane gives a wolf whistle that causes the guy waiting nearby to laugh.

I blush under their scrutiny, blinking even though the lenses are so soft and thin I can't feel them.

It's gorgeous out, so we decide to walk the High Line and find a spot to take photos for the dating website. "Who knows, I might even try it, too," Cassandra says, which sounds preposterous to me. I keep noticing men turning around to get a second look at both sisters as we walk down the street. All the sisters would have to do is pause on the corner and they could have a dozen dates.

Before we reach the High Line, I spot a gray cat curled up in the window of a little bookstore and my gut clenches. I pray the Moore sisters don't notice; they might ask me about my fictional dead cat, and I don't want to dig myself deeper into the stupid lie I created. I don't know why I didn't just admit I'd never seen Amanda before the day she died, but it's too late now.

So I point across the street at a Korean barbecue restaurant. "That place looks good."

A few seconds later, we're past the bookstore window and I breathe easily again.

We spend a couple more hours together, buying margarita-flavored Popsicles from a pushcart vendor, and trying on hats at a kiosk.

Both sisters keep directing me to pose as they snap photos of me with their phones. "Lift your chin and smile, you little vixen!" Jane says, making me laugh.

We finish with what feels like yet another celebration in a day of them: We share a bottle of rosé and a cheese plate at an outdoor café, laughing about potential lines for my dating profile.

I poke fun at myself, feeling a little expansive from the wine. "I'm quite the catch, you know. For my headline, how about 'Homeless, unemployed thirty-one-year-old looking for love'?"

They laugh along with me, then Cassandra puts her hand over mine. "You have to stop thinking this way, Shay. You *are* a catch. You're kind and funny and smart. Any guy would be lucky to go out with you."

Jane is nodding. My chest feels tight—full. As if it can barely contain all the emotions that are swelling in me. So I duck my chin and say thanks.

"We'll send you the best photos later!" Cassandra says as they get into a cab and I stand on the curb, waving.

Then I head toward the subway. As I pass a restaurant with floor-to-ceiling glass walls, I catch a glimpse of my reflection. I'm walking with my spine straight and shoulders back—the way Cassandra does. My hair is sleek and shiny, bouncing against my shoulders.

I notice one other thing: A guy on the other side of the glass, sitting alone at a table, is checking me out.

The temperatures are supposed to dip next week; it'll finally feel like fall. So I decide to swing by my apartment to grab a warmer jacket and a pair of leather boots that I like to wear with my jeans. I also want to pick up my black suit for my second interview, since I wore my gray one last time.

It's strange climbing the stairs again after a week away. It feels like I'm coming back from a much longer absence. When I turn down the hallway and reach for the door, I hesitate. I have my key out, but maybe I should knock.

I compromise by rapping my knuckles against the door as I unlock it.

"Hello!" I call as I step in and reflexively kick off my flats, the ones I got at Zara.

Sean pokes his head around from the kitchen at the same moment I notice the bench that used to be by the door is missing.

"Hey!" He wipes his hands on a blue-striped apron I've never before seen. He does a double take. "Wow, you look . . . different."

I touch my palms to the ends of my hair. "Yeah, I decided it was time for a change." I point to my eyes. "I'm wearing contacts now, too."

Jody appears, wearing a yellow-striped version of the same apron. "I love your hair!" she squeals, clapping her hands. "Where'd you get it done?"

"Cassandra and Jane took me to their place. Downtown."

I see Jody's eyes widen at the mention of the Moore sisters, but I don't give her any more details.

I look down at my flats and Sean nods toward the closet. "It was getting a little cluttered, so we started keeping our shoes in there."

"Ah." I move toward my bedroom. *Jody sure isn't wasting any time making her mark on the place,* I think. "Anyway, I just came back to grab a few things. I'm house-sitting for another week."

I expect Sean to accompany Jody back into the kitchen, but he doesn't. Instead, he follows me. "It's been weird not having you around. Wanna grab a beer next week and catch up?"

Even though I'm looking forward to meeting some nice guys online, seeing Sean standing in my doorway, with that silly apron on and his gingery hair sticking up in the back again, makes my stomach flutter. I remember the stat I jotted in my Data Book when I first began to fall for Sean: Forty percent of couples start off as friends.

The odds weren't bad, but they didn't tip in our favor.

"Sure," I reply. "Next week would be great."

He smiles, but before he can say anything else, Jody calls his name from the kitchen.

"I'll text you," he says.

I lay a garment bag on my bed and ease my black suit into it. I pack up the rest of the things I wanted and impulsively grab my makeup palette from the bathroom.

When I step outside again, I look around at the city that seemed to be aligned against me not so long ago. Now even it appears brighter and kinder. Yellow rectangles of light spill out from the windows of nearby buildings, the bustle of traffic and people feels comfortably familiar, and I can hear happy salsa music playing in a minivan idling at the curb.

Even though I walked for miles along the High Line with the sisters, my body feels light and energized.

My job interview is Monday. This time, I'll go in with confidence. Not because I've memorized data on the best way to make a good impression, but because I'm finally feeling it inside me.

I have other things to look forward to: Cassandra and Jane suggested we grab dinner one night next week.

Plus, there will be drinks with Sean.

I've suddenly got a social life.

I'm closing in on a job.

As soon as I get the photos from today, I'll put the finishing touches on my profile for the dating sites.

My streak of bad luck has finally broken.

The only open box left in my life is to find an apartment.

CHAPTER THIRTY-FOUR

CASSANDRA & JANE

AMANDA'S GHOST IS WITH them in the apartment.

Jane walks through the dusty room, her footsteps echoing. Cassandra stands with her back to the window, staring at the space that once held Amanda's blue IKEA couch and floral curtains but now contains nothing but memories.

She can almost smell the cinnamon, vanilla, and butter that used to permeate the air. She can see Amanda flopping on the couch, putting her feet on Beth's lap, complaining that her twelve-hour shift was going to give her bunions. And Amanda demonstrating how small the bathroom was: "I can't even open the freaking door without it hitting the toilet!"

Cassandra shakes her head, clearing it. They need to stay focused.

"Should we stage it so it looks more appealing?" Cassandra asks. "A few pieces of furniture, maybe a coat of paint?"

Jane considers this, then shakes her head. "We can't make it seem too good to be true."

"How's this for the ad: 'Cozy studio in sought-after Murray Hill. Close to subway, restaurants, and retail shops.'"

"One more line."

Once again, they are using words as bait, just as they did when they created the memorial service notice.

Cassandra smiles. "'Available immediately.'"

"Perfect. Valerie will post it on Apartments.com tonight."

The sisters already cleared out Amanda's studio in the weeks following her death. Now they do one final check, peering into kitchen cupboards and opening the dishwasher.

Cassandra opens the oven. A lone cake tin rests on the bottom rack. "She really did love her sweets." Cassandra pulls out the tin. She tucks it under her arm.

Nothing of Amanda remains here anymore.

Jane nods. "At first I thought she might be too soft—this gentle-looking nurse with her plate of desserts."

"But she had a bite to her." Cassandra remembers how they'd heard about the ER nurse from Valerie, who'd gone to City Hospital after fracturing her ankle stumbling off an uneven curb.

Amanda was on call that day. As she tended to Valerie, she'd talked about another patient, a badly beaten teenaged boy who'd been brought in hours earlier. The boy's parents had thrown him out of the house after he'd come out as gay, and he'd been living on the streets when he was attacked. Even after they'd learned their son was in a medically induced coma, the parents refused to come see him.

I'd like to go after his parents with a baseball bat, Amanda had said. *And then find the gang that did this to him.*

Valerie had taken a second look at the nurse who was tenderly wrapping her foot and lower leg in an Ace bandage. Two days later, Amanda had gone to Sweetgreen to grab a salad. Valerie had entered the restaurant moments after Amanda, feigning surprise to see her. They'd ended up sharing a table and talking.

I get a good vibe from Amanda, Valerie had said to the rest of the women—Cassandra, Jane, Beth, Stacey, and Daphne—during their next meeting. *You've all spent a little time with her by now. I think she's one of us.*

Let's vote, Jane had suggested. *All in favor, raise your hand.*

Stacey was the last to lift her arm, but when she did, it was unanimous—which was the rule for proceeding to the next step.

The vote didn't mean Amanda would be invited into the group.

It merely meant the six women had decided to test her.

Now Jane touches Cassandra's arm, drawing her back to the present. "Ready?"

Cassandra nods.

They walk through the door, leaving the memories of Amanda behind.

Although the rental market is tight, this particular apartment will remain vacant until Shay submits an application. The five thousand dollars in cash the sisters put in an envelope and handed the landlord earlier today will ensure this.

"Her name is Shay Miller," Cassandra had told the landlord, who jotted it down on the back of the envelope. "She'll be an ideal tenant."

CHAPTER THIRTY-FIVE

SHAY

Rental apartments comprise 63 percent of New York City's total housing.
But that doesn't mean it's easy to find one. The vacancy rate is notoriously
low. Last year it was 3.63 percent—almost half of the national vacancy rate,
which is 6.9 percent.
—Data Book, page 42

THE APARTMENT IS UNREAL.

It's just a few blocks from the place I shared with Sean. It's an alcove studio, which is perfect, because I've recently discovered that I love living alone.

It isn't big, but it's clean with a large south-facing window. And the rent is surprisingly affordable. It's only two hundred dollars more a month than I've been paying.

Plus something else happened today that makes it seem as if the fates are conspiring to put me in this new apartment.

I didn't get the job at Avenues Agency—they went with someone else.

I got an even better offer.

A woman from human resources at Quartz Inc. reached out to me on LinkedIn. They need a forty-hour-a-week freelance researcher, at a rate that exceeds what I made in my last job.

Before I phoned her, I looked up the company, which is based in Palo Alto. This small but innovative marketing and advertising firm is led by a guy who began his career at Google.

After we spoke, she set up a call with her supervisor, Francine DeMarco—who offered me the position at the end of an interview that lasted nearly an hour.

I couldn't help asking why they needed someone in New York when California had plenty of data analysts. I guess I was a little nervous that they might replace me with someone local.

Francine had laughed: "We're looking for eighteen researchers, and we need them all to start as soon as possible. It hasn't been announced yet, but Quartz just took on an enormous project, so we need a lot of hands on deck."

She also strongly hinted the job could turn into a permanent position.

My start date is next Monday.

Now I click through the photos on Apartments.com again, noticing the tiny bathroom—typical for New York—and the surprisingly modern appliances in the galley kitchen. It isn't nearly as luxurious as the place I'm house-sitting, but it has everything I need.

Available immediately.

I could move in this weekend.

There's just one problem.

I didn't realize it at first—I clicked on the photos before I did anything else—but when I read the fine print, I recognized the address immediately.

It's Amanda's old apartment.

I guess it makes sense that a few weeks after her death her place has just become available. And that I would find it, since I've been scouring rental websites nearly every day.

But how could I ever live there?

I pose that question to Sean when we meet for drinks the next night.

"A nice studio practically around the corner for that price?" He whistles. "You'd be crazy to pass it up."

"It's probably already been rented." I pull out my phone and go to the site I've bookmarked.

But Amanda's place is still available.

"Look, I get that it might be weird for your new friends to see you there." Sean leans back in his chair, splaying out his legs the way tall guys do. "But all rules go out the window when it comes to real estate in New York. You could look for six months and not find anything close to this good."

I take another sip of my Sam Adams, thinking of the mousetraps and water stains and the wail of the baby I heard through the thin walls of the last apartment I checked out. He's right.

"The thing is, I can picture myself there." I brush away the thought that it's a little unsettling that my life is intersecting with Amanda's yet again.

The waitress comes by and Sean orders another round. "It's on me." He clinks his glass against mine. "Congrats on the new job." Then he laughs. "I still can't get used to you without your glasses."

"Me, too. I keep trying to push them up on my nose, but they're not there."

"You look good. But you looked good before, too."

I'm wearing the Zara outfit I bought for drinks with Cassandra and Jane, but I've swapped the flats for my leather boots. I guess that even though I know he's with Jody, I still wanted to look nice for Sean.

You look good, too. But I don't say it.

"Here's what I would do," Sean says, and I remember how much I've always appreciated his gentle, straightforward advice. "Call your friends. If they have a problem with it, you'll just keep staying with me until you find something else. But maybe they won't mind at all. Maybe they'll even be happy for you."

He's about to say something else when his phone, which is on the table, buzzes with a new text. I glance down reflexively and see Jody's name.

"Sorry, hang on a sec." He types something quickly.

I wonder if Jody knows we're out together. If I don't at least try to get Amanda's apartment, I'll be back with them in just a few days.

Hearing her giggle, seeing them snuggling on the couch, and tiptoeing by their closed bedroom door.

"Do you think I should check with Jane and Cassandra now?" It'll be a little awkward to call them in front of Sean, but if I don't, I'm worried I'll miss this chance.

"Sure." He puts his phone faceup on our table. "I'm going to run to the bathroom."

I dial Cassandra's number. While I listen to it ring, I glance down and see Sean's reply to Jody: *Be back soon.*

I look away quickly. I didn't need the reminder that Sean is just on loan to me for a couple of hours.

Cassandra picks up my call and I can hear street noises in the background. "Hey, Shay! What's up? Jane and I are just heading into yoga."

"Um, I have kind of a weird question. I feel a little uncomfortable even asking this, but I need your opinion on something."

"Sure."

"I found this apartment for rent." I absently play with the sugar and Sweet'n Low packets in the metal holder on our table while I gather my thoughts.

"Oh, that's so great!" I hear her say something in the background, then Jane's slightly muffled response. "Awesome, where is it?"

"That's the weird part." There's no way to ease into this, especially since they're in a hurry. I can also see Sean walking back toward our table. "I didn't realize it at first . . . but it's Amanda's old apartment."

There's dead silence. I feel my insides tighten.

"Oh?" It's impossible to gauge Cassandra's tone.

Sean slides into the seat across from me. He raises his eyebrows and wiggles his thumb up, then down.

I shrug. "I don't even know if I'd be comfortable with it. But I wanted to check with you two first. . . ."

"Hmm, wow," I hear Jane saying. Her voice sounds closer now, as if Cassandra is holding her phone up between them. "That is a little tricky."

"I shouldn't even have asked," I say quickly. "It was a bad idea."

"Hang on, Shay," Cassandra says. "We were just surprised . . . but I guess it makes sense the landlord put it up for rent. I can see how you would've stumbled across it. You've been searching Apartments.com every day."

I can't remember telling her that, but I must have. It's the truth.

"I can find something else."

"The thing is, it's really hard to get a good studio in Manhattan," Jane says. "And Amanda loved it. It's such a cozy place."

Sean takes another sip of his beer, then leans in. I can tell he's curious about their response, so I tilt the phone toward him.

"Jane, I think she should do it," Cassandra says. "Someone's going to live there. It might as well be Shay."

I hold my breath.

"It actually makes me happy to think that someone we like is going to be there," Jane says. "Can't you just see Shay coming in from a run and making one of her banana smoothies in that great little kitchen?"

Sean smiles and gently nudges me with his elbow. He knows my banana-smoothie addiction well.

"Totally!" Cassandra says. "Shay, you've got to grab it before it's gone. What are you doing talking to us? Go call the landlord!"

I laugh, so relieved my body feels weak. "Okay, okay. I'll do it now."

"Text us and let us know if you get it!" Cassandra says. Any trace of discomfort or surprise is gone from her voice; she's bubbling with excitement. "You'll have to have a housewarming party."

"Definitely," I say before hanging up. "Have fun at yoga!"

I look at Sean, incredulous.

"That went well," he says. "Guess you have one more call to make."

By the time we finish our beer and head out, I've got an appointment to see the apartment tomorrow at nine A.M.

Bring a check for the security deposit, the landlord told me. *If you're really serious, I'd like to finalize this on the spot.*

"Seems like everything's going your way," Sean tells me as he gives me a hug goodbye.

I turn and walk in the other direction, imagining my bed in that alcove and the kitchen all set up with my teakettle and wok on the gas stove burners and my fruit bowl on the counter.

I can also see myself opening the door and welcoming in Cassandra and Jane.

CHAPTER THIRTY-SIX

CASSANDRA & JANE

Seven months ago

"Come in, come in!" Amanda had said, pulling open the door.

"I just gained ten pounds from the smell in here alone!" Jane had laughed as the Moore sisters hugged Amanda and shrugged off their coats.

Amanda had baked up a storm for her gathering: lemon bars, caramel brownie bites, chocolate-chip cookies, and a strawberry-rhubarb pie with homemade crust. Her apartment smelled heavenly.

"I can feel the butter sticking to my hips already," Beth had groaned as she'd inhaled deeply and grabbed a cookie.

All six of the women in the group were present: Cassandra, Jane, Valerie, Beth, Daphne, and Stacey.

For the first half hour or so, they drank wine, devoured the sweets, and wove questions into the conversation, asking Amanda about her childhood, her relationships, and how she filled her spare time.

Then it began.

"So, guess what I learned the other day?" Beth had looked around at the others, her expression revealing it wasn't happy news. "My ex has a poetry reading next week at Slam."

"Are you kidding me?" Cassandra said, even though this wasn't the first the sisters had heard about it.

"A mutual friend of ours posted about it on Facebook," Beth said. "I unfriended her immediately, but it's too late. I can't get the details out of my head."

"What's this about?" Amanda asked.

Beth told the whole story about her ex to Amanda, starting with her breast cancer diagnosis and ending with her ex-husband's abandonment.

Amanda touched Beth's hand, but Amanda's expression was angry—that mix of steel and softness Valerie had noticed in the ER.

"I've seen a lot of people mess up when loved ones suffer," Amanda said. "But that is one of the worst stories I've heard."

"Beth moved here for this guy, she supported him all those years while he sat on his ass and wrote his little rhymes, and he left her all alone," Cassandra said, watching Amanda carefully. "She had to take an Uber to and from her chemo treatments. She was down to ninety-eight pounds."

"So you didn't have anyone with you?" Amanda asked incredulously.

"A few friends offered, but I could barely drag myself out of bed some days." Beth shrugged, but her face twisted at the memory. "I was sick and hurting and depressed and I just didn't want anyone to see me like that. I couldn't summon the energy to put on an act. But Valerie lived in my building back then, and one day when I was struggling to get in some groceries, she helped me. Then she knocked on my door the next day to check on me."

Valerie interjected, "She knew I wouldn't take no for an answer."

Beth pushed away her plate, even though she hadn't taken a bite of the pie she'd just served herself. "I was so angry for so long. I thought I'd gotten past all that, but the idea that he might be succeeding . . . And get this: I still have to pay him alimony."

"That is unbelievable." Amanda spit out the words.

Beth shook her head. "What I wouldn't give to see him fall flat on his face." Her voice was shaking. "Apparently one of his poems is titled 'Cancer.'"

Jane reached over and rubbed Beth's shoulder. "I'm so sorry, sweetie."

"We should show up and heckle him," Valerie said.

Cassandra took a sip of wine. Her tone was contemplative. "It would be a shame if he was told the time of the reading had changed and he arrived too late to do it."

The test had begun.

Jane smiled. "Or if he got so nauseous he couldn't stay onstage."

Beth threw back her head and laughed. "Oh, sweet justice! That would be perfect. But how could we make that happen?"

Everyone fell quiet. It was important to see if Amanda took this further.

Amanda took a bite of her gooey caramel brownie. She didn't seem uncomfortable with the sudden silence. She appeared to be thinking.

"Syrup of ipecac," she said. "People used to give it to their children to induce vomiting if the kid swallowed something poisonous. They don't recommend that anymore, but it's still around. Some people with anorexia use it, unfortunately."

Cassandra had felt a tingling course through her veins. On the walk home later that night, when she discussed the moment with Jane and Valerie, she learned they had, too.

Valerie leaned forward, her brown eyes flashing. "How would we do it?"

"Slip some in his drink." Amanda shrugged. "A little goes a long way. Too much can be really dangerous, and even a small amount will make someone violently ill. As in, puking uncontrollably and running for the toilet. So you have to be careful."

"But how would we even get it?" Cassandra asked.

"It's available over the counter. I could pick some up from a drug-store," Amanda said.

The others had looked at one another.

Amanda didn't know it, but she'd just passed with flying colors.

CHAPTER THIRTY-SEVEN

SHAY

The chances of anyone having an indistinguishable look-alike somewhere in the world—meaning all eight measurable facial features are identical—are exceedingly rare; the odds are roughly one in a trillion. But because people see the entire face of whomever they are looking at, rather than scrutinizing each individual part, they often find striking resemblances between those who don't actually share many measurable facial similarities.
—Data Book, page 44

WARM WATER SLUICES DOWN my back and I reach for the bottle of lavender bodywash. As I adjust the shower setting, making it a touch hotter, I look down at my hand on the big silver knob. I had a manicure yesterday after I finished moving. My pink, oval fingernails don't look as if they belong to me.

They're the hands of someone more polished and feminine.

Like Amanda.

Amanda likely stood in this exact spot, twisting this same knob, every day. Including the day she died.

I yank my hand away from the faucet. I rinse off quickly, then wrap myself in a towel. My robe is still in one of the brown boxes stacked near my closet.

I change into sweats, pull my damp hair into a ponytail, and put on my glasses, since all I'm planning to do tonight is order in dinner and finish unpacking.

To chase away the lingering unease I felt in the shower, I plug my iPhone into a tiny portable speaker and put on a pop playlist.

I order a medium pizza with mushrooms and peppers via Seamless, then I quickly text my new landlord to remind him to drop off my key to my mailbox in the lobby. There are two rows of ten little bronze boxes, one for each of the twenty tenants in the building. I've already filled out a change-of-address form at the post office, so I should start receiving mail any day now.

Next I grab a pair of scissors and slice through the top of the nearest packing box. I start filling my dresser drawers with my T-shirts and sweaters, then I move on to the closet. I hang up my jackets and I'm starting on my pants when my doorbell rings.

The chime is a lower note than it was in my old place, and for a moment I mistake it for part of the song I'm listening to. Then it sounds again.

I climb to my feet and walk to the front door, peeking through the peephole.

I expect to see the pizza guy, but instead, a woman stands there, a bottle of wine in her hand. She's fortyish, with a round face and warm eyes.

"Hi, neighbor," she says when I open the door. "I'm Mary."

"Hey, I'm Shay."

She hands me the bottle of Merlot.

"Thanks." I'm not sure if she wants us to drink it together, so I ask, "Would you like to come in?" I open the door a little wider.

She shakes her head, smiling. "Nobody wants a guest on moving day. I just wanted to welcome you to the building."

She gestures to the open door across the hall. "I'm right here in case you ever need to borrow a cup of sugar or anything."

Then Mary looks past me, into the living/dining area, which is already filled with the couch I brought from the old place I shared with Sean and a small round table with two chairs that I picked up at a discount store.

Her expression shifts as sorrow fills her eyes.

"I know what happened to the woman who lived here before me," I blurt out. "I mean, in case you were friends—I just want you to know I'm sorry. . . ."

Mary sighs heavily. "I did know Amanda. It's not like we were super-close, but every once in a while we'd have a glass of wine, and sometimes when I traveled, she used to feed my cat."

Mary's voice seems to fade away as I flash to the lies I told Cassandra and Jane—about meeting Amanda because we shared a veterinarian, and about my fictional dead cat.

A sense of dread begins to creep over me.

"Amanda had a cat, too, right?" I blurt. She was holding a calico cat in the photo at the memorial service. I'm certain of that. It was the genesis for the lie I so regret, the one that keeps snowballing.

Mary looks surprised.

Foreboding is gripping me now; I feel a twitching in my chest.

"No, Amanda didn't have any pets."

Of course she didn't, I think. In all of the conversations I had with Jane and Cassandra, they never mentioned Amanda leaving behind a cat.

Something's still not adding up, though.

"But your cat," I say almost frantically. "It's a calico?"

Maybe Amanda held Mary's cat in the photo. Mary could have taken the picture.

Mary shakes her head, looking confused. She turns back and calls, "Felix!" Then she makes a clicking sound with her tongue. I hear a soft meow, and a small gray cat winds through the open door and comes to stand by Mary's leg.

"This is Felix." Mary scoops him up. "He's a little stray. I found him outside one night last winter. Took two weeks of my leaving out food before he trusted me enough to let me catch him. Anyway, we'll let you get on with your night. See you soon!"

She disappears back into her apartment. I close my door and lean against it, breathing hard.

Cassandra had to have known there was no way I could have en- countered Amanda at the vet's. But Cassandra hadn't looked at all sur- prised by my story; she didn't frown or ask a single question or challenge me. On the rainy day when we had tea together, I deepened my lie by telling Cassandra and Jane my cat had died. Jane had appeared to swallow my story at face value, too.

The Moore sisters knew their dear friend Amanda didn't have a cat. So they must also have known I was lying all along.

CHAPTER THIRTY-EIGHT

SHAY

Rates of anxiety and depression are at an all-time high in a number of countries—including the U.S. Along with therapy and medication, exercise can help combat these mental health challenges by producing endorphins and enkephalins. Three or more sessions a week are generally regarded as the minimum effectiveness, with a baseline of thirty minutes per session.
—Data Book, page 46

THE MOORE SISTERS MIGHT have decided not to call me out on my lie about sharing a veterinarian with Amanda for so many reasons.

But the most likely one is kindness.

When I deepened my fabrication right after I bumped into them unexpectedly in the rainstorm, I was badly shaken.

They probably didn't want to embarrass me and make me feel worse.

The day I saw what I know now was just an illusion of Amanda heading to the subway was my rock bottom. I'd been under so much stress, plus the Ambien could've toyed with my mind. I've heard stories about people who sleepwalk—cooking meals or even driving cars—on Ambien. So it's not a stretch to think that those pills affected me, too.

But I haven't taken Ambien in a couple of weeks. I don't need it; I want to see the world with clear eyes now. Last night was my first night in my new place. And even though I don't have curtains or blinds yet—I taped brown packing paper over my bedroom window to keep out the light—I slept for a solid eight hours.

I spent most of today getting organized. I've got all my packing boxes broken down for recycling, and my kitchen is set up just the way I like it, with my blender on the counter, next to my bowl of bananas, and my cupboard stocked with almond butter, dark roast coffee, pasta, and protein bars. And, of course, chocolate.

My old life is back, but it's a better version, I think as I step off the subway and onto the platform. I push through the turnstile, reveling in my steady heartbeat, my dry palms. I smile when I remember Anne making the joke about her vibrator. My panic has been wiped away, as cleanly as if it never existed.

I sling my gym bag higher up onto my shoulder as I head for the stairwell and begin to climb up. It's nearly six forty-five, which is when I'm supposed to meet Jane. The last time I saw her, she'd asked if she could join me for a CrossFit class. "I've got to do something," she'd said, pinching her flat stomach. I'd laughed and told her I wanted her secret, but I was thrilled she wanted to try it out. The class at seven P.M. tonight is hard, but I'm good at it. I can lift heavy barbells and do power squats without needing many breaks. I guess I'm excited for Jane to see me in my element.

But right as I reach the studio, she texts, *So sorry, something came up at work. I'll have to take a rain check! But in the meantime, here are the best photos from the other day. Can't wait to hear what happens when you put up your profile.*

No worries and thanks! I write back, even though I'm disappointed.

The photos are good: They captured me laughing as I tried on a straw hat, and looking a little more serious as I glanced out at the water. But there are only four of them, and I recall the sisters taking dozens. I guess they just sent me the most flattering ones.

I tuck away my phone, change in the locker room, and walk into the studio. I find a spot in the second row. The class is crowded, as usual, since the teacher has a huge following.

Forty-five minutes later, I'm drenched in sweat. My arms are shaking and I know my legs will be sore tomorrow. But my mind feels gloriously uncluttered.

I walk into the locker room and head to the sink to splash cool water on my face and wash my hands. When I raise my head again, I notice the woman at the sink to my left.

She looks a lot like the redhead I saw at Amanda's memorial service.

Our eyes meet in the mirror and she appears surprised. Maybe it's because she caught me staring at her.

I smile. "Hi."

She just nods.

It could be the wrong woman; I didn't get that close to her. Even if it is her, she probably didn't recognize me. I'm no longer wearing glasses, and my hair is lighter and shorter.

I quickly turn away and gather my things.

When I exit the studio, she's right in front of me, pushing open the door. She looks back reflexively as she holds it, the way people do to make sure they don't let the door close on someone, and I step through.

"Thanks."

"Sure." Her Boston accent sharpens the word.

Pahked ya cah in Hahvad Yahd. . . . It must be her.

She's still looking at me a little funny, as if maybe she can't quite place me yet. I'm about to bring up the connection, then I imagine how our conversation would go: *I saw you at a memorial service. . . . No, I didn't know Amanda, but I've become friends with her friends . . . who I think are your friends, too?*

It sounds weird.

When I step onto the sidewalk, she's still in front of me. But she isn't moving in either direction. She seems to be waiting. So I just turn to the right and head for the subway.

I don't look back. But I swear I can feel her eyes on me.

By the time I'm climbing the steps out of the Thirty-third Street station, I've mostly put her out of my mind. I'm excited for what I'm going to do tonight: cook a healthy dinner, then activate my dating profile.

I chat with my mom as I walk down the street, telling her more about the research position at Quartz and promising to come home for Thanksgiving. I even feel ready to endure a weekend with Barry.

But the oddest thing happens; I guess it's muscle memory, or some pattern in my brain that needs rerouting.

I walk into my old building before I remember I don't live here anymore.

I don't even have the keys; I gave my set to Jody.

I stand in the lobby, looking around for a moment. Then I push back out the door.

The woman I was when I lived here is gone.

CHAPTER THIRTY-NINE

CASSANDRA & JANE

"DataGirl," Jane says as her fingers move across her laptop's keyboard. "Stacey said Shay activated her profile less than an hour ago."

The sisters are secluded in Jane's Tribeca apartment, a few blocks away from Cassandra's residence. They're still in work clothes, though they've kicked off their heels, and the delivery sushi they ordered for dinner is laid out on the kitchen's granite island. Neither woman has touched it.

Cassandra's slim black pants slip down low on her hips as she paces in loops from the living room through the open kitchen and back again. Jane's cat—the one Amanda used to adore—leaps onto the couch and rubs her head against Jane's leg. Hepburn has been unusually affectionate lately, as if sensing her owner's distress.

"Found her," Jane says.

Cassandra moves toward the sofa, and Jane tilts the screen so they can view it together. "Nice pic," Cassandra remarks, her tone holding an edge.

In the profile photo Shay uploaded onto Cupid, she's exuberant. She's trying on a floppy straw hat and laughing, her face tilted up toward the sun.

That shot of Shay is strikingly similar to one of Amanda doing the exact same thing, at the same kiosk, on the High Line last spring. Jane took that picture as well. Amanda posted it to her Facebook page a couple of months before she died.

It was easy to maneuver Shay: After they'd led her onto the High Line, Cassandra had paused at the kiosk. She and Jane had grabbed a few hats, Jane pushing a straw one into Shay's hands before directing her on how to pose.

It could prove invaluable later to have public evidence of Shay's unrelenting desire to replicate elements of Amanda's life.

But it won't be enough.

An even more urgent element must be established: The other women in the group must be led to believe Shay is obsessed with Amanda—and that her preoccupation has only been growing since Amanda's death.

Earlier tonight, the sisters tried to plant the seeds establishing Shay's fixation by sending Beth and Shay on a collision course. Jane made separate dates with them to meet at the same CrossFit class. Jane canceled a few minutes before it began, pleading a fabricated work emergency.

Both women thought they alone were to meet Jane at the exercise studio.

The best-case scenario, the sisters had agreed, would have been for Beth to notice Shay—to recognize her from Amanda's memorial service or from the photograph Cassandra had distributed before it. Even if Beth hadn't remembered Shay, she might still have been spooked by Shay's resemblance to Amanda.

It seemed unlikely the opposite would happen, that Shay would recall Beth from the service and approach her. But if she did, the sisters could use this to their advantage as well: It would be evidence of Shay's dangerous obsession.

Unfortunately, the text Beth sent immediately after CrossFit made no reference to anything unusual occurring: *I'm never going to forgive you for signing me up for this torture and then backing out. I can barely walk!*

The sisters need to come up with something else, quickly. The police surely homed in on the discrepancy between the story Daphne told them and the one they heard from Kit. Daphne may not hold up well if she is summoned for further questioning.

All that they've built could be destroyed.

Cassandra collapses on the deep chenille cushion next to Jane, tucking her feet beneath her. She reads from Shay's profile:

"'Looking for someone who is active, but is also happy relaxing on the couch, sharing a pizza and talking, or watching a movie. . . . It would be great if you were at least as tall as me (I'm five feet ten, but I rarely wear heels). . . .'

"She wants a guy like Sean," Cassandra remarks, then continues:

"'My friends say I'm kind and smart—a great catch. Who am I to argue with them? :) If I sound like someone you'd like to meet, maybe we can start with a friendly drink and see where things go. . . .'"

"I think the 'great catch' line is a direct quote of yours," Jane points out.

"She's pretty malleable." Cassandra looks at Shay's photo again. There are so many eerie overlaps between her and Amanda now.

But their styles are different: In the pictures, Shay wears jeans and a plaid flannel shirt, which Amanda would never have chosen.

"Shay's wardrobe could use some tweaking," Cassandra muses. "We should take her shopping."

Jane nods slowly. "Or we could suggest she visit a certain boutique where she could pick up some great outfits for when she starts dating."

A smile spreads across Cassandra's face. "Genius. We'll send her to Daphne's. There's no way they can miss seeing each other."

CHAPTER FORTY

SHAY

*According to the Bureau of Labor Statistics, a typical person will have
ten different jobs before the age of 40. One reason why people switch
employment is because raises average just 3 percent per year in most
occupations—but moving to a different company can mean a more
substantial increase in salary. Women hold almost as many different jobs as
men throughout their lifetimes, despite the fact that women typically take
more time out of their careers for child-raising activities.*
—Data Book, page 51

AT 5:30 P.M. I PULL on my jacket as I step outside. The temperature is
starting to dip into the high forties, and it'll be dark soon, but I've been
inside all day and crave fresh air.

I spent the day filling out forms for Quartz's human resources department, then I began research for my first assignment: analyzing
different energy drinks on the market and outlining the various similarities and differences between them.

The hours flew by as I lost myself in compiling each brand's charac-
teristics and market share.

I'd set my phone to Do Not Disturb mode so that I wouldn't get
distracted, only allowing in calls and emails from Quartz. If I wanted
this to turn into a real job, I'd reasoned, I needed to treat it like one.

Now, as I head south on Second Avenue, I scan my email and text messages. There's nothing interesting, so I pull up the app for Cupid.

A little cupid emoji has a heart-shaped bubble coming out of its mouth with the word *Four!*

I click on it and see four messages. There's a little flutter in my chest. I haven't been on a date in months. And now *four* guys might be interested in me?

I can't wait to see who has reached out. I glance around and see an inviting-looking new bistro on the corner ahead. I head there, keeping my phone in my hand.

Plenty of tables are open this early, so I ask for one by the fireplace. As soon as the waiter takes my order for a glass of red wine and a hummus plate with veggies and pita, I open up the app.

It feels a little like Christmas morning and I'm about to unwrap the bows on mysterious presents. Anything—or more accurately, anyone—could be inside.

I deflate a bit when I read the first message. His profile handle is SilverFox. And his opening line is *Ever consider an older man?*

Not one old enough to be my father, I think.

I go on to the next message. This guy attached a photo, which I click on to open.

Then I recoil. It isn't too graphic—it's just a shirtless selfie—but it's so generically cheesy. His message doesn't make a better impression. All he wrote was *Hey.* I imagine him doing this to almost every woman on the site.

The third guy is wearing sunglasses and a baseball cap in his lone photo. *I've got a really busy schedule, so I'm not looking for anything serious. But want to meet up for a drink one night?*

I wish he'd written more about himself, so I check out his profile. It's pretty spare. It's hard to get a sense of who he is. Could he be married? I wonder. I think about it a little and decide to write back, *Can you tell me more about yourself first?*

But before I do, I check out the final message. The first thing I notice is the photo—of a guy with brown hair, a shy smile, and horn-rimmed glasses. He looks slender and fit. Appealing, but not intimidating. His username for the site is TedTalk.

A swooping feeling is in my stomach.

Hi DataGirl, I'm Ted. I'm definitely active—I love pickup basketball and hiking—but I also enjoy quality time with a good pizza.

"Excuse me," the waiter says, and I glance up to see him holding my wine and hummus plate.

"Sorry." I pull my arms back off the table. I hope he didn't see what was on my screen. Even though it seems like everybody does online dating these days, I still don't want a stranger knowing something so personal about me.

The waiter spends far too long arranging my cutlery and offering me more water. All I want to do is get back to Ted.

I go back to his message the moment the waiter leaves: *Heels won't be a problem for me, since I'm six foot one. Anyway, if you'd like to chat more, you know where to find me.*

I immediately click on his profile.

His information is listed: thirty-five years old, never married, mechanical engineer, lives in Manhattan. The category of relationship he's seeking is Serious.

I'm beaming. He sent the message at eleven-thirty this morning. So it's been more than six hours. I won't look overly eager if I reply.

I'm not good at flirting in person, but it seems easier here, in the darkened bar. I think for a minute, then write back, *Hi Ted, Here's an important question: Thick or thin crust? DataGirl/aka Shay. P.S. I like hiking too, but there aren't many places to do it around here. Unless you know of some secret spot?*

I've asked him two questions. That was deliberate, to keep the conversation going.

I dig into my hummus plate, suddenly ravenous. While I crunch on a carrot stick, I begin to scroll through photos of other available men who meet the parameters I set: between the ages of twenty-eight and thirty-eight, single, within twenty miles of me, and seeking a serious relationship.

It's unbelievable how many there are: So many guys want the same thing I do. I've probably passed a few of them on the street or stood next to them in line at the deli or on the subway. There could even be one in this bar.

Some universally known signals indicate when people are off the market—an engagement ring, a wedding band, even a claddagh ring—but no similar items let the world know you're looking.

I scroll through more photos. Quite a few guys are appealing, even after I've discounted the ones in muscle shirts flexing, or others who seem to be trying to show off their status by standing next to expensive cars or boats.

I read through dozens of profiles. Some are funny, some are straightforward, and a lot are so spare they're little more than biographical details.

But no other seems as attractive as Ted.

Just as I think this, the cupid icon bursts onto my screen. *One!*

I quickly click on the number, and the moment I see Ted has replied, I realize that's exactly what I was hoping for.

Shay, that's a tough one, but I'm an equal opportunity pizza connoisseur. Anything but anchovies. So where's your favorite place to get pizza? I'm pretty new to New York—I just moved here from Colorado a couple of months ago—and I'm still trying to learn more about the city. Kind of a culture shock, but I like it, even though my current apartment is the size of my old closet, haha.

I feel my lips curve into a smile. Ted only waited about fifteen minutes before responding. I like that; he isn't playing games. And if he just moved here from Colorado, he probably doesn't know many people. Maybe he's lonely, too.

I'm not going to play games either. Still, I wait until I've finished my wine before writing back.

I totally agree with you about the anchovies. Who puts fish on pizza? ;) My favorite place to go is Grimaldi's in Brooklyn—classic thin crust. You've got to try it if you haven't already.

I hesitate, thinking about what to write next. I could ask him more about his job, but I don't want to make him feel like his occupation or income level is important to me.

So I continue, *I've only visited Colorado once, when I went skiing with my college roommate and her family. It was so beautiful. I'd love to go back someday.*

Ask him another question, I remind myself. I look at his pictures again—he seems even more appealing now—and notice he's got a coffee mug by his left hand in one of them.

I write, *Are you a lefty?*

Then I backspace over it. I don't want him to think I've been scrutinizing his pictures. I'm so new at this; I don't know what the rules are.

I play it safe, choosing this question: *Do you ski?*

Then I hit Send.

I pay my bill and step back outside. It's even colder now, and completely dark, but the city feels vibrant. I wonder where Ted is right now; maybe in his closet-size apartment. Or maybe he's still at his office. He could be in any of the buildings I pass.

Knowing he's around makes the city seem smaller, somehow, in a good way.

Superstitions aren't logical, but I can't help playing a little game with myself: If I don't check my phone until I get back to my apartment, he'll have written back.

I reach home, and as soon as I've slipped off my coat and shoes, I take out my phone.

Ted has written back. He asked two questions of his own:

How about we continue this conversation in person? Can we meet for a drink Friday night?

CHAPTER FORTY-ONE

AMANDA

Two months ago

A TRICKLE OF BLOOD ran down Amanda's shin.

She cursed and reached for her washcloth, pressing it against the small cut, then turned off the shower. She'd rushed while shaving her legs because she was late. Just as she'd been getting ready to end her shift, a delivery truck had rear-ended the back of the Explorers Camp bus on the FDR. A half dozen kids had been rushed to the ER with injuries ranging from whiplash to bruises to the most severe, a fractured wrist and possible concussion. She couldn't leave with crying children filling up exam rooms as parents flooded in.

It was the worst possible time for the bus accident.

She'd stayed an extra hour, comforting a little boy whose arm was in a sling, until the boy's father arrived. She snuck the child a lollipop on her way out the door, feeling guilty that she'd rushed through the release paperwork.

She was due at a bar called Twist near the northern part of Central Park in a little over an hour. She was going to be late.

Normally, if she was heading out for a night on the town, she'd style her hair, creating gentle waves around her shoulders. But now she quickly blow-dried it before pinning it in a loose twist. She spent precious time on her makeup, applying tinted moisturizer and darkening her brows with a light brown pencil. Luckily she'd already picked out her outfit: a wheat-colored sundress with wide shoulder straps, gold hoop earrings, flat sandals, and a small purse.

She filled it with a burner phone, some cash, a credit card, and a pair of black cat-eye glasses with clear, nonprescription lenses, since her vision was perfect. She opened the cabinet beneath her bathroom sink and reached behind the extra toilet paper, feeling around until her fingers closed on the little plastic mouthwash bottle. She double-checked that the cap was secured before she slipped it into her bag.

She straightened up and glanced in the mirror, dabbing her fingertip below her right eyebrow to remove a smudge of mascara. Then her eyes widened. How could she have forgotten her lip gloss? That simple mistake could have derailed everything. She reached for a tissue and wiped off the peachy-pink shimmer.

She hadn't been able to eat anything all day. She knew she should nibble on something, especially because she'd be drinking soon, but her stomach was clenched in knots.

She took a last look around her apartment. Tupperware containers on her kitchen counter held the evidence of her sleepless night: lemon poppy-seed muffins, cream cheese brownies, and classic chocolate-chip cookies. Cooking was her therapy.

She stepped out into the sweltering evening.

She'd imagined this night many times. Now that it was finally here, it took on a surreal quality. Her senses heightened: She flinched at the blaring horn from an idling Uber and turned her head away from the noxious smell of the puddle left by the Labradoodle being walked a few feet ahead of her.

The air felt thick and dense, as if it wanted to hold her back.

Perspiration began to gather under her arms, but she couldn't hail a cab just yet. She needed to put a few more blocks between her home address and the pickup stop. She stopped on the busy corner of Park and Thirty-second and raised her hand. It was rush hour, and even in August, with the city's quieter rhythms, it took another precious four minutes for one to stop.

She slipped into the backseat and gave her destination, then ducked her head, pretending to be busy on her phone. Normally, she engaged cabdrivers in conversation. She enjoyed hearing their stories: She'd chatted with drivers who'd been cruising the streets of Manhattan for decades and had the thick Brooklyn accents to prove it, immigrants who'd worked as engineers in their home countries, and cabbies who'd ferried around celebrities and loved recounting their brushes with the famous.

Tonight the only noise in the cab came from *Jeopardy!*'s Alex Trebek on the touchscreen: "The title of this popular Netflix show about female prisoners references two colors."

A jitney bus pulled sharply into their lane, making the driver slam on his brakes.

"Sorry, lady," he said, catching Amanda's eye in the rearview mirror.

"It's okay," she muttered, ducking her head again.

The bar was approaching; the distinctive red awning was just two blocks away.

"This it?" The cabbie pulled over in front of a Mexican restaurant. The fare was $15.60. She gave him a folded twenty and slipped out.

She waited until he was halfway down the block before she slipped on the glasses she'd purchased for tonight and began to walk briskly.

She entered Twist twenty minutes behind schedule. She stood in the doorway, letting her eyes adjust to the dim lighting. Coldplay's "Yellow" played through the sound system, and the click of a cue hitting a pool ball came from the back of the room.

She spotted Beth at the far end of the big, L-shaped bar, a glass of white wine in front of her. Beth's eyes skimmed over Amanda without stopping.

The bar was moderately crowded; it was a Thursday night. If she'd made it here on time, there might have been more empty stools.

But the only unclaimed ones were at the end by Beth.

She looked around again, as if deciding where to plant herself. A couple of men played pool in the back room. Other people were scattered at tables and booths.

She took a deep breath and moved toward the bar, wedging herself into the small spot between two occupied stools. She smiled at the bartender, who was filling up a glass with beer from a tap. He gestured that he'd be right over to help her.

She felt dizzy. Her lack of sleep, the two cups of coffee she'd consumed during her shift, her empty stomach—it was all conspiring against her.

She tensed her leg muscles to try to stop them from shaking, then leaned against the bar, jostling the man to her right. He turned around reflexively.

She leaned forward and pressed her arms to her sides so the V-neck of her dress plunged more deeply. "Sorry," she said just as the bartender came to take her order. "What are you having? That looks good!"

The guy on the stool—late thirties, broad shouldered, thinning blond hair—lifted up his nearly empty glass. "Whiskey and soda."

Amanda nodded to the bartender and handed him a twenty-dollar bill: "We'll take two."

"Hey, thanks." The man spun around a quarter turn to fully face Amanda. He looked her up and down, appearing to like what he saw. "I'm James."

CHAPTER FORTY-TWO

SHAY

Four indications people may be uncomfortable with you:
1. *They touch their neck (where there are nerve endings; this can unconsciously help calm them down).*
2. *Their feet are pointed away from you.*
3. *They avoid eye contact or wince.*
4. *They cross their arms or physically withdraw and place an object between you (such as pulling a pillow on their lap).*

—Data Book, page 53

NORMALLY, I'D NEVER WALK INTO a boutique like this. You can tell from the outside the clothes are pricey and chic. I can see why Cassandra and Jane shop here, but I'm out of my element.

When I step inside Daphne's, however, my shoulders instantly relax. It smells delicious—like fresh citrus. Upbeat music is playing, something with a great rhythm, and yummy-looking mini-cupcakes are set out on a platter. The little store has an aura of happiness.

A woman approaches and I recognize her instantly: She's the glossy girl from Amanda's memorial service—the one with shiny hair, skin, and nails. Today she's in wide-legged dark-rinse jeans and a camel-colored silk blouse.

"Welcome," she says as she draws closer. She falters, her eyes widening, as her smile dims. "I'm Daphne."

"Hi, I'm Shay." I wait expectantly, but my name doesn't seem to ring a bell.

Perhaps Cassandra and Jane forgot to mention I would be stopping by.

"Shay. Nice to meet you . . ." She looks me up and down. Maybe she's wondering why someone like me would be in this posh boutique.

"Are you looking for anything special?" she finally asks.

Now I am certain she has no idea who I am. Cassandra and Jane suggested I come here to get an outfit for my date with Ted. *Her things are expensive, but she has really terrific sales—you never know what you're going to find,* Cassandra had said. *And you're going to love Daphne!*

"Uh, I have this date coming up. And our mutual friends Cassandra and Jane suggested I come here. . . ."

Daphne looks surprised again, but she recovers quickly. "Oh! How wonderful. They're two of my favorite people."

"Yeah, they're really great."

She can't seem to stop staring at me. Then she gives her head a little shake, as if to clear it. "So, a date," she says briskly. "Where are you going?"

"I'm not sure yet. It's actually a first date. We're just grabbing a drink."

"I've got some pretty tops over here." She leads me to a rack and flips through a few. She holds one up against me. It's a bold blue with a low, asymmetrical neckline. "This would go great with your coloring."

She continues going through the rack, pulling out a few more for me to try on. She carries them into the dressing room, which has a soft, tufted chair, a huge mirror, and sleek silver bars on the walls. She hooks the tops of the hangers on the bars, then closes the curtain. I'm pulling off my sweater when I hear her voice close by. She must be just on the other side of the curtain.

"So how do you know Cassandra and Jane?"

I have to sidestep that question. There's no way to easily explain our convoluted friendship. "Oh, through a mutual acquaintance." I tell myself it isn't a complete lie. I keep talking so she doesn't ask me for more details. "We've actually been hanging out a lot lately. We had drinks the other day."

She's silent for a moment. I wonder if she's still just outside the curtain.

I try on the blue top first. I would never have chosen it for myself, but Daphne is right: It looks good on me.

Then I check the price tag. It's $280—more than I've ever spent on a shirt before.

I look at the tags on the other ones and see they cost even more. I'm not going to bother trying them on.

I gaze at myself in the mirror again. I imagine walking into the bar to meet Ted in this pretty top. I picture him smiling, pleased to see me.

Plus, I feel like I have to buy something.

I slip the shirt off and hang it carefully on the padded hanger. I put back on my simple gray sweater, then I step out of the dressing room.

Daphne is over by the cash register, typing something on her phone. She slips it facedown on the counter when she sees me.

"That was fast. Did anything work for you?"

I hold up the hanger and give it a little waggle. "You were right. This is perfect."

She smiles—it looks a little forced—and takes it from me. "Great." She rings me up.

She isn't making conversation now. She seems to be concentrating on folding the top into tissue paper. I slide my credit card into the chip reader, suppressing a wince.

A silver pen is on a pretty notebook splayed open on the counter. I see people have written their names, addresses, and emails in neatly outlined rows. A little sign is nearby: PLEASE SHARE YOUR DETAILS WITH DAPHNE TO BE THE FIRST TO HEAR ABOUT OUR UPCOMING SALES AND PRIVATE EVENTS!

Daphne is still busy tucking the tissue-paper bundle into a bag and tying the handles with a bow. Without much thought, I pick up the pen and add my name to the mailing list.

Then I get to the column for my address. I automatically begin to write my old address. Then my hand stops.

I don't live there anymore. I live in Amanda's apartment—one that Daphne likely visited.

She'll probably recognize the address. How could I ever explain *that?*

With Cassandra and Jane, everything has unfolded in a series of steps: First, I confessed to them how I'd encountered Amanda on the subway platform and was affected by her death. That was when we got tea after unexpectedly seeing one another on the rainy day when I was at my lowest and had conjured a vision of Amanda. A few days later, we met at Bella's so I could return Cassandra's raincoat. We drank Moscow Mules, and I explained how I'd found the necklace. When I learned it was actually Jane's, I got it back for her, which all led to us getting together again. They learned more about my living situation when they met Sean and Jody, which resulted in them offering me a house-sitting gig and introducing me to their friend Anne. And then, when Amanda's apartment came up for rent, they encouraged me to take it.

It all happened so organically. Still, there's no way I can explain it to Daphne; I can barely keep it straight in my own mind.

I cross out what I've written and jot down my email address.

I look up and notice Daphne's sharp green eyes on me again. She slides my bag across the counter.

"Thanks," I say. "Hope to see you again sometime. Maybe with Jane and Cassandra."

She stands behind the cash register with her arms at her side, appearing a little reserved. Perhaps that's just her personality, I tell myself. Then I remember her at the memorial service, laughing through tears and hugging her friends.

Daphne doesn't respond to my comment. Instead, she merely says, "Have fun on your date."

CHAPTER FORTY-THREE

CASSANDRA & JANE

CASSANDRA AND JANE ARRIVE at the restaurant twenty minutes before the others.

They dined here earlier in the week to get a sense of the space. The best table, they agreed, is the circular booth in the back right-hand corner. It can comfortably fit five. Every member of the group will be in attendance tonight except for Valerie, who has another obligation.

The booth affords a slightly obstructed view of the bar. Anyone sitting at the bar—which is oriented against the left wall as one walks into the restaurant—will have their back to the far right corner of the room. The lighting is dim, which will provide further cover.

Beth walks through the door first, which is surprising, given that she's usually the last to arrive. One of the tails of her shirt is untucked and her blazer is a little wrinkled.

Both sisters slide out of the booth to give her affectionate hugs.

"What a long week." Beth flops down on the leather seat and tucks her heavy briefcase under the table. She leans her head back and sighs.

Jane reaches over and squeezes Beth's hand. "Let's get you a drink."

Beth is a bit frazzled tonight, but that's typical—her job keeps her scrambling, but otherwise she seems upbeat. Beth beat cancer, and now her flaming-red hair is as thick and frizzy as ever; more important, her spirit is stronger than it was before her diagnosis.

As the waiter approaches and the women order cocktails, Cassandra catches sight of Stacey arriving. Cassandra stands up and waves, glad to see it takes Stacey a moment to spot her. Their table is truly unobtrusive.

Cassandra slips out of the booth so Stacey can claim a seat with her back to the wall, as is her strong preference. The women catch up while they wait for Daphne to arrive. Beth discusses a new case, then Stacey mentions she has landed a big corporate client, setting up the software for a new branch of the company. When the other women toast her, she gives one of her rare smiles, which makes her look younger than ever—especially in the vintage Wonder Woman T-shirt and Levi's she's wearing.

Daphne strides in at six-forty, apologizing for being late: "Sorry, my assistant had to leave early so I needed to close up."

A glass of Pinot Noir waits in front of the empty spot in the booth. They all know Daphne's beverage of choice, just as they know she prefers to sit at the edge of the booth. Her slight claustrophobia is another legacy from James's attack.

Daphne reaches for the goblet gratefully and takes a sip. Cassandra and Jane give her a few moments to settle in before steering the conversation to the reason why they asked the women to gather.

"Valerie couldn't make it, but we'll fill her in later," Cassandra explains. "Daphne, why don't you go ahead and tell everyone what happened the other day."

Daphne sets down her glass and takes a deep breath. She begins with the moment Shay walked into her boutique, claiming Cassandra and Jane had sent her there, and ends by recounting how Shay said she hoped to see Daphne again soon, maybe with Cassandra and Jane.

Daphne doesn't leave out any relevant details, including the one that struck her most: "She looks so much like Amanda." Daphne shivers and reaches for her wine again.

Beth's gaze ping-pongs from Cassandra to Jane to Daphne. "Wait, so you guys *didn't* send this chick?"

Jane shakes her head. She pulls something out of her purse and lays it flat on the table. "Remember this woman? You all saw her at the memorial service."

Shay's face stares up at them from the photo, her eyes wide and a little hesitant looking behind her tortoiseshell glasses, and her long brown hair swinging forward over her shoulders.

"Could she be the one who came into your boutique?" Cassandra asks Daphne.

"Yes, yes! I didn't recognize her until now. But that's the crazy thing: She looks different. She changed her hair and got rid of her glasses. And she was so subdued and meek looking at the memorial service. But when she breezed into my boutique, she was smiling and chatting . . . at least at first. When I got spooked, she shut down a bit."

"Smiling and chatty?" Stacey repeats. "So she's not just trying to look like Amanda. She's trying to act like her, too."

Beth is silently studying the photo. She picks it up and turns it into the light.

"You guys all know that when we approached Shay at the service, she told us she and Amanda went to the same veterinarian, which is obviously a lie," Cassandra says. "What we haven't shared with you yet is that we bumped into Shay a few weeks ago. At the time we thought it was a coincidence. We took her to tea to see if we could get any more information from her. And she admitted something shocking." Cassandra looks around at the intent faces of the others. "Shay was with Amanda on the subway platform right before Amanda died."

Daphne gasps as her hand flies to her mouth.

"Shay admitted that's why she came to the memorial service," Cassandra continues.

"What the—" Stacey begins.

Beth cuts her off. "Now I know where I've seen her!" Beth turns to Jane. "She was at that CrossFit class the other night, the one we were supposed to go to together."

Jane's eyes widen. "Are you sure?"

Beth jabs her finger toward the picture. "She wasn't wearing glasses and her hair is shorter. She had it pulled up in a ponytail. She didn't look exactly like this, and she didn't look exactly like Amanda. But she was sure somewhere in between."

Cassandra leans back against the booth. So Beth *had* seen Shay after all. Everything is working beautifully. Even though Cassandra and Jane don't enjoy deceiving the other women, it's necessary to protect them. If they are ever questioned by the police about Shay—and if all goes well, they may be—their answers will be forthright and honest. They'd even pass a lie detector test if need be.

As for Shay, she must be sacrificed. She will be a necessary, though unfortunate, casualty.

"This is even creepier than we thought." Cassandra's voice is hushed. She leans forward, her gaze scanning the other women's somber faces. "Shay has been trying to insinuate herself with us. We made the mistake of giving her our phone numbers the day we had tea. She seemed fragile, a little lost. She said she'd been really shaken up by what she'd witnessed that day in the subway. I guess we felt sorry for her. But now . . . she texts and calls, trying to come up with excuses to get together."

"Why would she want to look like Amanda?" Beth asks. "Why is she stalking us?"

Cassandra shakes her head, simultaneously casting a discreet glance at her watch: 7:02 P.M. It's time.

Precisely one minute later, the door opens and Shay walks in.

Jane gives Cassandra a quick, significant look. The Moore sisters are the only two women at the table who noticed Shay's arrival.

It would be better if one of the others pointed out Shay's presence.

Cassandra clears her throat. "I think we have to consider a few things. Let's start with the facts: We know what Shay has told us, and we know how she has acted. We need to be wary of accepting her story. She could be lying about anything, or everything. Her actions, however, speak far louder than anything she has said, and these actions are documented."

The others are nodding.

"So what do her actions tell us?" Daphne asks.

"I don't say this lightly." Cassandra looks around the table at her close friends, the women she considers her sisters. She would do anything for them. She *has* done things she would never have thought possible only a year ago. "Something is deeply wrong with her. She seems . . . unhinged."

"I agree. If you saw someone commit suicide, why would you ever want to look like them and be around their friends?" Daphne says. "Nothing about this makes sense."

The women continue discussing Shay and her possible motivations.

Then Stacey abruptly rises from her seat and points toward the bar. "Is that her?" Stacey cranes her neck and starts to push her way out of the booth, but Cassandra blocks her.

"Oh my God, it *is* her!" Daphne hisses.

"Stacey, calm down. We've got to think this through." Cassandra puts a hand on Stacey's arm. "If Shay truly is crazy, and that *is* her, we need to be careful."

Jane reaches for her phone and quickly types a text beneath the cover of the table: *They've seen Shay.* She sends the message to Valerie, who is on the same block, but out of view. Although Cassandra and Jane created the fake profile for TedTalk and have been communicating with Shay on Cupid, tonight it will be Valerie who takes over Ted's role.

Stacey is still on her feet, breathing hard. "She must have followed one of us here. She's tracking us!"

"She isn't even looking at us," Daphne says. "It's like she's pretending she's here for another reason."

Just then Shay puts away her phone, slides off her stool, and grabs her coat and purse. She quickly exits the restaurant, never looking back. But as she turns to go out the door, everyone in the booth catches a quick glimpse of her face. She's a few dozen yards away, and the lighting isn't great, but it's unmistakably Shay.

"We should follow her," Stacey says. But she sinks back into her seat.

There's silence for a moment.

"This is beyond strange," Beth says. "I didn't see it as clearly at the gym, but you're right. She's trying to look just like Amanda."

Daphne shudders. "How worried should we be?"

"I don't get the sense she's violent," Jane says. "Just . . . disturbed."

"If she follows me again . . ." Stacey's chin juts out.

Beth speaks up. "It seems like Shay keeps trying to step into Amanda's life. Does she want to replace her somehow?"

Exactly, Cassandra thinks as her eyes meet Jane's.

Shay will soon serve as a kind of replacement. Just not in the way the other women suspect.

CHAPTER FORTY-FOUR

SHAY

More than half of Americans believe in love at first sight, with younger
people being more likely to hold this belief. Four in ten Americans say they
have fallen in love at first sight. One survey found that almost three-quarters
of Americans believe in "one true love."
—Data Book, page 54

I WALK IN THE DOOR of Atlas at a few minutes after seven.

Ted had suggested we meet at the bar, so I scan the customers already in the tall, high-backed chairs. But no tall, slender guys are sitting alone.

I take a seat by the far end, so I can keep an eye on the front door. I put my coat and purse on top of the chair next to mine.

"What can I get you?" the bartender asks, wiping down the space in front of me.

"Just water for now. I'm meeting someone."

He fills up a glass from the spigot and adds a wedge of lime to the rim, then puts it on a coaster in front of me. I smile and thank him and take a small sip.

I'm nervous. More than I expected. The last date I went on, a few months ago, was a setup. Mel's husband wanted me to meet one of his old college buddies. I didn't feel any chemistry, and it's safe to say he didn't either. We had a nice talk, but once we ran out of stories about Mel and her husband, our conversation ran dry. Neither of us reached out to the other after our date.

I realize I'm slumping a little and I sit up straight. I spent the day doing more research for Quartz—this time on the variety of "clean" beauty products currently for sale and the market share each claims—but at five sharp, I started getting ready. I changed into my new blue top and my favorite jeans. I spritzed on one of the perfume samples I got when I bought the lip gloss at the Sephora counter. I even added a little eyeliner and mascara. I worried I'd overdone it with the mascara—it kept smudging off just below my brows—so I swiped a little off with a tissue.

I glance at my watch: 7:07 P.M.

Ted and I have been messaging sporadically all week. After he asked me out, he told me he'd find a good place. We also exchanged phone numbers.

I pull my phone out now and check, but there's no new text from him. The last one came in yesterday: *Looking forward to seeing you tomorrow night.*

I scroll back through our previous texts to make sure I'm at the right place. But the name and address he gave me are on the menus I see stacked on the counter at the end of the bar. And he definitely said seven P.M.

I take another sip of water, then reply to a text my mom sent earlier today, asking how my new job is going.

Really good so far! I type—which is true. I'm working on a few campaigns already, and I've chatted on the phone with Francine, my boss, a couple of times. She seems smart and capable. I think I can learn a lot from her. She's coming to New York next month, and she suggested we meet for lunch.

The bartender swings by again. "Ready for something else?"

I smile brightly. "No, I'm good."

I scroll through my other recent texts so I appear occupied. Beneath my exchanges with my mom and Mel and Sean, who all asked about my new freelance job, there's my last conversation with Cassandra and Jane. I'd sent the Moore sisters a group text after I visited Daphne's boutique: *I found a really cool top! Can't wait to show it to you!*

Only Jane had written back: *Great!*

I haven't heard anything from either sister since.

I'm sure they've had a busy week. It's nothing personal.

I consider sending them a quick message, something breezy or funny, but something holds me back.

It's 7:17 P.M.

New York traffic is so unpredictable, and subways are always delayed. Ted could also have gotten stuck at work. He's probably rushing here right now.

But why couldn't he have sent a text to say he was running late?

There's a pit in my stomach. He'd seemed so friendly and polite in our messages. More than that, he always wrote me back quickly. He acted sincerely interested in me.

Is it possible he met someone between yesterday and today? He seems like such a catch. I can't be the only woman he reached out to.

As I'm staring down at my phone, a text pings in. It's from Ted.

I'm so sorry! Work emergency—I'm going to be here for hours. I wanted to text you earlier but my boss grabbed me as I was walking out the door.

It's 7:25 P.M.

I blink against the prickly feeling in my eyes. I understand why he couldn't make it. I'm just so disappointed. I guess I wish he could have let me know right when his boss first approached him. But maybe he didn't have his phone, and his boss could be a nightmare.

No problem, I write back. *Rain check!*

I slide five dollars onto the counter beneath my coaster and grab my coat and purse, not even taking the time to put the coat on.

I hurry out the front door.

It's Friday night, and all around me on the sidewalk people are in pairs and groups—couples walking hand in hand, a cluster of twenty-somethings laughing on a corner as they wait for a light to change, two guys in business clothes giving each other a high five.

At least I have my own place to go home to.

But I don't want to be alone tonight, so I take the subway to Athena's.

It's crowded when I walk in, but Steve waves me over and squeezes me into a tiny table in the back. "Haven't seen you lately, pretty girl. Where are you going all fancied up with that new hairdo?"

"Oh, I was supposed to meet a friend for a drink but he had to reschedule," I say brightly.

Steve looks at me a little more closely and puts his hand with its slightly gnarled knuckles on my shoulder. "Save room for dessert. I've got some fresh baklava for you."

I'm not that hungry when my food arrives, after all, but I force myself to eat a little more than half. I leave a big tip for my waitress—Steve's granddaughter, who just started working here a few weeks ago—and ask her to pack up my leftovers.

I let myself into my apartment around nine, carrying a little white bag with not just the rest of my falafel, but a big square of baklava that Steve insisted on giving me.

A plain white envelope is on my floor, just inside the door, like someone slid it underneath.

It looks just like the envelope I gave to Detective Williams, the one containing the necklace.

My name is on the outside, written in such a messy scrawl I barely recognize the letters.

I pick it up. It's light, but something small and hard is inside. It feels like metal.

I tear it open and see the mail key. I guess the landlord finally got around to dropping it off, after I left him another message yesterday to nudge him.

I reach for my key ring and attach it. I doubt anything important is waiting for me in the mailbox downstairs. Still, I should probably check.

But first I change, carefully hanging up my blue top. I pull on a hoodie and sweatpants and slip on flip-flops, since I'm only walking up and down the stairs.

The mailboxes are in double rows, one on top of the other, twenty in total. I find mine—3D—and slide in the key. I have to wiggle it a little to get it to turn. I pull the little bronze door open, and a few envelopes fall to the floor. It's crammed full of mail.

I remove the catalog that's on top and see it's addressed to Amanda.

Her mail is still coming here. I should have expected that. How could companies and marketers know what happened to her?

I reach into the small rectangular space again and again, piling bills and letters and more catalogs into my arms. Wedged in the very back is a fat manila envelope that has been forced into a curve against the walls and floor of the mailbox. I use my fingernails to pry it free.

I take the stack of mail upstairs and lay it all out on my little wooden table. I start to sort it into two piles: Amanda's and mine.

Almost all of it belongs to her. I could send it to her mother, since I have the address—although it might be jarring for her to open that package. I decide to ask Cassandra and Jane what they think I should do.

When I finish with the last piece, I don't have two piles. I have three.

The fat manila envelope that was wedged in the very back of the box doesn't have a name on it. There's no address or stamp or postal mark. It's completely blank.

It was so far back that it must have been in the box for a while, because when the mailman delivered the newer pieces, he would have pushed the envelope farther and farther away from the opening.

How could this unaddressed package end up in a mailbox, though? The only three keys to it, according to what the landlord said, were Amanda's, the mailman's, and the master key, which the landlord finally got copied for me.

So one of them must have put the package there. I can rule out the mailman, since there's no postage or delivery information.

Possibly the landlord left it for me and didn't put my name on it. He's not the most responsible guy; it took him a week to get me a copy of the key.

But it seems more likely Amanda left it there.

Why would Amanda store something in her own mailbox?

I reach for the envelope and turn it over in my hands. It feels soft and bulky. It isn't sealed. Just the little metal butterfly clip is engaged through the hole in the flap.

It would be easy to quickly check and close it right back up. Maybe one of the other neighbors, like Mary from across the hall, gave it to the postman while he was filling up my box. Maybe it *is* for me.

There's only one way to find out. I pinch together the ends of the metal clip and open the flap.

Inside is a big Ziploc bag, with something else sealed within. It looks like a plain blue towel, folded up into a messy square.

Nothing about this makes sense. Maybe something is wrapped *inside* the towel.

I pull apart the seal on the Ziploc and use my fingertips to slide out the towel. As I take an edge to pull it open, a shot explodes outside my window.

I recoil, cringing.

I listen for another sound—a yell or another shot. Then I hear a motor revving and realize it was only a car backfiring.

I take a deep breath and straighten up. *I should be used to the city's noises by now,* I chide myself.

I pull open an edge, but the towel is still folded in half. Now it's a rectangle instead of a square. A tiny drop, what looks like a rust-colored stain, is by the bottom edge.

The hairs on my arms are standing up. Some instinct is telling me to shove the towel back in the Ziploc and throw it away. I don't want to see what's inside.

But I can't stop my fingers from reaching out again, grasping the very tip of the towel.

I pull it open and flinch.

I can't stop staring at the rust-colored stain in the middle of the towel, and the small scalpel—the kind doctors use during surgeries—lying in its center. The scalpel also has brick-color stains on it.

It looks like dried blood.

CHAPTER FORTY-FIVE

AMANDA

Two months ago

"HI, JAMES," AMANDA SAID. "Nice to meet you."

The bartender delivered their whiskey and sodas and Amanda took a small sip. It burned her throat—she rarely drank, and when she did, it was usually just a single beer—and she suppressed a grimace.

"Haven't seen you here before." James's hand closed around his glass. The image of his fingers clenching burned into her eyes; she had to pull away her gaze.

"Oh, I've come once or twice," she lied. "But you must not have been here, because I would have noticed you."

The sisters had told her James was a regular at the Twist bar on Thursday nights: He usually showed up around six, was feeling good by seven, and didn't seem to have a type.

"You'll have to wing it," Cassandra had instructed her. "Play to his ego."

James stood up. "Take my seat."

She smiled as she slid onto the wooden stool, which still held the warmth of his body. He wore a white oxford shirt with the sleeves rolled up; his blue blazer was slung across the back of his chair. He rested his forearm on his jacket, encircling her. The room was crowded, but he didn't need to be so close. She suppressed a shudder.

So far so good.

Amanda's eyes flitted across the room as she fiddled nervously with one of her earrings. A guy was leaning forward, waving his credit card as he tried to get the bartender's attention.

Her heartbeat accelerated when she realized the guy was blocking her view of Beth.

James lifted his glass again and drained it, then reached for the one Amanda had ordered. "Mmm. You smell good."

He was so close she could see the broken capillaries around his nose. Her mom had those, too, a legacy of heavy drinking.

The guy with the credit card leaned back. Beth's chair was empty.

Amanda's body stiffened. She hadn't expected things to move this fast. She pulled her purse onto her lap and said, "So tell me what keeps you busy." She stared up at James while her hand slid into her bag and felt for the tiny mouthwash bottle.

She already knew James's background well enough to write his bio: divorced several years ago, one elementary-school-aged daughter, from a wealthy family in a smallish town in upstate New York, squandered most of his inheritance, spent Mondays through Fridays in the city trying to build a new business selling custom sporting equipment.

Some of this information came from watching him. Other pieces of it were gleaned after Stacey briefly got ahold of his cell phone and installed spyware on it.

"So, yeah, I try to keep active," James was saying.

Amanda nodded to encourage him to keep talking as she groped around for the little plastic bottle.

Then she saw a flash of frizzy red hair.

It's too soon! she wanted to cry out. *I'm not ready!*

But Beth was already putting a hand on James's arm. "Doug!" He twisted around to look at her. "I thought that was you!"

Amanda finally touched the bottle. Working under the lip of the bar counter to shield her actions, she tried to pinch the sides of the cap and untwist it.

Her fingers were trembling and uncoordinated; the cap refused to yield to them.

"Sorry, my name's not Doug. You've got the wrong guy."

Beth laughed. "I'm sure it's you! That convention in Dallas a couple years ago?"

Amanda finally removed the cap. She needed more time. But James was starting to turn away from Beth.

Amanda's heart leaped into her throat. She had the open mouthwash bottle in her left hand. If James glanced down, he'd see it.

Panic roared through her.

"Maybe I got the name wrong. Hold on, I've got a picture of us at that dinner!" Beth held up her phone, drawing James's gaze back to her.

This wasn't part of her script; Beth was improvising.

Amanda grabbed her drink with her free hand, wincing as the ice cubes clinked, and pulled it under the lip of the bar.

Was the bartender looking over at them? Beth's voice was loud, the only evidence of her nerves.

This was the critical part. Amanda couldn't falter or make a mistake; she had to do it perfectly. She poured the sixty milligrams of liquid morphine from the mouthwash bottle directly into her whiskey and soda, avoiding splashing any of the precious medicine onto the floor.

Then she slipped the empty bottle back into her purse. But it wasn't over yet.

"Wait, wait, I know it's here," Beth was saying.

James just repeated, "Wrong guy," and turned around.

Beth looked at Amanda, her eyes widening.

Amanda was still holding the doctored beverage, but she hadn't had time to swirl around the swizzle stick to mix up its contents, or to switch the drinks.

She needed ten more seconds.

Beth tapped James on the shoulder.

He ignored her and raised an eyebrow. "I promise I'm not using an alias. My name isn't really Doug."

Beth melted away, into the crowd. Back to her position at the bar.

Amanda was on her own.

James reached for his drink—the wrong drink.

She could jostle his arm and try to spill his whiskey and soda and offer him the other one, or—

Cassandra's calm, authoritative voice floated into her mind: *Play to his ego.*

Amanda reached out and put her hand on James's, trapping it. "That kind of thing must happen to you a lot. That gorgeous blonde back there"—Amanda lifted her chin to indicate a direction behind him—"has been checking you out since I got here."

James's head whipped around. She gave her drink a quick stir, then put it on the bar and slid it close to him. The two glasses were indistinguishable—but if she hadn't forgotten to wipe off her lip gloss, a telltale crescent would have marred the rim.

She grabbed his beverage and held tight to the cold glass as she raised it to her lips and pretended to take a sip.

"You're the only woman I've got eyes for," James said as he turned back. "With that sexy librarian thing you've got going on."

The liquid was still swirling slightly in the glass in front of him. But he didn't seem to notice.

He clinked it against hers. "Bottoms up!"

Then he took a deep drink.

Twenty minutes later, he set down his empty glass.

"Another round?" The medicine was beginning to take effect; his words were slightly slurred. Or could that just be from the alcohol?

Amanda leaned closer and whispered in his ear, "Would you mind if we went somewhere quieter?"

He made a little checking motion in the air with his index finger, and the bartender nodded and delivered the bill for the drinks James had consumed before Amanda's arrival.

James paid with a credit card and squinted down at the receipt as he pulled a pen out of his breast pocket, blinking repeatedly. Amanda knew his limbs were likely beginning to feel heavy. His speech was about to grow almost unintelligible. Soon he'd have difficulty walking.

She had to get him out of here fast.

She stood up the moment he signed the check. Then she heard a tiny, almost imperceptible plinking sound. Her hand instinctively went to her ear. It was bare.

She didn't have time to retrieve her earring, she decided. It was just a basic gold hoop; nearly every woman in New York had a pair. It would probably be swept up at the end of the night along with crumpled napkins and swizzle sticks and food crumbs and tossed into the trash can.

James stumbled slightly as he stepped down onto the sidewalk, nearly bumping into a man talking on his cell phone.

"I'm tipsy," Amanda giggled, hanging on to his arm.

"Sh'we get a cab?" he suggested, his voice garbled.

"Would you mind if we walked a little first and got some air?" Amanda reached for his hand, but she was the one guiding him.

They entered Central Park. It was the shadowy hour that preceded darkness. Dog walkers and joggers and even a few late commuters were walking through other parts of the park, but this area was empty. A breeze cut through the summer night, raising goose bumps on her arms.

She led James toward a bench in a secluded area, under the overhang of a giant oak tree's low-lying branches. She knew exactly where to go; she'd practiced this route before.

James's knees buckled just as they reached the bench, and he fell heavily onto it.

He slumped to one side, his head lolling on his neck, his eyes closed.

Amanda turned and walked briskly away, letting her hair down, then slipping off her glasses and tucking them into her purse.

In less than ten minutes, she'd enter a restaurant that bordered the park and request a table for one. She'd ask to be seated toward the center of the room; she didn't want to be invisible tonight. She'd engage the waiter in conversation before ordering, and she'd pay with a credit card bearing her name.

She moved faster, her breath coming quickly. Her part was finished.

She was nearly at the edge of the park when her burner phone rang and Stacey's voice rushed the line. It held something Amanda had never before heard in it: fear.

Amanda stopped short.

"Something's wrong," Stacey blurted. "Get back here."

CHAPTER FORTY-SIX

CASSANDRA & JANE

"SHAY JUST READ TED'S new text apologizing again for standing her up," Jane says the next morning, showing Cassandra the burner phone. "She hasn't replied, though."

"Give it until tonight. Ted can grovel a little more." Cassandra reaches out and touches the buzzer for 3D. A moment later, they hear Shay's voice: "Come on up!"

The sisters climb the steps to the landing for the third floor. When they turn the corner and step into the hallway, both stop short.

Shay is standing in Amanda's doorway, smiling broadly.

The sisters' shared sense of déjà vu is overwhelming. They've seen Shay a few times since her makeover, but the image of her in the precise spot where Amanda used to wait to welcome them is still jarring.

"It's so good to see you!" Cassandra says.

Shay ushers them over the threshold into the apartment as they look around. The open kitchen is less cluttered than when Amanda lived here: She kept pans on every stove burner and a Cuisinart, bread maker, and tins of flour and sugar on the kitchen counter. Both women chose the same place for their sofas, but Shay's coffee table is square, whereas Amanda's was round.

"Can I get you something to drink?" Shay offers.

"We've got a little prezzie for you first," Jane says as Cassandra extends a heavy box, wrapped with a silver bow. Jane is holding a plain brown shopping bag, which she casually sets down on the floor by the couch, where it's partially concealed from view.

"It's a combo gift to celebrate your new job *and* your new place," Cassandra says.

Shay looks down at the box. "You guys really didn't need to bring me anything."

"Open it!" Jane orders, laughing.

Shay unfurls the bow and removes the box's lid to reveal a sea-blue leather purse. It's much more feminine and luxurious than the simple tote she uses.

"Oh my gosh!" Shay stares at it, not even touching it. "It's gorgeous!"

"Take it out," Cassandra says. "One of our new clients designed it, so we each got one, too."

Other than the colors—Jane's is a dusky rose and Cassandra's is black—the hobo-style bags are identical.

Shay carefully removes hers from the box. She lifts the strap and hangs it over her shoulder.

The tracker is hidden inside the lining, which was sewn back up expertly.

"It's perfect with your new look," Jane says.

"I love it!"

"Let me take a picture to show our client," Jane says.

Shay smiles awkwardly while Jane lifts her phone and snaps one.

"Now check inside," Cassandra tells Shay.

She unzips the bag to reveal a sugar-cookie-scented Nest candle, with notes of Tahitian vanilla and bourbon-infused caramel. "Just looking at this makes me hungry!" Shay laughs.

The bag also holds Warby Parker sunglasses, a gauzy floral scarf, and a peachy-pink lip gloss.

"This is too much—" Shay starts to protest.

Cassandra cuts her off. "We have a closet in our office filled with this sort of stuff. A lot of companies send us their products because they want our clients to wear them. So you're just helping us do a little seasonal cleaning."

"Promise us you'll use it all," Jane says. "Especially the purse. There's no point in having a beautiful bag just hanging in your closet."

"Don't be afraid to carry it all the time," Cassandra adds. "This is your new everyday purse."

Shay looks a little overwhelmed—maybe from all the gifts, or maybe from the sisters' concerted effort to quash any objections she might have to accepting them. "I will. I've had that old tote forever, and I'm going to switch everything out today." She gives them each a hug. "Thank you so much." Then she takes the candle out of the box and sets it on her kitchen counter. "How about some iced tea?"

"Love some," Cassandra says. "Do you mind if I use your bathroom?"

"Of course. It's right—"

Shay cuts herself off, clearly remembering that it isn't the sisters' first visit to the apartment.

As Cassandra opens the door to the tiny bathroom, Shay recovers with a joke: "The other day I dropped my washcloth in there and suddenly I had wall-to-wall carpeting."

Both sisters laugh as Shay cuts lemon wedges and puts them on the rims of the tall, matching glasses, along with little sprigs of mint. She's also set out a cluster of dewy red grapes in a little bowl, next to another of almonds.

Cassandra closes the door on that image. She runs the water in the sink to cover the sounds of her movements as she eases open the medicine cabinet. Just as she suspected, the bottle of Ambien that the sisters noticed while they were surveilling Shay in Valerie's apartment sits on one of the shelves. Cassandra twists open the childproof cap; the bottle is almost completely full. She removes four capsules and slips them into the pocket of her jeans.

Her task is complete, but she takes a moment to scan the other items in the medicine cabinet: Tom's peppermint toothpaste, contact lens solution, and the usual toiletries. She pulls open the door to the tiny shower: nothing of interest. She bends down and opens the small cabinet beneath the sink. It's filled with cleaning supplies, extra toilet paper, and Kleenex. She's about to close it when something catches her eye. It looks like the edge of a large manila mailer.

Jane is talking loudly, relaying a story about a terrible date she'd been on the previous night. "The guy asked zero questions about me, but I learned all about his fancy clients and first-class trip to Istanbul.

It's so hard to find a good one, isn't it?" Her voice provides cover for Cassandra's movements.

Cassandra's hand closes around the manila envelope. She unclasps the metal fastener and peeks inside, sucking in a sharp breath when she spots the stained blue towel.

She unwraps it and sees a bloodstained scalpel.

She recoils, rocking back on her heels, barely able to process what she's seeing.

Jane's voice filters through the door: "So, Shay, you're still liking the new job? And how's the online dating going?"

It seems impossible that Shay could merely have discovered the envelope: The sisters meticulously searched the apartment after Amanda's suicide, and again before Shay rented it. How had she obtained it?

Cassandra has to make a snap decision: Take the envelope, or leave it?

She can't carry it out of the bathroom; she has nowhere to hide it. They can come back for it if need be.

She puts the envelope back, making sure the tip of one edge is visible. Then she stands up and opens the door.

"I was actually stood up last night," Shay is saying. "Well, the guy claimed he had a work emergency, but I was already at the bar. . . ."

Jane catches Cassandra's eye. Something in Cassandra's expression tightens; Jane knows her sister well enough to sense that something is very wrong.

Cassandra touches her sun-charm necklace; it's time to go.

"Oh, no," Jane says. "Did that disastrous *Rolling Stone* review come out?"

Cassandra nods, hoping Shay doesn't notice that Cassandra isn't holding her phone.

Shay merely passes her a glass of iced tea. "What review?"

Cassandra turns to Shay, elaborating on Jane's spontaneous fib. "I'm so sorry we have to run. It's the nature of our job. There's this musician we rep and he just got panned. But let's have a quick toast!"

Both sisters look at Shay, who lifts up her glass. It covers a bit of her face, distorting her left eye slightly, making her features appear mismatched.

"Yes, a quick toast," Jane says. "To your new life!"

CHAPTER FORTY-SEVEN

SHAY

Some uses for a scalpel: surgery, anatomical dissection, and crafts projects. As many as 1,000 people per day are injured while providing medical care, with scalpel blade injuries making up 7 to 8 percent of accidental cuts and puncture wounds.
—Data Book, page 61

To my new life.

Those words seem to echo through my apartment even after Cassandra and Jane rush out to deal with their work crisis.

"A temperamental musician and a bad review are a dangerous combination," Jane explained as she gave me a quick goodbye hug.

Only after they're gone do I notice they left a plain brown shopping bag by my couch. I peek inside and see a stack of books by an author named Sienna Grant. The sisters had mentioned working on her memoir, and lately I'm seeing it everywhere—including yesterday, in a big window display at Barnes & Noble.

I quickly text Jane to let her know she's forgotten the books. Her reply comes almost immediately: *Shoot, can you hold on to them? I don't need them right away.*

Of course, I text back.

I begin switching out the contents of my tote bag into my new purse. I'm going to take their advice and use it every day. I run my fingers over the soft leather and inhale the rich aroma, then I place it on my little dining table. It's so bright and elegant, it's almost like the sisters left a piece of themselves behind.

I'm pretty sure I saw a bag just like this one in Daphne's boutique. It makes sense that she'd sell it, given her connection to the Moore sisters. I frown, wondering if Daphne ever brought up my visit to them. I don't plan to go into her boutique again, but it's possible I might see her if Cassandra and Jane invite me out with their group sometime.

I pick up Jane's shopping bag and tuck it onto a shelf in my bookcase, alongside the books and knickknacks I've collected through the years, such as the perfect conch shell I found on a beach with my ex-boyfriend, and the old world globe I bought at a yard sale when I was in grade school.

Then I putter around, putting our glasses in the dishwasher—Cassandra only had a single sip of tea after we toasted—and handwashing the pitcher. I dry my hands on the dish towel slung through the handle of my stove.

I'd thought about showing the envelope containing the stained blue towel and scalpel to the Moore sisters this morning. But they rushed out so quickly there wasn't a chance. Maybe that was for the best. I've brought too many strange associations with Amanda into their lives already.

I could just toss the envelope in the trash and be done with it. I don't need this tainted, unsettling package in my apartment.

I walk toward the bathroom to get the envelope, then pause. I turn around.

Amanda must have saved it for a reason. Something is telling me to hold on to it, too.

I'm on my couch that night, binge-watching *Game of Thrones* again, when my cell rings.

The number looks familiar—it's the local 212 area code—but I don't immediately recognize it.

"Shay?"

My pulse accelerates. I know this voice.

"It's Detective Williams from the Seventeenth Precinct."

"Hi." My voice sounds strangled so I clear my throat. A fear leaps into my mind: Could she be calling because she knows I stole the necklace?

Mail theft is a felony punishable by up to five years in prison, and up to a $250,000 fine.

"I was just thinking about you. I wanted to see how you're doing."

"Oh, I'm good," I blurt.

"Glad to hear it. You were pretty shaken up the last time we talked."

This can't simply be a friendly call, can it?

She lets the silence hang between us. My palms are sweating now; I jump up and start to pace. "Everything's much better now," I babble.

Another pause.

"I got a call from someone at City Hospital."

I squeeze my eyes shut.

"A woman who looks a lot like you went by the other day asking about Amanda's mother." Detective Williams's voice is as calm and steady as if she were giving me a weather report. "Know anything about that?"

How could anyone at the hospital have known who I was? My mind feels so jumbled it's hard to think straight. I have to tell Detective Williams the truth. Or at least a piece of it.

"It was me. I just wanted to write a condolence note to Amanda's mother."

Detective Williams sighs. I can picture her at her neat desk, in one of her plain suits, her forehead creasing into waves.

"You really think Amanda's mother wants a letter from a woman who watched her daughter die?"

I swallow hard. If that's all the detective knows, she can't arrest me.

"I thought about it later. And, um, I decided not to send her a note."

I hear Detective Williams exhale again. I have no idea if she believes me.

"You're not still hanging around Amanda's friends, are you?"

I can't pile on another lie. "I've seen them around a few times. They're really nice."

"I'm telling you to let this go, Shay. Understand?"

"Yes," I whisper.

"I hope I don't have to talk to you again." Then she hangs up.

It feels like a near miss; Detective Williams doesn't know that I actually went to Mrs. Evinger's house. That I stole a package from her porch while she slept a few feet away.

Then I remember the flowers. If Detective Williams talks to Mrs. Evinger, will she mention a mysterious visitor who came while she was sleeping? Nausea roils my stomach and I cover my hand with my mouth, fighting it back.

Maybe I should call back Detective Williams right now and confess everything. She might take pity on me. And Jane could confirm that the necklace belongs to her.

I could even give Detective Williams the bloody scalpel and towel.

I pinch the bridge of my nose between my fingers, trying to sort through it all. I can't just tell her all of this. She could arrest me on the spot.

I need help.

On Monday morning, I'm up and out the door by seven A.M. After I spoke to Detective Williams, I spent the rest of the weekend trying to find a lawyer who could give me advice. One of them actually responded to my call yesterday, and I scheduled a one-hour consult with him.

My new floral scarf is around my neck, and my new bag is slung over my shoulder with the envelope tucked inside. If the lawyer agrees it's a good idea, I'm going to deliver it to the police.

I'm twisting my key in my door to lock it behind me when I hear, "Good morning."

I turn around and see Mary, my neighbor across the hall with the little gray cat.

Before I can reply, she gasps and puts a hand to her chest. She looks like she's seen a ghost.

"Are you okay?" I ask.

She stares at me, her face draining of color.

"Shay," she finally says. "I—It's just that you look so much like . . ."

The name explodes into my brain as she says it: "Amanda."

That night when I'd been house-sitting and I'd gazed into the mirror, wondering who I reminded myself of without my glasses and my hair up . . . it was she.

No one would ever mistake us for twins, but the resemblance is undeniable. At least it is now, with my lightened hair, shorter cut, and contacts.

I can't believe I didn't realize this before.

I don't know what to say to Mary. It must be so eerie for her.

"I'm sorry," I finally mumble. "I didn't mean to startle you."

She takes a step closer and reaches out, as if she wants to touch my hair. "The color . . . your scarf . . . when I saw you before, you looked different. Didn't you have glasses?"

"I did—I do. I'd just gotten out of the shower so I had them on then."

I flash back to how I'd looked that night, in a hoodie with my hair up in a ponytail and my tortoiseshell frames covering part of my face.

Mary gives herself a little shake. She bends down to pick up a newspaper and tucks it under her arm; she must have just opened her door to grab it. "You surprised me, that's all," she says, but she gives me a wary look as she goes back into her apartment. I hear the lock click.

I quickly reopen my own door and hurry inside. I rush into the bathroom and take out my contacts, placing them in the little plastic case the optometrist gave me. I find my glasses in the medicine cabinet, put them on, and grab an elastic band to gather my hair into a low ponytail. Then I unclasp my Fitbit and shove it under the sink.

I lean close to the mirror, breathing hard.

If you really want a makeover, you've got to let us help! Jane and I live for this stuff, Cassandra had told me.

I totally see you in this color, Jane had said, handing me a tear sheet of a model in a shampoo ad to give to the hairstylist—the one the Moore sisters brought me to. Cassandra had asked him to shape my eyebrows, too.

When I'd mentioned I'd been toying with the idea of contact lenses, they'd squealed, *Do it!*—and pushed me to book an appointment.

They knew Amanda so well.

Could it simply be a coincidence that all of their suggestions make me look more like their dead friend?

Even if it wasn't their intention, they must see it.

Amanda's style does suit me; I know I look better now. Just as her apartment is perfect for me.

So why are my hands shaking?

I cancel my appointment with the lawyer, eating the $260 fee.

How could Detective Williams understand all the strange things I've done? I'm friends with Amanda's friends. I snuck onto Amanda's mother's porch and stole her mail. I'm living in Amanda's apartment. I even look like her.

It's safer that I leave it all alone.

CHAPTER FORTY-EIGHT

VALERIE

Two years ago

"Miss?"

Valerie turned around, expecting the silver-haired gentleman who'd placed his lunch order to modify it. Instead, he snapped his fingers and pointed at her. "I just figured out who you are!"

She stood there in her black slacks and crisp white shirt, the tray she'd used to deliver his iced tea aloft on her upraised palm.

"*Law and Order: SVU.* Am I right? I never forget a face!"

Valerie smiled and affected her best thick Brooklyn accent. "'Put back the Doritos, kid, I saw you stick them under your coat.'"

The customer laughed, then his expression changed. Valerie knew what he was thinking: another failed actress serving BLTs on Sunset Strip.

"I'll be right back with your sandwich, sir." She hurried off.

It wasn't the first time she'd been recognized, but it was years since it had happened. In her late twenties, she'd won a small recurring role on a daytime soap opera that went off the air due to low ratings, and she'd enjoyed signing autographs—once—for a pair of middle-aged women who were touring the studio lot.

It was hard to accept: That single-season part was the zenith of her career.

Too young, too old, too short, too tall, too pretty, not pretty enough, not quite right . . .

Her story wasn't exactly original: At the age of seventeen, she'd stepped off a Greyhound bus with only two suitcases and a few hundred dollars in cash, determined to make it in Hollywood. But Valerie wasn't only chasing a dream; she was running even harder from her past.

Arf-arf!

No matter how many miles spun under the wheels of the cramped Greyhound bus that reeked of the meatball sub the guy a few rows up was eating, she could still hear echoes of the taunts that had followed her as she'd walked down the long school hallway lined with lockers on both sides.

Heard you like it doggie-style! one of the football players had shouted while the guy who'd betrayed her—the asshole who was funny and popular and had seemed so normal—smirked and accepted a high five from the idiot football player.

It didn't stop there. Not that day, or week, or even the next week. The taunts and whispers spread through their high school like a virus.

Someone—she didn't even know who—threw a dog treat at her head in the lunchroom. She had the role of Rizzo in their school's production of *Grease,* but she abruptly quit. She knew the moment she walked onstage, the barking would begin, just as it did when she was called on in class.

She couldn't tell anyone the truth—that it hadn't happened that way at all, that their buddy was a liar and a bastard, that she was still a virgin.

Who would believe her?

No one. Not even her own mother, whom she'd tried to tell first.

She couldn't bear to remain in high school.

So, California. It was all the way across the country. No one knew her there. It was a chance to start fresh—to show everyone who she could become. She worked as a nanny, a personal trainer, in craft services, and as a bartender while she tried to earn her SAG card. She lived in small apartments with two or three other girls crammed in to split the rent—except for the year she turned twenty-one, when she was briefly married.

As marriages went, hers wasn't bad: Valerie lived with Tony rent-free in his one-bedroom while he slept on the couch. Tony, who was born in a small town outside Madrid, paid Valerie five thousand dollars, mostly in tens and twenties he'd saved from tip money, and got his green card. She kept a few fond memories and his last name, Ricci—which put even more distance between her and her past.

Valerie had a knack for accents and a formidable memory for her lines, which helped her land an agent. But as her twenties slid into her thirties, her opportunities diminished. Her most recent job had been in a local commercial as a young mom with a laundry problem, which didn't even cover her rent for a month.

Her agent hadn't phoned with so much as an audition in weeks.

Valerie scooped up the BLT from the kitchen and grabbed the pitcher of iced tea with her free hand. The restaurant charged for refills—a ridiculous rule—but she freshened the silver-haired man's drink and said, "On the house."

"Thanks, sweetie."

When she cleared his table a little later, she found a twenty-dollar tip and a scrawled note on his receipt: *Hang in there.*

Maybe he'd sensed she was thinking of giving up.

The problem was, she had no backup plan. Her bank account held less than a thousand dollars. She'd never attended college. She was living in a small apartment with two other women who were also trying to make it in the business—just as she'd done when she'd first moved to L.A. The only difference now was that her roommates were nearly ten years younger than she was.

That evening, as Valerie sat on the edge of the bathtub soaking her tired feet in hot water, she gave herself a deadline: Her thirty-fourth birthday was three months away. If she didn't have any leads by then, she'd find a real job. Maybe she'd stay connected to the business as a personal assistant to someone who'd actually made it in Hollywood. She dried her feet, reached into the medicine cabinet to sneak a little of her roommate Ashley's expensive face cream, and fell into bed, exhausted from her double shift.

Six weeks later, Valerie's agent called. She'd won an audition for a supporting part as a traumatized woman in an independent film by an up-and-coming director.

Valerie read the 116-page script in one sitting, then immediately flipped to the first page and began highlighting her sections.

She wouldn't have many lines. Most of her emotions would play across her face.

She rehearsed every chance she got, creating an elaborate backstory for her character as she rode the bus to and from her restaurant job, and envisioning her scenes in rich detail as she lay in bed at night. She strategized about what to wear to the audition, finally settling on black jeans and a plain black T-shirt: a simple background canvas that wouldn't distract from her acting. She carried the script with her everywhere, like a talisman.

She poured everything she had into the three minutes she was allotted to channel the character in front of the casting director and the producer. It felt as if the emotions she'd kept tamped down for so many years—the fury and pain and bitterness that had consumed her in the weeks before she quit high school—had finally been uncorked in the small, plain audition room.

It wasn't as if this part had been created for her, Valerie thought. It was as if she had been created for it.

Valerie saw the producer glance at the casting director and give a little nod just before she left the room, and she knew she'd earned a callback. She walked outside, into the bright California sunshine, tears still dripping down her face.

Her roommate Ashley was practicing yoga in the living room when Valerie's agent delivered the news that she'd made it to the next round, and Ashley heard Valerie's excited squeal. Blond, leggy Ashley was twenty-six—the part called for a woman in her midthirties—and Ashley looked more like a surfer girl than a haunted single mom. She and Valerie almost never competed for the same roles. Still, Valerie was evasive about the details, more out of a superstition about jinxing herself than wariness.

The director would be at the studio for her callback, which was scheduled for the following Tuesday at nine A.M. Valerie would have a full scene with one of the actors who had already been cast. She *became* her character in the days leading up to her second audition—dressing like her, walking like her, and thinking like her. She even had a nightmare that reflected her character's trauma.

But Valerie never made it to the studio that Tuesday. Before she had a chance to win the part, she learned it had been nabbed by another actress: Ashley.

A week later, Valerie broke her lease and flew cross-country, reversing the journey she'd made at the age of seventeen. It wasn't just that she now wanted to get as far away from L.A. as possible. She was running toward something again.

Her instincts told her to seek out Cassandra and Jane. Even though she'd only seen them a few times since she'd fled from their hometown, they were the touchstones of her childhood. The memories she held of them seemed like the only good pieces of her past: the three of them lying in a row on Valerie's bed, flipping through *Tiger Beat* magazine. Making batches of dough for chocolate-chip cookies—but usually eating most of it raw out of the bowl. Grabbing a hairbrush as a microphone and leaning in close together while they sang the lyrics to Madonna's "Holiday."

Plus, she had nowhere else to go.

She knocked on the door of Cassandra's apartment and saw the shock in her eyes. Valerie knew she looked terrible, as if the trauma she'd endured had wreaked havoc on her body, stealing the color and vitality from her face, sharpening her limbs, and aging her. She moved slowly and wearily. *A car wreck survivor,* a casting director observing her might think. *Or someone who barely escaped a terrible natural disaster.*

She sat between Cassandra and Jane on the couch, a vodka and soda untouched in front of her, as the words poured out of her: about the customers who yelled at her when the kitchen got their orders wrong, about the assistant director who'd slid his hand up her skirt, about the casting directors who'd looked Valerie up and down, then spoken a single word: *No.* Some of them wouldn't even bother to say anything at all.

Then Valerie took a deep breath and began to talk about her gorgeous, perky roommate, Ashley, who'd wished Valerie luck when Valerie had gotten the callback and then stolen her part.

"I woke up the day of my audition feeling so tired and heavy it was almost impossible to move," Valerie had said. "I could see the sun peeking through my shades. It was too bright to be early morning. I reached for my phone on the nightstand, where I always kept it. But it was gone."

Valerie told the rest of her story; she'd gone over it in her mind so many times by now that she could almost see herself running into the kitchen and checking the clock on the microwave. It was 9:07 A.M., seven minutes after her audition was supposed to begin, she told Cassandra and Jane.

Her missing phone held all the pieces she needed: Its alarm had been supposed to wake her up; its calendar contained the studio address and directions to the audition room. She couldn't summon an Uber, as she'd planned—or even call to say she'd be late. "My mind felt so thick and muddy," she told Cassandra and Jane. "Like I'd had way too much to drink the night before. But I only had a single glass of wine."

By the time she borrowed a neighbor's phone and reached her agent, she was hyperventilating. "Calm down, I'll see if they can get you in later today," he'd said.

"But my chance was gone," Valerie told Cassandra and Jane as sobs racked her body.

Later that afternoon, Valerie continued, her roommate Ashley arrived home. And a few hours after that, Valerie finally found her phone wedged between her mattress and box spring, with the ringer turned off.

"I was so naïve," Valerie had said, her voice raw. "I thought Ashley was a good person. But she fooled me. She's an actress, after all."

"She stole your phone?" Jane had said. "And could she have put something in your wine, like a sleeping pill?"

Valerie had shrugged. "I just wish someone could make her pay for what she did."

"I wish someone could, too," Cassandra had said, meeting Jane's eyes.

The sisters' plan was hatched that very evening. Cassandra and Jane had spent their careers cultivating media contacts, and they knew more than a couple of celebrities.

The stealth campaign they launched against Ashley was one of the most relentless and effective the Moore sisters ever conducted: whispers into the ears of some of their clients, off-the-record calls to entertainment reporters, the dissemination of horribly unflattering pictures they hired a photographer to surreptitiously take, including a series of Ashley appearing to be sneaking into the married director's trailer. Ashley's career crashed before her movie ever had a chance to launch it.

The immense satisfaction of seeing the effects of their vigilante justice opened the sisters' eyes to the sweet power of revenge.

Soon they began to notice atrocities everywhere. There were so many horrible misdeeds in the world. Why should innocent people suffer while perpetrators roamed free, continuing to amass victims?

Their way is more effective than the unpredictable and often disappointing legal system.

It's a lot faster—not to mention cheaper—than therapy.

It's more intoxicating than a runner's high.

They don't want to stop. But more than that, they aren't sure they can.

Their successes are completely addictive.

CHAPTER FORTY-NINE

SHAY

Blackouts represent episodes of amnesia and can be the result of excessive consumption of alcohol. The two main types of blackouts are en bloc and fragmentary. Some subjects who experience fragmentary blackouts—which are the most common form—can become aware they are missing pieces of events if they are later reminded about those events.
—Data Book, page 64

AT A LITTLE PAST 5:30 P.M., I begin preparing for my guests. The Moore sisters should be arriving soon.

They have a work event later this evening, but they suggested we have a quick drink in my apartment first when they swing by to get the books they forgot the last time they were here.

"We'll bring the wine," Cassandra had said. "A glass before your date will help relax you."

Your date.

I find myself singing along with Pink as I set out the food. Ted is coming by at seven-thirty to pick me up and take me out to dinner.

Nothing will keep me away this time, he'd promised in his last text, after I'd agreed to reschedule.

After so many nights alone, my Friday evening promises to be full of excitement.

By now, I've completely reframed my silly anxiety about the make-over that highlighted my resemblance to Amanda. The Moore sisters have done nothing but try to help me ever since we met. Maybe it's a little strange that they didn't bring up my resemblance to Amanda when I first walked out of the optometrist's office. They were probably a bit thrown, but perhaps they didn't want *me* to feel uncomfortable.

They couldn't have been trying to make me look like Amanda, unless it was subconscious. It's more likely that they were simply help-ing me become the best version of me.

And *I'm* the one who found Amanda's apartment up for rent; they had nothing to do with that. Maybe they even felt a little discomfort about me moving in here, but they hid it because they knew how badly I needed to find a new place.

How could there be anything sinister about all the kind things they've done for me? I've felt so much less alone since I met them.

I've picked up a bouquet of flowers to brighten my kitchen counter. I went to the same corner deli where I purchased flowers the last two times—the single yellow zinnia that I laid on Amanda's doorstep, and the bigger bunch I left with her sleeping mother.

This time, I chose orange alstroemeria.

I light the new chunky candle the sisters gave me and dim the over-head light, then survey the room. Everything looks perfect in my cozy new place, and the vanilla-and-bourbon-spiked-caramel candle smells like I've just baked something delicious.

Happiness bubbles within me, making my body feel light and tingly.

I'm not planning to let Ted up when he calls from the lobby later tonight—I'll just go straight downstairs to meet him. Even if the eve-ning goes as well as I hope it does, I won't invite him up after dinner, either—so my efforts are just for the Moore sisters.

When the buzzer sounds, I press the button to allow them in and open my door. As I watch them walk down the hallway, side by side, I'm struck anew by how stunning they look. Cassandra is in a fitted bur-gundy dress with ankle boots, and Jane wears a black jumpsuit belted at the waist with a gold chain.

I wonder if they've become inured to their reflections in the mirror, or if they still appreciate how dazzling they are. But I feel good, too—it's like their dazzle is contagious. I styled my hair and I'm wearing the shirt I bought at Daphne's boutique. I'm going to wear the floral scarf they gave me with my leather jacket tonight, too.

"Come in!" I say when they reach me. I point to the bag of books that I've placed by the door. "So you don't forget them again."

"Oh, thanks," Jane says as I close the door behind her. "Wow, that's a perfect first-date outfit."

"You look effortlessly chic," Cassandra adds.

"Thanks. I'm actually a little nervous. The last guy who chased after me was trying to sell me a fake Rolex."

They laugh, then Cassandra says, "Well, I've got something that can help with your nerves." She holds up a bottle of champagne. "A client just gave this to us, and believe me, we need it after what she puts us through. Total diva. Okay if I open it?"

"Of course. I don't have any champagne flutes, though. . . ."

I look at my kitchen counter, where I set out three of the new wineglasses from the set I bought earlier this week. They're pretty and feminine, with different-colored glass balls—amber, cobalt, and emerald—near the bottom of the stems. They look nice alongside the flowers and platter of snacks.

"Oh, Shay." Jane comes over to give me a hug. I smell her now-familiar delicate floral perfume and feel her soft hair brush my cheek. "You didn't need to do all this."

I think I detect a melancholy tone in her sweet voice, but it's hard to tell because Cassandra interjects, "But I'm glad you did!"

She walks over to the kitchen counter and pulls the foil off the mouth of the bottle of Dom Pérignon, then removes the metal cage. She twists off the top, and I reflexively wince as a loud pop fills the room. Froth instantly begins to bubble over the rim of the bottle. She expertly catches it in one of the glasses, then fills the other two.

I take a sip from the glass she handed me. I've never had Dom Pérignon before, and it tastes delicious.

I watch as Cassandra takes a long drink from her glass—she has the one with the amber ball, which complements her eyes—then she sighs. "I wish we could hang out with you tonight instead of going to this work thing." She helps herself to a slice of cheese. "I'd love nothing more than to collapse on the couch, drink and eat, and watch a movie."

I can't quite believe that the Moore sisters would prefer being here than at whatever fabulous event they're scheduled to attend, but maybe when you spend so much time out socializing, you yearn for the allure of a quiet evening in.

Jane puts a hand on Cassandra's arm. "We had some fun nights in this apartment with Amanda, too."

I don't know what to say at the mention of Amanda's name, so I just look down.

Cassandra adds, "We're really happy we're here with you now, Shay." She clears her throat softly. "As hard as Amanda's death was for us, the only silver lining is that it led you to us."

Her generous words pierce through my chest. I blink back the threat of tears. "I know how much you both loved her."

"We think about her every day," Cassandra says. I can see tears in her eyes, too.

"I still picture her in that green polka-dot dress, walking to the subway for the last time," Jane adds, sounding wistful. "I'd thought about calling her that morning, to check in. But I got busy—I can't even remember with what. I always wonder if maybe that could have changed the course of everything. . . ."

Jane sighs and takes another sip of champagne. I do the same. The only thing filling the silence is the music still playing from the little speaker I've attached to my iPhone, but by now Pink has yielded to Alicia Keys.

"Do you guys want to sit down?" I gesture to my sofa and the chair flanking it.

"Let me just top us off." Cassandra takes my glass and turns her back to me as she reaches for the champagne bottle.

"So, how was *your* week, Shay?" Jane picks up the platter and brings it to the coffee table. "Hopefully less hectic than ours."

Before I can answer, Cassandra turns back around: "Here you go." She stretches a drink toward me and I reflexively take it.

I know immediately this glass isn't the one I had before. This one has the amber ball on the bottom of the stem; I had the emerald-green one.

"Oh, I already drank from that one." I gesture to the glass in Cassandra's other hand.

I expect her to switch with me. But she just smiles. "Who cares?"

Jane raises her glass. "Cheers."

Then they both take a sip. So I do the same.

"Mmm, isn't Dom the best?" Cassandra says.

"Yummy," I agree. The bubbles take up half the glass and tickle my nose. I wonder if all expensive champagnes are so frothy.

Jane flops onto the far end of the couch, and Cassandra takes the chair. Which leaves the spot between them for me. I sit down, feeling my weight sink into the pillows. When I first bought this couch on Craigslist, I thought it was too soft and squishy. But tonight it feels heavenly.

I curl my legs beneath me and take another drink, reflecting on how I've lost some of my connections to my other friends, but now I have Cassandra and Jane. It sounds too corny to say, but I can't help thinking it: The Moore sisters saved me.

We chat for a while about my date with Ted, then I ask about their plans for tonight. As Jane explains they're going to a benefit for a battered-women's shelter, Cassandra fills up our glasses, which are all empty again.

I lean my head back against the couch, feeling more relaxed than I have in months, listening to Jane talk about the charity auction.

"Our friend Beth is a defense attorney—you might have seen her at the memorial service—and she occasionally does pro bono work for the shelter. That's how we got involved."

Beth, I think. I was pretty sure I saw one of their friends at CrossFit. Could it have been her? But it takes too much effort to form the question.

My eyes are so heavy that it's an effort to drag them back open after I blink. My legs and arms feel loose and weighty the way they do after a long run.

"Are you okay?" Cassandra's voice sounds so distant.

"Just a little sleepy," I murmur.

Jane gives a big yawn, and it's contagious: I do the same.

"You've had a long week. Here, why don't you stretch out and take a little catnap before your date? We need to get going anyway." Jane moves over and I uncurl my legs, resting my head on the arm of the couch.

My exhaustion is so overwhelming I'm not even embarrassed. *Yes, a quick nap,* I think. *That's all I need.*

Jane is spreading the throw I keep on the back of my couch over me. "It's kind of cold in here. This will keep you cozy."

Thank you, I try to reply. But all I can do is sluggishly nod.

My mind starts to drift again. I hear Cassandra and Jane move about my apartment as they speak in whispers. They're clearing away the platter and glasses and running water in the kitchen sink.

I'm blissfully cocooned. One of the sisters—I'm not sure which—rests a warm, soft hand on my forehead. It feels nice, almost maternal.

They loved Amanda. Maybe soon they will love me, too.

"Do you want me to turn off the lights and close the blinds?" Cassandra offers.

No, I think, *Ted will be here in a little while.* But I'm not sure if I actually say it. I must not have, though, because the room plunges into shadows. The only source of illumination is the sweet-smelling candle flickering on the coffee table.

My door softly opens and shuts. It's so quiet now.

I jar awake, out of one of those strange half dreams where I feel myself falling.

A woman is standing over me.

I can't see her face; she blends into the shadows, almost like a ghost.

Amanda? I try to cry out, but can only muster a croak. I blink a few times and she's gone.

Did I hallucinate her again, like I did that day outside the subway?

Jane also said she can still picture Amanda walking in her polka-dot dress for the last time.

But Jane wasn't there that day. It was just me and Amanda, listening to the rumble of the incoming train, I think hazily.

There's a tickle in my brain. It keeps pulling me back to the surface of consciousness. It has something to do with Amanda on the day she died.

Adrenaline battles my deep fatigue as I try to recall the piece of information that's eluding me. But my thoughts are too slow and clumsy to compete with the crushing exhaustion that grips me.

I hear a whispered voice: "Enjoy your rest while you can, Shay."

The detail I've been searching for finally floats into my mind just before I descend into a deep, black hole of sleep: *How could Jane know that Amanda was wearing a polka-dot dress when she died?*

CHAPTER FIFTY

VALERIE

VALERIE STANDS WATCHING OVER SHAY.

Shay's eyelids flutter, as if she senses a new presence in the apartment.

Valerie remains immobile, watching the candlelight flicker across Shay's face.

She whispers, "Enjoy your rest while you can, Shay."

Shay gives a soft sigh as her body surrenders to sleep.

The drug used on Shay—a double dose of the Ambien that Cassandra took from Shay's medicine cabinet just a few days ago and ground up before adding to Shay's glass of champagne—is certainly effective.

Cassandra and Jane are now in a taxi speeding away from the apartment, their books in hand, en route to the charity auction. Before they left, they washed and dried and put away the glasses and platter Shay so thoughtfully set out. Valerie passed them in the hallway after they buzzed her in; their eyes met but they didn't speak a single word.

Valerie carries a nondescript brown paper bag with supplies of her own. She enters the tiny bathroom and bends down to peek beneath the sink.

She sees the manila envelope, exactly where Cassandra told her it would be. She pulls it out with her gloved hand and checks the contents.

Valerie stares down at James's dried blood, remembering how he'd looked splayed on that bench in Central Park. It had taken so much work—countless hours of thought and planning and strategizing—to get James alone and vulnerable so that he could be punished.

Now Valerie wonders how Shay located the envelope containing evidence from the night James was finally punished, when Cassandra and Jane had carefully sifted through the contents of Amanda's apartment immediately after her death, then again several days later.

Valerie feels a bit of grudging respect for Amanda, who must have found a cunning hiding place.

Shay, however, left the envelope out almost in plain sight.

It's her own fault, Valerie thinks. Shay—so annoyingly tenacious—brought all of this on herself.

Valerie checks her phone. By now, Cassandra and Jane are mingling at the crowded charity auction. Establishing alibis.

Valerie exits the bathroom, passing Shay's inert form, and places the scalpel and towel on Shay's floor, near the threshold of the door. From the brown bag she carried into the apartment she removes the wheat-colored sundress Amanda wore on the night she led James into Central Park. She leaves two other items she brought on the floor beside the dress: James's wallet and watch.

Then she takes a hard look around the apartment, making certain no detail has been overlooked. She sees Shay's leather jacket hanging over a chair, along with the floral scarf that exactly matches one Amanda used to wear. Inside Shay's new purse are the sunglasses that are an exact replica of Amanda's favorite pair.

Shay, Valerie thinks, has no idea what's in store for her.

Valerie steps through the door, leaving it ajar, and disappears into the hallway, her head ducked low.

She exits the building and walks unhurriedly down the street. Smiling at the shopkeeper sweeping the sidewalk as he closes up for the night. Inhaling the crisp late-fall air. Feeling better than she has in a long, long time.

PART
THREE

CHAPTER FIFTY-ONE

SHAY

Ambien is one of the most popular sleep aids in the United States. Twice as many women as men use this prescription drug; 77 percent of those who take Ambien do so incorrectly.
—Data Book, page 65

I AM NOT ALONE.

A male voice is calling my name: *Shay Miller!*

I open my mouth to answer but I can only make a croaking sound. My tongue is thick and fuzzy feeling. A horrible taste fills my mouth.

I lift my groggy head from the end of the couch. Everything is blurry, and my eyes feel painfully dry. I blink a few times, until my living room comes into focus. I must have fallen asleep with my contact lenses in.

For a moment I think the voice belongs to Sean. Then I remember I'm not in my old apartment.

I try to sit up, but a wave of dizziness forces me back down. My blinds are closed but bright light seeps through the cracks between the slats. It must be morning.

What happened last night?

"Shay Miller!" The man's voice is more insistent now.

I look toward my doorway and see two uniformed police officers. One has his hand on his gun holster.

I slowly push myself to a sitting position. "What's going on?" My voice sounds raspy.

"Why don't you tell us?" says the officer with his hand on his gun. He has dark, flinty eyes and a lined face.

I'm still in my jeans and blue blouse. The last thing I clearly remember is Cassandra popping the cork on a bottle of champagne.

I've never blacked out from drinking too much, not even in college. But my head is splitting, and last night is a jagged hole in my memory.

"I was with my friends—I must have fallen asleep."

Then I jerk back.

The bloody scalpel and towel that I'd hidden under my sink are splayed across my living room floor. So is a man's wallet and a gold watch I don't recognize.

A crumpled tan sundress with a rust-colored stain on the hem is next to my coffee table. I've never seen it before.

The officers are staring at me intently, not coming any closer.

"Wh-what is all this?" I stutter.

My body starts to shake. I wrap my arms around myself and rock back and forth.

"Take a deep breath," says the younger officer, the one who isn't touching his gun. "We're just here to try to figure out what's going on."

How did someone get into my apartment and put all this stuff around me?

I had plans to go out with Ted last night. He was coming to my lobby to pick me up. Is it possible I let him in? Could he have done all this?

I look at the wallet and watch again. "I was supposed to have a date. Are these things his?"

"Who was your date with?" the older officer, the one with the harder face, asks.

"This guy named Ted." I realize I don't even know his last name. "I met him online."

The vanilla-bourbon candle on the coffee table is almost completely burned out; the air smells cloyingly sweet. My stomach heaves. "Could I please get some water?"

Then I hear the creak of a footstep in the hallway.

A moment later, a tall, lean woman with a close-cropped Afro appears behind the two officers.

She scans the room, her gaze roving over the scalpel and towel and dress.

Then her eyes fix on me. They widen with shock.

"Shay?" Detective Williams asks.

An hour later, I'm in one of the small blue rooms at the Seventeenth Precinct that I passed not long ago when I came here to give the necklace to Detective Williams.

I can't stop shivering, even though Detective Williams gave me a blanket and brought me a cup of hot coffee.

"Why don't we start at the beginning." She pulls out the chair opposite me. The metal feet scrape across the linoleum floor. "Would you mind if I recorded this?" She gestures to the camera in the corner.

"I guess that's okay." I pull the thin black blanket tighter around me.

Detective Williams must have been stunned to see me in Amanda's old apartment—looking a lot like Amanda. I'm still not entirely clear why the police showed up, but from what I can gather, a neighbor who noticed my open door and saw the bloody towel near the threshold dialed 911.

My phone is tucked in my bag, and this room has no clock. I feel completely disoriented.

"Is it Saturday?" I blurt.

Detective Williams nods. "Yes."

At least I haven't lost a bigger chunk of time.

She is staring at me with that impassive expression, the one that makes me think she can handle hearing anything. So I finally confess to her, even revealing how I went to Amanda's mother's house and retrieved Jane's necklace.

Detective Williams takes notes while I talk. When I mention my makeover, her pen pauses on the page and her gaze rises to roam over my face. She seems to be scrutinizing everything from where I part my hair to the cleft in my chin.

I have no idea what she's thinking.

I take another sip of coffee. It's lukewarm by now, but at least the caffeine is clearing away the fuzziness from my brain. The sensation reminds me of how I felt when I took Ambien—I was so sluggish the morning after.

Is it possible that I took Ambien last night?

Hallucinations. Lack of memory. Altered consciousness. And women are more susceptible to the effects. All of this is in my Data Book.

I've read cases of rare instances of people sleep-driving, cooking meals, and even having sex with no memory of these activities.

Did I let Ted in without knowing it? Or did I open my door to someone else?

I recoil from the thought. It seems impossible.

More flashes from the evening come to me, like shards of a dream: Cassandra topping off my glass. Jane tucking the blanket around me. The soft sound of a door shutting.

"Do you want to talk to my friends?"

Detective Williams tucks her pen into the spiral at the top of her pad. She regards me steadily for a long moment. "You mean Amanda Evinger's friends?"

My voice is shaking. "They might know more about what happened."

Instead of responding, she stands up. "I'm going to grab another coffee. Need anything?"

I shake my head.

She leaves, closing the door behind her.

Maybe she doesn't intend to call Cassandra and Jane, but that doesn't mean I can't. I grab my phone from my purse. I dial Cassandra first, then Jane. Neither answers so I leave them both messages: "Please call me back as soon as possible. It's an emergency."

Then I text Ted with the same message.

But none of them immediately replies.

I try to think about what to do next. I'm tempted to phone my mom, but then I imagine Barry answering, and I decide against it.

I look around the spare, hard-edged room. Nothing is in here other than the table, metal chairs, the camera in the corner, and a frosted pane of glass on one wall. I wonder if it's one of those mirrors that the police use when a suspect is being questioned.

I press my fingers to my temples, trying to piece together fragments of memories: Cassandra in her burgundy dress . . . Jane hugging me . . . the smell of her sweet perfume . . . delicious, foamy champagne . . .

My head spins.

Detective Williams has been gone a long time. The waiting is torture.

I finally walk to the door, the blanket still wrapped around my shoulders, and reach for the knob. I'll just stick out my head and see if I can spot her.

I pull but the door refuses to budge. I'm locked in.

I turn around, staring at the four walls. Are other police officers watching me right now?

My vision swims. My breath feels stuck in my throat.

I can't succumb to a panic attack.

Am I locked in this room because Detective Williams wanted to give me privacy?

Or am I a suspect for a crime I don't even know about?

CHAPTER FIFTY-TWO

AMANDA

Two months ago

AMANDA HAD PLANNED TO hurry to a restaurant right after leaving James on the bench in Central Park. She'd intended to sit as close to the center of the room as possible and ask the waiter about the night's specials and pay with a credit card. She'd wanted to be memorable.

Instead, she burst through her apartment door, stripped off her tan dress and left it crumpled on the floor of her bathroom next to her purse, and turned on the shower.

She stood under the hot spray, compulsively washing herself, attempting to dig the dried blood out from under her fingernails.

And struggling to push the images out of her mind: James's body, convulsing on the bench. Blood trickling down his face from the letter *R* that had been carved above his right eye. His lips swelling. His pale skin gleaming with sweat. And Stacey staring as Valerie stood over him, holding the bloody scalpel in her gloved hand.

Amanda shivered despite the hot water beating down on her. She couldn't get warm.

Call 911! Amanda had cried. *He's having a reaction to the medication!*

Valerie had merely bent over him again, wiping away the blood on his face with a small blue towel. She was clearing her canvas so she could finish carving the word into his forehead, the one that would tell the world what James had done to Daphne.

Stop! He could die! Amanda had cried.

Now she wrapped her arms around herself, shaking. She remembered the Nightingale Pledge she'd recited at her graduation from nursing school: *I solemnly pledge . . . to practice my profession faithfully. . . . I . . . will not take or knowingly administer any harmful drug. . . .*

They were supposed to punish James, not kill him.

She could hear a ringing over the noise of the shower. The burner phone the Moore sisters had given her was still in her purse, next to the bloody towel. Wrapped in the towel was the scalpel.

Amanda stared straight ahead, the water blurring her vision.

"Did he show Daphne any mercy?" Valerie had asked, finishing the *R*.

"Val, he's foaming at the mouth," Stacey had said.

James's movements had begun to slow down as his body gave up the fight.

From the pledge Amanda had recited as she'd stood onstage at her graduation, her posture straight and proud, and the sun brightly shining overhead: *I will dedicate myself to devoted service to human welfare.*

Amanda had tried to push Valerie aside. If James's airway was closing, it would be too late to save him by the time an ambulance arrived. But there was one chance: She'd spotted the pen in James's breast pocket, the one he'd used to sign the check at the restaurant. She'd seen doctors perform emergency tracheostomies before. She could cut a hole into his trachea with the scalpel, then use the tube of the pen to keep air flowing through his swollen throat.

"Give me the scalpel," she ordered.

Valerie ignored her and started on the downward slash of the second letter, *A*.

Cassandra and Jane, who had been serving as lookouts, came running over.

"Someone's coming. We've got to get out of here." Cassandra grabbed Valerie's arm, causing Valerie to drop the scalpel.

Amanda picked it up. "I have to help him!"

James's body gave a final shudder, then stopped moving.

"I think he's dead," Stacey said.

Cassandra didn't hesitate. "It needs to look like a robbery."

"With that letter on his face?" Still, Valerie reached into James's back pocket and slid out his wallet. Cassandra unclasped his watch.

Then Jane lifted a finger to her lips.

On the other side of the sprawling oak tree, a dog barked.

"We need to go, *now*," Cassandra whispered.

Amanda touched two fingers to James's neck. His pulse had vanished.

"No," she whispered.

She'd seen death many times in the hospital before; she'd fought it with her hands and instruments and skills. It was never easy to lose. But this was different.

She'd never before been death's accomplice.

She reached for the towel Valerie had left on his chest and wrapped the scalpel in it, then stuck it in her bag as Stacey grabbed her elbow, roughly pulling her away. "C'mon, Amanda. Move!"

The five women hurried toward the edge of the park. Ahead were the bright lights of headlights and restaurants and buildings. "Separate now," Cassandra directed them. Her expression was impassive under the glow of the streetlight. Her voice was steady and even. "Meet at my place."

Amanda watched as the others split in different directions—Cassandra and Jane hailing a cab, Valerie melting into the shadows along the edge of the park, and Stacey jamming her hands into the pockets of her jeans and heading toward the subway.

Amanda stood there, alone.

Then she began to run. But not toward Cassandra's apartment.

She ran home.

CHAPTER FIFTY-THREE

SHAY

About 50 percent of Americans say they rely on their instincts to help them determine what feels truthful and what doesn't. One in seven say they strongly trust their gut to make decisions, while one in ten rarely do.
—Data Book, page 66

WHEN DETECTIVE WILLIAMS FINALLY comes back into the room, she apologizes for the door being locked. "It automatically bolts when it shuts. You're free to go anytime you like."

"Oh, okay." I feel my sense of claustrophobia recede. "Do you have any update on what happened last night? Whose stuff is in my apartment?"

"We don't have any information about that right now."

But the wallet must have had something in it to indicate who it belonged to—a driver's license or credit card. Before I ask about that, though, Detective Williams sits down and leans forward, her forearms resting on the table.

Her tone doesn't change when she asks me her next question. But I feel a shift in the air, as if some sort of switch has been flipped.

"Where were you on the night of Thursday, August fifteenth, Shay?"

I blink and shake my head slightly. That was months ago.

"I don't know offhand," I whisper. I look down at my phone, which is on the table now. "Can I check my calendar?"

"That would be great, if you don't mind."

I pull it up. *Temp, dentist, 6-mile run.*

"I temped all day, then I had my teeth cleaned. I went for a long run that night. See?"

I tilt my phone in her direction and Detective Williams nods. But she's not glancing at my screen. She's staring at me.

The silence feels oppressive.

"Sorry it's not more exciting," I say, trying to ease the tension.

She doesn't smile. It's almost like she's waiting for me to tell her more.

"What's going on?"

"That's all for now," Detective Williams finally says. She stands up, and I do the same.

She leads me back to the front door. "I'll be in touch," she says as I step out.

I stand on the busy street, feeling disoriented. The last thing I want is to be by myself.

So I phone Sean. The moment I hear his warm, familiar voice— "Hey, Shay!"—I burst into ragged sobs.

I'm so grateful that for once Jody isn't around. She has an organizing job that's supposed to last all afternoon.

It's just me and Sean on his new couch—the one he got to replace the sofa I took away—with big glasses of water in front of us. I'm still feeling dehydrated, as I often do after taking Ambien. So maybe I did swallow a pill at some point last night.

We've been talking for a long time. Sean was so stunned by what had happened that I had to tell him the whole story twice.

It still doesn't feel real to me, either.

"So how did you leave things with the detective?"

I'm hunched over, with my legs pulled up and my arms wrapped around my knees. "She asked if I had any plans to travel out of the city, and I said no. She obviously knows where I live. I'm not sure I can go back to my apartment. I mean, what if the person who left all that stuff comes back?"

I can't suppress a shudder.

"So you'll stay here. Like old times." Then Sean smiles, and I can tell he's trying to get me to do the same: "Except you should know that Jody has turned your room into an office."

Of course she has, I think. When I look up again, Sean is staring at me with concern in his eyes. "Hey, have you eaten today?"

I shake my head. When I went into the bathroom at the police station, I'd recoiled at my reflection: Mascara was smeared under my eyes, and my hair was disheveled. I'd dampened a paper towel and run it under my eyes and splashed cold water on my face before trying to tame my hair. I'd taken out my contacts and put on glasses, thankful I'd been carrying them in my purse and that I'd thought to grab it before Detective Williams had driven me to the station.

"I'm not hungry."

"Come on." He gives me a little tap on the knee. "You've gotta stay nourished. How about I make you one of your favorite banana smoothies?"

I follow him the few steps into the kitchen.

"Do you want to try your friends again?"

I look down at my phone. Ted still hasn't replied to my text. And neither Cassandra nor Jane has returned my calls. So I text the Moore sisters again: *Please call me as soon as you can. Something awful has happened.*

I wait a moment, staring at my screen, but I don't see the three dots that would indicate one of them is typing a reply. "They're probably with a client or something."

Sean pulls a banana out of the fruit basket and begins slicing it up. "They're in PR, right?"

"Yeah." I can tell he's trying to get my mind off the past few hours, to give me an oasis of calm, but I can't make small talk.

He reaches for the almond butter in the cabinet and continues to chat, telling me about the new student he's tutoring. "So this helicopter mom called me the other day and said her son got a 1580 on the SAT. She wants me to help him get to a perfect 1600." Sean pulls vanilla extract from the spice drawer. I notice the drawers are now lined with brightly striped contact paper.

"Oh, wow," I say listlessly.

He puts his hand on my shoulder. "Should I stop talking?"

I shake my head rapidly. My thoughts are too unnerving in the silence.

"More talk coming up right after this intermission." The loud grinding noise of the blender startles me and I flinch. Sean notices and turns it off. "Sorry."

He pours the smoothies into two glasses and adds reusable metal straws. "Jody got us these. They're much better for the environment."

I flash to Cassandra handing me my glass of champagne last night, and the feel of a soft hand on my forehead. I suppress a shudder.

"Come on, have a sip," Sean urges me.

He takes a long drink and I do the same. The cool liquid feels good against my throat, but I don't know if I can manage to drink any more.

"What did I forget? They don't taste exactly like the one you always make."

"The cinnamon."

My phone buzzes in my jeans pocket. It's a text from my mom: *Sweetie! Mashed or sweet potatoes for Thanksgiving? Or both?*

I can't believe the world is still spinning on its usual axis—that people are thinking about holiday meals and reading the Saturday paper and jogging in Central Park.

"Was that from your friends?"

I shake my head.

"I remember they liked your smoothies, too." He takes another sip.

I frown. "Why do you say that?"

"That night when we met for a beer and you called them about the apartment, they mentioned it." He walks over to the couch and pats the cushion. "C'mon, you look a little pale."

I slowly walk over and sink onto it. My legs suddenly feel like they can't hold me up.

I never made a smoothie for Cassandra or Jane. I have no recollection of ever bringing up the subject.

"Shay?"

"Can you remember exactly what they said?"

He looks up and to the left—which a lot of people do when they're trying to retrieve a memory. I find myself holding my breath.

"One of them—I'm not sure which—told you she could picture you in your new kitchen, making your famous smoothie."

My skin prickles.

He looks at me. "Are you okay?"

"How did the Moore sisters know about the smoothies I make?" I whisper.

As soon as I say this out loud, another thought explodes into my brain. It's an echo of the question I hazily formed last night when I was lying on the couch: *How did Jane know Amanda was wearing a polka-dot dress on the day she died?*

There's no simple explanation. Jane had said she was busy at work; she'd meant to call Amanda, but she didn't. And although *I* knew what Amanda was wearing, I'd never discussed her outfit with them. I'm certain I hadn't mentioned the green polka-dot dress when I encountered the Moore sisters at the Thirty-third Street subway station on the day I saw an Amanda look-alike. I remember thinking it would make me sound crazy if I included that detail.

"Shay?" Sean is frowning. "What's going on?"

Another memory shard: Jane telling me to lie down on the couch and sleep. The exhaustion had crashed into me so suddenly last night I couldn't fight it. Even on the nights when I'd taken Ambien, it had never hit me so hard or fast.

"I have to call Cassandra and Jane again." This time I dial Jane first. My call goes directly to voice mail. "Jane, please, I need your help." My voice is shaking.

Next I phone Cassandra. When I finally hear her throaty voice come over the line, I blurt, "Cassandra, thank goodness I reached you. It's Shay. Something—"

She cuts me off, her tone so firm and cold I physically recoil. "Shay. I'm telling you for the last time, stop calling me and Jane. Stop following us. You need professional help. There's something seriously wrong with you."

Then she hangs up.

I hold the phone to my ear, shocked into immobility. It's hard to breathe.

Why would Cassandra say those things to me? Could I have done something awful last night—something I don't remember? I must have, for her to say those harsh words.

Tears fill my eyes as I reflexively start to call her back, to beg for her forgiveness.

"What did she say?" Sean asks.

"Wait a second," I whisper. My head is beginning to throb painfully again.

Nothing about the last eighteen hours makes any sense.

Cassandra sounds like she almost hates me now. She told me to stop pestering her and Jane.

But they're the ones who came to my apartment last night and brought champagne. Cassandra said she wished she could cancel their plans and hang out with me.

The same eerie, dreamlike sense I experienced on the day I followed the woman who looked like Amanda to the subway floods over me.

How could they have turned on me so quickly?

My stomach contracts and I run to the bathroom. I dry-heave into the toilet, then stand up and turn on the sink tap with shaking hands. I run cold water over my wrists and rinse out my mouth.

I stare at my reflection.

I don't look like the old me, or the new one either. The expression in my eyes belongs to a stranger.

Amanda's eyes looked empty on the day I saw her—as if she had nothing left. No joy, no hope, no one to care about her.

But the Moore sisters claimed to have loved her.

They'd acted like they cared about me, too—at least until a few minutes ago, when Cassandra's words ripped through me.

Everything is whirling out of control.

Think, I order myself frantically. I try to remember anything I could have said to Cassandra and Jane that they might have misconstrued, which could explain their animosity.

But instead, my mind spins back in time, to when I saw the Amanda look-alike shortly after Amanda's suicide. The Moore sisters just happened to be passing by that subway station as I clung to the post, trembling and hyperventilating. Feeling as terrified and unhinged as I do right now.

It had seemed like a miracle: What are the chances they'd be in that precise location at that exact time? And that they'd recognize me in an umbrella-carrying crowd, with my hair plastered over my face, after one relatively brief encounter? And that their meeting would be canceled, giving them a free hour to spend with me?

Almost infinitesimal.

Once I tried to look up how many people are in New York City during the daytime, when commuters flood in. The numbers are hard to verify, but one estimate put it at 175,000 people per square mile in Manhattan. And there are 472 subway stations in the city.

My breath comes more quickly as I grip the hard, cold edges of the sink.

Cassandra told me to stop following them. But they're the ones who showed up against all odds.

The Moore sisters said the Amanda look-alike didn't exist. But now they've turned me into one.

Nothing is adding up.

CHAPTER FIFTY-FOUR

AMANDA

Two months ago

AMANDA, CALL ME!

Amanda, are you okay?

Every few hours, her cell phone erupted with calls and texts from the other women.

Amanda, please pick up! We're worried about you!

She couldn't stop seeing James thrashing on the park bench as the life drained out of him.

Amanda, I'm right around the corner—can I pop by?

That text from Beth finally made her pick up the phone and dial Beth's number. Maybe Beth—the smart, warm lawyer—was having regrets, too.

"Hey, what's going on? Why aren't you talking to any of us?"

"I'm freaking out," Amanda whispered. Her voice was hoarse; it was now Saturday morning and she hadn't spoken to anyone in the thirty-six hours since James had died.

"Look, I know things didn't go exactly how we planned. But we have to stick together."

"We killed him, Beth." Amanda's voice trembled.

She could hear Beth slowly exhale. "We didn't mean to." Beth's tone shifted from friendly to authoritative. "And you know what he did to Daphne. He was evil."

"So no one else is having regrets?"

"It's too late for that."

Beth wasn't an ally; Beth wanted to get her in line.

"Why don't we get together and talk about it. We can come over. All of us."

Before, it had always been the seven of them aligned. But now it would be her against the other six women.

Amanda imagined them crowded into her small living room: Jane rubbing her back, Stacey a bit apart from the others with her arms crossed and her jaw tight, Cassandra leaning in close, Daphne and Beth adding their voices to the others—their words blending and overlapping and pressing in on Amanda as they all tried to stamp out what they'd consider her disloyalty. And Valerie, staring at her with flat brown eyes.

"I'm not feeling well," Amanda replied.

Amanda could hear Cassandra in the background, telling Beth, "Let me talk to her. We need to know what she did with the scalpel."

Amanda hung up and turned off her phone.

Sometime later—maybe an hour, maybe three—her buzzer sounded.

She flinched; now they were in her lobby.

She crept across the floor in her socks as quietly as possible, wincing when a board creaked, even though she knew they couldn't hear anything from two floors down. She slipped into the alcove and climbed into her bed, pulling up her rumpled sheets.

The buzzer sounded again. This time the loud, insistent noise lasted much longer. She covered her ears with her hands, but she could still hear it.

She lay there, her eyes squeezed shut, until finally the sound died away.

When she turned her phone back on late that night, it showed twenty-four missed calls.

The next day, a Sunday, Amanda was scheduled to work. She rose from bed feeling hollow eyed. She hadn't slept much or eaten anything other than a banana and a slice of toast.

She walked to her closet, her body aching, as if she really were ill. She reached over her laundry bin, where her tan sundress with rust-colored, streaky stains was crumpled on the bottom. She pulled out her Crocs and pink scrubs as her vow from the Nightingale Pledge ran through her mind again: *I will dedicate myself to devoted service to human welfare.*

She found concealer in the bathroom and patted it on the purple shadows beneath her eyes. In the cabinet under the sink, she'd hidden the scalpel and towel. She couldn't bear to look at the reminders of what they'd done. But she still felt the presence of the objects.

If she gave the scalpel to the other women, would they let her walk away?

No, Amanda thought. *They never would.*

The city felt different now—hot and angry. Pedestrians jostled her on the sidewalk; a swinging briefcase caught her painfully on the hip. The sun beat down on her relentlessly. She stepped into a crosswalk and a taxi whipped around the corner against the light, blaring its horn. She arrived at work and forced herself to smile at the hospital security guard as she lifted her hand to the wall panel to gain access to the ER.

Could he tell how different she was?

For the first hour or so she checked vitals and answered call buttons and helped treat a patient with pneumonia. But when she went to retrieve antibiotics from the cabinet in the medicine room, she froze, staring at the bottles of morphine and seeing herself swirl the liquid into James's drink.

"Amanda?"

Gina was standing in the open doorway to the medicine room. Amanda didn't know how long she'd been there.

"The IV for room five," Gina said. "You didn't change it."

"Oh, no, I—"

"I already got it," Gina said crisply. She frowned. "You okay?"

Amanda nodded. "Sorry." She hurried out of the room. Amanda felt Gina's eyes on her several more times during the day; she'd endangered a patient. If Gina hadn't changed the IV, the elderly stroke victim could have become dangerously dehydrated.

Amanda's shift seemed to stretch twice as long as usual. When she finally arrived home, she couldn't stop shaking.

The next day was worse.

She'd barely been at work for a half hour when someone handed her a message: "Hey, a call just came in for you. She wouldn't leave her name."

Amanda stared at the words on the little pink slip of paper: *Glad you're feeling better. We'll see you tonight!*

Her knees buckled.

She managed to get through most of her shift. But shortly before it ended, she was rushing to assist a doctor treating a gunshot victim when she lost her footing—her lack of sleep and food combined with her stress making her clumsy—and she fell against the patient, knocking out the chest tube that was helping his lungs expand properly.

The doctor swore, plugging the hole with his hands.

Amanda stared at the red blood covering the doctor's latex gloves. She couldn't breathe. She couldn't even move for a moment.

"Damn it, Amanda!" the doctor shouted. "Get a crash team!"

Gina ran into the room as Amanda backed away from the gurney.

Instead of helping her patients, she was now a danger to them.

"I have to go," she blurted to Gina.

Gina didn't answer; all her focus was on the young man whose chest had been torn apart by a bullet.

Amanda ran down the long hallway, her Crocs squeaking against the linoleum, and exited the building. She stumbled onto the sidewalk, her breathing ragged.

Then she saw a woman standing directly across the street, her sleek dark hair shining in the sunlight.

No. Amanda's pulse skyrocketed. She spun around and hurried back inside.

She pulled her phone out of the pocket of her scrubs, her fingers trembling, and ordered an Uber. She stood next to the security guard until the vehicle pulled into the circular ER driveway. She ran out and leaped into the car's backseat. "Hurry, please!" she cried.

When the Uber pulled up in front of her apartment building eight minutes later, her keys were already out. She raced up the steps and burst through her door, double-locking it and stretching out the chain to further secure it.

Her buzzer sounded minutes later.

The next few days bled together. She called in sick to work on the first day, then turned off her phone.

When she turned it back on, in addition to all the missed calls and messages from the group, there was one from Gina: "Amanda, we need to talk. Call me back."

But what could she tell Gina?

Sleep was impossible now; the other women were relentless. Sometimes she heard gentle knocking on her door. Once, in the middle of the night, a key scraped in her lock. While she stared, her body rigid, her door swung open until the chain stretched to its limit.

How did they get a key?

Sometimes the voice that floated through the door crack was kind and cajoling: "Let's talk this through. Sweetie, we're trying to help you. C'mon, unlatch the door."

Other times it was stern: "You need to snap out of this. We'll be fine if we stick together, like we promised to do. James would've hurt other women. You saved them, just like you save patients in the hospital. You've saved so many women you've never even met, Amanda. Open the door."

The worst were the hisses that seemed to curl through her mind like tendrils of smoke: "*You* were the one who stole the medicine. *You* drugged him. *You're* the one who will be blamed for all of this. If you don't start to cooperate, you'll go to jail for life!"

Was it real, or were the voices only in her head? she began to wonder.

She knew what the other women in the group were capable of, and the punishments they had inflicted, even against people they'd never met—like the parents who'd never bothered to visit their teenaged son as he lay in a medically induced coma after they threw him out of their house because he was gay. The women had waited for months, biding their time until late on a Saturday night after the lights in the parents' house on Long Island were turned off. Then they uncoiled the garden hose in the front yard. They slipped it through the mail slot and twisted the metal knob to turn it on. Thousands of gallons of water pumped into the main level while the parents slept—saturating the wood floors, seeping through rugs, leaking into the basement, and damaging the home's structure.

"Let's see how *they* like being homeless," Valerie had whispered to the others as they'd crept away from the house.

And slipping a bit of syrup of ipecac into the drink of the ex-husband who'd left Beth when she was diagnosed with cancer wasn't enough of a punishment for him, the group decided, even though they'd enjoyed viewing the footage Stacey had recorded of his disastrous event. He'd rushed off the stage just minutes into his poetry reading—but not quickly enough to make it to the bathroom. They'd also created a GIF of him throwing up on the café floor and uploaded it to YouTube, linked to his name, so it could live on in perpetuity.

"That GIF will show up anytime his name is googled," Cassandra had said.

And they'd gone after the abusive mother who'd lived next door to Stacey, first bribing neighbors to repeatedly call social services on behalf of the little girl. But that was justice, not the revenge they craved. So next they broke into her apartment and planted enough drugs to ensure that even the best lawyer wouldn't be able to spare her a prison sentence.

Jane made the anonymous call to the police.

Amanda had only known the Moore sisters for less than a year. Somehow it seemed as if she'd been swept up into their orbit for much longer. She'd been dazzled by their charisma, their warmth, the place in the close-knit group they'd opened up to her.

She hadn't realized how lonely she'd been before the other women had embraced her, filling the void she'd carried around since childhood.

But she wasn't truly one of them, after all.

They must know it now, too.

CHAPTER FIFTY-FIVE

SHAY

Common law enforcement misconceptions:
- *You can explain your way out of trouble.*
- *If you cooperate with the police, you won't be charged.*
- *You're safe if an officer didn't read you your Miranda rights.*

　　　　　　　　　　　　　—Data Book, page 67

SEAN HAD AN AFTERNOON consulting gig that he offered to cancel, but I told him to go ahead.

I could tell he was still worried about me, but I convinced him I wanted to take a long, hot shower and a nap.

He got me situated in my old room—the new office—pulling out the futon and setting out a pillow and set of sheets. He also gave me one of his hoodies and a toothbrush still in its plastic packaging.

"Jody will be home soon," he said just before he left. "I told her you'd be staying the night."

After I shower, I put back on my jeans and Sean's sweatshirt. I close my eyes briefly as I inhale his scent. Then I head into the study.

Jody has completely transformed the space. It's almost unrecognizable. One wall is painted a pale yellow, and a trio of black-and-white prints hang over the narrow desk.

I sit on the edge of the futon and open my Data Book, rereading all the dangling threads I can remember since meeting the Moore sisters.

They knew Amanda and I didn't meet through a veterinarian. They knew what Amanda was wearing on the day she died even though they weren't there. They appeared right after I spotted the woman in the polka-dot dress going into the subway, but they said she didn't exist. They made me over to resemble Amanda. They encouraged me to move into Amanda's apartment. They sent me to shop at Daphne's boutique, but they never told her I'd be coming. I fell into a strange, hard sleep after they came over and gave me a glass of champagne— which they switched with a different glass.

I add a few more lines: *The Moore sisters left my apartment—the door only needed to be pulled closed to automatically lock, just like the one in the police station—and I woke up the next morning with all those strange things on my floor. And now they've abruptly turned on me. . . .*

I hear the front door of the apartment open and my heart leaps into my throat. Then Jody calls out, "Hello?"

Before I can get up to greet her, she appears in the doorway.

I'm shocked when she hurries over and hugs me tightly. "You poor thing."

"Thanks," I murmur. Her words bring me close to tears again.

"Can I get you anything? Tea? Or something stronger?"

"No, I'm okay. Thanks for letting me stay here tonight."

Jody picks up my blue shirt, which I've left at the foot of the futon next to the set of sheets, and smooths it out before folding it into a perfect square.

"So what happened, exactly? Sean told me a little, but . . ."

I start to recount the story again, but a truncated version of the one I've relayed to Sean.

"Here, let me make up the bed for you," Jody interrupts.

I stand and walk over to the desk, to set down my Data Book so I can help her stretch the sheets across the futon.

Then I see it.

An unusual vase: an upside-down hand with a hollow wrist where the flower stems go, only Jody has filled it with pens and pencils.

I recognize this vase. I saw it when I house-sat for Cassandra and Jane's friend.

I blink hard, unsure if it's another apparition. Then I reach for it, feeling the cool china in my hand. It's real.

I spin around, still holding it: "Where did you get this?" I blurt.

Jody pauses in fluffing my pillow. "It's fun, right? A client of mine had one in her kitchen and I loved it, so I found it online. It's perfect for the room, isn't it?"

That vase. It's another coincidence. There have been too many lately surrounding my relationship with the Moore sisters.

"What was the client's name?" My throat is tight, making my voice sound a little strangled.

"Uh, Deena . . ." Jody frowns. "I can't remember her last name. She paid in cash. That part I do recall."

I never got the name of the woman I house-sat for. But I remember her address.

When I recite it, Jody pulls out her phone. "That sounds kind of familiar. . . ." She scrolls through her calendar. "Hang on, I've got it, I just need to find the day. . . . It was a couple of weeks ago."

She looks at me, her expression startled.

My legs give way and I collapse onto the edge of the futon.

"How did you know?" Jody asks.

I can't sleep that night. I lie awake for hours, staring at the ceiling, going over everything in my head until I'm dizzy. I finally doze off around dawn, but my rest is fitful.

I get up as quietly as possible, since Sean and Jody's door is still shut, then dress in Sean's hoodie and my jeans again. I don't want to carry the bag the Moore sisters gave me, so I tuck my cell phone and small folding wallet into the big front pocket of the hoodie. I also put my sunglasses on top of my head.

I leave the apartment at around eight-thirty on Sunday morning— the same day of the week and time as I did when this all started, only a few months ago.

Back then it was hot and muggy. Now it's bright and chilly. But I'm so churned up inside I don't even feel the bite of the wind against my face or my lack of a coat.

New puzzle pieces keep spinning around in my head. Jody was in the apartment on East Twelfth Street less than a week before Cassandra and Jane asked me to stay there. Yesterday, I peppered Jody with questions about Deena, the client who needed her closet reorganized. But Jody didn't know a lot; they'd only spent a couple of hours together. She did say the woman looked to be in her late thirties, was recently divorced, and had wanted to chat over a glass of wine.

"I never drink on the job, but I didn't want to offend a client," Jody had explained.

I finally got out of her that Deena had asked a lot of personal questions—some about Jody's relationship with Sean, and even about Sean's roommate. Me.

Jody had shied away when I'd pressed her to explain specifically what they'd discussed.

"I can't really remember." Jody avoided my eyes. "She might have asked what you were like . . . um, that was about it."

"What did you say?" I'd asked urgently. I didn't care about Jody's opinion of me, but I needed to know what information she'd put out there.

"I said you were nice!" Jody replied somewhat indignantly.

No matter how hard I tried, she wouldn't reveal more.

I round a corner, approaching my destination. I'm so agitated I'm walking at a much faster rate than usual. The city is awakening now. A bike messenger yells at a cabbie for cutting him off, and a mom urges along her lagging son, warning he'll be late for soccer practice. A bus pulls up at a stop next to me, exhaling loudly, and a weary-looking woman climbs aboard.

I know this neighborhood pretty well: I've bought bananas and strawberries from the fruit vendor on the corner I just passed. Cassandra and Jane's friend Anne met me on that same corner, too, before Anne helped me work through my subway phobia.

I realize the data points don't look good for me, even though no one arrested me and Detective Williams said I was free to go at any time. I need one more piece of information, and it might also help convince Detective Williams that I've unwittingly gotten wrapped up in something ominous.

I finally reach my destination, the flower shop.

I wait outside, shivering, until the shopkeeper unlocks the door.

What I'm about to do feels risky. Maybe I should be staying put at Sean's.

But playing it safe feels like the most dangerous thing I could do. I can't just wait for the next awful thing to happen.

"Are you searching for anything special?" the florist asks.

"Just a simple bouquet. It's a gift."

"We've got several arrangements on display around the store, or I could put something together for you."

I try to figure out what would be the cheapest option.

"Could I have a half dozen chrysanthemums?" I point to the yellow blooms in a bucket in a refrigerated case.

"Sure." She opens the door and selects the stems. Then she wraps them in cellophane and ties it all up with a ribbon. "That'll be twenty-four dollars."

I reach into my pocket and pull out my thin, folding wallet. I pay in cash.

Then I walk to the East Twelfth Street apartment, yet another nexus between me and the Moore sisters.

When I'm almost there, I stop and pull my hood over my hair and put on my sunglasses. Then I stride into the building.

"Hey there," I say to the doorman. "Delivery for . . ." I lay the flowers on the lobby counter and squint at my phone. "I can't see her name, but it's apartment 6C."

"Valerie Ricci. You can take it up in the service elevator."

But I'm already halfway to the door. "Sorry, gotta run." I hurry out.

I move at an angle behind a telephone pole and wait. I can't believe my ploy worked and I got her name. I was hoping for that, but I would've settled for just getting a glimpse of her face.

Who knows if the woman who lives in the apartment with the distinctive hand-shaped vase is even home? She could be traveling again. But the doorman told me to bring them up, so I'm optimistic.

Her real name may not even be Valerie Ricci. But that seems unlikely. She'd have to show identification to sign a lease, and she'd need a bank account to pay her rent.

I'm eager to confirm her name. But even more urgently I want to see her.

I don't have to wait long.

A few minutes later, I see a woman walk from the back of the lobby toward the doorman's desk. I can't see her face, but she has brown hair down to her shoulders.

He hands her the flowers and she looks at them, running her fingers through the stems. Probably looking for a card, but she won't find one.

She raises her head and I can see her mouth moving as she speaks to the doorman.

Then she turns, and for the first time I glimpse her features.

This time, the shock I should feel doesn't even register. I've become inured to the unbelievable twists that seem to infiltrate everything the Moore sisters touch.

I know this woman. She held my hand as she helped me down to the subway and made me laugh with her joke about a vibrator.

But she—*and* the Moore sisters—told me her name was Anne.

She's still looking in my direction, but I'm hopeful she won't recognize me with my hoodie up and sunglasses on.

I must have known I'd need to be invisible.

When she heads toward the elevator, I step out from behind the telephone pole and start walking back to Sean and Jody's.

I home in on the facts I need to add to my Data Book. I thought there were three different people: Anne, who took me on the subway; Deena, the client who hired Jody; and the mysterious woman I house-sat for.

But they all must be the same woman.

I was living in Valerie Ricci's apartment when she pretended to be someone else and met me to help me through my subway fear. It's so strange I can barely wrap my head around it. The Moore sisters obviously knew all of this, too; they set up both my house-sitting gig and that meeting.

In that very apartment I first began to think about changing my look. I stared into a big rectangular mirror in the entranceway, pulling up my hair and taking off my glasses.

I made banana smoothies there every morning, too. Were the Moore sisters somehow watching me?

I almost trip over a curb, grabbing the side of a trash can to prevent my fall.

It sounds crazy. But no crazier than anything else that has happened to me recently.

All this time, I've been fixated on Cassandra and Jane Moore. I've researched their PR company and clients, I've tried to be someone they'd want to hang out with, and I've even viewed them as my saviors.

But Valerie Ricci must have colluded with them to get me into that apartment. And she was the one who hired Jody and questioned her about me.

Valerie must be more than just a casual friend of Cassandra and Jane's, like they portrayed her.

She's not just a part of this. She's at the epicenter of whatever it is.

CHAPTER FIFTY-SIX

CASSANDRA & JANE

MAYBE IT WAS TOO MUCH to hope that Shay would be arrested on the spot for James's murder, after Valerie phoned the police with an anonymous tip about the open door and bloody towel in apartment 3D.

But at least it should have taken the police focus off Daphne. That text she'd sent to James: *I hope you rot in hell.* The letter *R* carved into his forehead, with the beginning of an *A* next to it. Had some shrewd investigator guessed at the word and envisioned a link back to Daphne?

Surely the police had already retraced James's steps on the evening of his death. They would have gotten a description of the woman seen leaving the Twist bar with him: tall, with golden-brown hair, wearing a tan sundress. Maybe a security camera affixed to a bank or nearby building had captured the image of the two of them departing and heading toward Central Park on that breezy August evening.

It could easily have been Shay. Especially once the dress—which the Moore sisters had removed from Amanda's laundry bin only hours after her death—was discovered on Shay's floor.

Shay should be holed up in Sean's apartment right now, still reeling not only from the drugs, but also from her subsequent police questioning, and Cassandra's searing rejection.

The last thing the sisters expected was for unassuming, gentle Shay to go on the offensive.

Immediately after Cassandra and Jane receive the call from Valerie—
"I think Shay was here; she tricked me into coming down into the
lobby"—they know they have to increase the pressure on her.

The tracker in Shay's new purse has remained at Sean's apartment.
But when Jane telephones Jody immediately after Valerie received the
flowers with no card, Jody confirms Shay left early that morning.

"Thank God we caught you alone," Jane says, speaking quickly to
circumvent Jody's questions—such as how the Moore sisters have her
cell phone number. "Cassandra and I are in your neighborhood; we
can be there in ten minutes. We have to talk to you."

Jody must have been looking out the window for the sisters because
before they can even press her intercom, she buzzes them in.

As soon as Jody closes the door behind them, Cassandra grips Jody's
forearm and speaks in a hushed, urgent tone: "We may not have a lot
of time. Listen, there's no easy way to tell you this. But you may be in
danger. We have reason to believe that your boyfriend's former roommate is seriously unhinged."

Jody gasps as her hand flutters to her chest. "*What?* Shay made it
sound like *she* was in danger. She said she had a date Friday night and
woke up surrounded by a bloody scalpel and a man's wallet! Sean
thought maybe the guy roofied her."

Jane slips her hand into her coat pocket. Her fingers close around a
four-by-six photograph. The Moore sisters have been in this apartment
once before to collect Amanda's necklace from Shay, but only in the
living area. They can see a few doors; they need Jody to lead them into
the room that Shay is using.

"I know," Cassandra continues while Jane nods. "But she's been
doing all this crazy stuff lately, like following us."

"She's stalking some of our friends, too," Jane adds. "Shay followed
one to an exercise class and went shopping at this boutique another one
owns."

"Oh my gosh," Jody whispers. "Does she have one of those split-
personality disorders? I saw this movie about it once. . . . I can't believe
I slept in the room next to her!"

A teakettle whistles and Jody hurries over to turn off the stove's burner. "I thought we could have some tea." Next to the stove are three china cups on saucers.

"Thanks, Jody, but I don't think there's time. We should check Shay's room in case she has a weapon or something," Cassandra says. "Just to be safe. I'm sure you're fine—I mean, you made it through last night."

Jody nods and heads for the farthest door, her movements quick and a little jerky. She's on edge now, just as the sisters want her to be.

"It's my office now." Jody twists the knob.

All Jane needs is a few seconds to hide the photo—and then they can guide Jody to it.

Valerie had suggested a compartment of Shay's purse, but if the bag isn't accessible, Jane plans to shove it between the pages of her Data Book or even under the mattress.

Jody is rambling. "I just can't believe it. Once there was this lady-bug in the kitchen and Shay carried it down the stairs and put it on a bush outside. . . . But isn't that the kind of person you're always hearing about on the news? Those unlikely suspects?"

Cassandra nods as she scans the room. It's clean and uncluttered, with a blanket stretched tightly across the pullout futon.

Jody flits around the room, peering under the futon, then lifting the pillows one by one.

Jane edges toward the bag and is about to reach for it when Jody looks up. "Should we check her purse?"

"Ooh, good idea," Cassandra replies.

Jody peers into the bag as she holds its handles open. "Nothing in here."

Jane slips the photo between the pages of Shay's Data Book, which is at the foot of the futon.

Jane opens the closet door. "Nothing here either."

"Should we look in her creepy notebook to see if she wrote any-thing recently?" suggests Cassandra.

Jane grabs it and begins flipping the pages. The picture flutters out.

Jody bends down to retrieve it. Cassandra holds her breath. Both sisters stare as Jody looks at the photograph of Amanda on the High Line, wearing a straw hat and tilting up her chin.

Jody looks up, her face creased in confusion. "Why would Shay draw an X over herself?"

Then she glances down and gasps. "It isn't her! I thought it was at first, but it's just a woman who looks like her!"

Cassandra and Jane edge closer to Jody, pretending to study the picture of Amanda—the one they printed out and drew the slashing black X over only days ago.

Cassandra sucks in her breath sharply. "That's our friend Amanda!"

Jody looks from Cassandra to Jane. "Why would Shay have her picture?"

"Shay knew her, too," Jane says. "But Amanda committed suicide in August." Jane shakes her head sorrowfully.

"That's actually how we met Shay," Cassandra tells Jody. "She came to Amanda's memorial service."

"Wait a second, this doesn't make any sense!" Jody cries. She presses the fingertips of her left hand against her forehead. "Shay saw someone commit suicide in August, in a subway station."

"Oh my God," Cassandra says as she takes a step back. Jane sinks onto the edge of the futon.

"That was Amanda who died in the Thirty-third Street station," Cassandra whispers as Jane drops her face in her hands. "Shay told us they shared a veterinarian, and that's how they knew each other. Are you telling us that Shay was in that subway station at the moment Amanda died?"

"A veterinarian?" Jody stares at them both, her mouth agape. "Shay doesn't have a pet! So why would she . . ."

Before Jody can continue, Jane's cell phone chimes with the special ringtone assigned to Valerie. Jane yanks her phone out of her left coat pocket and glances at the screen:

She's coming.

Valerie is staking out the front of the building. The warning means the sisters have only a few moments to get out of the apartment.

"Shay just texted to say she's almost home and wants Cassandra and me to come over," Jane says urgently. "We've got to get out of here!"

Jody backs out of the room. She starts to grab a coat and boots out of the closet by the front door.

"You don't have time to put those on!" Cassandra hisses. There isn't even enough time to make it downstairs.

The three women scramble up to the fourth-floor landing. They hear footsteps climbing up less than a minute later. Then comes the distant sound of a door opening and closing.

Jody is crouched on the bottom stair, still holding the photo. "I feel sick," she whispers. "I can't believe this is the woman Shay says she saw commit suicide."

"Jody, you've got to tell the police what you found," Cassandra urges.

Shay's history of stalking has already been established. She was fired from her last job, and she suffered a crushing romantic rejection. She has exhibited bizarre behavior, including trying to slip into the life of a dead woman.

Is it such a leap for anyone to believe Shay might also be capable of murder?

Jody stares down at the blue sky, the sunlight on Amanda's face, the jagged X drawn across her skin. "I'll call the police right now," she whispers.

CHAPTER FIFTY-SEVEN

SHAY

Some people contend there are two primal fears. The first and most basic is
the end of our existence. The second is isolation; we all have a deep need to
belong to something greater than ourselves.
—Data Book, page 68

RIGHT AFTER I SEE HER FACE, I google "Valerie Ricci" on my phone,
trying every possible variation of the spelling that I can think of. I
don't feel safe lingering outside her building, so I head a few blocks
away, to a diner I noticed when I house-sat, while I wait for the search
engine to pull up results.

I slide into a booth toward the back, choosing the side that lets me
keep an eye on the door, and order wheat toast. I'm still not hungry,
but I know I need something to absorb the acid in my nervous stomach.

My search has thousands of results: One is a lifestyle blogger in
North Carolina, another an attorney in Palo Alto, and there are school-
teachers, insurance agents, real estate brokers, and a self-published author. I can't chase every one of them down.

I click on the images link and begin to look through the pictures:
blond, blue-eyed Valeries, and lots of brunettes, and at least two red-
heads. Old Valeries and young ones, all shapes and sizes. As I scan

through them, I realize I am unconsciously looking for the woman who just accepted the flowers from her doorman. But Valerie could have metamorphosed into the woman she is now. I slow down, giving each picture a careful look.

Then I see a familiar oval face with straight eyebrows and chestnut hair.

I've found her.

By the time the waitress slides a plate of toast triangles in front of me, I'm scrutinizing an old image of Valerie on the set of a now-canceled soap opera. From there, I locate a few of her past addresses in L.A. She was an actress, which seems fitting: She certainly made me believe she was someone else—and she convinced Jody, too.

I also discover she has an ex-husband named Tony Ricci, who still lives in L.A. His number is listed. I make a note of it so I can call him once I come up with a cover story—or a role of my own, like the ones Valerie plays.

Maybe he can tell me Valerie's maiden name and hometown. If I have that information, I can try to trace her back in time.

My search turns up nothing about her in recent years, other than the address I just visited on East Twelfth Street. I can't even find out where she works. Not a single current photograph of her exists online. It's almost as if the person she used to be vanished when she came to New York.

I manage to finish a piece of toast and a half glass of water, then I slide out of the booth and walk back to Sean and Jody's, hunching my shoulders against the cold. I check behind me every block or so and even cross the street twice. But all in the city seem engrossed in their own lives; no one appears to be watching me now.

Sean and Jody were asleep when I left this morning, and I'm hoping Sean will be home alone now. But after I climb the stairs to the second floor and use the spare key he gave me last night, I realize the apartment is empty.

I stand there, looking around, wondering what to do next. I'm so cold I can't feel my toes.

Three flowered china teacups and saucers are on a little tray in the kitchen, along with a tiny china creamer and a box of chamomile.

Jody must be expecting company, I think, since Sean only drinks his beloved dark-roast coffee. Maybe she ran out to get cookies or scones.

A cup of hot tea sounds perfect, I think. I reach into the cupboard for a chunky mug and drop in a teabag. As I reach for the teakettle, my fingertips brush its metal handle and I jerk back. It's so hot I've burned myself.

I run the sink tap and put my fingers under the cold water.

Then I look again at the little tray Jody has set out. Why would she boil water for guests who haven't yet arrived?

I turn off the sink. "Jody?" I call out.

All three doors are open—the one to the bathroom, the one to Jody and Sean's bedroom, and mine. There's no way she wouldn't hear me if she were still here.

My head whips around to check my bedroom door again as something registers in my brain. The door to Jody's office—the room I'm using—is wide open now.

But I'm certain I left it shut.

I stand there, a wet paper towel wrapped around my throbbing fingers, staring at the open door.

Déjà vu: When I stayed in Valerie Ricci's apartment, I cut my finger slicing a red pepper and thought about opening her bedroom door to look for a Band-Aid. But I didn't; the door was tightly shut and I left it that way.

The next day, however, I noticed it was cracked open.

I'd texted the Moore sisters, wondering if the super had been in the apartment, and Cassandra immediately responded that he had been by to check on a leak.

I accepted that at the time. But now, it seems a little too convenient that she'd known the super had been in the apartment of one of her friends.

If it wasn't the super, then who came into Valerie's apartment while I was supposedly house-sitting?

It could have been Valerie. Cassandra and Jane also had a key—they used it when they first showed me the apartment. Or Valerie could have given another key to someone else entirely. While I was feeling grateful to have the beautiful apartment as a refuge, someone could have come in and rifled through my things or even watched me sleep.

I shudder and drop the paper towel onto the counter. Then I lift my head and slowly sniff the air.

I wheel around, hurrying back out the door.

I've felt many things in the city I've lived in for nearly a decade: hopeful, despondent, joyful, irritated, and deeply lonely.

But I've never felt the gut-wrenching, primal sense of fear I experienced just now when I inhaled the faint traces of the distinctive floral perfume Jane always wears.

I stay aboveground, my hoodie pulled over my hair. Even though the streets are relatively crowded, I still spin around every now and then to make sure someone isn't following me.

All I have are the clothes I'm wearing, my wallet, and my iPhone, but I know I can't go back to Sean and Jody's. I need to find a safe place to stay.

As I'm pondering this, I receive a text from Jody: *Hey, my grandmother is sick, so Sean and I are going to head out of town for a few days.*

I stare at the text, thinking about how I've never once heard Jody mention a grandmother.

I feel as if I've been punched in the gut.

Only yesterday, they were so caring and concerned about me. Why the abrupt change?

I blink back tears as I shove my hands deeper into my pockets. Maybe I misconstrued Jody's tone, which is easy to do in a text, I try to tell myself.

I begin walking aimlessly, thinking again of those three delicate teacups on the tray, and the still-hot kettle. Jody had pulled out her good china instead of simply taking mismatched mugs from the cabinet.

It's as if she wanted to impress her visitors. Now I understand why.

Did something happen to make her turn from caring to brusque? Or did some*one* make it happen?

Cassandra and Jane met Jody and Sean when they came by to pick up Jane's necklace.

Did the Moore sisters come to the apartment to convince Jody and Sean to turn against me?

Someone brushes past me and I whirl around. But it's just a teenager on a cell phone with a big backpack.

I look up at the buildings towering over me. So many windows. Anyone could be watching me.

I can't go to my new apartment or stay with my mom or Mel. The Moore sisters probably know their addresses, and I can't put anyone I care about in jeopardy—or risk having Cassandra and Jane turn the people I love against me, too.

I don't know what the Moore sisters have planned, but I doubt they're finished with me yet.

I dial Detective Williams's number, but she doesn't pick up. I hang up before leaving a message. What could I even say? *I know it sounds crazy, but I think Cassandra and Jane Moore—they're the friends of Amanda's that I've been hanging out with—are watching me. They know things about me, like what I eat or where I'll be. And they turned my old roommate against me.*

I have to collect more facts before I go to the police.

I wander the city for hours, until my feet are aching and my body feels numb. By the time dusk falls, I've figured out where I can stay tonight. I've seen enough movies to know that if I want to be untraceable, I have to pay in cash. So I stop by an ATM and withdraw the maximum $800.

Then I walk through Times Square and head west. It will be easier to be invisible in one of the most crowded places in the city.

It doesn't take me long to spot what I'm looking for—a seedy small hotel with a neon VACANCY sign blinking outside.

I try to pull open the door, but it's locked. A red buzzer is to my left, and I press it while I cast another look back over my shoulder.

At the loud humming noise I instinctively reach for the door again to pull it open. I step inside the dim lobby. The man behind the front desk barely glances up from his computer. He's got a fringe of gray hair over his ears and a matching mustache.

"Reservation?" he asks when I reach the desk.

"Sorry, no. But I saw the vacancy sign. . . ."

"We've got a room with a double bed on the second floor."

"Is there anything higher?"

"No elevator. Most people want lower."

"I don't mind."

"Got one on the fifth floor. Eighty a night. Just need a driver's license."

I pull the wad of twenties I've just taken out of the ATM from the pocket of my jeans and peel off five beneath the counter. "I was mugged. They got my wallet. I don't have a license." I slide the bills to him, making sure they're fanned out so he can see the extra twenty. "Is that a problem?"

"Not for me. One night, then?"

"For now."

He's barely even made eye contact with me. And if the Moore sisters—or anyone else—are looking for me, they may not know exactly how to describe me. I'm wearing my glasses again, and I used one of the scrunchies I borrowed from Jody's supply in the bathroom.

"Name?" He clicks on an ancient-looking computer.

Once I looked up the most popular baby names for girls born during my birth year, and I immediately recall a name that dominated in the late eighties and early nineties.

"Jessica. Jessica Smith." Smith is a perennial common surname in the United States.

He hands me a key. "Vending machines with pop back there." He points toward the rear of the lobby.

"Thanks." I look down at the heavy metal key. The clerk is already back on his computer, playing solitaire.

I want nothing more than to barricade myself in my room. But I don't have any food, or a change of clothes. So I force myself to head back out.

I find everything I need within a block's radius: a three-pack of underwear, a long-sleeved shirt, and a down vest on sale for twenty dollars. I then head to Duane Reade and pick up travel toiletries, a few Cup-a-Soups, some protein bars, and a burner flip phone with internet access and a prepaid SIM card.

I'm almost at the register when I remember something and whirl around and head toward the back of the store, where there are office supplies. I grab a cheap spiral notebook and a ballpoint pen before heading back to the register. I pay in cash, then return to the hotel.

I buzz again to gain entry, and the clerk gives me a vague nod as I pass him on my way to the staircase.

I trudge up, then unlock my door and look around. The room is tiny and utilitarian, with just a double bed, a straight chair, and two nightstands. I check under the bed and in the tiny bathroom before I even put down my shopping bags. I secure the flimsy-looking chain and blockade the door with the chair, wedging it under the knob.

I finally sink onto the edge of the faded bedspread. Breathing hard, I stare out the window that faces a brick building three feet away.

If I don't keep my mind busy, it feels like the weight of my fears will crush me. So I get to work.

I start by pulling out my phone and begin plugging terms—"scalpel," "New York City," "Cassandra and Jane Moore"—into a search engine.

I scan dozens of articles and pictures. Most of them I've already seen from my previous searches about the Moore sisters.

I expand my search, trying to picture the pages of my Data Book containing all the information I recorded about the Moore sisters: the name of the yoga studio Cassandra frequents. Bella's, the bar where we had Moscow Mules. Daphne's boutique. Thirty-third Street subway station suicide. The Rosewood Club, where the sisters hosted Amanda's memorial service.

I get tons of hits. I read until my eyes are gritty. But I can't find the missing link that will help me make sense of all this.

When heavy footsteps tromp through the hallway, I flinch. But they pass by my door without pausing, and a moment later I hear someone enter the room next to mine and turn on the television. The canned laughter of a sitcom seeps through the thin walls.

I don't want to turn on my television, which could mask the sound of someone trying to get through my door. I also don't want to leave my room. I'm not hungry, but I am thirsty. I should have known there wouldn't be a complimentary bottle of water on my nightstand.

The front-desk clerk had mentioned a vending machine in the lobby. *Pop,* he'd said, which is a regional term that a lot of people in the Midwest use. I think about walking down that dim hallway and descending four flights of stairs. Instead, I head to the bathroom and cup my hand under the sink tap and drink from it.

I should eat something, I realize, but my stomach feels too tightly clenched to handle even the soup I bought.

I lie down on the bed, listening to the distant wail of a siren. I've left on the bathroom light so I won't be in darkness.

I felt alone before I met the Moore sisters, when my biggest problems were a dead-end temp job and hearing Jody's giggle coming from Sean's bedroom.

Now I know how much worse things can become.

I'm convinced the Moore sisters set me up for something. But what?

Fatigue starts to overtake my body, as if someone has laid a weighted blanket on me. I think back to Jane laying the throw over my body, saying, *This will keep you cozy.* I've been in such a frantic state, but now I'm shutting down. My body and brain can no longer sustain the intense stress. I feel completely numb. I just want to disappear.

As I stare into the darkness, I wonder, *Is this how Amanda felt on the day she died?*

CHAPTER FIFTY-EIGHT

AMANDA

Two months ago

IT HAD BEEN TEN DAYS since James died. No, since *she* had killed James. The hissing voice was right: It was her fault.

Gina had left several more messages, but Amanda didn't respond. What could she say?

Then came a final call from City Hospital, this one from human resources, letting Amanda know she'd been fired.

Her life as she'd known it was over. But at least she could do one right thing.

Early on a Sunday morning she slipped on the first article of clothing her hand closed around in her closet, a green polka-dot dress. She found a manila envelope and filled it with the evidence she'd been hiding beneath her sink.

Then she stood by her door, listening intently. She heard nothing.

She unlatched the chain and peered down the hallway. It was empty.

She hurried to the stairs, taking them two at a time as she wound her way down to the lobby.

It was completely still—no other residents were picking up their Sunday papers or coming in with lattes in hand.

But that didn't mean someone wasn't waiting for her outside.

Amanda looked down at the bulging manila envelope in her hand.

What might they do to her if they knew she was planning to deliver it to the police?

They would intercept her.

They would destroy the evidence.

They would destroy her.

Amanda thought hard and carefully, concentrating as deeply as her weary, jumbled mind would allow. Then she spun around and walked back to her mailbox, using her key to open it. She shoved the envelope to the very back.

She reached for her phone and dialed the nonemergency police number. She wasn't going to tell the police everything. At least not yet. But she wanted them to know she was coming, just in case.

"My name is Amanda." Her voice shook. "Could I speak to someone in Homicide? I have evidence of a crime."

As she headed uptown, Amanda continually scanned her surroundings. Her ringer was turned off but her phone kept buzzing in the side pocket of her dress, like a furious wasp. It wasn't quite nine o'clock in the morning, but it was already so hot she felt her hair sticking to the back of her neck.

It was less than a fifteen-minute walk to the Seventeenth Precinct. She'd told the officer that she was on her way, though she didn't provide her last name or any details about the felony she said she'd witnessed.

"You say your name is Amanda?" the woman had said. "Ask for me when you get here. I'm Detective Williams."

But the detective had sounded weary and distracted, as if this was far from the first call she'd received from someone who sounded paranoid and made grandiose claims.

As Amanda traveled the city streets, the rancid smells of the summer-baked city swelled around her. Her phone buzzed angrily again and again, barely pausing.

Finally, Amanda couldn't stand it any longer. She answered the call. She remained completely silent, but she couldn't soften her heavy breathing.

"Amanda," Jane said in a soft, gentle tone. "I'm so glad you finally picked up. I'm here with Cassandra."

"Talk to us," Cassandra said. "We'll get through this. We'll help each other, like we always do."

"I can't bear it any longer," Amanda whispered. "I need to go to the police. I'll keep you out of it. I'll take all the blame."

"Don't be foolish," Valerie's steely voice cut in. "You'll rot in a jail cell."

"I'm sorry," Amanda gasped.

"Listen to me!" Valerie ordered. "Stay right there on that corner. Do not cross that street."

Amanda felt goose bumps rise on her arms. She spun in a circle, looking around.

"How do you know I'm on a corner?" she whispered.

Run.

The instinct slammed into her brain. She hung up and sprinted toward a deli. A man was arranging produce in baskets outside the door. She could ask him for help. Maybe he could hide her in a closet while she called the police again, she thought desperately.

But the sisters would find her.

Where else could she go? She'd almost reached the bodega when she heard the familiar whooshing sound beneath her feet: A subway train was approaching, spewing air through the sidewalk grates.

Amanda's head whipped around; her gaze homed in on the forest-green pole marking the Thirty-third Street station. She raced down the stairs and headed for the turnstiles, her MetroCard already out.

But the first machine she tried malfunctioned, refusing to read her card. She moved to the next one.

Six seconds. That's how long the delay cost her.

She raced onto the platform, her legs churning, her hand stretching out to try to block the car's doors from closing. But their edges swept just past her fingertips and closed.

The train pulled away, its breeze blowing against her face.

Amanda looked around, her mind roaring with panic. The LED display showed another train would be coming in just a few minutes.

She began to edge down toward the mouth of the tunnel, where she'd be closer to it.

They'd known she was on a street corner. But how?

Stacey had installed spyware on James's phone long before his death; maybe she was being tracked that way, too. Amanda hurled her phone onto the tracks, where the incoming train would destroy it.

Nothing else was in her possession that the Moore sisters could possibly use to locate her. She wasn't carrying a purse. She didn't—

She caught her breath.

Her hand rose to her neck, where a gold charm rested between her collarbones. Since the sisters had given the necklace to her months ago, she'd never taken it off; she'd forgotten she'd been wearing it. She ripped it off and let the delicate chain slide through her fingers to the concrete floor. Then she hurried toward a support beam that would help shield her from view.

A woman wearing khaki shorts and a red T-shirt came down the stairs, and for a moment Amanda's heart jackhammered—then she realized the woman was a stranger.

Amanda glanced at the LED display again. Time was behaving strangely; it seemed to be standing still.

The woman began to walk toward Amanda.

A bulb in one of the overhead fluorescent lights flickered. Trash overflowed from a can.

Amanda could feel the rumble of the approaching train; it swelled up into her body from the concrete beneath her feet.

The woman in the red T-shirt was close to her now. She was tall and strong looking, with a pleasant face. Her presence felt comforting to Amanda, somehow.

Then Amanda looked beyond her.

Valerie was standing at the bottom of the staircase, her dark hair gleaming under the lights, just as it had when she'd been waiting for Amanda outside City Hospital.

If it had been Jane coming for her, or even Cassandra, things might have been different. Jane would have wrapped soft arms around Amanda and asked her to come talk to the others. Cassandra's husky voice would have been sterner, but Cassandra would still have tried to reason with her.

But they had sent Valerie. They were cutting Amanda loose.

Valerie began to close the distance between them, her pace almost leisurely, her gaze locked on Amanda.

Amanda stepped close to the edge of the platform.

"Don't!"

Amanda turned to see the woman in the T-shirt and shorts staring at her, her hand outstretched.

But Valerie was closing the gap between them.

The roar of the incoming train filled Amanda's ears. She had no real family, no job, and now no friends.

You're going to lose everything, Cassandra had said.

I already have, Amanda thought.

She leaped up, her arms spreading out as she flew through the air.

For a brief moment, she felt free.

CHAPTER FIFTY-NINE

SHAY

*The murder rate in the United States dropped last year. New York City
isn't even one of the top 30 most dangerous cities in the country. And
according to one study, if you murder someone in the United States, there's a
60 percent chance you'll get caught. Although in New York City the chance
of getting caught is 85 percent.*
—Data Book, page 70

I AWAKE FEELING DISORIENTED for the third morning in a row.

On Saturday, when everything started to go horribly wrong, I came
to on my couch. Sunday I woke on the futon in my old bedroom at
Sean and Jody's. Now I'm in this strange hotel.

Last night was endless. Every time the radiator thrummed or the ice
machine in the hallway clattered it jolted me. I finally managed to drift
off for an hour or two, but I can still feel the ghost of the nightmare
that gripped me.

I fumble around on the nightstand until I find my glasses.

My burner phone is plugged into its charger. When I check it, I see
Tony Ricci still hasn't returned my call.

I climb out of bed and go into the bathroom, taking a quick shower
before dressing in my jeans and Sean's hoodie again. Then I email
Francine, my boss at Quartz, to let her know I'm sick and can't work

today. My contract calls for me to work forty hours per week. *Is it all right if I make up the hours?* I write. I know she won't be at her desk yet, since it's three hours earlier on the West Coast.

I climb back onto my bed—there's nowhere else to sit in the room, since the hard chair is still wedged under my doorknob—and pull out my new notebook. I turn to the first fresh, blank page. I begin to fill it with everything I recall about Cassandra and Jane. I try to re-create our past conversations—beginning with the moment I encountered them at Amanda's memorial service.

It's lucky, in a way, that I was so taken by the sisters. They made such a vivid impression on me that my memories of them are almost three-dimensional.

Please don't hesitate to reach out if you want to talk. Connecting with each other is one of the most essential things we can do . . . , Cassandra had said the first time we met.

The heat of her hand on my bare forearm. Those mesmerizing amber eyes. Jane's dimple flashing as she smiled up at me.

My throat thickens as I picture Cassandra putting her raincoat around my shoulders. I see Jane with a bright smile standing up to wave me over to the table at Bella's and, later, while we walked the High Line, making me laugh as she snapped the photo of me in the straw hat. *As hard as Amanda's death was for us, the only silver lining was it led you to us,* Cassandra had said on the last night we spent together.

Hot tears prick my eyes. They broke my heart.

My foot shoots out and kicks over the trash can.

I thought you were my friends, I want to cry out. *I trusted you, and you betrayed me.*

What the sisters did feels worse than getting fired from my last job, Barry's insults, or even watching the man I lived with and secretly loved fall for another woman.

I inhale a jagged breath and force myself to concentrate. I've filled pages of my new Data Book with my memories of Cassandra and Jane, but it's mostly superficial details—such as the fact that Cassandra drinks jasmine tea, and Jane favors a floral perfume.

I don't possess a lot of hard data about the sisters, not the way they do about me. They visited my last two apartments—three if you include the one where I house-sat. They've met Sean and Jody. They know about my subway phobia, my new freelance gig at Quartz, and even what I make for breakfast. They're aware that I want a serious relationship, and they have pictures of me on their phones.

What do I know about them? I've never seen the inside of their apartments, or their workplace. I don't know what keeps them up at night. And I have no idea why they acted like my friends, and then my enemies.

I don't even know if they really like cinnamon Altoids or yoga or Moscow Mules.

Maybe it was all for show.

Once I've recorded all my memories, I google the Moore sisters, reading through their company's website and jotting down the names of their clients. There's surprisingly little about them on the internet, and most of it I've already seen. Still, I write down whatever information I find.

I have no idea what to do next.

I pace up and down the channel next to my bed in my tiny hotel room, feeling like a caged animal. I try to make sense of the facts I've documented, but it's a jigsaw puzzle with missing pieces. The Moore sisters must have a reason for their bizarre actions. Yet it completely eludes me.

By early afternoon, my head is throbbing, probably from the lack of coffee. It's hard to ignore the sound of a man and a woman loudly arguing in a room down the hall. I check my messages but I haven't heard back from Francine. Ted hasn't replied to me either, so I text him again.

I'm down to less than six hundred dollars in cash. There's more in my bank account, so I can afford to stay in this hotel for a while longer. Then what?

I call Francine's work number to make sure she received my email. I get her voice mail and think about leaving a message. But I hang up before the beep. I'd rather talk to her personally so I can gauge her reaction.

I wonder if Francine is annoyed that I'm taking a sick day so soon after being hired. I'm a freelancer; it would be easy for her to replace me.

Anxiety gnaws at me.

I flip through my Data Book to try to distract myself, but it only makes things worse: Images of Cassandra and Jane—tossing back their shining hair, folding their shapely legs into a taxi, flashing their perfect teeth as they laugh—seem to rise off every page.

I need to get out of this room.

But if Francine phones back and I answer, the ambient noises of the city will be clear in the background. She might wonder how sick I really am if I'm outside.

I run my hand over my forehead. I could be stuck here all day waiting for her call.

I finally look up the main number for Quartz so I can relay a message to one of Francine's colleagues. I dial it and ask the receptionist if I can speak to someone in human resources.

"Transferring," she says, and a moment later a man answers, "Allen Peters."

"Hi, Mr. Peters." I haven't spoken since I checked in last night, so my voice sounds a little scratchy. "I'm sorry to bother you. I'm Shay Miller, the freelancer from New York City."

"Who?"

"Shay Miller. I was recently hired. . . . I report to Francine De-Marco."

"Who? You must have the wrong number. There's no one here by that name."

I drop the phone onto the bed and edge away from it, like it's dangerous.

I never had a job at Quartz.

My mind spins back to the first message I received from Francine. Quartz was part of her email address, and her phone number had a 310 exchange, which corresponds to the West Coast.

I researched Quartz, the company, after I thought I'd landed an interview. But not the woman who contacted me on LinkedIn, or Francine DeMarco.

I begin to tremble. The Moore sisters have to be behind this.

They're everywhere, I think.

And now they know so much more about me. I filled out a half dozen forms and sent them to "Francine." They've got my Social Security number, my birth date, my middle name, my mother's cell phone number, since she's my emergency contact. . . . What are they going to do to me next?

The room starts to swim; I'm hyperventilating.

I collapse onto the bed, fighting to even out my breathing. How many other areas of my life did the Moore sisters infiltrate that I don't know about?

The walls are pressing in on me.

I abruptly jump up and put on my down vest and stick my wallet, burner phone, and a power bar into its pockets. I scoop up my new Data Book and press my ear against the door before I open it. I hold my breath as I listen. The man and the woman in a room down the hall are still fighting, but their voices are quieter now. I yank open the door.

The corridor is empty.

I exhale slowly. I think about having to walk back down this dingy, creepy hallway when I return, and I remember a trick I once saw in a movie. I dash back in my bathroom and grab a square of toilet paper. I tear off a small piece.

I draw the door closed, but just before it latches, I slip the scrap of tissue between the jamb and the hinges, at exactly my eye height. The DO NOT DISTURB sign is hanging on the outer doorknob. The paper is almost completely hidden; just the tiniest sliver of white shows in the crack. No one would ever see it if not looking for it.

If it's still in place when I return, I'll know no one has breached my room. But if anyone opens the door, it'll fall to the floor. Even if it's seen falling, the person won't know exactly where I placed it.

It's all I can think to do to protect myself.

I descend the stairs to the lobby, ducking low and peering around every corner before I make the turns.

When I arrive in the lobby, a different clerk is on call. I hand him eighty dollars. "Another night. Room 508, please."

"Last name?"

I hesitate for a fraction of a beat. "Smith. Thanks."

Then I step outside, into a bracing wind.

CHAPTER SIXTY

VALERIE

SHAY HAS DISAPPEARED.

Despite the fact that Jody called the police to inform them about the unsettling photo of Amanda, Shay hasn't been arrested. Beth, whose job as a public defense attorney gives her access to law-enforcement databases, has checked.

Jody told Jane that Shay is no longer staying in the guest room. Jody reported that Shay texted Sean last night to say she was spending the night with another friend, and that she'd collect her things soon. Stacey has confirmed Shay is not staying at Mel's place in Brooklyn, or her mother's home in New Jersey. Cassandra and Jane stopped by the apartment that once housed Amanda but is now being rented by Shay, slipping in with the spare key they'd had made before Shay rented it, but Shay wasn't there, either.

It's as if Shay has been swallowed up by the city.

Valerie, who arrived at the Sullivan Street office of Moore Public Relations at dawn, reaches up to massage her temples. Her head is throbbing, and the bright lights in the office pierce her eyes. She has been running on only a few hours of sleep for the past few nights.

Maybe it will look worse for Shay if the police can't find her either, Valerie thinks.

Valerie starts when the phone on her desk rings. It's only a magazine columnist, hoping for a tidbit about a celebrity.

"I'll have Cassandra or Jane call you back," Valerie says, keeping her voice light and calm.

The sisters still have clients who need them, and an office to run, but they're canceling unnecessary appointments to open their schedules. They're keeping a few important ones—including with Willow Tanaka, the artist, who is coming into their office toward the end of the day to sign contracts for a lucrative branding partnership.

The Moore sisters plan to get Willow in and out as quickly as possible. Then, under the guise of heading out for a late meeting, Cassandra, Jane, and Valerie will once more return to Shay's apartment.

They have something else to plant there. They need to find a good hiding place, one the police will surely find if they obtain a search warrant to tear apart the residence of a suspected murderess.

Not *if* the police obtain the search warrant, Valerie tells herself. *When*.

It should be simple enough to find the perfect spot. They know the apartment well. And the final piece of evidence is featherlight and smaller than an index card.

When her personal phone rings again, Valerie thinks about letting it go to voice mail—she's surprised by how much Shay's absence is getting under her skin—but after the third ring, she picks it up and greets her caller warmly. "Tony! What in the world are you up to?"

Valerie has kept in sporadic touch with Tony in the fifteen years since he got his green card and she moved out of his apartment, but they haven't spoken since she came to Manhattan.

He cuts right to it: "I got a strange message from a 917 area code. There's a woman asking about you."

Valerie grows still. "Did she leave a name?"

"No." Tony's voice is high with anxiety.

"You don't have anything to worry about. As far as Immigration is concerned, your case closed long ago." It's a wonder he passed the grueling immigration interviews, given his nervous nature. "Can you give me her number?"

She doesn't recognize the combination of digits Tony recites, so she jots them down.

"If she calls again, just let it go to voice mail." Valerie hangs up and stands up, her eyes narrowing.

It has to be Shay.

She's circling ever closer. If she had caught Tony unaware, he could have revealed information Valerie has successfully kept hidden for her entire adult life.

Valerie takes a sip of coffee, then sets her mug on her glass-topped desk so roughly it nearly shatters.

Why haven't the police arrested Shay yet? Where has Shay gone?

Maybe they shouldn't wait for the police to act, Valerie thinks. Perhaps Shay should disappear permanently.

CHAPTER SIXTY-ONE

SHAY

An estimated 1,800 people go missing in the United States every day—
though most of those reports are later canceled. There are roughly 90,000
active missing person's cases in the U.S.
—Data Book, page 72

I DUCK MY HEAD against the wind as I walk through Times Square, passing a person in a Cookie Monster costume posing for a photo with a young boy, a tour-bus operator who tries to sell me a spot on a day trip to the Statue of Liberty and Ellis Island, and the flashing neon lights that never cease.

My footsteps are instinctively leading me toward the Moore sisters' office on Sullivan Street. I need to see something solid about the sisters, even if it's just their names on the company display in the lobby.

My job was fake, so perhaps theirs is, too.

I walk all the way to the Moore sisters' building, trying to burn off my edgy feelings and clear my mind. After the first half mile, my face and hands begin to feel numb, but at least I'm doing *something*.

I arrive at the address on the PR firm's website and stare up at the six-story structure with a plain but elegant façade. A little flag outside says MOORE PUBLIC RELATIONS. So at least one part of their story seems real.

It appears to be an ordinary Monday in Manhattan: Men and women are hurrying down sidewalks, talking into cell phones, many carrying to-go cups of coffee or bags with take-out lunches. It's hard to believe that only a week ago I was one of the 1.6 million people in the city doing the same thing.

Maybe I'll see Cassandra or Jane exiting the building. I could try to follow them and find out more.

I imagine them striding around their offices in their stylish clothes, their phone lines constantly ringing with people vying for their attention.

I wait and watch—just as I suspect they've been watching me.

Before long, I start to shiver. The cold rises up through the sidewalk and seeps through my body. I wish I could buy a cup of coffee to warm me, but I don't want to leave my post, even for a few minutes. I shift my weight from leg to leg, trying to get my circulation flowing.

At a little before 4:30 P.M., I see a woman approach the building. She's wearing red leather pants, a black wool cape, and high platform boots. Her white-blond hair is choppily cut to her chin, and her bangs look like broom straw across her forehead.

But it's not her striking appearance that draws my attention. I recognize her immediately from the photo on the Moore Public Relations website: Willow Tanaka.

I keep watching as Willow disappears through the revolving door. When she comes back out, I can try to engage her in conversation—perhaps she'll tell me something about the Moore sisters.

I know I'm clutching at air, but I'm desperate.

The sun begins to sink behind the city's tallest buildings, casting giant shadows over the streets. I tuck my hands deeper into my pockets and stamp my numb feet against the concrete.

About twenty minutes later, I see that distinctive hair and a flash of red leather.

Willow is exiting the building.

I push away from the pillar I've been leaning against and take a step toward her.

Then I see the woman emerging from the revolving door directly behind her.

I recoil.

It's Valerie Ricci.

She's wearing gray slacks with a fitted wrap sweater, and her hair is up in a twist. She looks neat and efficient—as if she's transposed a new persona over the warm, talkative, slightly bawdy woman I knew as Anne. I watch as she and Willow stand together on the sidewalk. Then Valerie hails a cab, raising her hand with a crisp flick of her wrist, and Willow climbs inside the vehicle.

Valerie spins on her heel and walks back into the building.

Cassandra and Jane described Valerie as a friend when they told me she'd help me overcome my subway phobia—and they used the same word when they described her as the tenant of the apartment they got me to "house-sit." And when I first met her, she gave me the impression she was a stay-at-home mom.

Now I wonder if Valerie actually works for the Moore sisters, even though I never came across the mention of her name on their website.

It seems crazy that they would have paid her to take me on the subway and use a fake name and temporarily move out of her home so I could sleep in her guest room. But maybe it isn't; the Moore sisters have done far more outrageous things to me.

While I'm digesting this, the three of them—Cassandra, Jane, and Valerie—exit the building. I shrink behind the pillar.

I don't think they can see me; a busy street is between us. I watch them approach the curb, then lose sight of them briefly when a delivery truck rumbles by. When my line of vision is clear again, a taxi is pulling up for them.

I begin to jog, keeping my eyes fixed on their yellow cab as it merges back into traffic and starts to blend in with dozens of others. When it idles at a red light, I scan the street, holding my hand up. But all the taxis that approach are full. It takes me three more blocks of running until I can catch one.

"Can you follow that cab, please." I point. "The one with the Chanel perfume ad on the roof."

We pass Washington Square Park, then head north past Union Square Park, my cab jerking and weaving through traffic. I keep my eyes fixed on the perfume bottle atop the vehicle I'm chasing. On Park

Avenue South we briefly lose them when we get stuck at a red light, but their cab stops at the next light, so we catch up.

Finally my driver manages to edge directly behind them. I can see three sleek heads in the backseat. For a moment it's hard to tell who is who, then I realize Valerie is in the middle, with Cassandra to her right and Jane to her left.

We're getting close to the apartment I used to share with Sean and Jody; we pass the Thirty-third Street subway station, and the Starbucks on my old corner.

A few blocks later, we turn east. My body grows rigid. I know this route well; I've traveled it many times.

It feels surreal, but I know exactly where they're going.

Their cab pulls over and stops, and they climb out—first Cassandra, then Valerie, then Jane.

They walk to the front door of the building directly in front of them and use a key to gain entrance. I slump low in my seat so they won't see me if they suddenly turn around.

"Lady?" My cabbie's loud voice makes me flinch. "You getting out?"

The Moore sisters are in my new apartment building—the one that used to belong to Amanda. They have a key to the main entrance. Do they also have one to my alcove apartment?

Jane and Valerie disappear inside, but Cassandra remains by the entryway, like a guard.

"Can you pull up to the end of the block?" I fumble in my wallet for one of my precious twenties.

I give it to the driver and slip out of the cab. Enough people are on the sidewalk to provide camouflage, but I still move as close as I can to the pharmacy on the corner, glad it's dark enough out that I blend in with the shadows.

What are they doing in my apartment? Could they be trying to catch me there?

Not five minutes later, I see all three of them approach the curb again and hail another cab. I duck into the pharmacy and try to look out the floor-to-ceiling window to see where they're going, but I can't tell which vehicle holds them.

I wait another few minutes, then I step back out onto the sidewalk, wishing I had thought to use my burner phone to snap a picture of them with my building in the background as proof.

When I'm a few feet away from the entrance where Cassandra stood only minutes ago, I pause. I'm afraid to go inside.

Then I see a young couple I vaguely recognize with a baby strapped to a carrier on the man's chest approaching. I'm pretty sure they live one floor above me. That little slice of normality gives me the security I need to move forward. I follow them into the building.

When I reach my floor, the strong overhead bulb lights the hallway brightly, and I can hear laughter coming from Mary's place across the hall.

My door is shut. Nothing on the outside of my apartment looks out of the ordinary. And surely the police took away the bloody scalpel and other strange items.

Still, I'd be even more reluctant to go inside if I didn't hear Mary's cheerful voice resonating from across the hall. I unlock my door and slip in, immediately flicking on the light switch.

I scan my apartment quickly, then close the door and draw the chain across it. I don't want to spend long here. But nearly every time I've been with the Moore sisters, they've either left me with something or taken something from me: Cassandra's business card. Her raincoat. The necklace they retrieved. The tear sheet from the magazine. The photographs on the High Line. The bag of books Jane forgot at my new place on the first night I welcomed them here. The fancy purse and other gifts.

And, of course, the man's watch and wallet and the tan sundress that I'm now convinced they planted in my apartment.

If they took or left something again, I need to know what it is.

I start in my kitchen, methodically going through every drawer, cupboard, and cabinet. I even check my freezer and the oven racks. Luckily I'm neat by nature, and since I moved in only weeks ago, my place is uncluttered. I work my way from the front to the back of the apartment. Within an hour, I'm in the alcove, peering under my bed and shaking out my sheets.

I yank open the drawer of my nightstand, where I keep an extra set of headphones, a scrunchie, and an old iPad that I use to watch movies.

Those items are all intact.

But something new is beneath my iPad: a small piece of paper. When I pick it up, I see that it's a receipt from a bar I've never heard of, called Twist.

The bar's phone number and address are printed at the top by the logo of a lemon twist, above the tally for two Seagram's and sodas.

I shudder, imagining Valerie or Jane sliding open my nightstand drawer, their hands lifting up my iPad.

I don't have time to figure out why they planted this now. I fold the receipt carefully and tuck it in my wallet. I finish searching my bedroom, moving as quickly as possible, but I don't see anything else amiss.

I grab a fresh sweatshirt, jeans, and socks, shoving the items into a duffel bag. I'm halfway to my door before I remember how cold I've been, and I hurry back to my closet to get my black puffer jacket, which I trade for my thin down vest.

I peer out my peephole. The hallway appears to be clear. I unlatch my chain and race out, hearing my door slam shut behind me as I tear to the stairs, taking them two at a time, and burst through the entranceway door onto the street. I keep running, all the way to the next block, then I finally slow to a walk.

I spin around to look behind me every minute or so. I cross the street and switch back over half a dozen times. I pop into a little bodega and stare at the passersby, searching for a familiar face. But I don't see anyone who appears to be following me.

I feel as if I'm in a pinball machine as I weave through Times Square, dodging the woman scalping theater tickets to *Hamilton,* the guy pushing fake Ray•Bans toward me, muttering, "Ten dollars," and a man pressing flyers into the hands of tourists.

I finally reach my hotel. Before I unlock my door, I look for the edge of the white toilet paper.

It's gone.

CHAPTER SIXTY-TWO

SHAY

When it comes to violent crime, especially murder, Americans are at much greater risk of falling victim to someone they know, perhaps someone they know intimately. According to a landmark study by the Bureau of Justice Statistics, between 73 and 79 percent of homicides during a fifteen-year period were committed by offenders known to the victim.
—Data Book, page 73

I'M HUDDLED IN A BOOTH in a diner about a mile from my hotel. I ran all the way here, my heart pounding and my duffel bag banging against my hip.

It could just have been a maid ignoring my DO NOT DISTURB sign. But I can't erase my fear that Cassandra, Jane, and Valerie were waiting for me in my room.

"Freshen up your coffee?" a waitress with electric-blue eye shadow asks, startling me.

She fills my mug before I can reply.

I've already had two cups, and I forced myself to eat half of a grilled-cheese sandwich to justify taking up this table for so long.

I'm facing the door of the restaurant, and I've positioned my body sideways, so my back is to the wall, even though the only people near me are the elderly couple sharing the booth behind me.

I have no idea what to do or where to go. Not a single place in this city feels safe.

My body begins to shudder with the sobs I've been holding back. I feel as if a noose is slowly tightening around my neck.

I take off my glasses and wipe my tears with my sleeve, then put them back on. I don't have the luxury of indulging my feelings.

I pull my Data Book out of my duffel bag, then remove the receipt from my wallet. I start recording new data: *Twist bar, two Seagram's & sodas, Aug. 15. . .*

The voices around me seem to fade. I feel like I've been plunged underwater.

When I sat in the sterile room at the police precinct, Detective Williams asked me, *Where were you on the night of Thursday, August fifteenth, Shay?*

My fingers tremble as I reach for my burner phone.

"August 15," I type into a search engine.

It yields countless hits.

I narrow it by adding "New York."

There are still hundreds of millions of results.

Something important happened on that date. That must be why Detective Williams asked me about it in the sterile questioning room.

I close my eyes and see the bloody scalpel. When I first glimpsed it, I'd guessed that Amanda had taken it from work. I'd rolled around different theories in my mind, each more unsettling than the next: Maybe Amanda had used it in an earlier suicide attempt, but had changed her mind. Or it could be evidence of some malfeasance at City Hospital— maybe a surgeon had operated on the wrong patient with it.

There are other possibilities, though.

I add one more search term to further refine my results: "Twist bar."

A headline bursts onto my phone screen: BUSINESSMAN FOUND DEAD IN CENTRAL PARK.

My eyes move frantically down the screen: James Anders was found murdered in Central Park just a few months ago—on Thursday, August 15.

"He looked like he'd been butchered," a police source told the paper.

Butchered. The horrifying word seems to pop off the screen.

I grab my notebook and start recording facts. My hands are shaking so violently my words are barely legible: He was thirty-seven. A divorced father of one. From a town called Mossley in upstate New York. No suspects.

I click on a few more links, writing down everything I can find about James Anders. The obituary from his local paper, *The Courier,* described how he attended Syracuse University and married his college sweetheart. After his divorce, he'd begun to split his time between Mossley—where he'd lived his whole life—and Manhattan as he tried to start up a new business selling custom sporting equipment.

This article also has a picture. I squint at the grainy photo of a man wearing a suit and tie.

"Hey, hon, we're closing up in a few." The waitress puts the check on my table. It's signed with her name—Shirley—and a smiley face.

I lean back and briefly close my eyes. It seems like I should be inured to shock after the events of the past couple of days, but what I've just learned feels like a blow to my solar plexus.

I hear the door to the diner rattle and my eyes snap open. It's just a customer exiting.

Still, it reminds me of how vulnerable I am. *Keep moving,* my brain tells me.

In a few hours the city will begin shutting down. I don't want to be wandering around, trying to find bars that close late and diners that open early. Hotels no longer feel safe.

I need a different place to hide. Somewhere I won't be disturbed, so I can think. Some place unexpected.

I check the time on my phone. It's almost nine P.M., and I've got 68 percent of my battery left. I'm down to less than a few hundred dollars.

I know one other thing, too: I'm being set up for a murder.

The subway sways along the tracks, its wheels rumbling, as I head out to Far Rockaway in Queens for the second time tonight. When I reach the end of the line, I'll cross the platform and ride the thirty-one miles back to 207th Street at the northern tip of Manhattan again.

Then I'll do it again and again, until dawn breaks.

The subway in New York never sleeps.

I made one phone call just before I descended the stairs to the turnstiles. I called the number on Detective Williams's card. She didn't pick up, maybe because I used the burner phone and she didn't recognize the number, or maybe because she was busy with a case.

My words rushed out uncontrollably in the message I left: "I know Amanda's friends are setting me up for the murder of James Anders, but I didn't do it! They planted that stuff and more in my apartment—you've got to believe me, please. I'm innocent!"

I probably sounded completely crazy to her; I might even have made things worse for myself.

Now I look out the window of the train and see the graffiti painted on the walls of the city's tunnels has yielded to a suburban landscape since we've moved aboveground: We whiz by trees, single-family homes, and glowing porch lamps. A kid's bike propped up against a railing. A doghouse.

I'm sitting in the middle of the train, as close as I can to the conductor, who pays me no notice. I know exactly where the emergency buttons are in this car. My duffel bag contains my change of clothes, wallet, burner phone, a power bar, and my Data Book and pen. My arms are wrapped around it, and my eyes never stop moving as commuters get on and off the train. I scan every single face.

The people who appear and then disappear around me are like a microcosm of the city: late-night Wall Street workers in expensive suits mix with equally weary-looking cleaners in blue aprons, and a woman carrying a guitar case sits across the aisle from a guy in a Jets jacket, while voices from the boisterous party crowd—women in skirts and sequins laughing as they take selfies, a group of guys heckling their drunk buddy who fell over when the train lurched forward—soar over it all.

But as the night wears on, the crowds grow thinner.

Right now it's just me in the subway car. I look at the conductor again, then clutch my duffel bag even tighter.

It must be two or three o'clock, but I turned off my phone to preserve the battery when it hit 26 percent. Reception is so spotty on the subway that I ate up a lot of battery looking up everything I could find on James Anders, and my charger is back in the hotel room, along with my iPhone.

A young guy wearing layers of dirty, frayed clothes enters my car at the next stop. I tense up, feeling my eyes widen, when he begins to head in my direction. He smiles, revealing a few missing teeth, and briefly holds up his hands, as if to show me he means no harm. Then he turns and takes a seat toward the opposite end.

I feel bad about my instinctual reaction; I hope I didn't hurt his feelings. He's tall and beefy, and I actually feel a little safer with him around. We ride together as the hypnotic, rushing sound of the train's movement fills my ears again.

I know things don't look good for me. I have no alibi for the night of August 15. I went for a long run—that much was in my phone's calendar, which I showed to Detective Williams. But I can't remember the exact route, or what I listened to on my headphones, or even what time I arrived home.

I didn't kill James Anders. So who did?

Someone who knew him. Statistics I found earlier tonight show that between 73 and 79 percent of homicides were committed by offenders known to the victim.

One of the articles I read noted that James Anders's wallet and watch were stolen, but that he'd paid for his drinks at Twist right before leaving.

So whoever killed him must have taken those items.

I can still see the brown leather wallet and gold watch on my floor, by the tan sundress with dried bloodstains on the hem.

The Moore sisters were in my apartment earlier that night, plus they—or Valerie—have a key to it. I'm convinced they planted those items. Every bit of data I've amassed tells me they must have killed James, too.

But why?

I have to find out how their lives intersected with his.

I turn back on my phone and use some of my waning phone battery to search their names all together again—Cassandra and Jane Moore, Valerie Ricci, and James Anders—but nothing comes up.

It seems logical that they must have crossed paths in New York. James lived here part-time for the past year, traveling to his home in Mossley on the weekends.

They could have met him anywhere in the city—at a bar, at the gym, at a restaurant, on the street. Could he have been one of their lovers? If so, surely the police would have investigated them.

I've gone over it a thousand times in my head. But I can't figure out how to connect them. I underline James's address in New York and the name of his company, my pen pressing hard against the page. Maybe the name Moore will mean something to one of his coworkers.

The train pulls into another station and the doors hiss open. But no one gets on. By now the guy toward the far end of my car is snoring gently. The doors close and we move on.

I look down at my phone screen again and read another obituary for James Anders, this one a brief few paragraphs created by the funeral home that handled his service. I've already written down the names of the people who survived him: his daughter, Abby; his mother, Sissy Anders; and his ex-wife, Tessa. His father predeceased him, the obit said. Except for the four years he spent at Syracuse, James resided in Mossley all his life.

I click on a few tabs one by one: The first allowed people to buy flower arrangements to be displayed at the church during his funeral. The second provided information about where mourners could donate to an educational fund for Abby. The final one served as a "tribute wall" where people wrote condolence messages.

I start to read through the notes. Someone quoted a line from the Bible about angels, another expressed outrage that James's killer hadn't yet been caught, and one wrote Billy Joel lyrics: "Only the good die young. . . ."

Some of the tributes are anonymous, unfortunately. I begin to jot down the names of those who signed theirs.

When the train plunges back underground, my phone's connection cuts out. I hold my breath when the lights flicker, but they quickly stabilize.

When we're aboveground again, I scribble down as many of the names on the tribute wall as possible. I keep getting kicked off the internet, but by the time my battery dies, I've recorded a few that seem like promising leads.

A man signed his comment "Principal" Harris—which I'm guessing refers to James's old high school—and a few buddies referenced poker games, cookouts, and epic parties at the river. One signed his full name, Chandler Ferguson, and it's unusual enough that I might be able to find him. He could be a link to James's other friends, or maybe I could ask to see his old high school yearbook to collect more leads. A woman who signed only the name Belinda wrote, "You've always been like a son to me. God bless." She could have been a next-door neighbor, or even a relative.

If I can figure out a way to get the people who knew James best to answer my questions, they could unveil the connection between James and the Moore sisters.

When my battery finally dies and my phone goes dark, my hand aches from writing so furiously, and pressure has built up behind my eyes.

I didn't know the Moore sisters when James was murdered. I only met them after another violent death—their friend Amanda's. So they couldn't have been planning all along to set me up for this.

Why did they target me?

It was the purest of coincidences that led my path to cross with Amanda's at such a horrible moment. They couldn't have engineered that; if I hadn't stopped on that muggy August morning to tie up my hair and lost twenty-two seconds, I would've caught the earlier train.

I lean my head back, trying to imagine what the police meant by butchered. I can't see Cassandra or Jane killing anyone—let alone so brutally.

We're approaching the end of the line; I recognize the twisted tree trunk on a street corner from seeing it earlier tonight. I stand up, hearing my joints pop.

The young man in the slightly frayed clothes is still sleeping. I reach into my duffel bag for my last power bar, then walk quietly down the middle of the train and lay it on the empty seat next to him.

The train stops. I check the platform to make sure it appears safe. Then I step off, cross to the other side, and wait for the one heading back to Manhattan.

CHAPTER SIXTY-THREE

CASSANDRA & JANE

Nineteen years ago

AT FIRST, NOTHING SEEMED out of the ordinary on that Wednesday night.

Cassandra and Jane ate roast chicken and green beans at the kitchen table, while their mother sipped a white wine spritzer and prepared a plate of what she called "crudités" for their stepfather's arrival. Their homework was finished; their backpacks waited in the front closet for a new school day.

They'd lived in their stepfather's house for more than a year by now, and the unspoken routine was firmly established: When he arrived home, they became invisible.

Usually, that occurred around seven P.M. on weeknights.

But Cassandra had barely swallowed her last forkful of beans when the front door swung open and the sound of footsteps approached the kitchen.

Their mother grabbed her purse off the counter and swiped on a fresh coat of frosted pink lipstick, using the shiny refrigerator door as a mirror.

"You're home early!" she cried when their stepfather appeared, wearing one of his three-piece suits. It was her fake happy voice; Cassandra and Jane had heard it a million times before—like when Jane had given her a multicolored macaroni necklace she'd made at school, or when Cassandra had told her she'd signed up her mom to bake homemade cookies for the class Christmas party, or when their retired next-door neighbor struck up a conversation about his tomato garden.

"I was eager to see you," their stepfather replied, but his voice didn't sound normal either. When their mother walked over to kiss him, the girls noticed he turned his head to one side.

"All done?" She pulled away the girls' plates. Jane wasn't—she'd been saving the crispy skin of her chicken for last—but she didn't protest.

Something strange was in the air.

Cassandra felt it, too. "C'mon, let's go upstairs," she said, taking Jane's hand.

Their stepfather's nasally voice carried clearly after them: "So, how was your day?"

"Good, good," their mother replied. "Let's get you a drink."

As the girls climbed the stairs, they heard the sharp crack of ice cubes coming free from the tray.

"And did you enjoy step aerobics?" their stepfather asked.

Silence. Then the cubes clattered into a glass.

"Wait," Cassandra whispered, pressing Jane's hand. They crouched on the top step, huddled together. The girls could smell the lemon Pledge the housekeeper had used on the banister earlier that day; their socks pressed into the soft, plush wall-to-wall carpet, the one their mother had forbidden them to walk on wearing shoes.

"Yes, it was fine," their mother answered. There was a pause. "Is something wrong with your drink?"

Another pause. A strange current ran through the house. It made the sisters feel like they'd stepped into a scary movie.

Something was looming; about to pounce.

"Is he angry?" Jane whispered.

Cassandra shrugged, then put her index finger to her lips.

"So, chicken for dinner?" their stepfather asked. "I thought you'd be more in the mood for steak."

Cassandra squeezed Jane's hand.

"Sweetie, what are you talking about?" Their mother's tone was shrill now. "We don't eat red meat in this house . . . remember what your doctor told you?"

"Yes, but I wondered if you wanted a little variety today."

Jane turned to Cassandra and scrunched up her face. Their stepfather was speaking in code.

But their mother seemed to understand it. "My love—"

He cut her off. "I had a bit of a surprise this morning. I received a letter. Someone slipped it under the front door of my office building."

"Who was it from?"

"There's no signature."

"What—what did it say?" their mother stammered.

"Here, I'll read it to you." The girls heard a rustling sound, then he cleared his throat. "'Check out where your wife really goes on Wednesdays when she pretends she's taking a step aerobics class.'"

There was dead silence.

Then their voices grew louder, with his squashing hers down. He used a few bad words the girls knew—and one they'd never before heard. Their mother began to cry.

The last thing their stepfather said was "I want you all out of here by the morning."

Nothing was ordinary after that Wednesday night. Their family broke apart; now it was just three of them—Cassandra, Jane, and their mother—living in a small rental house. They returned to their old public school, and their mother began working full-time again. There was no more Dover sole or fresh seashell-colored paint.

But they didn't have to take off their shoes and carefully place them in the closet every time they entered the run-down small house with the chain-link fence surrounding it. They no longer had to become invisible at seven P.M. And Cassandra and Jane got to share a bedroom once more, where they could whisper late into the night and be reassured by the other's steady breathing if a nightmare came.

Sometimes—especially after dinner, when she was smoking Virginia Slims and elevating her tired feet—their mother would speculate about the author of the anonymous letter.

"Who would have sent that note?" she'd ask, stubbing another butt stained by her frosted pink lipstick into the ashtray. "It's like someone wanted to punish me."

A silent gaze would pass between Cassandra and Jane.

CHAPTER SIXTY-FOUR

SHAY

Even newborns show heightened interest in faces and develop the capacity to recognize them quickly. Many areas of the brain are involved with facial recognition, with the frontal lobe playing a large role.
—Data Book, page 75

WHEN THE DOORS TO THE New York Public Library on Fifth Avenue and Forty-second Street are unlocked at ten A.M. sharp, I'm the first person to step inside. I've been waiting between the two marble lions that flank the entrance. Long ago, they were nicknamed Patience and Fortitude because the New York City mayor Fiorello La Guardia felt citizens needed to possess those qualities to survive the Depression.

I take a deep breath as I walk through the stately Rose Main Reading Room, which is illuminated by chandeliers and small table lamps. Gracefully arched windows line the walls, and the ceiling is like a work of art, with murals inlaid between gilded curls and twists. Amid all this old-school grandeur are computers available to anyone with a library card.

Earlier this morning, after I left the subway and found an electronics store that opened at seven A.M., I bought a new charger for my burner phone. Then I went to a diner and asked to be seated by an outlet before ordering coffee and eggs. While I waited for my phone screen to come alive, I dozed off, awakening with a jerk after my head dropped down. I haven't slept since I caught a couple of hours of fitful rest in the hotel room two nights ago.

My fatigue is numbing; when a waitress dropped a plate that shattered on the floor, I barely flinched. My body feels heavy and sluggish, and I have to keep blinking to clear my vision.

I drank a cup of black coffee straight down before I played the single message that was left on my phone sometime during the night.

Detective Williams's voice was even more brusque than usual. "Shay, where are you? We need you to come in. Call me back the moment you get this."

I have two missed calls from her, too. She's intent on reaching me. When she told me to come in, it sounded like an order.

I don't know what the Moore sisters and Valerie have done since they left my apartment, but they may have engineered something to make me look even guiltier. They may have somehow swayed Detective Williams. Just as they apparently swayed Jody and Sean.

A wave of nausea grips me as I realize I have to acknowledge the real possibility that I could be arrested.

I'm worried the police can track me by my burner phone, now that Detective Williams has the number. So I want to keep it off as much as possible. But I have more research to do, which is why I came here, to the public library.

I slide into a seat before a waiting laptop and position my fingers above the keyboard. It's a relief to no longer have to squint at a tiny screen. The first name I plug into the search engine belongs to James's mother, Sissy Anders. I have to explore several channels to get a phone number for her, but I finally locate it through her Facebook page. His ex-wife, Tessa, has a listed number that I write down, even though I doubt she knew much about James's life in New York. It's also easy to find the phone numbers for James's new business in New York, his home address in Mossley, and the management company for his apartment building on East Ninety-first Street.

An older woman with a pair of reading glasses on a chain around her neck and a pile of textbooks slips into the chair next to mine. I reflexively check her face, then move on to the names I found on the funeral home's tribute page. I input "Harris," along with the terms "Mossley" and "principal." It yields an instant hit: Mossley Prep Academy. I navigate to the school's website and see Harris Dreyer listed as a former principal. He's probably retired by now, I think.

I continue researching the names from the funeral home's page. I can't find a Belinda Anders, which seems to reduce the possibility that she was related to James. But I do locate Chandler Ferguson, who's now a real estate agent in Mossley. Maybe like James he never really left his hometown. I put a star next to Chandler's name in my Data Book; they could have been close friends.

When I check the timer on my computer screen, I see I've only got four minutes left before the computer kicks me off to free up the system for other users. I forgot about the forty-five-minute limit. But maybe I have enough.

At least I can begin making phone calls now.

I pack up my things and head to the restroom. I've been in these clothes for days, and the filth of the subway seems to be clinging to me. I duck into a stall and lock the door and pull my sweatshirt over my head. I'm just unbuttoning my jeans when I hear the click of high heels against the floor.

Someone is standing a few steps in front of my stall, her toes pointed away from me. I see alligator pumps, gracefully arched feet, slim ankles. . . .

My heart jackhammers.

The sink water turns on.

I lean forward as quietly as possible, peering through the sliver at the side of the door. A fitted coat, blond hair cut in a bob . . . I glimpse the woman's face as she turns off the water and dries her hands while checking her reflection in the mirror.

She's a stranger.

I exhale as her heels click back across the floor and she exits the bathroom.

My legs are so weak and trembly that when I stand on one foot to take off my jeans, I have to grab at the stall's side wall to keep from falling over.

I bundle up my old things and shove them into the duffel, then change into my clean clothes. I exit the stall and turn on the sink tap and rinse out my mouth. I splash some cold water onto my face and wash the lenses of my glasses.

I glimpse myself in the mirror and quickly turn away. My hair is lank and a little greasy, and my skin is sallow.

I exit the library and begin walking, grateful my puffer coat is now keeping me warm. My body feels heavy and a little clumsy; I see double before I blink and shake my head to clear it.

I desperately need rest; my body and brain won't be able to function much longer without it. My concentration is already slipping and I'm showing signs of deep sleep deprivation. After three nights with no sleep, people can begin to have hallucinations. I'm not too far from that point.

When I reach Bryant Park, I find an empty bench and begin making calls on my cheap phone.

The number for James's new company has been disconnected. I track down a former colleague who was working with James on his custom-sporting-equipment business, but he says he has never heard James mention Cassandra or Jane Moore, or anyone named Valerie. The manager of the apartment building where James rented a one-bedroom tells me no women with those names live in the complex. When I call the Mossley real estate agency and ask for Chandler Ferguson, my most promising lead, I get sent to his voice mail. While I'm leaving him a message, an incoming call makes my phone buzz.

It's Detective Williams again.

I don't answer.

Instead I turn off my phone for a few minutes while I leave the park and walk a few blocks away, to a bus stop. I sit on the bench inside the little shelter and turn on my phone again. I dial one of the numbers left on my shortening list, for James's ex-wife, Tessa. She doesn't answer so I hang up.

Next I call James's mother, Sissy Anders.

She picks up on the second ring.

I begin by telling her the lie I've created—that I went to Mossley Prep with James and that we alumni want to honor him with a small ceremony.

Uttering those words makes me feel sick; my stomach clenches so tightly it hurts. It feels even worse than stealing back Jane's necklace from Amanda's mom.

When Mrs. Anders finds out there's no ceremony planned, it'll be like salt in her wounds. But maybe she'll forgive me if I can find out who murdered her son.

I'm about to launch into the next bit I've practiced. I need to lob out the names of Cassandra, Jane, and Valerie to see how Mrs. Anders reacts. If she recognizes them—if James ever mentioned having a date with a gorgeous woman named Jane in the city, or if he told his mom he'd gone to a networking event and met a Cassandra who works at a fancy PR firm—I'll have all the proof I need.

But before I can say another word, Mrs. Anders spits one out at me: "Vulture."

"Ex-excuse me?"

"What are you trying to get, money or something?" she snaps. "Mossley Prep already held a small service and planted a tree in my son's honor last month."

She slams down the phone, leaving me breathless.

A tear slides down my cheek and I wipe my nose with my sleeve. Everything I do seems to be wrong, and I'm sinking deeper and deeper into something I worry I'll never be able to climb out of.

Only one contact is left: Harris Dreyer, the former principal.

He answers my call in a deep, rich voice, giving his full name, as if he's at an office.

I can't tell him the truth, either.

"Hi, I'm so sorry to bother you. I'm calling about James Anders. I was hoping you could tell me something nice about him for his college alumni magazine."

"Oh, James, what a tragedy." Harris sighs. "You know, unfortunately, I can't talk about a former student other than to tell you I have warm recollections of that wonderful young man."

"His best friends," I blurt. "Could you just tell me who he was close to?"

It's hard to find statistics on how many people stay in touch with their high school friends, but given James's strong ties to the area, it's certainly possible that he kept in close contact with his closest buddies from Mossley Prep—maybe even the ones who moved away.

"I wish I could help, but I can't give out any information on any of my old students. I hope you understand."

I thank him and hang up. Then I wrap my arms around myself and rock back and forth on the hard wooden bench.

All my work was fruitless.

I have to keep trying to find the link. It feels like the only thing that can save me.

I push off the bench and begin to walk in the direction of James's East Ninety-first Street apartment building. Maybe I can find one of his neighbors, or perhaps I'll see something that will finally click— similar to when I spotted Valerie coming out of the PR firm.

While I walk, I phone the Syracuse University Office of Alumni Engagement because I have no idea where the Moore sisters or Valerie attended college. "I'm just trying to track down a few of your graduates," I say. But the woman who answers the phone tells me none of them attended Syracuse.

I finally reach the building where James stayed when he was in New York. I wait by the entrance, my duffel bag at my feet, hoping someone comes in or goes out.

But it's the middle of the workday, and although I'm there for three hours, the only people who enter the building are a dog walker and a UPS deliveryman, both of whom look at me quizzically when I ask if they knew a James Anders who lived here.

Maybe this is the wrong approach, I think. James had only been in New York for less than a year. I can't imagine he developed strong ties in that short time. The people who knew him best are all in Mossley.

I pull out my Data Book and look down at my scrawled list of names—but they're first names, and other than Belinda, they're all fairly common ones: Kevin, Sam, Robin, Kathy, Matt. If any of them are former high school classmates, maybe there's a way I can cross-reference them by finding a Mossley Prep yearbook.

I've been sitting on the steps leading up to the door of James's building. I pull myself up heavily and head down the street, stopping at the dry cleaner's a few doors down and showing the picture of James on my tiny screen to the woman behind the desk. She doesn't recognize him or his name, but I leave my number, and she promises she'll have the manager call me later today. I also stop at the burger restaurant on the corner and the liquor store across the street. It's a long shot that anyone at these places would know James, let alone have spotted him with one of the Moore sisters. But I have to try.

I resume walking toward the Apple Store. On my way, I dial Tessa, James's ex-wife again, but she doesn't answer. For all I know, she's out of town. Chandler doesn't pick up either.

The store is crowded—the new iPhone was just released—so I have to wait a few minutes to get an open computer. I keep my duffel bag clenched between my feet as I navigate to the Mossley Prep website and try to find a link to old yearbooks.

There aren't any. But I do discover the high school newspaper, the *Tattler,* is archived online—and the issues go back exactly twenty years. James would have been seventeen then, probably a senior.

I begin to scan the pages, searching for names in bylines and photo captions that match those on my list. I scroll through dozens of pages before I get my first hit in the homecoming edition of the paper: A guy named Kevin O'Donnell was homecoming king. He might have been the same Kevin who wrote about epic parties at the river.

I keep scanning through the old black-and-white pages, then I see a picture of a group of guys playing soccer under the headline THE LIONS PREPARE FOR ANOTHER VICTORY!

I look at the picture of the players, but I can't tell if James is in it. He could be the blond guy chasing the ball, but his face is in profile. And all I've seen is one grainy black-and-white picture of him as an adult.

I rub my burning eyes, then continue to scan the pictures and articles. I find two Kathys—one who wrote a piece about the debate team, and another who won a cross-country meet. I write down both of their last names.

"Miss? Do you need any help?" I look up to see a guy in a navy blue T-shirt with an Apple logo standing next to me. I'm suddenly aware of how I must appear: I spent the night on the subway and I didn't brush my hair today, let alone shower. More than that, the agitation and fear roiling off me are probably palpable.

"Just looking," I say, and return my gaze to the screen.

Five pages later, I scan a large photo of student actors rehearsing for the senior fall play. A dozen kids are onstage, but only two are named in the caption: "Lisa Scott, who plays Emily Webb, and Andy Chen, who plays George Gibbs, get ready to wow the audience on opening night!"

I jot down those names, then I scan the faces of the other teenagers, looking for James.

My tired eyes skip over a dark-haired girl sitting on the edge of the stage, her legs dangling. Then my gaze jerks back.

Straight eyebrows. Features that are unremarkable yet somehow familiar. An intense stare at the camera.

My peripheral vision turns black; I feel like I'm about to pass out. I take deep breaths, fighting off the sensation.

It looks like Valerie Ricci.

If she and James went to Mossley Prep together, I've found the hidden link.

Valerie was an actress, I remember as my pulse accelerates. She lived in L.A. before moving to New York. It stands to reason she'd perform in the school play.

I lean forward, my face close to the screen. This photo is twenty years old. It looks like it could be a young Valerie, but I couldn't bet my life on it.

More than three thousand counties are in the United States. What are the odds that Valerie would just happen to have been from the one James lived in?

Essentially impossible. People also have a roughly one-in-three-thousand chance of getting struck by lightning in their lifetime, and I've never known anyone that has happened to.

I begin to whip through the old newspaper archives again, a fresh surge of energy fueling me as I search for any other indication of Valerie's presence at Mossley Prep. This is what I've been desperate to find—it could prove my innocence and get Detective Williams to investigate the true criminals.

The final issue of the school year contains a double-page spread featuring the graduating class with the names of all the students listed.

I begin to tremble as I read through each one.

She wouldn't have been Ricci back then, but there is no one named Valerie at all.

I search through the faces. But the girl I saw on the theater stage is missing.

Did I imagine seeing her?

Hallucinations don't begin until after three nights with no sleep. I'm not there yet.

I go back to the first page of the paper, determined to find some trace of Valerie at the school.

When my phone rings, I glance down reflexively. It's Detective Williams again.

I'm tempted to answer and blurt out what I think I've stumbled across, but it would be far better if I can phone her back with hard evidence. I let it go to voice mail.

I consider calling Mossley Prep, but it's dark out now; past closing time for any high school, and I doubt they'd give me information about a former student anyway.

I'm so close to figuring all of this out.

My phone rings a second later, but this time it's a number with the Mossley area code. I snatch it up.

It's Chandler Ferguson, the real estate agent.

"Thank you so much for calling me back!" I blurt. My voice sounds borderline hysterical. "You went to Mossley Prep, right?"

"Yes?" he says, drawing out the word into a question.

"I—I—I'm trying to get some information about one of your former classmates, Valerie Ricci. But she would've had a different last name back then. Did you know her?" My words are running into each other.

He pauses.

"I really need to find Valerie," I whisper. "Please."

"Excuse me," a woman says loudly. "I'm waiting for that computer if you're not using it."

I step away, leaving my duffel bag on the floor.

"Valerie?" he repeats. It sounds like I'm on a speakerphone in his car; I can hear a tinny echo. I hold my breath.

"If that's who I'm thinking of, yeah, she went to our school briefly." He gives a little laugh. "Piece of work, that one."

My vision swims. The ground tilts beneath me.

Cassandra and Jane didn't know James. Chandler has just confirmed it was Valerie who had the connection to the murdered man. They probably grew up in the same town. They attended the same high school.

"What do you mean 'piece of work'?" I gasp.

I feel someone tap me. "Is this yours?" The woman who claimed my computer points at my duffel bag. I scoop it up with my free hand and move away. It's so noisy in the store that it's hard to hear Chandler when he asks, "Sorry, who did you say this is?"

"I'm just an old friend of hers."

I hear him honk and curse softly. "The highway is filled with idiots tonight. Didn't mean to offend you. Sorry, I didn't really know Val and I haven't seen her in twenty years. Now, if you're interested in buying a house . . ." He gives a little laugh. I hear the connection click, as if he has an incoming call. "Look, if you really want to find Valerie, I think her mom still works at Ribeye. I'm pretty sure she served me a steak last time I was there. You could ask her."

"What's her mom's name?" I ask urgently.

"Belinda. Gotta run, good luck."

I stand in the middle of the store, my phone still to my ear, people swirling all around me.

Belinda is Valerie's mother.

My brain is so jumbled now I almost can't make the connection. I flip back in my Data Book, which is normally tidy but now has lines slashed through and arrows connecting bits of information. I search for Belinda's name. *You were like a son to me,* she wrote on the tribute page.

Were Valerie and James high school sweethearts?

I have to get to Belinda. She's holding the final puzzle piece.

———

"Who did you say you were again?" Belinda asks.

I've been pacing the streets, holding my phone, waiting for her to call me back at the end of her shift, as her manager at the steak house promised she would.

It's almost nine P.M., and fatigue and adrenaline are wreaking havoc on my body. I'm so weak I'm nearly staggering. All I've eaten today is a few bites of scrambled eggs, and I'm severely dehydrated. But I can't stop moving; I feel like I'll collapse if I do.

"Hi, I'm Lisa Scott, and I went to Mossley Prep with your daughter Valerie," I say, using the name of the girl who appeared on the theater stage with Valerie. "I'm trying to track her down. . . ."

"Oh, Valerie's living in the Big Apple now."

I grip the phone more tightly. "It's just that I'm organizing a special memorial for James Anders at our next reunion, and I understand they were friendly."

Take the bait, I think urgently.

But she doesn't immediately reply.

"Uh, I was—I'm wondering about Valerie so I can send her an invitation. . . ."

"Friendly?" Belinda finally responds, sounding surprised. "Valerie wasn't just *friendly* with James. I was married to James's father for a little while. So he was her stepbrother."

I'm stunned into speechlessness.

"But Valerie probably wouldn't go to James's memorial," Belinda continues.

This is it. I have the piece of evidence I need to give the police. Detective Williams will surely investigate Valerie now.

My body begins to tremble and I feel tears slide down my cheeks.

"They weren't close, you see. And Valerie was always out of the house at play rehearsal or with her friends. You know how girls are at that age."

I'm barely listening as Belinda continues. All I want to do is hang up and phone Detective Williams.

"If any of my daughters would want to attend, it would be the other two."

The hair on my arms stands up as an electric charge courses through my body.

"Valerie has two sisters?" I whisper.

"Yeah." Belinda sounds surprised. "Cassandra and Jane."

I squeeze my eyes shut, seeing those three sleek heads close together in the back of the cab.

"Thank you, Mrs. Moore," I finally manage to reply.

"So where did you say this memorial for Trey will be? I mean James—Trey's his old nickname, so it's how I always think of him. Anyway, is it just for classmates, or . . ."

Belinda's voice is fading away.

"Hello?" I hear her say, just before I hang up.

CHAPTER SIXTY-FIVE

VALERIE

Nineteen years ago

It was the best day Valerie had experienced since she'd transferred to Mossley Prep, the school for rich kids in her town.

She didn't know anyone well yet—it sucked to start at a new high school during senior year—but right before lunch, the drama teacher posted the cast list for the spring production of *Grease*.

She'd won the part of Rizzo, with its showstopping solo.

"Congrats," said Lisa Scott, the spoiled little blonde who always got the leads. She'd be playing Sandy.

"Thanks," Valerie responded, thinking, *I'm going to make everyone forgets you're even onstage.*

Valerie was walking home, breathing the crystalline air and humming along to the music in her mind, when her stepbrother pulled up in his Audi convertible. "Wanna ride?"

Trey was cute in a preppy kind of way, but he wasn't her type. Plus, it was gross to think about him that way. They were related now, even though they barely saw each other at home. He was only around every other weekend, and she spent as little time as possible in that stuffy house with her weird stepfather. Whenever she had free time, she'd go visit her friends from her old high school, the ones she'd been torn away from when her mother remarried.

Still, occasionally when Trey visited and they crossed paths, he'd hold up a joint and waggle his eyebrows, and they'd sneak into the woods bordering their backyard. He'd imitate their classmates and sometimes slip her a copy of an upcoming test that he'd somehow obtained. Trey could be fun.

She hopped in the car.

A joint was in the ashtray of his Audi today, too. "Let's stop by the river." He took a drag and passed the joint to her. She inhaled, holding the smoke in her lungs.

"Nah, I should go home." She wanted to start memorizing her lines.

"C'mon." He turned the wheel in the direction he wanted to go. "Everyone's there."

She shrugged. "Whatever."

Everybody *was* at the river that afternoon—including a guy Valerie liked, another senior named Mateo, who was into black-and-white photography and played bass, which was cool.

Feeling bold from her triumph at school and from the joint, Valerie went to sit beside Mateo, leaving Trey to hang with his buddies. She felt Trey's eyes on her, and once he called out for her to come grab a beer, but she waved him off.

Barely a half hour after they arrived, Trey walked over and stood staring down at her. "Time to go." She was leaning against Mateo, admiring on the screen of his Nikon photographs he'd taken.

Valerie had to shield her eyes when she looked up at Trey; the sun was behind him, turning him into a dark silhouette.

Mateo's leg was pressed against hers, and its warmth felt delicious. "Not yet," she told Trey.

He stood there another minute. Then he said, "I'm leaving."

Valerie rolled her eyes at Mateo. But he was looking at his watch. "Damn, I've gotta go, too."

So Valerie stood up, brushing off the back of her skirt. "Hold on, I'm coming," she called as she hurried to catch up with her stepbrother.

The moment she slipped into the passenger seat he revved the engine and peeled out. Her door wasn't even fully shut.

"Jeez, Trey. What's the rush?"

He didn't answer. Instead, he drove around a bend.

"You're going the wrong way."

He jerked the wheel, pulling the car into a dead end. "You're such a whore," he spit out.

She stared at him in disbelief; was this some kind of a joke? His face was all red and the cords in his neck stood out.

Her hand, almost of its own accord, crept toward the door handle. But before she could open it, he propelled himself over the console, moving so fast he was on top of her before she fully realized what had happened.

"Trey! What are you doing?"

He straddled her while simultaneously grabbing the lever on the side of her seat to jerk her down into a reclining position.

She was too stunned to immediately react. Then she yelled, "Get off me!"

His mouth crushed hers. His hand pulled up her skirt and clawed at her skin. His fingers jammed their way inside her.

She fought back, squirming away from his fingers, trying to push him away. But his athletic body was so big and strong it easily over-powered her.

"Whore," he muttered again as he captured both her wrists with one hand, pinning them above her head. He ground his groin against hers.

Trey was reaching down to unzip his jeans when her knee knifed up through the air. He stopped moving and made a high-pitched, strange sound. She somehow managed to push him off and grabbed the door handle, sliding out from beneath him.

She fell roughly onto the gravel street and scrambled back up, cutting through backyards. Running toward safety.

A little later Valerie pushed through the front door of her step-father's house, still breathing heavily. She could smell the roast chicken her mother—who was such a fake little housewife now—had made for dinner.

She stormed into the kitchen and grabbed a can of Diet Coke from the fridge, popping the tab and spilling a few drops on the white tile floor.

She shuddered. She could still feel Trey's tongue pushing into her mouth while his fingers invaded her body. She wanted to punch him, to hurt him again. She took a long sip of Diet Coke, trying to erase the taste of his tongue in her mouth.

"You're late," her mother scolded. "And you know you're not supposed to drink my soda."

Valerie locked eyes with her mother and took another sip. Her little sisters, Cassandra and Jane, were sitting at the wooden table, their napkins in their laps, glasses of milk in front of them, still wearing their school uniforms.

"Hi, Val," Cassandra piped up.

"Guess what? I got a hundred on my spelling test!" Jane said.

Valerie exhaled. "Good job," she muttered. Normally she'd go over and give them both a hug. But she couldn't bear to be touched right now.

"Dinner's ready," their mom said.

"I'm not hungry," Valerie mumbled.

If her mother would just take a good look at her instead of fussing over the salad she was preparing for her new husband, she'd notice what had to be written all over Valerie's face.

He hurt me.

Her kneecaps stung, and dried blood was still on her palms from when she'd landed so roughly on the gravel road.

Her mother sighed heavily, bending down to wipe up the drops of Diet Coke. "I'm not in the mood for this tonight, Val."

Valerie turned and ran upstairs, slamming her door. She desperately wanted a shower; she was already pulling off her jean jacket. She flung it across the room, where it hit a lamp and knocked it over.

Her mother pushed her door back open a moment later without even knocking. "Young lady! Your father is going to be home any minute now! You need to get your act together."

"He's not my father!" Valerie's whole body felt hot and jittery and somehow alien, as if Trey had altered it. She needed to wash everything away.

Her mother stood in the middle of the bedroom, not even seeing her. "If you don't change your attitude right now, you're grounded."

Valerie took a deep breath. "You don't understand." She wrapped her arms around herself. "Trey—he grabbed me." She felt her chin tremble. Tears pricked her eyes. "He wanted to—he was on top of me—"

Her mother picked up the jean jacket Valerie had thrown and began to fold it. "Valerie, don't be so dramatic. That's ridiculous."

"He wouldn't stop!" Valerie blurted. Finally, she was able to put words to what had happened: "He tried to rape me!"

Her mother laid the jacket on the bed and smoothed the already-neat comforter. "Trey could have any girl he wanted." She could have been talking about the weather; her tone was conversational. But a remote coldness came into her eyes just before they slid away from Valerie's.

"I'm sure you got this wrong," her mother continued briskly. "Why don't you take a shower and try and calm down. I'll keep your dinner warm in case you want it later."

Then she exited the room, quietly closing the door behind her.

"Mom," Valerie whispered.

But her mother was gone.

A few weeks later—after enduring Trey's leers, and the rumors he'd spread that made his buddies in the school bark when she passed by, and watching her mother beam up at Trey every time he entered a room, as if he were the perfect son she'd always dreamed of having— Valerie was gone, too.

Trey was a charmer, a star athlete, a solid student who called his teachers "sir" and "ma'am." She was a teenager who wore short skirts and heavy black eye makeup and struggled to get B's and had spent more than a few afternoons in detention for skipping classes. Guys like James Scott Anders the Third—with their pedigrees and trust funds— always won. Who would believe her word over his?

Not even her own mother.

She stole all the cash she could from her stepfather's wallet and her mother's purse and bought a bus ticket to Hollywood.

She did one final thing on the morning she fled town.

She wrote an anonymous letter to her stepfather, using her left hand to disguise her handwriting, telling him his new wife was sleeping with the manager of a steak house on Wednesdays when she pretended to be taking step aerobics.

It took years for Cassandra and Jane to finally learn the truth about Valerie.

Their big sister hadn't fled Mossley because she no longer cared about any of them. She didn't write that letter to their stepfather out of spite, as the younger Moore sisters had suspected.

On the night that Valerie left Los Angeles after what she described as the second-worst betrayal of her life, she finally told Cassandra and Jane her secret. She explained she'd written the anonymous letter because she hoped it would make their stepfather divorce their mother and get them away from Trey.

Valerie knew at the center of her soul that he would target Cassandra or Jane next. Valerie had to get them out of that house.

She had been their secret protector all along.

CHAPTER SIXTY-SIX

SHAY

According to one comprehensive survey, the odds of having three children in one family who are all girls is 21 percent. In the 1920s, Alfred Adler— himself the second of six children—studied birth order and how it shaped personality. He theorized that the oldest child can develop a "taste for power" and can dominate younger siblings.
—Data Book, page 75

THREE MOORE SISTERS. Not two.

The city is swimming around me, with streetlamps and cars throwing off elongated, wavy streaks of light. A siren starts to blare, the noise echoing in my skull.

Cassandra, Jane, and Valerie had a stepbrother. His nickname was Trey, but he went by James as an adult. He was murdered in New York a few months ago. The revelations explode in my brain, one after another.

I have to get to somewhere safe.

I step to the curb and hail a cab. When one pulls up, I give the female driver the address of the Seventeenth Precinct.

If Detective Williams isn't in, I'll wait all night for her on one of those old wooden benches—at least there'll be an armed officer a few feet away.

As I sit down on the bench in the cab's backseat, a fatigue descends over me. I feel almost as groggy and weak as I did after I drank the champagne I'm now certain the Moore sisters doctored with some drug.

The driver catches my eye in the rearview mirror. She doesn't smile. *Could she be in on all this, too?* I wonder.

I don't latch my seat belt, and I check the locks to make sure they're not engaged. But a moment later the driver pulls away her eyes and I see a picture of her children on the dashboard.

I'm being paranoid, I tell myself.

Still, I wonder if I should call Detective Williams to let her know I'm coming in.

I flip to a clean page in my Data Book and begin to write down exactly what I want to say to her. I need to sound cogent and believable.

I've barely written two sentences when a call comes in on my burner phone from an unfamiliar 917 area code. I hesitate, then pick it up and press the button to accept the call.

"Shay Miller?" The woman sounds middle-aged and has a deep New York accent.

"This is she."

A lot of noise in the background—a mechanical rumbling and clattering and distant voices. "It's Detective Santiago from the NYPD."

Detective Santiago's next sentence feels like a bombshell. "I'm the lead homicide detective on the case of James Anders. Look, I know you've gotten wrapped up in something crazy. Things are moving fast. We're reopening the investigation into Amanda Evinger's suicide."

"What?" I gasp.

"There's no doubt she jumped. We have a clear view of that from our surveillance cameras in the subway. But we have reason to believe someone was pursuing her. And we've been investigating the Moore sisters ever since Amanda's death."

"They were James's—"

"Stepsisters. We know. Sorry, hold one second."

I hear the sounds of a subway train pulling into a station; then a man shouts, "Santiago!"

"One minute!" she shouts back. "Shay?"

"I'm still here."

"We need you to come down to the Thirty-third Street subway station as soon as possible and show us exactly where you were standing in relation to Amanda and walk us through the scene. How quickly can you be here?"

I wonder if she can also hear noises in my background—the sound of a heavy engine and the drone of traffic.

Everything she says sounds believable. And I'm only a couple of blocks from the subway station now. I could be there in five minutes.

But I'm going to verify Detective Santiago's identity first. And I'm definitely not doing anything until I've spoken to Detective Williams.

The lie springs to my lips so easily it astonishes me. "I'm actually just driving back to the city." I know she can probably hear the sounds of the car. "I was visiting my mom in New Jersey. I'm not too far away, though."

"Oh. Which exit are you near on the freeway?"

I pause. "Just about to pass Newark, so I'm forty-five minutes away. I'll get there as soon as possible."

The moment I hang up, I dial Detective Williams.

I drum my fingertips against the cover of my Data Book while I wait for her to answer.

CHAPTER SIXTY-SEVEN

VALERIE

VALERIE STANDS BY THE green pole marking the entrance to the Thirty-third Street station, watching passengers, mostly gray-faced men and women trapped in the kind of small, colorless lives that Shay inhabits, travel up and down the stairs.

In less than an hour, Shay will return from New Jersey and hurry to this exact spot, expecting to meet Detective Santiago. Shay will be breathless and hopeful, convinced that she has finally outsmarted the sisters and that justice will prevail.

Shay hasn't shown a great deal of aptitude in anticipating the threats that have befallen her, though it was clever of her to track down Belinda—Valerie no longer thinks of her as "Mom"—and learn about the sisters' connection to James. That move won Shay a bit of grudging respect from the oldest of the three sisters.

Still, Shay bumbled by not expecting Belinda to report the strange female caller who'd hung up midconversation after finding out about Valerie's relationship to James. "Wouldn't she have known that if she was really in Val's class?" Belinda had asked Cassandra.

Cassandra and Jane are en route to a hot new restaurant now. By the time Shay arrives at the subway station, they'll be seated and ordering drinks surrounded by other customers, their alibis secure.

Valerie thinks she could have orchestrated all this without her younger sisters, but she's glad she didn't have to.

Growing up, Cassandra and Jane were inseparable—they were closest in age, and temperamentally suited. Sometimes Valerie would let them bypass the KEEP OUT! sign on her bedroom door and flop down on her comforter to tell them what it was like to French-kiss boys, or how to shave their legs. Her younger sisters were a rapt audience; they've always been impressionable.

As adults, their loyalty to Valerie intensified a thousandfold when she moved to New York and finally revealed what had caused her to leave their hometown. She hadn't been rejecting *them*, she explained. She'd pulled away because it hurt too much to have reminders of her past.

The story Valerie shared about their stepbrother, Trey, was true—every last bit of it, down to the feel of his fingers hurting her and the slightly derisive look on Belinda's face when she committed the ultimate betrayal against her oldest daughter.

But the other tale Valerie relayed on the stormy night when she reunited with Cassandra and Jane—the one in which she played the role of the innocent victim who was tricked by her conniving roommate Ashley—was tweaked and altered for dramatic effect.

Valerie is an actress, after all.

Ashley hadn't drugged Valerie or hidden her phone on the night before her big callback. Those details were a complete fabrication. Or, as Valerie prefers to think of it, creative license.

Valerie didn't make it to the callback because Ashley won the part, fair and square, during her own callback, which took place on the afternoon before Valerie's was scheduled. Ashley hadn't even known Valerie was chasing the same role.

In her heart, though, Valerie believed the part belonged to her, and she to it. Her devastation was genuine.

Maybe Valerie should have felt guilt when her supportive younger sisters used their influence to ruin Ashley's career. Ashley might have been able to survive the horribly unflattering photos that were leaked to the tabloids, but the rumors about her sexual perversities were so depraved and vile it seemed no one in the industry could look past them.

Today Ashley is married and living in the Valley; that was a much better role for her.

Perhaps Valerie should feel guilty about what will befall Shay—another innocent woman who got in the way.

But she doesn't.

Valerie has a new purpose now, one that is more meaningful than hitting her marks and channeling a character, and even more rewarding than hearing an audience's applause.

She began to feel fully alive again when she watched Trey—or James, as he'd shed his childhood nickname when he went to college—die on that park bench.

Who knows what atrocities she can guide her sisters and the other women to avenge in the future?

Ever since the three sisters reunited, Valerie has been a powerful stealth influencer, shepherding Cassandra and Jane in an exciting new direction. Valerie is the invisible architect of every act of vengeance their larger group has perpetrated. After being alone for so long, she relishes having her sisters by her side.

There's just one more loose end to tie up.

Valerie lifts her head slightly as she catches sight of a woman in a black puffer coat approaching the subway station. Valerie smiles.

Shay has finally arrived.

The other women in the group think Cassandra and Jane are the leads, and that Valerie plays a supporting role.

But Valerie has been the star all along. This is *her* stage.

CHAPTER SIXTY-EIGHT

SHAY

The Double Jeopardy Clause in the 5th Amendment means no one can be tried twice for the same crime. There is no statute of limitations when it comes to murder. There are currently 54 correctional facilities in New York. They hold about 47,000 prisoners.
—Data Book, page 78

IT'S NEARLY TEN P.M. by the time I enter the Thirty-third Street station.

A dull roaring sound floods my ears; I'm so dizzy I have to concentrate to simply walk in a straight line.

I look around for the police as I grip the railing and slowly begin to descend the steps. But I don't see them.

Unease fills my body.

Though people are on the street above me, the stairs are empty.

Even though that's not unusual at this time of night on a weekday, my legs are trembling, and I almost miss a step.

As I reach the landing, a woman hurries toward me, as if she is rushing up to exit.

But instead of passing me, she spins around and grabs my arm above the elbow, hard, causing pain to shoot down my forearm. At the same moment, I feel something hard press into my waist.

I know even before I glimpse her face that it's Valerie.

We were here together, in this precise spot, only weeks ago. Valerie held my arm then, too, as she laughed and joked and got me over my fear of the subway.

But she was wearing a friendly mask then. Tonight I see her real face.

Her expression is composed, yet her brown eyes glitter. "Shay, come with me. We're going to take a ride."

My heart begins to thud. My body is limp with terror.

"The police are here!" I blurt. "I'm meeting them!"

"Sorry I had to trick you to get you here, Shay." But it's not Valerie's voice coming out of her mouth. It's Detective Santiago's heavy New York accent.

Then she smiles.

If I was scared of Valerie before, now I'm terrified.

Valerie begins to walk toward the platform, maintaining the painful pressure near my elbow joint. I have no choice but to keep pace with her; I haven't looked down yet, but I'm certain she's pressing a gun against my torso.

A man carrying a briefcase passes us going the other way and I try to catch his eye, but he's looking down at his phone. Even if he did see us, what would he notice? We look like two girlfriends huddled close together, maybe because of the cold, heading out to a late dinner or concert.

We approach the platform. "Look, Shay, I'm not going to hurt you."

Half a dozen people are milling around—a few businesspeople, a young woman wearing bulky headphones, and a mom absently rolling a pink stroller back and forth. But they all seem lost in their own thoughts.

Valerie's voice is soft and gentle now; I'd almost believe her if I didn't know what she is capable of. "Cassandra and Jane and I just need to talk to you."

It's eerily quiet down here, between the rush of trains.

"I know you and Cassandra and Jane are sisters, and that you had a stepbrother named James." My lips are so dry and rigid it's hard to form the words. "But why did you set me up for his murder?"

"Cassandra and Jane want you to know it was nothing personal."

Valerie leads me farther down the platform, by the support beam. She pulls me to a stop not far from where Amanda stood when I first glimpsed her, then positions herself directly behind me.

Time seems to be slowing down. I'm acutely aware of my breath shuddering in and out of my lungs and what must be a gun against my ribs as Valerie adjusts it a little higher.

I could jerk away from her and try to run back up the stairs. I read somewhere that it's difficult to shoot a moving target. But I'm so weak and my brain is so foggy that I can't risk it. I'll never be able to outrun her. Plus that little pink stroller is somewhere behind me . . . if Valerie fires her gun, the bullet could go anywhere. With so much metal down here it might ricochet.

Valerie's hair brushes against my cheek as she leans closer to me. "Come, Cassandra and Jane are waiting for us. We'll get this all sorted out as soon as we see them."

The LED display shows the next train is due in two minutes.

A woman in gym clothes strolls toward us, appearing bored, one of her hands in her pocket and the other swinging free.

"Not a word," Valerie whispers, her breath warm against my ear.

But the woman isn't even looking at us. It's like no one in this city sees me.

I glance around. There's no escape. I feel a faint vibration beneath my feet.

One minute, the LED light announces.

The woman is closer now, but she's glancing at something back in the shadows beneath the overhang of the stairs. She casually raises her right hand, running it over the top of her hair, as if smoothing out her ponytail.

My body is completely rigid as I hear the rumbling of the train.

Valerie takes a big step, forcing me toward the edge of the platform. *Too close.*

Suddenly I know what she intends to do. Cassandra and Jane aren't waiting for us. Valerie wants this to look like I committed suicide; she's replicating Amanda's last moments.

She's truly trying to turn me into Amanda.

Valerie's gun is digging into me, and the oncoming train is almost in front of me. I'm trapped between two horrible fates.

The thunder of the train fills my ears.

Then I hear a shout: "Police! Valerie Ricci, put your hands up!"

The command comes from behind us. Valerie's head whips around as she twists slightly away from me and momentarily lowers her gun.

In that moment my instincts take over, marshaling every bit of my remaining strength as my legs and core tighten and keep twisting, continuing the rotation as I pull Valerie in a half circle with me. Then I ram my elbow into her chest, pushing her away from me.

The train appears in the mouth of the tunnel as Valerie falls backward onto the tracks.

The train whips past, erasing her, as I collapse onto the platform. I squeeze my eyes shut as the subway cars frantically grind to a stop, making shrieking noises that sound horrifyingly human.

People are shouting and rushing toward me, but I just lie there, feeling numb. When I finally open my eyes, I see the overturned pink baby stroller—with a plastic doll dangling out of it.

The woman pushing it was a cop, like the woman in exercise clothes, I realize.

I was never alone down here on the platform, just as Detective Williams promised when I called her from the cab.

A hand on my shoulder, her steady, familiar voice in my ear: "You're okay now, Shay."

It's good she heard everything, I think as she gently unzips my coat and checks the wire she outfitted me with shortly before I arrived at the subway station.

After all, two other sisters need to be punished.

EPILOGUE

SHAY

Two months later

> *Three things that saved me:*

1. *When Valerie, the former actress from L.A., pretended to be Detective Santiago by channeling the detective's thick Brooklyn accent, she asked which exit I was near on the "freeway." That's a West Coast term, as I once noted in my Data Book when I jotted down regional terms like* bubbler *for "water fountain" and* gravy *for "tomato sauce." Anyone born and bred in New York would have said "highway."*

2. *The woman who was with James Anders on the night he was murdered— by now she has been identified as Amanda Evinger—wore hoop earrings and dropped one as she left Twist. The bartender spotted it and called after her, but she didn't hear him. The real Detective Santiago collected it when she questioned the bartender following the discovery of James's body. She knew I couldn't have been with James at Twist. My ears aren't pierced, as Amanda's were.*

3. *When Detective Santiago asked Jody to bring her the picture of Amanda that was planted in my Data Book, Sean accompanied Jody. He described how the Moore sisters had set me up with a house-sitting gig, how shocked I was when they knew about my smoothies, and how he'd listened during my phone call with the sisters as they urged me to take Amanda's vacant alcove*

studio, in a location and with a rent that seemed too good to be true. He
also told the police he'd stake his life on his certainty that I was a victim in
whatever was going on. When I finally got my iPhone back from the sketchy
hotel, I saw he'd left a half dozen messages.

—Data Book, page 84

I STEP ONTO THE subway car just before the doors close and grip the overhead metal bar, my body swaying as the train picks up speed.

My old tote bag, containing my Data Book, is slung over my shoulder again.

I look around, collecting details the way I always do. Thirty-five other people are in this car. So out of the thirty-six of us, twelve—or 33 percent—likely consider themselves very happy, according to one survey on the emotions of Americans. A different study says four, or about 11 percent, are probably deeply unhappy.

As we pull into the station on Forty-second Street, I slide onto an open seat. I'm on my way home from my new job at Global Metrics. The person they hired right after I botched my interview didn't work out, so I went after the position again, and this time I won it. I'm looking forward to a quiet night in my studio apartment on the Upper West Side. It doesn't have the charm of Amanda's place, but at least the memories there are all my own.

On the happiness spectrum, I'm somewhere in the remaining 56 percent.

A guy across from me is staring. I don't think it's because I'm his type, though. My face was plastered on the cover of the *New York Post* when the paper broke the story of the Moore sisters' arrests for being accomplices in a homicide. Cassandra and Jane are currently being held without bail as they await trial, along with the other women in their group. They're going to be convicted, Detective Williams assures me; there's an awful lot of evidence against them.

I look a little different these days. I'm growing out the layers in my hair, though I've decided to keep the highlights, and I alternate between contacts and glasses depending on my mood. It's like I've taken on some parts of Amanda; the new me is a hybrid of the two of us.

Though I think about the sisters less and less, I'm still frequently reminded of them. Like when I see a trio of women sharing a bottle of wine and laughing, or when I remind myself to stand up straight instead of hunching, or when I watch friends link arms as they walk down the street.

It's hard to admit this, but even after everything they did, a part of me misses them. When they were around, I never felt alone.

I also remember all three sisters whenever I step onto a subway platform.

What are the chances that I would bear witness to two violent deaths in the same precise spot, only months apart?

But I try not to dwell on that data.

There's also a stat I've thought about a lot lately: that the average person will walk past sixteen killers in the person's lifetime.

I watch as a woman moves down the subway aisle.

I keep staring at her as she passes my seat. I wonder if she will walk past fifteen others during her lifetime.

I've never told anyone about how after the police officer yelled for Valerie to put up her hands and she reflexively turned, I continued twisting, forcing her between me and the platform. The body I used to try to minimize by shrinking into myself was my greatest ally in that moment; I needed my bigger limbs, stronger muscles, and extra few inches of height to overpower her. Then I used my last bit of strength to push her away.

I glimpsed her eyes as she was falling onto the tracks. They were wide open, glittering with a silent accusation.

Some people might consider me a murderer. But I hope most would say I acted in self-defense.

My subway car grinds to a stop and the doors wheeze open. A few people get off, and others crowd aboard.

I watch them move in and out of view. Some will get raises during the next year, while others will be asked for a divorce. A percentage will suffer physically—anything from a broken bone to the diagnosis of a terrible disease—while others will fall in love. The numbers tell me so.

As for me, I don't know what the future holds. But I choose to believe that the statistics are now in my favor.

ACKNOWLEDGMENTS

From Greer and Sarah:

Our thanks goes first to our brilliant editor and publisher, Jennifer Enderlin, who deftly steered us toward finding the right way to tell this story and whose creative vision elevated it immeasurably. Her support and enthusiasm for us and our writing are appreciated every day, and we feel so lucky to have her at the helm.

Our passionate publicist, Katie Bassel, is like a ray of sunshine, and she goes above and beyond to promote us and our books.

The incredible crew beside these two women nurture our novels through the publication process with meticulous care, boundless energy, and limitless creativity. We are so lucky to have them working on behalf of our books. Thank you to Rachel Diebel, Marta Fleming, Olga Grlic, Tracey Guest, Jordan Hanley, Brant Janeway, Sallie Lotz, Kim Ludlam, Erica Martirano, Kerry Nordling, Gisela Ramos, Sally Richardson, Lisa Senz, Michael Storrings, Dori Weintraub, and Laura Wilson.

To our new family at William Morris Endeavor: Jennifer Rudolph Walsh, Margaret Riley King, Sylvie Rabineau, and Hillary Zaitz Michael, thank you for taking us on and hitting the ground not just running but sprinting. We are elated to be working with you.

Our gratitude to all of our foreign publishers who have shared our work around the globe, especially the charming and hilarious Wayne Brookes at Pan Macmillan UK.

A big thanks to Victoria Sanders, Bernadette Baker-Baughman, Jessica Spivey, and Diane Dickensheid.

And to Benee Knauer: Your enthusiasm and insights always make us feel better!

A special shout-out to Holly Bario, Mia Maniscalco at Amblin Entertainment, as well as producer Jared LeBoff, for their guidance, support, and patience as we wrote the screenplay for *The Wife Between Us*. We are thrilled to be on your team.

Our deep appreciation to Shari Smiley, Lindsey Williams, and Ellen Goldsmith-Vein. And to Carolyn Newman, Jackie Secario at eOne,

USA Network, and screenwriters Josh and Rachel Abramowitz: We are so grateful for your work in bringing *An Anonymous Girl* to the screen.

And last but never least, a huge thank-you to our readers. We love connecting with you, so please find us on Facebook, Twitter, and Instagram. And to sign up for our very occasional newsletters, please visit our websites, at www.greerhendricks.com and www.sarahpekkanen.com. We'd love to stay in touch with you.

From Greer:

Sarah, I have two words for you: BETTER TOGETHER! Whether we are joyously celebrating a success or struggling in the trenches (cake toppers, timelines, cats), there is no one I would rather be with on this magical journey. With you by my side I am never alone!

I am deeply appreciative of my friends both inside and outside the publishing industry who come to readings, host events, and recommend our books. I am especially grateful to Marla Goodman and Alison Strong (who did double duty as early readers), Karen Gordon, Gillian Blake, and my Nantucket Book Group.

Thanks also to Georgeanne Dinan, Patty Allocca, and Detective Will Acevedo, who helped with some of the research. And to Kirsi Insalaco and the team at SoulCycle East 83rd, who keep me physically fit and mentally sane.

Extra-special thanks to my family: the Hendricks, the Alloccas, and my incredible parents, Mark and Elaine Kessel.

Robert Kessel: Little brother, this one's for you. Your love and support over the years have meant the world to me. Rabble Rabble, my special friend!

Paige, our tech adviser, your intellectual curiosity and smarts made this a better book. Alex, I can always count on you to lift my spirits with your generous heart and good cheer. And finally to John, who lives through each book from its inception through publication and beyond. Even the sky isn't the limit with you by my side.

From Sarah:

Greer, what a ride we've been on! I'm so grateful we have each other to cling to during the scary dips, and that we get to soar to heights side by side—often wearing outfits that we didn't plan to be matching!

So many dear friends assisted with this book, beginning with Susan Avallon, who provided a smart critique that improved our pages. Thanks to my sister-in-law Tammi Lee Pekkanen, who helped us come up with a breakthrough plot twist, and to early reader Jamie des Jardins.

Retired Montgomery County, Maryland, Police Chief Tom Manger patiently explained police procedure to me over a delicious breakfast. We took a few liberties in this novel in the name of creative license, but you grounded several key scenes in fact. I owe you another breakfast—this time with the lovely Jacqueline, too!

My gratitude to Russell and Lisa Pompa for their assistance, and to Amy and Chris Smith, Cathy Hines, Joe Dangerfield, and Rachel Baker for always being there. And to Glenn Reynolds, for being a terrific co-parent.

Laura Hillenbrand, a special thank-you for your generosity and for always listening. P.S. Your books aren't half-bad, either.

My parents, John and Lynn Pekkanen, fill in the gaps during deadline weeks by picking up my kids from soccer practice and drum lessons and dropping off pizzas. They're also among my earliest readers and biggest champions, as are Robert, Saadia, and Sophia Pekkanen—the West Coast Pekkanens—who are all stellar writers themselves. Ben and Tammi Pekkanen have given me so much support and laughter—as well as a perfect nephew, little Billy.

Roger Aarons, thank you for making me laugh every day, for always planning new adventures for the two of us, and for reading every single draft of this book and catching errors with an eagle-like intensity. Most of all, thank you for making me so happy.

And finally to Jackson, Will, and Dylan, my three sons, who fill my days and my heart with pride and love.

OUT NOW

The Wife Between Us

By Greer Hendricks and Sarah Pekkanen

When you read this book, you will make many assumptions.
It's about a jealous wife, obsessed with her replacement.
It's about a younger woman set to marry the man she loves.
The first wife seems like a disaster; her replacement is the perfect woman.
You will assume you know the motives, the history,
the anatomy of the relationships.

You will be wrong.

★

'Fans of *Gone Girl* and *The Girl on the Train* will adore this
classy domestic noir set in New York' *Daily Express*

'With shocking twists, this intricate thriller proves all is not
what it seems for the discarded first wife and the woman about
to marry her ex. Addictive' *Woman & Home*

OUT NOW

An Anonymous Girl

By Greer Hendricks and Sarah Pekkanen

Seeking women aged 18 to 32 to participate in a study on ethics and morality.
Generous compensation. Anonymity guaranteed.

When Jessica Farris signs up for a psychology study conducted by
the mysterious Dr Shields, she thinks all she'll have to do is answer
a few questions, collect her money, and leave. But as the questions
grow more and more intense and invasive, and the sessions become
outings where Jess is told what to wear and how to act, she begins
to feel as though Dr Shields may know what she's thinking . . .
and what she's hiding. As Jess's paranoia grows, it becomes clear that
she can no longer trust what is real in her life, and what is one of
Dr Shields' manipulative experiments. Caught in a web of deceit
and jealousy, Jess quickly learns that some obsessions can be deadly.

★

'Tackling big issues of morality and ethics, the story explores what
happens when boundaries are crossed and creepy obsessiveness takes
over from cool professionalism' *Psychologies*

'A thriller not to be missed' *Candis*